Readers love ARIEL TACHNA's
Partnership in Blood novels

I0614800

http://www.dreamspinnerpress.com

By Ariel Tachna

All For One (with Nicki Bennett)
Best Ideas
Château d'Eternité
Checkmate (with Nicki Bennett)
Fallout
Her Two Dads
Highland Lover
In Search of Fireworks
The Inventor's Companion
The Matelot
Music of the Heart
Myths and Magic: Legends of Love (Dreamspinner Anthology)
Once in a Lifetime
Out of the Fire
Overdrive
The Path
Rediscovery
Revelations in the Dark
Riding Double (Dreamspinner Anthology)
Rose Among the Ruins
Seducing C.C.
Stolen Moments
A Summer Place
Sutcliffe Cove (with Madeleine Urban)
Testament to Love
Under the Skin (with Nicki Bennett)
Why Nileas Loved the Sea

THE EXPLORING LIMITS SERIES (WITH NICKI BENNETT)
Exploring Limits • Stretching Limits • Refining Limits
Breaking Limits • Transcending Limits • No Limits

GAMES LOVERS PLAY
Amorous Liaison • Best Behavior • Ride 'em Cowboy

HOT CARGO
Hot Cargo (with Nicki Bennett) • Something About Harry (with Nicki Bennett)
Healing in His Wings

LANG DOWNS
Inherit the Sky • Chase the Stars • Outlast the Night • Conquer the Flames

PARTNERSHIP IN BLOOD
Alliance in Blood • Covenant in Blood • Conflict in Blood • Reparation in Blood
Perilous Partnership • Reluctant Partnerships • Lycan Partnership • Partnership Reborn

AVAILABLE AT DREAMSPINNER PRESS
http://www.dreamspinnerpress.com

Partnership Reborn

A Partnership in Blood novel

ARIEL TACHNA

Dreamspinner Press

Published by
DREAMSPINNER PRESS

5032 Capital Circle SW, Suite 2, PMB# 279, Tallahassee, FL 32305-7886 USA
http://www.dreamspinnerpress.com/

Partnership Reborn
© 2014 Ariel Tachna.

Cover Art
© 2014 Catt Ford.
Cover content is for illustrative purposes only and any person depicted on the cover is a model.

ISBN: 978-1-63216-362-2
Digital ISBN: 978-1-63216-363-9
Library of Congress Control Number: 2014948693
First Edition October 2014

Printed in the United States of America
∞
This paper meets the requirements of
ANSI/NISO Z39.48-1992 (Permanence of Paper).

To my sisters,
who have stood beside me for ten years
and helped make this dream a reality.

Prologue

"STOP PACING and come sit with me."

Jean looked toward the bed he and Raymond had shared for so many years. His eyes saw the shock of pure white hair and the lines age had etched into Raymond's skin, but his heart still saw the man his wizard had been when they first met: strong and vibrant, young but not that young, a man in his prime, so eager to defend, so desperately in need of love. Jean had given it to him in every way possible, and now he was about to be taken away.

"If I do that, I have to think about what's going to happen."

"If you don't do it, it will still happen," Raymond said, coughing a little as he struggled to speak. "I'm an old, old man, Jean. Nothing can change that, and nothing can stop it. I need you with me."

Jean had never been able to refuse Raymond anything, so he crossed to the bed, pushing aside his grief.

"Don't make Orlando's choice," Raymond ordered. "I don't want my death to be the end of you. I want to look down on you from the next life and know you're still here, cherishing every memory and maybe someday finding someone else to love."

"You're talking nonsense."

"No, I'm telling you I love you enough to let you go, just like you have to love me enough to let me go now," Raymond said. "You've kept every promise you ever made to me. Now I want you to make one more. I need you to go on, whatever that takes, with whomever you find to make the days a little more bearable. Don't forget me, but don't use that as an excuse to lock yourself away from the world. The world needs you too much."

"Fuck the world and what it needs," Jean spat. "What about what I need?"

"I would give it to you if I could," Raymond said, "but immortality is beyond me. I love you."

Raymond fell silent after that, though his chest continued to rise and fall fitfully. Jean clung to his hand, the skin dry and brittle beneath his touch, his fingers finding the pulse point at Raymond's wrist for reassurance that his love was still holding on.

He heard noises in the living room beyond the closed door, but he ignored them. They could wait, because Jean would not give up even a second of the time he had left with Raymond for anything or anyone. Raymond's pulse grew weaker, and his breathing slowed. Jean tried to ignore the signs, but even Raymond's formidable will could not stave off death, and with a last burst of pure, sweet love, the heart that had given Jean life for so many years flickered out.

The howl that left Jean's throat was not human, a sound echoing a pain so pure and unadulterated that he wondered how it did not destroy him in its intensity, but his voice gave out and nothing had changed. Raymond lay unmoving in their bed, his hand growing cold in Jean's as the sun rose on what would undoubtedly be a beautiful spring day. The kind of day Raymond loved. The kind of day Jean would never be able to see again without his wizard at his side.

Jean nearly tore the bedroom door from its hinges in his haste to escape, to flee a fate he could not change. He ran smack into hard arms that crushed him in an embrace, keeping him from rampaging. Soft hands joined them as two voices murmured words of condolences and comfort.

"Let me go." He struggled against their grips.

"No," Sebastien said, shaking Jean a little. "Not when you're this upset."

"What do you care?" Jean spat. "Just let me go. What are you doing here?"

"Every vampire in Paris is mourning right now," Sebastien said. "Some may hate you, but every one of them loved Raymond. You can rage at me all you want, but I'm not letting you go—and neither is Angélique. We're going to stay here until you get control of yourself again. We already lost one friend. We can't lose another."

"How long do you really think you can keep me here?" Jean demanded.

"As long as it takes," Angélique replied. "Raymond made sure there were spells on the doors to keep you inside and safe until you calmed down. When you're no longer in danger of doing something stupid, someone will let us out—but until then, it's just the three of us."

"You'll starve before then."

"I'm not that self-sacrificing," Angélique said. "My employees are on call and will come as needed."

"Then I'll starve before then."

"And leave the Cour in chaos?" Sebastien asked. "I never took you for a fool."

Jean struck out at him, but Sebastien saw it coming and sidestepped easily, catching him in a tight grip again. On any other day, Sebastien would have been no match for the older, stronger vampire, but exhausted as Jean was by grief, he could not get away.

Jean slumped into Sebastien's arms, sobs welling up in his chest. His eyes prickled with unshed tears, that sign of grief denied him by his undead nature, but nothing could stop the heaving of his chest or the broken cries that escaped him. The beast inside him, quiescent for more than ninety years, paced restlessly now that the calming touch of Raymond's emotions no longer kept it in check.

It would be so easy to rampage, to give in to the rage only Raymond's love had ever eased, but that would serve no purpose. He had made a promise to Raymond, accepting it in his heart even if he had not said the words aloud, and he could not break that. He could not be less than the man Raymond had loved because to do that would negate all of Raymond's trust in him. Raymond had spent their entire partnership doing everything he could to convince the world that vampires were not monsters but rather men and women like anyone else, capable of a full range of emotions and as much self-control as any mortal. Jean could not undo that in one careless moment of grief, no matter how overwhelming. He would not sully Raymond's legacy because of his own self-indulgent need to release some of the pain inside him.

"You can let me go now," Jean said softly. "I need to see to Raymond. He deserves the ritual he gave to so many others, during the war and since then. He deserves to have his ashes interred with honor. He deserves…." His voice broke, and he could not finish his sentence, because Raymond deserved so much more than Jean would ever be able to do for him. Raymond would not want it. He had always preferred anonymity to fanfare, but Jean had not spent more than ninety years at Raymond's side without learning how to work around his lover when necessary.

"I need to call Olivier," he said, thinking of the director of l'Institut Marcel Chavinier, who had taken over after Raymond retired. "He should be the one to conduct the rites."

"I'll call him," Angélique offered. "Go see to Raymond. We'll handle the rest. I don't know Olivier as well as you do, but I can still call him."

Jean nodded and returned to the bedroom. Raymond's body lay where he had left it. No surprise, really, but he would have given anything in his power to have a few more hours with Raymond. He could hear his lover now, telling him not to be ridiculous, that a few more hours would not have changed anything, but Jean disagreed. A few more hours might not have changed Raymond's ultimate fate, but they would have been worth any sacrifice to do without the yawning maw of emptiness inside him now. He teetered on the precipice, only his awareness of Raymond's desires keeping him from falling into a pit of despair blacker than the deepest ocean trench. He had seen vampires lose people in the past, and he knew what lengths their grief could drive them to. He could not do that, though. He could not give in to any of the emotions ravaging him because if he did, he would betray Raymond's trust in him.

"You owe me for this," Jean muttered to Raymond as he crossed the room to the closet. Raymond had picked out the suit he wanted to wear for his final rituals, ignoring Jean's shudder at the macabre discussion. Jean was glad of it now. It saved him having to think about how to prepare Raymond's body. He could not clean him with a spell as Jean had watched Raymond do for others in the past, so he would have to see to his lover the old-fashioned way.

The body he bared when he pushed aside covers and pulled off pajamas was old now, bearing the wrinkles and age spots of a man well over a hundred and twenty, but Jean lingered as lovingly over it as he ever had when Raymond was young. The scar that paralleled Raymond's spine had faded over time, as if the magic of Jean's mark had leached it of its potency, but nothing could erase it entirely. Raymond would have, Jean knew. If he had the power, he would have removed his mark of Cain, but Jean had always seen that scar differently. For Raymond, it had been testament to a moment of blindness. For Jean, though, it was proof of Raymond's strength in breaking away from the tyrant who had scarred him and terrorized

Paris for more than two years. It shouted to all the world that Raymond had seen the error of Serrier's ways and turned on him to help bring him down.

The second mark had not faded a bit from the moment Jean etched it into Raymond's skin. His mark, the symbol of his office branded into Raymond's skin, announced to anyone who saw it that they were bound together for eternity: one heart, one soul, one body. Raymond was Jean's sole source of sustenance from the moment he'd claimed his Avoué. And Jean was the only lover Raymond took from that day forward.

"How am I supposed to feed from someone else?" he asked the empty room. "How am I supposed to go from him to… anyone else?" Raymond's blood had been a banquet for him, as complex and layered as the finest wine, full of love and lust, rich with devotion and the occasional jolt of deviousness. In ninety-four years, Jean had never once felt any craving for a different taste. Now he had no choice. He would be trading a five-star restaurant for a fast-food joint, and even before the first drop, it tasted like dust in his mouth.

He finished with Raymond's back and rolled him so he could wash his front. The scars there were of less import than the ones on the back, the signs of an active life rather than any specific event, but Raymond's chest bore one mark that nearly brought Jean to his knees. On the left side of his chest, above his heart, were the twin punctures left by Jean's fangs. He had bitten Raymond there, and despite the speed with which Raymond healed from Jean's feeding, they had never healed. Raymond had never allowed them to heal. Each time they started to fade, he had goaded, begged, or otherwise seduced Jean into opening them again until they had become almost a piercing, the sides of the holes open permanently and only the bottom a new break in the skin each time Jean fed.

Grief welled up inside him again as he cleaned that spot. He leaned forward, his forehead coming to rest on Raymond's still chest. "I hate you," he said against Raymond's skin. "Why did you have to make me promise to go on? The Cour doesn't mean anything to me, despite what Sebastien thinks. I'll never be able to step back into that role without you. It might take a few months before anyone takes advantage of the fact that I'm alone again, but I've gotten spoiled having you at my side. Even if I wanted to, I doubt I'd be able to hold onto my position—not after being out of le jeu des Cours for so long. There's nothing left for me here without you." The Aveu de Sang he shared with Raymond had elevated him above the cutthroat maneuverings of the Cour for too many years to step back into the fray easily.

He had not truly understood Orlando's decision four years ago, when his friend had chosen to stay at Alain's graveside and face the rising sun rather than retreat to safety. Now he needed no explanation. Were it not for his promise to Raymond, he would do the same.

Forcing himself to focus, he finished cleaning Raymond's body and dressed him in the suit he had chosen. Then, haunted by memories of other, better times, he fled the room. He could not go beyond the confines of the apartment, but at least the other rooms had associations with people besides Raymond, even if Raymond was a fixture there as well. The bedroom had only ever been his and Raymond's, a sanctuary they had never allowed anyone else to penetrate. In the living room, he might be inundated with memories of Raymond as they entertained Alain, Orlando, Sebastien, and Thierry, but that was far different than the memories the bedroom held. They had plighted their troth there, pledging their very existence to one another in an Aveu de Sang, a ritual so old it extended beyond the reach of history and legend, a tenet of vampire lore so central and yet so rare that having two couples perform it in the same generation was unheard of.

They had very nearly had three.

"Is he…?"

Jean shrugged. He had no more words to describe the situation than Sebastien did. Words had always been Raymond's strong suit, whereas Jean had preferred action. Not that Raymond hesitated to act when necessary. On the contrary, Jean had seen him move with ruthless speed and determination when the situation demanded it, but Raymond had also been a master of diplomacy, keeping conversations going when matters would have otherwise devolved into violence. Sebastien had not exaggerated when he spoke of the Cour loving Raymond. They had respected him in a way they rarely respected mortals or even other vampires.

"Angélique is talking with Olivier now," Sebastien said when Jean did not answer him. "Everything should be set to perform the ritual tomorrow night at the latest."

"Thank you." Jean's voice broke as he spoke, but he could not bring himself to care. At one time, he and Sebastien had been enemies in le jeu des Cours, but now Jean knew Sebastien would be his staunchest supporter if Jean decided to reenter the fray. His lapse in control would not hurt him here.

Sebastien simply patted Jean's shoulder and let him grieve. He had been there too, not so long ago that he had forgotten the feeling of grief. Although his bond with Thierry, created in secret with only their closest friends as witness, had not been an Aveu de Sang—the most sacred bond a vampire could create with a mortal—it had been no less meaningful to him. And the searing loss of the one person the beast inside of him recognized as anything other than his next victim had not been an easy one to accept. Sebastien could hear Thierry's voice in his head telling him to suck it up and deal with what could not be changed. It brought an entirely inappropriate smile to his face, but Jean's head was bowed beneath the weight of his grief, and he did not see it.

Sebastien wanted to offer words of consolation, but experience had taught him well that no words could soften the blow—and promises of time healing the pain, while true, were no encouragement either. Time had eased the loss of his Avoué—the man he had bound himself to, forsaking all others—but only slowly. He had been able to feed from others again after his Avoué's death, but it had taken Thierry—sarcastic, combative, snarky Thierry—before he had truly moved on. Thierry had extracted much the same promise from Sebastien that Raymond had from Jean, and so Sebastien soldiered on, trying to find meaning in his life again without his partner there to bring light and laughter to his soul. Already Sebastien could sense the darkness creeping in around Jean. Sebastien could not bring light to his friend the way Raymond had done, but he would not let the darkness take him.

THEY GATHERED an hour after sunset, arriving in the Père Lachaise cemetery in groups of two or three, an occasional solitary figure or larger group swelling the ranks. They came in silence, every one, even the ones who had numbered among Raymond's detractors in life. In death, they came to pay him the respect his lifelong dedication to their cause had surely earned.

Only the faces in the nearer ranks were familiar, etched with varying echoes of the same grief that rent Jean's soul, but the numbers continued to grow, wave upon wave of mourners come to pay tribute to a man who had touched their lives whether he knew it or not.

"Who are all these people?" Jean whispered to Sebastien and Olivier.

"Vampires, wizards, werewolves, faeries, and members of every other magical race touched by Raymond's tireless quest for their equality," Olivier replied. "They didn't have to meet him personally to mourn his loss."

Jean looked back over the sea of faces, barely illuminated by the waning moon and the ambient light of the city. Raymond might not have appreciated the fanfare that accompanied his last rites, but he would have appreciated the way everyone had come together, regardless of their differences. Their presence was a fitting tribute to Raymond's legacy.

"Shall we begin?" Olivier asked.

Jean never wanted this to begin. He never wanted to say a final good-bye to his Avoué, but putting it off a few more minutes would not change reality. He gave his assent, and Olivier turned to the assembly.

Jean barely heard the words Olivier spoke in memory of the president of l'Association Nationale de Sorcellerie, founder of l'Institut Marcel Chavinier, researcher and activist, friend and mentor. Raymond had been all of those things, of course, but none of them mattered to Jean. He had seen deeper than those surface attributes. He had read into Raymond's soul and bound his own to it until he thought he would go mad with Raymond's absence.

Olivier summoned air to wrap around them, commending Raymond's breath to the elements. Jean choked back a sob. He had witnessed Raymond's last struggling breath. He did not want the air to take it but to return it, to push life back into his body again. Water came next, Raymond's element, and as the fine mist settled over Raymond's skin in ritual cleansing, Jean was reminded of all the times Raymond had lost control at the end of their lovemaking and covered them in the same soft mist that coated him as much as Raymond. His eyes burned, but no amount of grief could return what his making had stolen from him, so no tears fell to wet his cheeks along with the mist. Olivier called fire next, returning Raymond's body to the dust from which it was made. As the flames devoured his lover's remains, Jean's knees gave out, and he would have fallen if Sebastien had not caught him. He bowed his head, unable to watch the end of the ritual. He had seen it played out multiple times as Raymond presided over the rites of their friends and loved ones. He knew Olivier would turn the earth, burying Raymond's ashes in the soil at the base of his gravestone. When it was done and the power of the ritual released, people would come to pay their last respects, to offer words of condolences to the ones left behind. He had stood at Raymond's side as he comforted the grieving for more of these ceremonies than he cared to count. He had supported vampires as they said good-bye to their partners. He probably could have recited the words of the spells along with Olivier, not that his words would have any effect. None of that familiarity helped him now, though, as Olivier consigned his lover's ashes to the earth.

"Send them away," he told Sebastien hoarsely. "I can't—" Grief closed his throat, leaving the sentence unfinished, but Sebastien understood. He left Jean to sink to his knees and placed himself between Jean and the rest of the mourners. A moment later Angélique joined him, followed quickly by Fabienne, Denis, Pascale, and Mireille. Together they formed a barrier between their grieving friend and any who would disturb him. Sebastien took note of each name and face in case a time came when Jean wanted to know who had come to share in his grief, but he remembered all too well how lost he had felt when Thierry died, how incapable of dealing even with his friends. The sympathy of strangers would have been intolerable.

Jean buried his hands in the newly turned dirt, clinging as long as he could to that last tangible connection with Raymond. He vaguely registered the sound of voices and movement behind him, but they required nothing of him, and he gave them nothing in return. He could not. He had nothing left to give. Everything good in his life, in his soul, lay now in eternal slumber, mingled with the earth beneath his fingers. He was hollowed out, purged of every emotion but grief. The beast within him, that awful demon kept in check by Raymond's devotion, howled at the absence of its mate. The elements themselves seemed to echo that cry, wind and water whipping around him as the earth beneath his hands churned. He only needed fire now to come and reduce him to dust as it had done to Raymond so that he could rest forever with the man he had loved. But no flames rose around him to end his agony—only a high, keening cry that tore from his throat to echo the pain tearing through his soul.

Silence finally descended as his voice gave out, his throat raw from his screams. He shivered in the cool night air. His clothes were soaked through, with the mist Olivier had called before or some new source, he could not have said. He glanced back, relieved to see the cemetery empty now except for Sebastien and Angélique, who stood at a respectful distance.

He turned back to face the fresh grave again. He could feel the passage of time, his senses warning him of the coming dawn. He had an hour yet, but he could not linger much longer and still keep his promise to Raymond. It would be so easy to stay where he was and let the sun rise and do what the flames had not. The protection of Raymond's magic had worn off in the two days since his death. He would not need to feed for some time yet, but the Aveu de Sang only extended the time he could go between feedings, not the time Raymond's magic protected him from the sunlight. If he stayed, the sun would incinerate him the moment its rays touched his unprotected skin. He had watched it take Orlando. A flash of joy and pain and then nothing but ash. A moment of agony and then sweet reunion and an eternity with Alain. He had not gone often to Alain and Orlando's grave after that night, but the few times he had, he had felt a breeze on his face on even the calmest days and had heard again the echo of joyous laughter. They were together. His faith had taught him that—but he did not need faith, not with that kind of proof.

"He'd never speak to you again," Sebastien said, as if reading Jean's thoughts. "You'd spend all of eternity trying to convince him to even acknowledge you."

"He would ignore me out of spite, wouldn't he?" Jean said bitterly. "At least I'd be with him."

"Come on," Sebastien said. "It's time to go home. If you can't face your apartment right now, you can come home with me, but we need to leave soon."

Jean bent forward and pressed a final kiss to the ground before rising with none of his customary grace. Grief had apparently stolen that from him as well. He let Sebastien lead him through the empty streets to the car Olivier had put at their disposal for the night. Jean gave his address woodenly, too exhausted to summon any emotion now.

He ignored Sebastien and Angélique as they followed him inside. They could stay or go. He didn't have the energy to care. He trudged through the living room and into the bedroom. Sebastien started to follow even there, but Jean shut the door. Raymond might be gone, but this would always be their haven, and Jean would not share that with anyone else. He sank down onto the bed, heedless of his wet clothes or the dirt stains on his knees. He pulled the duvet over his shoulders, closed his eyes, and willed his mind into oblivion.

Chapter 1

Thirty years later

"TELL ME again why we're doing this?"

Raphael Taravaud looked up from his perusal of his closet, where he had been searching for the perfect shirt to wear when they went out. Kylian Raffier, his best friend since childhood, leaned casually against the doorframe, looking far too good for Raphael's peace of mind. Kylian had long, straight black hair and just the hint of a beard, exactly the kind of man Raphael would go for, except for one small detail: Kylian wasn't for him. He had tried more than once to translate that into words everyone else could understand, but he had never managed, even to his own mind. He could only say that he knew. The very essence of his being cried out for its mate, and Kylian was not it.

"Because I've looked everywhere else I can think of," Raphael replied. "The same vampires show up at l'Institut practically every time they have their dinners, and none of the others want partners. He's out there somewhere, Ky. I just have to find him."

"So you're going clubbing in Paris in the hope of miraculously running across him, and you're dragging me with you because I have nothing better to do on a Friday night than follow your sorry ass around from club to club," Kylian scoffed. "This is your worst idea yet."

"Then come up with a better one," Raphael challenged. "You think I enjoy this? You think I enjoy walking around feeling like half of me is missing?"

"You're so damn sure," Kylian said with a shake of his head. "How do you know this?"

"I don't," Raphael admitted, because for Kylian, he would try again to do what he had yet to manage for anyone. "I just know something's missing—and from everything I've learned about partnerships, that's what it feels like, except my partner isn't here. You remember some of the accounts we studied of partners who were separated during the war, or later for various reasons? How the bond helped them find their partners again by sense alone? I have that sense.

I feel that tug, except I've never met the man on the other end. I've tried following it, but it's too nebulous to lead me anywhere."

"You're so sure it's a man. What are you going to do if it's a woman?" Kylian teased.

"I guess I'll learn to like tits," Raphael said with a shrug, but he was not worried. He could not explain the connection he had felt—and missed—for as long as he could remember, but he was done waiting for his partner to find him by conventional means. His vampire was out there somewhere, and he was going to find him. Whatever it took.

"I still say you're setting yourself up for disappointment," Kylian said. "Even if you find your partner, the kind of bond you're looking for is incredibly rare. It wasn't just any separated partners who found each other again by sense alone."

"Not as rare as it used to be," Raphael replied. "There were two in the previous generation."

"And one is dead, and the other now lives completely retired from society," Kylian reminded him. "Not a great recommendation for anyone considering that choice."

"But what grand love stories they were!" Raphael said. "Like you wouldn't jump at the chance for that kind of love if it came your way."

"*If* being the key word," Kylian said. "But if it came my way, I'd think about it. I'd discuss it with my partner and maybe we'd consider it, but it's a huge step. You know the stories. When Alain Magnier died, Orlando St. Clair sat at his grave until the sun took him, and when Raymond Payet died, Jean Bellaiche collapsed with grief. He's hardly been seen in thirty years. I'm not sure I'd want to do that to someone I loved."

"It's better to have loved and lost…."

"Is it?" Kylian challenged. "I'm not so sure, if that's the price for that kind of relationship. I can't think of any vampires who have found a second partner, and some of them lost their partners forty or fifty years ago."

"Which is nothing to a vampire," Raphael pointed out. "Even most of the young ones are hundreds of years old."

"They still have to live each day," Kylian said, "and you're talking about them watching the person they love grow old and die while they remain unchanged. It's not all hearts and flowers. There's self-sacrifice in that kind of commitment."

"Your grandmother only had ten years with your grandfather before he died, and she never remarried. Do you think she regrets those years for a moment?" Raphael asked.

"No, I know she doesn't," Kylian said.

"Then why are you so sure the vampires regret it?"

"You said it yourself. It's the same batch of vampires every time they have a dinner at l'Institut, and they are all newer vampires who haven't had a partner before. Can you think of a single instance where a vampire has taken a second partner after the first one died?"

"No, but I don't know every vampire or every pair. I'm sure there are some," Raphael insisted. "And even if there aren't, I don't need a vampire who had a partner before. I just need a vampire to be my partner now."

"And so you're going to drag me around Paris to every club vampires are known to frequent in the hope of meeting the one vampire who might be your partner and getting him to feed from you, and you're going to do all this hoping said vampire doesn't hate you for trapping him into a partnership without realizing you're a wizard before he feeds from you," Kylian summarized. "This may be your most brilliant plan yet."

"Sarcasm doesn't become you," Raphael retorted. "If I had an idea for a better plan, believe me, I'd go for that instead—but I have to do something."

"Why?" Kylian demanded. "That's the part of this I just don't get, Raph. I don't understand why you feel like you have to do this."

"Because he's missing," Raphael said. "I don't know how else to explain it, but he's out there somewhere instead of here beside me where he's supposed to be. Don't tell me it makes no sense. I know it makes no sense. There's no way I should miss someone I've never met, but I do. I look for him without thinking when I want to share good news. I reach for him during the night, only to find empty space next to me in bed. I dream about him without quite being able to see his face, but I can tell you everything else about him. He's thin but wiry, not tall, like maybe he was turned generations ago when people didn't grow as tall as average now. He's serious, but I know there's a wicked sense of humor underneath that."

"If you do manage to meet and recognize him, what then?" Kylian asked. "You have this all built up in your head of how he'll be and how things will work, but this isn't a story in some book. This is reality, and you don't know that he'll return your interest. Even if he's never had a partner before, even if he's not opposed to the idea of having one, you still have to win him over, and you're talking about doing it after you've tricked him into feeding from you and creating a bond he may not want."

"I don't know, all right?" Raphael said. "Are you happy now? I have no idea how it's going to work out, but I have to do something. If you have a better idea, I'll take it."

Kylian shook his head. "Not really. The only thing I can say is, tell him what you are and what you want before he bites you the first time. I know it's a great story about St. Clair and Magnier meeting in the cemetery, and St. Clair biting Magnier and just knowing they were meant to be together. I've read the accounts just like you did, and the idea that their love was so all-encompassing that St. Clair couldn't go on alone adds to it, but that's not the only account we studied. Many of the others, even the ones who settled into solid bonds, said they wouldn't have done it if they'd known what they were getting into before they started. It goes against everything we stand for to trap someone into a relationship that way. When the war was going on and the partnerships were first forming, they didn't know what they were doing. You do."

"I can't lose him," Raphael said.

"If you trick him into a relationship, how do you expect to keep him?" Kylian replied.

Raphael slumped onto the bed. "I don't know. I just know I have to find him."

"So we'll search," Kylian said. "We'll keep looking until we find him. Just tell him the truth before he bites you. You can seduce him if it feels right. You can both walk away from that, but neither of you can walk away once he's bitten you. What if you're wrong, and you end up hating him? You'll be as stuck as he is."

Raphael knew Kylian was right, objectively anyway, but he had lived with his phantom lover from his earliest memories. As a child, the man in his dreams had been a playmate rather than a lover, but his first wet dream had featured the same faceless man he searched for at every dinner he attended at l'Institut Marcel Chavinier and in the face of every man he met wherever he went.

"Just promise me you'll think before you rush into anything," Kylian said when Raphael didn't immediately reply.

"I promise," Raphael said. He could give Kylian that much. Not much else, but at least that much.

"IT'S TIME, Sebastien," Angélique said.

"It's past time," Sebastien agreed, "but it's still all I can do to drag him here twice a week. Do you really think he'll agree to go hunting with me? It's only been thirty years. If I take him to the clubs, he'll be recognized, and he'll argue that being out in public will set him up in opposition to Fabienne."

"That's bullshit, and we all know it," Angélique insisted. Jean would never challenge the new chef de la Cour, and Fabienne would hand the Cour back over to him in a heartbeat if he wanted it. "Yes, he might be recognized in some of the clubs, but he was never one to frequent them, even before Raymond. He ran the Cour, but in a city this size, not everyone chose to attend meetings. He's not as recognizable as he used to be. Scout out some of the smaller clubs. There's bound to be one he can go to."

"You realize we could be doing this for nothing. Monsieur Lombard has lived in retirement for far longer than Jean."

"You didn't," Angélique retorted. "Either time."

"Thibaut wasn't a wizard, and Thierry wasn't my Avoué," Sebastien countered.

Angélique snorted. "So more than ninety years of sharing his life, his bed, and his blood doesn't count? Pull the other one."

Sebastien scowled at her, but he could not deny that what he had shared with Thierry had surpassed even what he had shared with his Avoué. They had no name for the bond they had created between them—more than a partnership but not an Aveu de Sang, because that magic only worked once—but their bond had given him peace of mind, if nothing else. Sebastien's inner beast had recognized Thierry after they completed their private ritual. Sebastien had learned to relax again after that, finally free of the fear he would lose control and hurt Thierry again.

"It's not the same."

Angélique didn't look convinced, but Sebastien let it go. She had enjoyed her partner, and David had been totally devoted to her, but she had always kept the upper hand and kept one small step back so that David's death saddened her rather than gutted her. Sebastien envied her occasionally, but then he remembered all the joy of his years with Thierry and pitied her instead.

"Since you brought it up, I assume you have suggestions for clubs I should look into," Sebastien said.

"As a matter of fact, I do."

He chuckled when she pulled a list from under the pillow of the divan she was reclining on and handed it to him. The list contained ten clubs, neatly annotated in her elegant handwriting. "I'll check them out."

SEBASTIEN ALMOST turned around to leave the first club on Angélique's list before he ever made it in the door. He had decided not to announce his presence, as so many of the vampires did at the clubs, choosing instead to join the line of people waiting to get inside. The bouncer had come down the line, checking IDs, and stopped cold when he saw Sebastien's name on his ID card. "Sebastien Noyer? *The* Sebastien Noyer? Why are you in line out here? You don't have to wait."

"It's fine," Sebastien demurred. "I don't mind waiting with everyone else."

"No, no, I insist. My boss will have my job if he finds out I let you wait out here. It's spring, yes, but it's not warm yet. Please, come inside."

Sebastien let the bouncer lead him to the door, ignoring the whispers of the people he passed. He did not see a way out of going inside now that he had been identified, unless he created an even bigger scene. He could do that, but he had hoped to avoid attention. Protesting would only draw even more. He would take this club off his list for Jean, though, because if they recognized his name, with as little as he had been in the public eye in the later years of Thierry's life, they would know Jean instantly, and that defeated the purpose. Jean would never consent to go somewhere he might be recognized.

The inside of the club was nicer than Sebastien had expected, the walls done in understated dark wood rather than in the garish colors many of the clubs currently favored. Sebastien had seen fads come and go in his long existence. The colors would go out of style in a year or a decade. If the club stayed open long enough, it would not need to redecorate in a year or two as styles changed. The bar area itself resembled any of a hundred other bars around the city, but the young man propped up against the bar resembled no one Sebastien had ever seen before. A jolt of lust hit him before he could tear his gaze away.

He made it halfway across the room before he realized he had moved, but his new position allowed him a better view of the young man's face. Sebastien had never been good at guessing age, but he would have put the man between twenty and twenty-five, old enough to be legal but young enough to make Sebastien feel ancient.

You are *ancient,* he told himself, *no matter how young you look.*

It was not the man's age or physical beauty that held Sebastien's gaze as he kept staring. No, it was the look on his face, a mix of cynicism and amusement, as if the man could not decide if he wanted to laugh at or scorn the world around him. Sebastien had not seen that particular expression in thirty-three years.

Bile rose in his throat at the thought. He had begun hunting again since Thierry died, refusing to break his promise to Thierry by isolating himself as Jean had done, but those assignations had been about feeding his body, not about replacing Thierry. No one could replace Thierry, just as Thierry had not replaced Thibaut. Sebastien accepted that he might meet someone and fall in love again, but it was too soon. Even more importantly, he would not sully Thierry's memory or his new relationship by claiming someone purely because he reminded Sebastien of Thierry.

Maybe a woman this time, he thought as he focused his gaze elsewhere. The mortals in the club appeared of an age with the one who had caught Sebastien's interest, all of them dressed to draw attention, either with collars missing or turned down to show the smooth, enticing skin of their necks, or with plunging décolletage to offer even more. He had fed well the day before. He should not have been hungry again, but the sight of so many nubile young bodies on offer whetted his hunger, and he felt his fangs drop. The club would not suit for Jean, given the way Sebastien had been recognized, but Sebastien was already here. He saw no reason to deny himself a taste of one of the succulent offerings.

"Hunting, Noyer?"

"What else would I be doing here?" Sebastien summoned his best polite smile for the vampire who had called him by name.

"I don't know, but these aren't your usual hunting grounds."

It took Sebastien a moment to place the vampire, but he finally recognized Stéphane, one of the vampires who had challenged Jean frequently at the beginning of the alliance. He had never found a partner, if Sebastien remembered correctly.

"I wasn't aware you'd become as territorial as a werewolf," Sebastien drawled. After all the help the Morvan pack had given him and Thierry, the comparison would not have insulted him, but the other vampire would not take the words so lightly. He bared his fangs threateningly, but Sebastien ignored him. His bond with Thierry had not lifted him outside le jeu des Cours, but his years with Thierry and as Jean's right hand had cemented his position in a way this upstart could not hope to threaten.

"Is there a problem?"

Sebastien turned to smile at the bouncer who had escorted him out of the line and inside. "No problem. I was just deciding where I wanted to sit," he said.

"I'll clear a spot for you at the bar," the bouncer offered. Sebastien refrained from shooting a triumphant look back at the vampire he had just bested. Jean had taught him that it stung the loser more if he did not even acknowledge his victory.

Chapter 2

KYLIAN BARELY glanced at the man who joined him at the bar. He had already decided Raphael was insane for suggesting they come here. He had been to meat markets that put a more delicate spin on what was being offered. But he could certainly see the appeal such a place would hold for a vampire. Whatever their tastes, they would find someone here to fit their desires, and the mortals crowding the dance floor and the bar would not be here if they were not willing prey. That last part was what Kylian had trouble understanding, even after all the classes they had gone through at l'Institut and all the partnered wizards and vampires he had talked to. Nothing he had seen or heard had convinced him of the value of turning himself into dinner for a vampire.

Raphael would not agree, although so far he'd had the good sense not to throw himself randomly at the few vampires who had come in. Kylian hoped it would continue that way. He did not relish the thought of having to pull Raphael out of trouble if he did meet someone he thought would fill the missing place in his soul.

Kylian smothered a snort at the thought. He had spent the past twenty years trying to break Raphael of his romantic streak, but nothing worked. To the depths of his being, Raphael was an idealistic romantic. He believed in the happy ending, in the greater good, in all that was wholesome in the world. Kylian had accepted this and come to the conclusion that he would protect Raphael from the cold, cruel world that might take the shine off his innocence.

Even if it meant following him from bar to bar every night until he found his elusive soul mate. Not that Kylian would let anyone get close until he knew such a person would be good for Raphael. It would be far too easy for an unscrupulous vampire to take advantage of Raphael's naïveté. Kylian did not know if a partnership bond could be faked, but with Raphael's happiness on the line, Kylian would not take the chance.

"I'll have a Courvoisier."

Nothing in the order itself or in the man's voice should have caught Kylian's attention, but he turned nonetheless as the bartender walked away to prepare the drink.

"Not the usual order around here," Kylian said.

Sebastien turned to face the young man he had been trying to ignore and shrugged. "I learned from a man with expensive tastes." He ignored the bite of grief at the memory of evenings he and Thierry had spent with Jean, Raymond, Alain, and Orlando, drinking expensive brandy and discussing anything and everything they could think of—from politics to the ancient lore of as many magical races as would talk to them.

"You don't look old enough to sound that world-weary," Kylian commented.

Sebastien shrugged again. "Around here, looks can be deceiving. I'm more than five hundred years old."

Kylian blinked in surprise as that sank in. At all the dinners he'd attended at l'Institut, the vampires had never consumed the offerings, only sat at the tables and talked. "I thought vampires only drank blood."

"Vampires are only nourished by blood," Sebastien corrected. He kept hoping that fallacy would fall out of popular belief, but it lingered. "We can eat and drink anything we want."

"But what's the point if you don't feel it?" Kylian asked.

"Spoken like a true youngster," Sebastien drawled. "A good glass of cognac is about the experience—the bouquet, the friends, the ambiance. Nobody drinks Courvoisier to get drunk, not even to get buzzed. If that's what you want, stick with cheap wine."

Kylian bristled, but he could hardly argue his age or even his experience. His twenty-eight years were nothing compared to the vampire's long life. "If you're going to be insulting, you can go somewhere else and do it."

"Last I checked, it was a free country."

Before Kylian could argue more, the bartender returned. "Here's your drink, monsieur Noyer."

Kylian's ears perked up at that. "Noyer? Like Sebastien Noyer from l'émeute des Sorciers?"

"Yes, what of it?" Sebastien demanded. He had only been at the club for half an hour, and he was already fed up with the fawning. He had escaped much of that after the war, since Thierry had never been one to play at politics, and then they had moved to l'Institut and stayed there for the rest of Thierry's life. But all his avoidance had come to naught.

"Nothing," Kylian said. "Nothing at all. It's just… I grew up hearing stories about you, in history classes or from my best friend, who idolizes the heroes of that war. I never imagined I'd get to meet you someday."

"We weren't heroes," Sebastien replied. It was an old familiar argument, one he had lost far more often than he had won, but that did not stop him from making it again. "We simply did what needed to be done."

"Isn't that the definition of a hero?" Kylian insisted. "Someone who does what needs to be done when no one else can or will?"

Sebastien rolled his eyes at that, but Kylian thought he saw a hint of a smile lurking around the corners of his mouth. It only spurred his determination to win a real smile from the taciturn vampire. "What brings you out to a place like this?"

"If that's a pickup line, you need a new one," Sebastien said, ignoring the renewed stirring of interest in his gut. Even if the kid was interested, Sebastien could not allow himself to follow through. He had more important things to do than pick up a pretty young piece of ass. "If it's a conversation starter, find a better one. If you really have to ask, what are *you* doing here?"

"I'm here because my idiot best friend insisted on coming, and I'm not about to let him anywhere near vampires unsupervised," Kylian replied without thinking.

Sebastien's scowl deepened at the implied insult, but before he could take umbrage, Kylian rushed on. "I didn't mean that the way it came out. I meant he doesn't have an ounce of common sense. Without someone to keep an eye on him, he'd get himself into trouble without even trying."

"You definitely need to work on your delivery," Sebastien said, but his scowl had faded and amusement colored his voice. "If you'd said that to the wrong person, you'd be in a world of hurt now."

"He's the careless one, not me," Kylian replied coolly. He ran his hand along the wooden surface of the bar. It would not rise to his hand the same way earth would, but it was close enough to prove his point.

Sebastien's eyes narrowed. He had spent enough time in the presence of wizards to recognize the current of magic and the way the wood shimmered. Not only a wizard, but one tied to the earth, if Sebastien had to guess. Thierry would have things to say to the kid for the lack of subtlety in his actions, but it had served its purpose. Sebastien now knew exactly what he was dealing with. "You're a wizard."

"You're not the only one full of surprises," Kylian said.

"And your friend?"

"He is as well," Kylian confirmed.

"You're playing a dangerous game, coming here where vampires hunt at will," Sebastien warned.

"I'm not playing anything," Kylian said defensively, never mind that he had warned Raphael about the exact same thing, "and I don't think it's any of your business even if I were."

"Maybe you're not, sitting here at the bar alone," Sebastien conceded, "but you wouldn't be at this club at all unless one of you wanted to meet vampires—and you aren't interested in it from a purely academic standpoint, or you'd have gone to l'ANS or to the Cour. It's well known that the chef de la Cour parisienne is friendly toward wizards, even if she doesn't currently have a partner of her own. But you didn't go to either of those places. You came here, and that implies a different kind of interest."

"You have to understand. We grew up on stories of you and your colleagues. You're the heroes not just of the war but of popular culture. You're our generation's Grace Kelly and Prince Rainier," Kylian explained. Sebastien squirmed a little at the thought of being held up as any kind of role model, but especially as a romantic one. "Your lives have colored Raphael's perception of romance for as long as I can remember. He's in love with the idea of finding a soul mate. I can't dissuade him. The best I can do is protect him."

"Then he should be at l'Institut Marcel Chavinier, not here," Sebastien said, his voice harsher than he intended as he remembered meeting Thierry for the first time and all that had transpired from there. They had not known then what they had later learned about the volatile combination of wizard and vampire. Sebastien would not have changed a moment of it, but he knew others who had not felt the same. "The vampires here aren't looking for partners, much less a mate. Your friend's going to get himself in trouble if he tricks a vampire into bonding with him."

"I told him that, and he's already tried l'Institut," Kylian said. "But he doesn't listen to me. He'd listen to you. Maybe you could warn him what could happen. I know he's an idiot, but he's my best friend. Please? What could it hurt?"

Sebastien could think of plenty of reasons to refuse, but the kid— he really had to ask his name—was so earnest in his concern for his friend. Over the years, Raymond had driven home their responsibility in educating others about their bond—the partnership bond, not the private one he and Thierry had consecrated later—so often, that Sebastien could not refuse now.

Before he could agree, though, the man at his side cursed under his breath and bolted across the room toward a blond young man sitting half wrapped around Stéphane. Stéphane looked ready to bite the blond's neck right there in public, making Sebastien wonder how much things had changed since he last spent any time with the greater vampire community. If feeding in public was now acceptable, the privacy provided by Angélique at Sang Froid was looking better and better again. Some things were private, as far as he was concerned. The wizard had his friend under control, but Stéphane looked thunderous. Sebastien took that as his cue to depart. He had not come to cause problems for the club owner or for Fabienne. He might not be as involved in the Cour as he once was, but his actions still carried weight, and more confrontation with Stéphane would have repercussions he was not willing to incur.

No matter what anyone said, he was no one's hero and no one's role model. Raphael could learn his lesson from someone else.

"WHAT ARE you doing?" Raphael hissed as Kylian dragged him away from the booth where he had been getting to know Stéphane.

"Keeping you from making a monumental error," Kylian snapped back. "Besides, I have someone I want you to meet."

"You don't know it was an error," Raphael insisted. "Maybe he was the one I've been looking for."

Kylian rolled his eyes at that. "Really? Even I could tell he was trolling, and that was from across the room. Look, just come talk to this vampire I met. If you really want to go back to that vampire"—disdain dripped from his voice—"after that, I'll let you go."

"You don't have to be like that," Raphael said, sounding so hurt that Kylian nearly relented right then. He had never been proof against Raphael's pout. Fortunately his friend was too honest to take advantage of Kylian's weakness.

"I'm sorry," Kylian said, "but you know I'm a better judge of people than you are, and you'll really want to meet—" He bit back a curse when he realized Noyer was no longer standing at the bar where he had left him.

"Meet who?" Raphael asked.

"You wouldn't believe me if I told you," Kylian said with a sigh. "For whatever reason, he's gone."

"Monsieur?" The bartender caught Kylian's attention.

"Oui?"

"Monsieur Noyer asked me to make his excuses. He paid your tab by way of apology," the bartender explained.

"Noyer?" Kylian should not have been surprised Raphael latched onto the name.

"Yes, Sebastien Noyer," the bartender said. "This is the first time he's ever been to our club. We were honored he would choose to come here."

"And you didn't come get me right away?" Raphael demanded, turning on Kylian. "I'd give anything to meet him."

"That's why I was coming to get you," Kylian said. "Well, that and I didn't like the way that vampire was looking at you, but I was coming to get you so you could meet him. I thought he was going to stay so he could meet you, but I guess I read him wrong." That galled Kylian terribly, because he was usually a fairly good judge of character—hence his concern with the way that vampire had been coming on to Raphael—but he had apparently been wrong about Noyer.

"So what was he like?" Raphael said. "You can't just tell me you met him and stop there."

Kylian sighed and tried to sum up his encounter with the famous vampire. "Not what I expected," he said finally. "I said something about the war and him being a hero, and he brushed it aside completely, like it was what anyone would have done, and we know that's not true. Plenty of people stood by and did nothing."

"But?" Raphael prompted.

Kylian could not suppress a smile at that. As well as he knew Raphael, Raphael knew him just as well. "But he left when I told him I was going to get you so he could talk to you."

"Maybe he's shy," Raphael said. "Or maybe he got a call and had to leave. Or maybe he didn't want a scene, because as much as I would've tried to be cool about it, I probably would have ended up making one."

"I'm still sorry you didn't get to meet him," Kylian said. Raphael's explanation took some of the heat out of Kylian's temper. Perhaps Kylian had come on too strong, and Noyer had feared it getting worse with Raphael there as well. He doubted they would ever meet again, but if they did, he would try a gentler approach. He had not let himself think it while he was talking with Noyer, but the man was attractive in that ageless way vampires sometimes had, and he certainly had enough presence to fill an entire room if he chose. Kylian wondered how it would feel to be the sole focus of the hazel eyes that had scanned the room so constantly. Alert for what, Kylian could not have said, but alert nonetheless. He shivered at the thought.

So much for his disinterest in vampires. It seemed he'd never met the right one until now. Too bad he had picked one who had already buried a partner he had loved almost as famously as the two epic love stories of the war.

"I DIDN'T expect to see you tonight."

Sebastien rolled his eyes when Angélique greeted him at the door to Sang Froid. He had hoped to be early enough that her manager would still be on duty, but luck had apparently deserted him tonight. "I tried one of the clubs on your list. They'd identified me before I even made it in the door. Not somewhere I can take Jean," he told her. "Is Florence free? I need to feed."

"You were at a club surrounded by willing prey," Angélique said. "You should have fed there."

The only interesting face at the club had been the wizard, whose name he had not even asked. Feeding from him had not been an option.

"You didn't answer my question. Is Florence free?"

"For you, I'm sure she'll make time," Angélique replied, "but we will talk about this when you're done."

"There's nothing to talk about," Sebastien insisted.

"And yet here you are, paying me for something you could have gotten easily for free at the club," Angélique pointed out. "You've been hunting for yourself more often than not. Why is tonight different?"

Because all he could see tonight was long black hair and dark brown eyes—and no matter how appealing they were, he could not have them, not when they belonged to a wizard.

"I didn't go to the club to hunt," Sebastien replied. "I went to see if it was somewhere I could take Jean to hunt, which it's not."

"That's not a reason," Angélique insisted. She forestalled the retort on his lips with a wave of her hand. "Let me check on Florence, but do not try to leave without coming by my office. You won't let Jean succumb to his misery, and I won't let you succumb to yours."

Sebastien should have denied it, but Thierry had been much on his mind that evening. It was part of the reason Sebastien had not tried to hunt at the club. He could have found someone, but the emptiness of it had left him cold. At least with Florence, it was a business transaction, nothing more, and they both left the experience with exactly what they wanted from it. He had enough blood to sustain him for a few more days, and she had enough money in her wallet to pay her rent for another week. He liked her, and he thought the feeling was mutual, but neither of them imagined it was anything more than that.

Angélique returned a few minutes later with a smiling Florence behind her. Sebastien ignored Angélique and offered his hand to Florence. She laughed at him as she always did and leaned in to kiss both his cheeks. "We know each other too well for that," she scolded when she had finished.

He could hardly argue with that. He had visited her regularly for ten years now. She was not always available when he needed to feed, and he did not always come to Sang Froid, but he always asked for her first when he did. "I suppose we do," he agreed, though he would leave it to her to cross the line from acquaintances to friends the next time he came as well. "Do you have some time free for me tonight?"

"Of course I do," she said with a smile. "Come, we will find a quiet place to be together."

They would talk, and he would feed, and that would be the extent of it, but the turn of phrase she always used left him missing Thierry each time. Sometimes he thought she did it on purpose, to remind him of what he had shared with Thierry and to remind him he could have, if not that, then something meaningful, again. He had never asked if Angélique put her up to it. He was not sure he wanted to know.

He followed her through the warren of halls and rooms to the one she was using that evening. "What's on your mind?" she asked as soon as the door shut behind him.

He slumped into a chair. "I don't even know where to start."

"At the beginning, of course," she replied, taking a seat opposite him on the elegant divan. "Where else would you begin a story?"

He chuckled a little. So like her to go straight to the heart of the matter. "Angélique and I are worried about Jean. It's been thirty years, and he's made no effort to return to any kind of normal life. I know he loved Raymond, and I know that kind of loss doesn't just go away, but he's stuck in limbo—not dead, but not living either—and that isn't what Raymond wanted."

"Would it be kinder just to let him go?" Florence asked. "I know you want to pull him back and to see him return to the man he was, but have you considered that it might not be possible?"

"More than once," Sebastien admitted, "but he isn't the first vampire to lose an Avoué or to lose a wizard partner, and we've all learned to go on."

"But he is the only surviving vampire to lose both at once. You've told me repeatedly how the Aveu de Sang makes everything between a vampire and his lover more intense. When you add to that the benefits of having a wizard as a partner, it's no surprise he's still grieving."

The reminder of losing Orlando pinched at Sebastien's heart, but he had understood Orlando's choice then in a way Jean had not. Orlando had only ever loved Alain. There had never been anyone else for him, and there never would be. Jean had loved before, and Sebastien truly believed he would love again if he would only open himself to the possibility.

"Not quite," Sebastien replied slowly. "My second bond with Thierry might not have been an Aveu de Sang in name, but it mimicked every root characteristic we could think of, and I'm still here."

"As you say. Your concern for Jean isn't new. What changed tonight?"

"Angélique convinced me to check out a list of clubs where I might be able to take Jean hunting," Sebastien explained.

"And you thought this was a good idea? You realize her taste is somewhat skewed, don't you?"

Sebastien had heard rumors over the years, but he had never been invited to Angélique's bed and probably would not have gone even if he had been. "It was a perfectly normal club. The only problem is that I was recognized before I even got in the door. I can't take Jean somewhere like that. Not at first, anyway."

"So you turned around and left," Florence said.

"No, I stayed and had a drink and met... someone," Sebastien said slowly.

"Someone?" Florence repeated. "That's intriguingly vague."

"A man," Sebastien specified. "I didn't get his name, but we talked, mostly about his friend, who is determined to snare a vampire. It wouldn't have been anything out of the ordinary, except that he's a wizard."

"You didn't get his name, but you found out he's a wizard? There's something backward about that," Florence observed.

"That's sort of the way the conversation went," Sebastien said with a shrug. "In retrospect, everything about it was backward from the minute I saw him."

"Oh, so that's the way it is," Florence gloated as she leaned forward. "Tell me more."

Sebastien almost refused, but he had to talk to someone, and Jean would not want to hear about it. Jean wouldn't say anything, but then he rarely said anything no matter what Sebastien did. The silence said far more about his state of mind than any words could have done, so Sebastien tried to respect that as much as he could. Angélique would listen, but he would have to put up with that damned knowing smile she always wore when anything personal came up in conversation.

"I don't know what to say," Sebastien replied. "That's the problem. I've hunted since Thierry died. I've been attracted to people since then. I've had sex since then. Going to a club and seeing an attractive young man shouldn't have been a problem—but I've been completely unsettled since I first laid eyes on him, and I can't figure out why."

"Could it be because he's a wizard?" Florence asked.

"Possibly," Sebastien admitted. "With anyone else, feeding is just feeding and sex is just sex, but with a wizard, there's the chance of it being more. I stumbled into my relationship with Thierry and was lucky to find someone I could work with and eventually love. Not everyone was as lucky, and I don't want to take the chance of my luck running out this time."

"That's why you get to know him first," Florence said. "It's what the rest of us mortals do before we make a commitment to someone. We go out, we talk, we get to know each other, and we decide if we're compatible. If we are, we keep seeing each other. If we aren't, we stop."

"Once I bite him, it's all over if he's my partner," Sebastien said. He could find out if Kylian was his partner with a wave of his wand, of course, since his partner's magic wouldn't work on him, but that didn't resolve his issue with whether to act on the attraction.

"Then don't bite him until you know if you can be with him," Florence said in exasperation. "Really, you'd think a vampire of your age would have enough self-control to go out with someone or even sleep with someone without feeding from him."

Chapter 3

SEBASTIEN COULD not decide whether to laugh or cry when the first person he saw as he walked into the second club on Angélique's list the next night was the same dark-haired young man he had talked to the night before. He took a deep breath and reminded himself that the man's presence was not a reason to turn around and leave. He had not been recognized at this club, an improvement over the last one, and the man's presence did not make it a bad choice for Jean or even, really, for Sebastien himself. He could talk to the man or not, as he chose. Nothing about being in the same place required anything of either of them.

Pretending he had not noticed the man's presence, he found a spot at the other end of the bar and ordered a Courvoisier.

"You have predictable taste in drinks, even if you aren't predictable in any other way."

Sebastien turned at the sound of the man's voice. Choosing the other end of the bar had not helped him. "Bonsoir. I didn't see you here."

"Is the lighting in here really that bad? I thought vampires saw better in the dark."

"I wasn't looking for you either," Sebastien lied.

"Of course not. You disappeared last night without an explanation. If anything, you were looking to avoid me."

Sebastien bit back his automatic retort, since the words were true. "Look, we got off on the wrong foot yesterday," he said. "Could we pretend it never happened and start over?"

The man took a moment to consider but finally nodded. "Hi, I'm Kylian Raffier."

Sebastien let out the breath he had not realized he was holding. "Hi, Kylian. I'm Sebastien. Nice to meet you." He held out his hand, hoping Kylian would take it. When he did and the familiar need jolted through him, Sebastien resigned himself to a long, torturous night.

Kylian, though, just laughed, unaware of Sebastien's troubles. "We didn't do that yesterday, did we?"

Sebastien shook his head. "And I spent the rest of last night wishing I'd at least learned your name."

That surprised Kylian. "You thought about it?"

Sebastien flushed even as he nodded. Merde, he was out of practice with anything outside the realm of hunting. After Raymond's and Thierry's deaths, he had severed all ties to l'Institut and the wizard community. It had hurt too much to contemplate being around wizards with Thierry gone. "Yes. It's been a long time since I've spent any time talking with a wizard."

Kylian had not thought about it that way. "I can see how that would be disconcerting. I didn't mean to run you off with my insistence you talk to Raphael."

That had not been the problem. Not the heart of it, anyway. The problem had been Sebastien's attraction to Kylian himself. He no longer knew how to handle that. It gave him a convenient excuse, though. "Is he here tonight? I promise not to run off this time."

"He's here," Kylian said. "I wouldn't be here otherwise. This is not my typical choice of hangout."

"So what is?" Sebastien asked. "If you weren't following your friend around for his own safety, where would you be on a Saturday night in April?"

"On a night like tonight? I'd probably be at one of the cafés in le Marais or maybe at the movies. Or I might have looked for a concert to attend in one of the small places that caters to local groups. Before I moved to Paris, I played bridge pretty regularly, but I haven't found a partner here. Raphael knows the basics, but he doesn't have the patience for the subtleties."

"There's a lot of strategy in bridge. It's not an easy game to learn," Sebastien observed. The rest came as no real surprise for a man of Kylian's age, but in Sebastien's experience bridge was not a common game among that set.

"There's not a lot else to do when you grow up in Chamberet," Kylian said wryly. "It was bridge or pétanque, and bridge requires actual skill, not just luck."

Sebastien had a flash of Thierry insisting he explain le jeu des Cours, claiming he could learn any game of strategy—even one as complex as the one that ruled the lives of vampires. In the end, Sebastien had learned more from Thierry than he had taught.

"Did you stop Raphael from making a mistake last night?" Sebastien asked, unwilling to continue that line of thought. "That vampire he was with is not one I would trust with anyone I cared about."

"I lured him away with the promise of meeting you," Kylian said. "He was disappointed you had left."

"I won't disappear tonight," Sebastien assured him. "I'll even go with you to talk to him, if you want."

Kylian smiled so brightly Sebastien felt his heart stutter. Damn. He had it bad and they barely knew each other.

"Let's see if the lure of talking to one of the original vampires to form a partnership is enough to get him out of here and somewhere a little more to your tastes," Sebastien added on impulse.

"What about why you're here?" Kylian asked. "I don't want to drag you away from your hunt."

"I'm not hunting," Sebastien said. He was all too afraid he had found what he was looking for—even though he hadn't realized he was looking. "Let's get your friend. We'll go somewhere with a less... cutthroat ambience, and we'll talk."

Sebastien winced at how pathetic he sounded, but Kylian did not seem to notice or mind. Sebastien was intimately familiar with the helpless fascination vampires felt for their partners. Even before he and Thierry had become lovers, Sebastien had been captivated, confounded, and completed by him in a way that defied explanation. He was not sure he wanted to go through that again—but it had already started, and he did not know if he was strong enough to stop it.

"There he is," Kylian said as he lifted a hand to catch Raphael's attention. Raphael was Kylian's foil—blond, curly hair cropped short, where Kylian had long, straight black locks—but when Raphael joined them, Sebastien swore he could see the bond between the two. He wondered for a moment if they were lovers, but Kylian had said Raphael was searching for a partner, and the researchers at l'Institut had long since learned that a deep romantic bond precluded the formation of a partnership since the magic that allowed the partnership to form created a romantic bond between the new partners almost immediately. If their relationship was more than platonic, Raphael's quest was doomed, a fact he would already know if he had been to a seminar at l'Institut. Sebastien would have to make sure they both knew the risks before he let things go any further.

"I thought you were shitting me last night," Raphael said as he stared at Sebastien with a mixture of awe and fascination that made Sebastien squirm. Raphael was on the hunt for a partner, and Sebastien did not want to be considered for that role. He was not sure he was ready for another partner, but if he was, he would be choosing a different wizard entirely. "You really did meet him!"

"Raphael, meet Sebastien. Sebastien, this is Raphael Taravaud."

"It's an honor to meet you, monsieur," Raphael said, offering Sebastien his hand.

Sebastien shook it, pleased to note he did not have the same reaction to Raphael's touch as he did to Kylian's. At least his susceptibility was limited instead of leaving him vulnerable to all wizards. "Please, call me Sebastien. There's no need to be formal."

"But what about—"

"That's all in the past and doesn't have any impact on the present," Sebastien interrupted. He was off-kilter already. Listening to a recounting of his life with Thierry through the eyes of an idealistic child—for Raphael's obvious naïveté made him one, no matter his age—was more than he could bear.

"Sebastien suggested we find a quiet café where we can talk," Kylian said, saving Sebastien from his embarrassment. "I don't know much around here, but there are some places near my apartment."

"Do you know anywhere close we could go?" Raphael asked Sebastien.

"I haven't lived in this part of Paris for a number of years," Sebastien replied. "Wherever you want to go is fine with me."

"And yet we've run into you two nights in a row," Kylian said. "How did that happen?"

"Luck?" Sebastien joked, though he already knew it was more than that. Damn the fate that seemed to drive vampires to their partners. "Let's get out of here. I'll explain when we get somewhere quieter."

"THIS IS a nice place," Sebastien said, looking around the café Kylian had brought them to. Le Marais was not a part of town he had frequented even before meeting Thierry, so he had no expectations. The quiet hum of conversation would provide a background of white noise to give them some privacy.

"I like it," Kylian said. "Raph says it's boring."

"I do not," Raphael protested. "I just don't know anyone here the way you do."

"Children," Sebastien said, feeling more ancient by the minute. Thierry had never made him feel this old.

"Sorry," Raphael said, his face flushing. "It's an old argument."

Sebastien wanted to ask how old it could really be, but he did not want to know how young Kylian was. As long as he did not know, he could delude himself about not taking up with someone too young for him.

The waiter at the bar waved at Kylian as they found a table in the back and came up to them a moment later. "Bonsoir, Kylian, messieurs. What can I get for you?"

"An espresso," Kylian said.

"As usual," the waiter said with a smile. Sebastien had to fight back the urge to snarl at the man for flirting with Kylian.

Kylian shrugged. "I like what I like."

"And for you, messieurs?"

Raphael ordered an espresso as well, so Sebastien followed suit.

"Kylian tells me you're looking for a partner," Sebastien said after the waiter had left. Any conversation had to be better than dwelling on the way the waiter had looked at Kylian.

"Kylian talks too much," Raphael said with a glare for his friend.

"What?" Kylian said. "He asked why I was at the club last night. I told him I was with you and you were looking for a vampire. What was I supposed to say?"

"Something a little less personal, maybe?"

"I wasn't aware it was a secret," Kylian retorted.

"I'm sorry I brought up something I wasn't supposed to know, but that's all the more reason for me to say this," Sebastien interjected. "Make sure any vampire you're interested in knows you're a wizard before he or she bites you. Make sure you're both willing to make that commitment before you take a step that can't be undone."

"I've been to l'Institut," Raphael said. "I've heard it all before."

"But did you listen?" Sebastien pressed. "That vampire you were with last night…. I don't know if he was your partner, but he has spoken out against the partnerships from the very beginning. He never gained any ground because Jean was too entrenched and the success of the equal rights legislation was too far reaching, but I wouldn't put it past him to kill to get rid of an unwanted partner. The seminar at l'Institut discusses the benefits and drawbacks of partnerships, but they only work when both parties are willing—and Stéphane wouldn't have been."

"I'm not stupid, you know," Raphael said defensively. "I know you both think so, but I'm really not. I'd already figured out I wasn't going to get what I wanted from him yesterday before Kylian came to get me, but I can't find him if I don't look."

"That's an interesting way of putting it," Sebastien observed.

"It's also none of your business," Raphael said. He tossed some money on the table. "That'll cover my coffee. I'm not feeling social anymore."

"Raphael, wait," Kylian said, but Raphael ignored him and left the café.

"I'm sorry," Sebastien said. "I didn't mean to offend your friend."

"No, if anyone should be sorry, it's me. I knew how he felt about finding a partner. I shouldn't have said anything about it without his permission. I'll talk to him tomorrow when he's had a chance to calm down. His temper is a flash in the pan—bright and loud when it happens, and over just as quickly."

The waiter arrived with their espressos. "Your friend left?"

"He wasn't feeling well," Kylian said. "Don't worry. One of us will drink his coffee."

"Only if you're sure, Kylian. I wouldn't have minded if you didn't."

Sebastien's nostrils flared along with his jealousy as he inhaled sharply at the blatant flirting. Kylian seemed oblivious, though, and simply smiled at the waiter. When he had left again, Sebastien summoned a smile for Kylian. "He likes you."

"Who, Paul? No, that's just the way he is."

With you, Sebastien thought.

"Besides," Kylian went on, completely unaware of Sebastien's turmoil, "he's not my type."

"What is your type?" Sebastien asked, feeling daring.

Kylian laughed. "Are you fishing for compliments?"

Sebastien drew in another sharp breath. "Are you offering them?"

Kylian smiled and leaned closer. "Raphael is the one who's looking for a partnership, not me, but I like you. I wouldn't say no to seeing what develops between us."

Sebastien swallowed hard. "I'm not looking for a partner either, but I wouldn't turn down a friend, and maybe more."

Kylian's smile widened. "Then I suppose I should say my type is a sexy brunet vampire."

Lust hit Sebastien hard, and his fangs dropped. He ignored the desire for blood. He was not going there, partnership or no partnership, not until they were both sure they wanted it. He wrestled his inner demon into submission until his fangs subsided. Only then did he lean forward, close enough to share breath with Kylian. "That makes me a very lucky man."

Kylian flashed another smile before he leaned the rest of the way in, their lips meeting swiftly before Kylian pulled back again. "I'd say it makes us both lucky men."

RAPHAEL DID not let himself run as he left the café. He would not sink to the level of fleeing his best friend, but it was a near thing. He made for the banks of the Seine, as he always did when he needed a place to think. The water flowing serenely past calmed his soul and grounded his magic. He did not lose control of it often, but when he did, it was always because of Kylian. Nobody knew him like Kylian did, so nobody could push his buttons, however unintentionally, the way Kylian did.

He found a bench in a secluded little park, hidden from the eyes of any passersby on the sidewalk above. He was still visible from the river, but at this time of night, only a few boats moved along the waterway. Even then, the shadows protected him from all but the bateaux-mouche whose bright lights lit the riverbanks for tourists as they passed.

He felt like an idiot now that his good sense was regaining the upper hand. Yes, it hurt that Kylian had revealed even part of his deepest secret to a stranger, but he had not specifically asked Kylian not to say anything. It had simply never occurred to him that Kylian would have a reason to say anything about it. After all, who would he tell?

Sebastien Noyer, apparently.

Raphael groaned at that thought. Of all the vampires in all the world, Raphael could only think of one he idolized more than Sebastien, and Jean Bellaiche had not been seen in thirty years. Raphael was not sure he was even alive, which meant Sebastien was it as far as Raphael's heroes were concerned—and Raphael had just made a complete fool of himself in front of the man.

He cursed the luck that led Kylian to befriend Sebastien, of all vampires, but he could do nothing about it now other than admit to a rather unbecoming surge of jealousy that Kylian, who had never wanted a partner or had any real interest in vampires, should be the one to capture Sebastien's interest. Sebastien was not the one Raphael was looking for—he had known that almost immediately, just as he had known it with every other vampire he had ever met—but this was still Sebastien Noyer they were talking about. If anyone could help Raphael find his partner, it would be Sebastien. He had to know every vampire in Paris, and probably in most of the country, after the war and all his time at l'Institut and helping Bellaiche with the Cour and….

"Stop it," he muttered aloud. A bateau-mouche passed by, and he flinched away from the light. He had not wanted to share his turmoil with Kylian. He certainly did not want to share it with random strangers. "You're being stupid."

Kylian had never shown any interest in a partnership. Whatever was going on with him and Sebastien, it would not be that, and Raphael would not be jealous, because whatever it was, it did not affect him or his friendship with Kylian. It was Kylian's business, not Raphael's, and nothing would come of it anyway. Kylian would not want anything to come of it, even if Sebastien had decided he wanted a new partner. Raphael could do this. He could hash things out with Kylian and accept whatever friendship developed between Kylian and Sebastien and maybe even stop feeling embarrassed every time he and Sebastien met.

Now, if he said it enough times, maybe he would even believe it.

Chapter 4

KYLIAN'S LIPS were still buzzing from the kiss he and Sebastien had shared when he finally left the café and went in search of Raphael. Theoretically, Raphael could be anywhere by now, a wave of his wand enough to take him wherever he wanted to go, but Kylian suspected Raphael had not gone far at all. With his affinity for water, he had almost certainly gone to the Seine. Kylian would find him on one of the benches that lined the river. It was only a question of how far he had gone before he went to ground.

Hopefully enough time had passed for Raphael to be calm again and ready to listen to Kylian's apology—but even if he was not, Kylian would find him and let Raphael yell until he felt better. Better to lance the hurt between them so it could heal rather than let it fester.

He would have to tell Raphael about the kiss, too, which would not go over well. After years of Raphael dreaming of finding a partner, Kylian, not Raphael, had caught the eye of a vampire. Not as partners, but even the kiss was more than Raphael had gotten.

He reached the fence that bordered the sidewalk at street level above the Seine. Leaning over it, he peered into the darkness below. "Raphael," he called softly, "come out, come out, wherever you are."

The startled laugh that drifted up to him on the night wind brought a smile to his face. If Raphael could laugh at the childhood memory of playing hide-and-seek together, he could not be too angry at Kylian. Kylian vaulted the fence and dropped down next to the bench, barely missing the bushes that grew against the stone wall.

"You could have walked down the path like a normal human being," Raphael said.

"When have I ever been a normal human being?" Kylian retorted. "I'm sorry about Sebastien. I shouldn't have said anything to him."

Raphael shrugged. "I didn't ask you not to."

"You shouldn't have had to ask," Kylian said. "It was obvious how much it mattered to you when we talked about it before we went out last night, but I was bored. He asked why I was there, since I clearly wasn't interested in the vampires, and it seemed the most natural thing in the world to answer him honestly. And for what it's worth, I don't think he intended to criticize your desire. I just think he wanted to be sure you knew what you were doing, that you were being safe about it. I could have told him you knew, but he didn't ask me."

"Why did it have to be him?" Raphael asked. "Of all the vampires in Paris, why did he have to be the one I made a fool of myself in front of?"

"You didn't make a fool of yourself," Kylian insisted loyally. "You were upset and you left. He understood that."

"Did you stay and talk to him for a while after I left, or did it take you this long to find me?" Raphael grinned as he got the dig in. Kylian had never been known for his sense of direction, and Raphael had frequently eluded him as children when they played hiding games.

"I found you the first place I looked," Kylian shot back. "I stayed and talked to him. I know it's all backward, with you wanting a partner and me meeting a vampire, but I like him, Raph. He's… different from all the other vampires we met at l'Institut and elsewhere. I don't know how to explain it, but something about him is compelling."

"Of course he's different," Raphael said. "He had a partner and lost him."

Maybe it was that, Kylian mused. Certainly Sebastien had an air of gravitas around him, a shadow that never seemed to lift from his eyes.

"I suppose he must feel a bit like everyone he knew is gone, one way or another," Kylian replied, "between losing his partner and Bellaiche disappearing from society. In all the histories, it was always the six of them—Magnier, St. Clair, Bellaiche, Payet, Dumont, and Sebastien—and he's the only one still alive and active. I always wondered why he didn't take the Cour after Bellaiche stepped down, but now that I've met him, it makes sense."

"Does it?" Raphael asked.

Kylian winced at the sudden tension in Raphael's voice. He had given away more than he intended to without explaining things to Raphael first. "It does. He isn't one to put himself forward." He took a deep breath and steeled himself for Raphael's reaction. "He kissed me after you left."

"What?" Raphael's voice exploded between them, making Kylian wince. He had known Raphael would be upset, and he had kissed Sebastien anyway.

"I kissed him back."

"Fuck you," Raphael spat. "You don't want a partner. Why would you do this?"

"I've never felt the drive to find a partner the way you do," Kylian agreed, "but kissing him wasn't about finding a partner. It was about meeting a man I'm attracted to and acting on it. He's not *your* partner, is he?"

"I wouldn't know, would I?" Raphael said bitterly. "I never got a chance to find out."

"Do you think he's the one you're searching for?" Kylian pressed. "Really and truly, not just because you're hurt and angry at me? Because if you honestly believe he's the vampire you've been searching for, I'll step back and you can have him. I won't stand between you and your happiness. But think seriously before you answer that question, because you could be standing between me and mine."

Kylian's stark declaration startled Raphael out of his snit. He had expected Kylian to back down, but he had not expected it to cost him anything.

"You've met him twice," Raphael said slowly. "Are you that sure already?"

"No," Kylian admitted, "but I know I'm interested in him. Everything I've learned about him makes me want to learn more. Maybe it will work out, maybe it won't, but I want the chance to find out. But I won't see him again if you truly believe he's the one for you."

"He's not," Raphael said. "I shouldn't have made you think he might be, when I knew right away." He hesitated for a moment. Given how badly he had reacted to the reminder to be careful, he felt hypocritical even thinking about warning Kylian. "You were so worried I'd rush into something. You will follow your own advice, won't you?"

"A kiss is hardly enough to form a partnership," Kylian replied. "He isn't looking for a partner, and neither am I. Whatever this might be, it isn't going there. I'd have to let him bite me for it to happen anyway, and I simply won't. There. Problem solved."

Raphael doubted it would be that simple, but he let it go for now. Kylian was an adult. The decision was his to make. "Are you going to see him again?"

"I gave him my number. We'll see if he calls," Kylian replied. "I'm going to enjoy it for what it is and not worry about it."

"Why didn't you get his number too?" Raphael asked.

"Because he's the one who lost his partner," Kylian explained. "He's the one who has to be ready for a new relationship. I can't pursue him and expect it to work. He knows I'm interested. The next step is up to him."

"He kissed you, didn't he? That's a good sign."

"I thought you didn't want me to be with him."

"I'm jealous," Raphael admitted, "but if he can make you happy, that's my problem, not yours. You being with him has no bearing on me finding my partner. If anything, it might help me if he's willing to introduce me to other vampires."

Kylian frowned.

"No, I'm not suggesting you bring it up," Raphael assured him quickly. "If you do end up together, it will happen naturally or it won't."

"Thanks," Kylian said. "I don't want him to question my motives for being with him, and I don't want your hopes to be crushed if it doesn't work out between us."

"So is he a good kisser?"

Kylian grinned. "He's hundreds of years old. He's had time to perfect his technique."

Raphael laughed, amazed at how easy it was to be happy for Kylian after his temper had cooled. Yes, he was jealous, but he would not let that affect their friendship. He couldn't. "Imagine what it'll be like when he takes you to bed."

"If," Kylian corrected, although he could imagine it all too easily. He didn't want to get his hopes up, but if it ever happened, he knew it would spoil him for anyone else. "It may never get to that point."

"He kissed you," Raphael reminded him, as if Kylian needed the reminder. "I'd say that's a good first step."

"We'll see," Kylian said. "I don't want to rush into anything. It's worth doing right."

"I've never heard you talk about someone like this," Raphael said. "That's the kind of thing I'd say, not you."

"So maybe I understand you a little better now," Kylian replied. "Maybe next time you talk about your soul mate, I won't be so quick to dismiss you."

Raphael wouldn't complain about that, but it only made him worry more for Kylian.

SEBASTIEN STARED at the phone in his hand. He had started to call four times in the past ten minutes, but each time he chickened out before the call could go through. Thierry would laugh himself silly if he could see Sebastien now, mooning over a kid like he didn't have more than five centuries of experience to guide him in approaching someone. That would be much more reassuring if he had ever started a relationship the normal way. Instead he had lifetimes of experience in hunting and then seducing his chosen prey into giving him what he needed to survive, one instance of a lover pursuing him into an Aveu de Sang, and a partnership he had stumbled into, ignorant of the depth and breadth of such a relationship until it was too late to do anything but cherish it for the rest of Thierry's life. None of that helped him in the slightest when it came to calling Kylian to arrange to see him again.

He should have done it before Kylian left the café, but he had been too off-kilter from the kiss to think beyond that moment. He couldn't say it was the best kiss he'd ever had. First kisses were rarely all they were hyped up to be, noses getting in the way and lack of familiarity making it harder to find the right angle or the perfect pressure. They were often special, but rarely perfect, and the kiss the night before had been as awkward as any other first kiss. It shouldn't have left him reeling the way it did, and he couldn't explain why it had. But it had, and even now his hands trembled at the thought of seeing Kylian again.

"Am I overreacting?" he asked the empty room. "I know you're laughing at me, Thierry, so stop and help me figure this out. You made me promise to go on with my life, so now you have to help me keep that promise."

The silent room provided no answer, but asking the question aloud helped settle him, as it always did when he spoke to Thierry this way. "You'd like him," he went on. "He's got your sense of humor, sharp and sarcastic and painfully blunt, but he has enough charm to pull it off. He would have fit well with us back then—although if he'd been there, I wouldn't have noticed him the way I have now because I didn't have eyes for anyone but you."

He took a deep breath and looked down at the phone in his hand again.

"I don't know why I'm so nervous about this. He couldn't have been any clearer in his interest when he gave me his number. If he says no when I call him, it'll be because he has a conflict, not because he doesn't want to see me again. I know that as surely as I know your name, but it doesn't help. Something about him has me completely off balance, and you know how I hate feeling that way. It's probably why you took such pleasure in throwing me off balance all those years. He isn't doing it on purpose the way you did, though, so I can't get annoyed at him for it. Not that I could ever stay annoyed at you for long either. You always took such delightful advantage of it when you managed to really get me going. It was almost worth it."

He could practically hear Thierry's scoffed "almost?" in reply, but even now, he wouldn't give Thierry the satisfaction of knowing how much Sebastien had enjoyed those moments when Thierry had him twisted in knots and then took him to bed to thoroughly ravish him out of his annoyance.

"It isn't like that with him. I don't think he even realized he'd done it. It certainly wasn't intentional. Or if it was, he's a lot better actor than I gave him credit for. It's just… I've kissed a lot of people over the years, and I've learned how to pick out the ones who might be special pretty quickly. I kissed him on impulse, really just a buss of his lips, little more contact than I'd have sharing les bises with Angélique or Fabienne. I wanted to know how he'd react. I didn't expect my own reaction. It was all I could do not to kiss him again right away, and when he kissed me back…. Fuck, Thierry, I haven't felt like that since you died. He isn't the first person I've kissed since then. He isn't even the first man I've kissed, but he is the first person to make me feel alive again. I want this. I want him."

So what are you waiting for?

He had spent hours talking to Thierry since his death. Probably years, if he added up all the discussions he'd had with an empty room when he needed to think something through and couldn't get there on his own, or when the weight of being alone finally became too much. In all that time, he had never heard Thierry's voice in his heart that clearly. As crazy as it made him feel, it also gave him the courage he'd lacked.

"Merci, chéri," he said to the empty room. "I love you."

He took one more deep breath and called Kylian's number one more time. This time he didn't end the call before it could go through.

"Allô?"

"Hello, Kylian. It's Sebastien. From last night?"

"I remember," Kylian replied, his voice warm even through the connection. "I'm not likely to forget you."

"I'm glad to hear it. I was hoping we could see each other again. I have a commitment I can't break for tonight, but I'm free tomorrow."

"What time?" Kylian asked.

"Any time after sunset," Sebastien answered. "My night is yours if you want it."

He heard Kylian's sharp intake of breath and wondered if he'd rushed and lost his chance with the wizard, but before he could think of a way to backtrack and save the conversation, Kylian spoke.

"I have to work the next morning, so I can't take the whole night, but I'd love to see you again. We could meet at the same café and decide where to go from there."

Sebastien took a moment to calculate the distance from his apartment to le Marais. "I'll meet you there at seven thirty," he said. "That will give me time to get there after it's dark enough for me to move safely. Is it tomorrow yet?"

"I wish." Kylian's breathless voice twisted Sebastien's insides. If he thought Jean would take care of himself if Sebastien didn't show up, he would suggest they meet tonight instead, but his promise to his old friend outweighed his attraction to Kylian. Maybe a time would come when that wouldn't be the case, but for now, Jean had to come first.

"Did you find your friend after you left last night?" Sebastien winced at the banal turn of the conversation, but he had to say something to keep Kylian on the phone a little longer.

"I did," Kylian replied. "And I was right. Once he'd calmed down, he was fine. We talked for a while, mostly about you."

Sebastien flushed at the thought of what they might have said. "Nothing bad, I hope."

"Of course not! I told him how much I'd enjoyed meeting you and talking with you."

"We did more than just talk." Sebastien's voice dropped in register at the memory.

"We did." Kylian's tone darkened to match Sebastien's. "I hope we'll have a chance to do it again."

"I think that can be arranged," Sebastien replied. It was all he could do to refrain from suggesting Kylian come over right now so they could see just what they could do with time and a little privacy. He cursed silently. This wasn't how he wanted their relationship to start. He wanted to get to know Kylian and appreciate him for himself before he focused on his body or his blood. "Within reason, of course. We agreed not to rush into anything just last night."

"I know," Kylian said. "I didn't expect it to be this hard. I don't know what it is about you that makes me want to throw caution out the window."

Sebastien swallowed hard. One of them had to stay in control, and from the sound of it, it would have to be him. That made the evening with Jean tonight even more important. He *had* to sate his beast enough tonight that he could be a gentleman with Kylian tomorrow night.

"If it helps, the feeling is mutual," Sebastien said softly.

"I'm not sure if that helps or makes it harder," Kylian replied. "How am I supposed to behave myself knowing you feel the same way?"

"By remembering that if we rush too much, we could end up with something we can't undo," Sebastien said.

"It's not your fangs I'm interested in."

Sebastien knew that, but if he lost control of his beast for even a second, his fangs could drop and he could score Kylian with them unintentionally. And if Alain and Orlando's story could be used as a guide for anyone else, even the smallest taste would be enough to forge a partnership if they matched. Sebastien would not do that to Kylian without his consent, and that meant staying in control of himself, no matter the provocation. He'd never had to worry about it with Thierry. By the time they first made love, their partnership was already fully established, and by the time they'd performed the ritual to deepen their bond, only Sebastien's fear of savaging Thierry again kept him from devouring Thierry every time they kissed. After the ritual, even that hadn't been a concern. To have to rein himself in again would be all the more difficult for having known true freedom.

"I know, but I'm a vampire. Those fangs are a part of me, no matter how carefully I try to control them."

"We'll cross that bridge when we come to it," Kylian said. "For now, I just want the chance to get to know you better."

"Then we'll meet at the café and sit and talk," Sebastien said. "I can't very well bite you in public."

"That's not the only thing you can't do in public," Kylian retorted.

"I know," Sebastien said. "That's why we should stay at the café. Less chance of either of us doing something we'll regret later."

"I'm not sure I'd regret it even if we did."

Sebastien inhaled sharply. Kylian hadn't said that. He couldn't have. Not after their discussion of not wanting a partnership, of not wanting to rush into anything, of taking the time to get to know each other. Sebastien's beast roared inside him, hungry for blood, sex, and submission. He wouldn't take any of them from Kylian. Not until he could do so in good conscience.

Before Sebastien could formulate a reply, Kylian cursed under his breath. "My boss is coming, and he gets really annoyed if we're on the phone when we aren't on break. I'll see you tomorrow night."

He ended the call before Sebastien could even say good-bye.

Sebastien set the phone down and stared blankly at the wall. "What the hell just happened?" he asked Thierry or the empty room, but neither had a reply.

Chapter 5

SEBASTIEN LET himself into Jean's apartment, feeling the familiar brush of Raymond's magic as he turned the knob. He still expected it to have faded each time he arrived, but the wards were as strong as ever. Sebastien wondered if Thierry's wards still protected the house they had shared, but he had sold it soon after Thierry's death and hadn't been near it since. A part of him hoped Thierry's magic still lingered in the world, but he wouldn't torture himself with it. He couldn't, not if he wanted to stay sane. Talking to Thierry's spirit, if it lingered, was bad enough.

"Jean," he called when he was inside, "it's time to go."

He received no reply, but he rarely did. If he got Jean to say more than a few words to him each time he visited, he counted it a success. He crossed to the bedroom and knocked on the door. He never went inside, but he would keep knocking until Jean came out.

The door opened on the first knock this time, and Jean stepped into the living room. "You're late."

He was, but he hadn't expected Jean to notice. "I got a late start tonight. I didn't realize you were expecting me at a particular time."

"I wasn't," Jean replied, "but you always arrive anyway."

"Someone has to keep you fed," Sebastien replied with a shrug. He still hadn't decided how much to tell Jean about Kylian.

"I don't know why you insist on it," Jean said, "but since you're here, let's go. The sooner we leave, the sooner you'll leave me alone again."

Sebastien led the way out of the building and toward the quarter where Sang Froid waited. He watched Jean surreptitiously as they crossed the city. He was wan and listless, as always. Sebastien searched each time for some returning spark of hope, of interest, of life, but Jean showed no sign of paying any attention to his surroundings beyond putting one foot in front of the other.

"You seem different tonight," Jean said eventually. The comment surprised Sebastien into stopping.

"What do you mean?"

"I don't know," Jean said. "You just seem… lighter."

Sebastien considered that for a moment. He hadn't thought about it in those terms, but his grief didn't weigh him down the way it had since Thierry died. "I suppose I am," he said finally.

"What changed?"

"You don't want to know," Sebastien said. "You won't like it, and I don't want to argue with you."

"You met someone," Jean surmised. "That's the only thing you wouldn't want to tell me."

"And if I did?" Sebastien challenged. "It's been thirty-three years for me, Jean. I didn't go looking, but Thierry made me promise to go on and not to let his memory keep me from living again if the opportunity arose. I've mourned him. I've stayed faithful to him, probably more than he would have wanted. He wouldn't begrudge me a new chance at happiness."

"Is that all he meant to you?" Jean asked bitterly. "More than ninety years and a bond you fought to create, brushed aside like it's nothing?"

"You know that's not true," Sebastien shouted. "I loved Thierry. He was my mate in every way, the only one whose blood could sate my beast. You were there when we performed the ritual, when I could finally let go for the first time. You know what that meant to me. I'll never have anything like that again, and I wouldn't want to, but that doesn't mean I can't have something. Bordel de merde, Jean, I barely even have friends anymore, and none outside the vampire community— half of which is in mourning for their lost partners and the other half of which thinks we were fools to get involved with wizards in the first place. I just want a few hours without all of that dragging me down. Where's the crime in that?"

Jean sighed. "It's not a crime. Nothing in our laws prohibit it, but then you know that. It's more that I don't understand. I can barely breathe. Anything else is an effort too great to even contemplate. You talk about wanting a friend again. I can't even make sense of those words. I haven't felt anything since he died. I'm dead inside. The beast doesn't even stir in me. If you didn't drag me out to Sang Froid, I'd have perished years ago. I can't be your friend, because I've forgotten how. I've forgotten everything that isn't him."

"I know," Sebastien said. "I do. I'd tell you it gets easier, but you'd know I'm lying. It doesn't get easier, except that one day my heart started beating again. It hurts. It hurts like hell when it does. It's like losing him all over again because the one thing I have left of him is my memories, and any new memory takes away from the old ones. But even knowing that, the new memories happen whether I want them to or not. This is the second time I've done this. I know how it goes, and I know it will eventually reach a point where his voice, his touch, his taste will be indistinguishable again, so indistinct in my memory that I can't recall them except as the vaguest of sensations. I dread that day, but it will come whether I fight it or not."

"So you just let it happen? I can't. He was my soul."

"I know. Thierry was mine."

"Then how can you even consider someone new?" Jean asked, voice rough.

"Because to not do so is a worse betrayal of his memory," Sebastien replied. "Kylian is not a replacement for Thierry. He's a breath of fresh air. A chance to feel something besides grief. That's what Thierry wanted. It's what Raymond wanted for you too."

Jean shook his head. "I can't. I won't tell you not to, but don't ask it of me. The grief is still too fresh."

Sebastien had not hoped for even that much. Now to tell Jean the rest.

"I met Kylian when I was looking for a club where I could take you to hunt. It's time, Jean. You don't have to meet anyone new, but you have to take that first step."

"What gives you the right to make that decision?" Jean demanded.

"Nothing," Sebastien admitted. "But that doesn't mean I'm wrong. Angélique agrees."

"Meddling bastards, both of you," Jean grumbled.

"This is the most emotion I've seen you show since we buried Raymond. I'm not proposing anything that would betray Raymond's memory. You never hunted him. He was your partner before either of you admitted to wanting anything else. How would hunting be any different than going to Sang Froid?"

"If I go to a club, they will expect more than just feeding me," Jean reminded him. "Or have things really changed that much since the last time I went to one?"

"No, nothing has changed," Sebastien said, "but their expectations don't control you. You're offering what you're offering, end of discussion. You don't have to do anything that would betray Raymond's memory, although I don't think he'd mind if you did. He wouldn't want you to suffer like this."

"That assumes that I could," Jean said. "I haven't felt anything like desire since he died."

"Then hunting at a club should be simple," Sebastien said. He wasn't surprised by the admission, only that Jean would voice it. It had taken years after Thierry's death before he could look at anyone else with interest, and for a long time, it had only been women. That had changed before he met Kylian, but they had only been momentary fancies, over as soon as he'd sated his need for blood and sex. Kylian wouldn't be as simple. Sebastien knew that much already. "Nothing to remind you of Raymond or to betray his memory. Come with me tonight?"

"I thought you met someone," Jean said. "Why do you need to hunt?"

"Because I met him. I didn't feed from him," Sebastien said.

"That doesn't make sense. What aren't you telling me?"

"He's a wizard," Sebastien admitted. "I don't want another partnership. And maybe he wouldn't be my partner, but I'm not going down that road. I'll see him. I might even sleep with him eventually, but I won't bite him until I'm sure it's the right thing for both of us."

"What does he think of this?"

"He doesn't want a partner either," Sebastien said.

"Then where in the world did you meet him?"

"He was trying to keep his best friend out of trouble," Sebastien replied. "He looked bored, which isn't a look you usually see on people's faces at that kind of club. If they're bored, they go home. I asked what he was doing there, and we got to talking. Things went from there."

"Oh really?" Jean drawled, and for a moment, Sebastien could see the old chef de la Cour in his friend's eyes. "And where did they go?"

"To a cup of coffee and a kiss," Sebastien said. "That's all."

"Are you going to see him again?"

"Tomorrow," Sebastien said. "Tonight was already set aside for you. I need to feed, and so do you. Come hunting with me."

"You know, I just realized we've never hunted together," Jean said. "All the years with our partners, we never needed to."

"And before that, we weren't exactly friends," Sebastien agreed. "We don't have to go to a club if you'd prefer another place, but I need to hunt. Tonight Sang Froid won't be enough."

"He has you that worked up?" Jean asked.

"As embarrassing as it is to admit, yes," Sebastien said. "I feel like I'm newly turned all over again. The beast is restless, and I don't want to lose control tomorrow night. I don't want to scare Kylian off before we ever get started."

"You didn't scare Thierry off."

"No, although I still don't know by what miracle I was that lucky, but he loved me by then, enough to stay and fight for me. Kylian has no reason to stay if I lose control with him."

"Do you really think you would?"

"Normally I'd say no, of course not, but I told you, I'm restless in a way I haven't felt since before…." He couldn't bring himself to give voice to the ritual that had bound him and Thierry, but Jean did not need it. He had been there as they had taken the leap of faith that the cobbled-together blend of traditions would be enough to do the impossible and force Sebastien's inner demon to recognize Thierry as his mate.

"Is it because you're hunting again?" Jean asked.

"I've been hunting for the past ten years," Sebastien replied. "I don't think that made a difference."

"Your new young man, then?"

"He's not mine," Sebastien protested. "Not yet, anyway."

"But you want him to be, and that could be enough to summon those instincts. They have a target and you're denying them. We're base creatures beneath the bonds of civilization we put on."

"All the more reason to sate every appetite I can tonight," Sebastien replied. "That way I'll be less tempted tomorrow."

"Then we will hunt," Jean said. Sebastien had to stop to marvel at the power of their friendship. What Jean would never do for himself, he offered to do immediately when he realized what it would mean to Sebastien.

Chapter 6

As AGREED, Sebastien met Kylian in the same café where they had shared coffee and conversation two nights previously. As soon as he walked in, he checked to see if the same waiter was working. To his relief, he saw no sign of the man. Controlling his beast would be easier without the prod of irrational jealousy.

Kylian was already waiting for him, ensconced at a table in the back. Sebastien joined him, his breath catching at the smile that lit up Kylian's already handsome face when he saw Sebastien. It felt odd to see him without Raphael at his shoulder, but Sebastien couldn't complain about having Kylian to himself for the evening. The possessive thought troubled him, but he pushed the worry aside. He had never been a possessive man except where his Avoué and Thierry were concerned, but dwelling on it would serve no purpose except to spoil the evening.

"Bonsoir, Kylian," Sebastien said as he shook Kylian's hand. Kylian squeezed his fingers as he lingered over the handshake, and when Kylian finally drew his hand back, he trailed his fingers over Sebastien's palm, sending a frisson of need along Sebastien's nerves.

"Bonsoir," he replied as Sebastien sat down. His voice teased across Sebastien's skin like a caress. Putain, this was going to be a long night. Even knowing the night would not end with his fangs buried in Kylian's neck did not quell the sudden longing for it. Sebastien smiled back and forcefully tamped down on the beast within.

"How have you been?" he asked, trying to get himself back on even footing.

"If I tell you I spent the past two days missing you, would you take it the wrong way?" Kylian asked.

"No," Sebastien said hoarsely. "I felt the same way."

"This is insane," Kylian said with a shaky laugh. "We don't know each other well enough to feel this way."

"It does feel rather sudden," Sebastien agreed, "but I can't make myself regret it."

"Have you ever had this happen before?" Kylian asked. "Because I'm usually way too cynical or sarcastic for the guys I meet to come back for more."

Sebastien didn't let himself hope that meant no one had ever touched Kylian. He couldn't let his thoughts go there or he'd never let Kylian walk away from him again.

"Their loss," he said instead. "And yes, I've felt this way before, but only a couple of times." Two, to be precise. Once when Thibaut ramrodded him into an Aveu de Sang almost before he could breathe, and once when a grieving wizard had held out his wrist for Sebastien to bite and changed Sebastien's life forever. That didn't bode well for ignoring his attraction to Kylian.

Kylian didn't reply right away, but when he did, it wasn't at all what Sebastien had expected. "I know too much about you from the history books without you telling me much of anything. I don't know what I'm allowed to ask or say."

"You can ask what you want," Sebastien said. "I may choose not to answer. I know a large chunk of my life is a matter of public record. Even if we tried to keep the private portions to ourselves, it wasn't always possible."

"Was monsieur Dumont one of the times you felt this way?" Kylian asked in a rush of words.

"Thierry," Sebastien corrected. "His name was Thierry, and yes, he was one. Everything about him caught me by surprise and fascinated me at the same time."

"You still love him."

It wasn't a question, but Sebastien answered anyway. "Yes. I'll always love him, but I've accepted that he is part of my past now. He didn't want me to be alone. He was very clear about that."

"Does that mean you're looking for a replacement?" Kylian asked bitterly.

"No," Sebastien said, grabbing Kylian's hand in his urgency to make Kylian understand. "Not at all. No one could ever replace him because no one will ever be him, but that doesn't mean there's no room for someone new. He was my life while I had him, but he died, and I'm ready to move on."

Kylian flinched at his words, making Sebastien wonder what he'd said wrong.

"I'll never measure up," Kylian said. "Even if you're ready for someone new, I have nothing to offer. I'm not a hero. I'm not an officer. I'm not any part of l'ANS, much less high-ranked within it."

Sebastien stopped Kylian's words with a brush of his lips. When he leaned back, Kylian looked as starstruck as Sebastien felt. It shouldn't feel so right to kiss someone he barely knew, but he couldn't bring himself to complain.

"Yes, Thierry was all those things, but that's not why I loved him. If you told me you weren't cynical to the bone and as sarcastic as the day is long, you might have something to worry about, but you already told me you were those things. If you told me you weren't protective of your friends, I might have a problem, but I've seen you with Raphael. If you told me you hated all magical races outside your own, that might be enough to dissuade me—but you're here with me now, so you obviously don't feel that way about vampires at the very least."

"Is that really how you see me?" Kylian asked.

"It's how you've shown yourself to be," Sebastien replied. "Actions speak louder than words. Thierry always told me that, but I knew it even before him. We vampires have a game, I suppose you'd call it. Le jeu des Cours. It governs status within our numbers, and it's all about actions and repercussions and how to twist other people's actions to your own benefit. Mostly I think it's a bunch of bullshit these days, but then, I'm hardly active in the Cour now either. Jean was a master at it until he retired."

"If actions speak louder than words," Kylian said slowly, "why are we here in a place where all we can do is talk?"

"Because neither of us is ready for our actions to do the talking," Sebastien said. "You don't want a partner, or that's what you told me before. I don't want to be trapped with a partner I might not care for the way a partnership requires."

"You're assuming we're partners," Kylian said. "What if we aren't? There'd be nothing to hold us back then. It's simple enough to test."

Sebastien hadn't even considered the idea that Kylian might not be his partner. Everything about their reactions to one another fit the studies Raymond and Jean had spent their life together working on. "Do you have a pen?"

Kylian set one on the table between them. Sebastien drew a line on the back of his hand and rested it on the table in silent offering. Kylian hesitated for so long that Sebastien thought he'd changed his mind, but then he drew his wand and cast the familiar erasing charm across Sebastien's skin. The line of ink didn't even fade, much less disappear.

"Now we know," Sebastien said quietly. The brush of magic lit a fire in his gut. During the war he'd avoided magic as much as possible, since most of it was meant to kill or maim, and after it was over, he'd come to associate the sensation with his closest friends. Since Raymond's death, the only magic he'd encountered was the wards on Jean's apartment. Raymond's magic was nearly as familiar to him as Thierry's had been, although never in as intimate a setting. More than once, Sebastien had felt the explosion of Thierry's magic across his skin as they found their release together. Kylian's magic felt different, but so very right, in a way that defied words.

"I guess that answers the question of whether a vampire can find a new partner," he said slowly. "I should let someone at l'Institut know. After Jude died, Adèle found a new partner in Pascale, but I'm not sure any other vampires besides me have."

"I'm not your partner yet," Kylian said.

"No, and you might never be," Sebastien agreed, "but you could be, and that's more than we knew before, unless someone has found a new partner without me hearing about it."

"Is that likely?" Kylian asked.

Sebastien shrugged. "I don't keep up with the latest research the way I did when I lived there. With Thierry gone and our partnership broken, it seemed more like self-flagellation than anything else, and I've never been one for unnecessary pain."

Necessary pain was a completely different story. He didn't bear the marks left by the ritual that had made Thierry his mate, but he had felt the pain at the time. It had been worth every ounce of agony to know they were bound.

"That makes sense, I suppose. No one mentioned a vampire finding a second partner when I attended the seminar there, but that was eight years ago."

"That long?" Sebastien asked. "I wouldn't have pegged you as being old enough for it to have been that long."

"I'm twenty-eight," Kylian said. "I know that's nothing to you, but I'm not a child."

"I didn't think you were," Sebastien replied. "I met you at a club, remember? But I did think you were younger than you are." It was a relief to hear. He had enough worry over what was happening between them without adding Kylian's youth to it. Twenty-eight wasn't old, but it was old enough for him to make up his mind about a relationship.

"I get that a lot," Kylian said. "The scruff is supposed to help, but I'm pretty sure it just makes me look like I'm trying to appear older instead of actually helping."

"I like it." Sebastien reached out to stroke the soft whiskers on Kylian's cheek. Except for the last harrowing days of the war, Thierry had always shaved, so it was an unfamiliar sensation on his skin. "It suits you, whether it makes you look older or not."

"My mother says I look disreputable."

"Roguish," Sebastien countered. "They're not the same thing."

"Semantics," Kylian insisted.

"Not to me," Sebastien said. "And remember, I saw the courts of Louis XIII and beyond. The courtiers, the ones who were soldiers as well as noblemen, were the epitome of roguish, with their devilish smiles and the swords on their hips to back up their words, but they were never disreputable. They valued the king's favor too much to do anything that would tarnish their reputations. You remind me of them, especially the ones who eschewed the wigs that were so in fashion and wore their hair naturally long instead. Maybe not quite as long as yours, but long enough that they could put it in a queue, powder it, and have it not offend the matrons of the time who ruled the fashion of the court with an iron fist."

"I can't even imagine the things you must have seen in your lifetime."

"I've seen good and bad," Sebastien said. "I've seen delights you could never imagine, and I've seen horrors I would never inflict on my worst enemy."

"I thought vampires tended to be insular, at least before l'émeute des Sorciers," Kylian said.

"We did, and even now we still are to some extent, but the histories you studied left out one piece of the puzzle," Sebastien explained. "I wasn't part of the Cour for most of my existence. I only became a real part of it during the war. Before that, I was on my own, and that meant finding ways to fend for myself."

"Why?" Kylian asked. "All the stories portray you and Bellaiche as inseparable."

Sebastien snorted. "Someone needs to rewrite those books. Jean is my closest friend now, without a doubt, but it took the war, the partnerships, and a fair bit of diplomacy on Raymond's and Thierry's parts to get us to that point. He hated me."

"Really? Why?"

Sebastien's turmoil must have shown on his face because Kylian immediately backtracked. "I'm sorry. That's too personal a question to ask so soon. Forget I brought it up."

"No," Sebastien said. "You have the right to know. If we're going to be involved, you'll hear it again anyway." He took a deep breath, trying to decide where to begin. "I wasn't born or made in Paris, but the town where I grew up was too small for me to stay once I was turned. I came to Paris with every intention of joining the Cour and becoming part of vampire society here. Jean was already chef de la Cour, although new to his role, and the Cour was a flourishing, vibrant place. It was easy to get lost in Paris at the time, to hide in plain sight. As long as we didn't leave a trail of bodies behind us, no one even thought to consider our existence. In many ways, it's a heyday that may never come again. I had been in the city a week at the most when I met Thibaut. He recognized me as a vampire, offered to let me feed, and seduced me in the process. He convinced me to form an Aveu de Sang with him. What he didn't tell me was that he had likewise been courting the chef de la Cour but that Jean had hesitated to give him the bond he wanted. Jean saw only that the man he had considered his mate now belonged to someone else, a nobody from the country who hadn't even been properly introduced to the Cour. He hadn't made a formal claim on Thibaut, so he couldn't banish me outright—but he made it very clear I was not welcome, and the other vampires followed his lead. It wasn't until the war that Jean listened to the story from my perspective. Even then, it took time for him to trust me. Not that I blame him."

"Wow," Kylian said. "I had no idea."

"Few people outside the Cour do, and I see no reason to change that," Sebastien said. "Those years have no bearing on my position within the Cour now, and even less bearing on what belongs in the history books. They're memories I would prefer to forget most days."

"The stories, the popular ones, not the historical ones, always present your relationship with Thierry in the same light as they do messieurs Bellaiche and Payet, or messieurs Magnier and St. Clair. But I thought if a vampire had an Avoué, that was pretty much it for him or her."

Sebastien sighed. "It is, usually. I don't know if the difference is that Thierry was a wizard or that I made Thibaut my Avoué because he wanted it, not because I did. I did love him, and I mourned him when he died, and I kept mourning him until I met Thierry." Sebastien didn't say that he'd mourned Thierry until he met Kylian. It simplified the situation too much, for one thing. More than that, though, he didn't think Kylian was ready to hear it.

"And now?"

Or maybe he was.

"Losing Thierry tore a hole in the very fabric of my life," Sebastien said, "but some days I swear I can feel him yelling at me to get over it and get on with my life. It won't be what I had with him, just like what I had with him wasn't what I shared with Thibaut. It will be something else. Something good, I hope. Something better than the emptiness he left behind. It won't stop me from missing him, just like loving him didn't stop me from missing Thibaut, but it will be its own thing. As it should be."

Kylian leaned forward and kissed him, heedless of the other customers in the café. Sebastien closed his eyes, the better to enjoy the feeling of Kylian's beard against his lips, a permanent reminder that he was kissing Kylian, not Thierry or anyone else from his past. Kylian wasn't a nameless source of relief, the way so many others had been since Thierry died. Kylian deserved better than to have Sebastien's mind substitute anyone else in his place. He lifted a hand to Kylian's shoulder and felt the brush of long hair against his fingers, another reminder of who he was kissing.

Kylian pulled back after a moment and studied Sebastien's face. Sebastien summoned a smile, even as he struggled to regain his internal balance. He had so rarely kissed the men and women he fed from, his mouth—and fangs—being otherwise occupied, but kissing Kylian felt right. Like he had come home after years of absence.

The thought unnerved him. Even with Thierry, it had taken longer than this, and he had marveled at the time how easily he had slipped into a relationship with his partner.

"Do you really want coffee?" Kylian asked softly. "Because I'd like to be somewhere alone with you."

Sebastien was quite sure that was a phenomenally bad idea, but he nodded despite himself. "We could walk along the Seine. It's only a few blocks away. Nobody uses all those little parks at this hour."

"I know them well. They're Raphael's favorite places in the city," Kylian said. "He likes to be close to the water."

"Where's your favorite place in the city?" Sebastien asked.

"Anywhere you are."

Sebastien smiled at the earnestness of the reply. It should have come across as trite, but he could see the truth of the words in Kylian's eyes, just as he felt the truth of them resonate within him. "And before you knew me?" Sebastien pressed. The Seine was close, but nowhere in the city was inaccessible with the Métro. They could go to Kylian's favorite place easily enough.

"The bois de Boulogne, but that's not close," Kylian said. "We could go to the jardin du Luxembourg if you don't want to walk along the Seine, but I have earth beneath my feet no matter where we go."

"Then let's go down by the river," Sebastien said. "We'll go to the bois de Boulogne another time."

They paid for their untouched coffee and left the café. As they wended their way from the place des Vosges toward the river, Kylian slipped his hand into Sebastien's and squeezed gently. The contact vibrated up Sebastien's arm. His pulse tripped for a moment before settling into a new, faster rhythm. He couldn't explain his reaction, but it felt too good to question. He felt *alive* again.

When they reached the river, Sebastien looked for one of the small green spaces with a bench where they could sit, but Kylian kept walking, so Sebastien followed along. "Are we going somewhere in particular?"

"No," Kylian said, "but it's a beautiful night to walk along the river." He paused for a moment. "If we go down to one of the benches, I'm not sure I'll be able to stop myself from kissing you again."

"You assume I'd want you to stop."

"It wouldn't stop at kissing."

Kylian's hoarse tone snapped something inside Sebastien. He pushed Kylian against the nearest lamppost, uncaring that the circle of light would draw the attention of every passerby, and brought their mouths together. They had kissed before, mostly gentle brushes of lips, but those chaste kisses wouldn't satisfy Sebastien now. He needed to feel the press of Kylian's body along the length of his. He needed Kylian's lips to part beneath him so he could delve deep. He needed to taste, to claim. He fought to keep his fangs from dropping. He couldn't bite Kylian, no matter how badly he needed blood. When he lost the battle with his fangs, he pulled back, panting harshly. "You can't say things like that."

"Why not?" Kylian asked. His pupils were completely dilated, his features lax with pleasure. Sebastien thought he'd never looked more appealing.

"Because when I lose control, my fangs drop," Sebastien said. He bared his teeth so Kylian could see the sharp points. "It only takes a few drops of blood to create a bond we both agreed we didn't want."

"Then maybe I should do other things with my mouth besides kiss you," Kylian purred as he shifted against Sebastien. He could feel Kylian's erection against his leg, and it set the beast inside him howling for sex and blood. He pulled back abruptly. He had to put some distance between them before he did something they'd both regret.

Kylian remained where he was, leaning against the lamppost, his body on display. Sebastien's mouth watered, but he resisted. He couldn't trust himself right now, and Kylian was no help at all.

"You're playing with fire," he warned.

"I'm an earth wizard," Kylian drawled. "Earth smothers fire every time."

Sebastien took an involuntary step forward. Kylian might be an earth wizard, but he drew Sebastien like a moth to a flame. Sebastien knew how that story ended, though, and he wasn't going to make the moth's mistake. Not until he knew he could survive the flames unscathed. Giving in to Kylian, whether it remained purely sexual or became a partnership, would leave its mark on him, and suddenly he wasn't sure he was ready for that.

"I'm sorry," he said. "I can't do this."

After one last searching look, as if the vision Kylian made weren't already imprinted on his memory, Sebastien turned and fled.

Chapter 7

"FUCK!" KYLIAN cursed when Sebastien left. He knocked his head backward against the lamppost. "You screwed that one up, Raffier."

He pushed away from the post and stalked back toward the place des Vosges and home. He couldn't believe he'd gotten so carried away. He liked sex as much as the next man, but he considered himself civilized enough to not jump a potential partner in the middle of the street. Sebastien had shattered that veneer with a single kiss, leaving Kylian a seething mass of lust with no other goal than to seduce Sebastien into fucking him into oblivion. And wasn't that another surprise? Kylian preferred to top as a rule, although he'd been known to bend if his partner insisted. With Sebastien, he didn't even consider it. If he closed his eyes, he could all too easily imagine the dark vampire hovering over him, pinning him to the bed with his superior strength—not that Kylian wanted to get away—tantalizing him until he was begging, and then pounding into him with all that harnessed power. He ached for it, for Sebastien.

Kylian could feel his magic sparking around him in his need. He'd told Sebastien he could feel the earth beneath his feet anywhere they chose to walk, but the concrete sidewalk blocked a deep connection, and Kylian needed that now if he didn't want to explode from the power that surged beneath his skin with no outlet. The fences along the sidewalk kept him out of the bushes, where he could have reached dirt instead of concrete. He sped up as he searched for the entrance to the nearest park. His urgency grew with each step, every instinct he possessed screaming at him for letting Sebastien get away. "It's only for now," he chanted to himself. "I'll see him again. I'll have another chance."

He hoped that was true. If he had ruined everything between them, he didn't know what he'd do.

He found an entrance to one of the parks and ran down the path until he reached the river's edge. The paved sidewalk gave way to gravel. He breathed a sigh of relief as he sank to his knees and rested his palms flat against the ground beneath him. If he trusted himself to cast a spell to take him to the bois de Boulogne, he could strip and press his entire body into the earth—but he had no guarantee of privacy here. He would have to make do with just his hands.

He tried to focus—as he had learned to do as soon as his magic manifested—so he could channel the energy into the ground where it would rest, ready to strengthen him again when he needed it. It was the first thing a wizard learned and the last he forgot, but Kylian could barely concentrate through the storm raging inside him. He had never felt this out of control, not even in the early days when he'd had no idea what he was doing. His body shook with the effort to hold in his magic and spin it outward through his hands. Ants crawled under his skin, disrupting his concentration even more. He couldn't think. He couldn't breathe. He couldn't do anything but spiral out of control. He dug his fingers into the gravel, seeking the dirt below. If he could just touch the dirt, earth instead of stone, he could settle himself. He could let out this incomprehensible surge. He could find surcease.

His fingers found dirt and he cried out in exquisite pain as his magic poured out of him. His back arched from the sheer force of it, an explosion that started deep in his gut and radiated outward. Panting, he collapsed onto the ground, unable to support his own weight through the onslaught of sensation. He lost all track of time and his surroundings, his vision graying out as he shook in the throes of release.

When he finally came back to himself, he rolled to the side and tried to gather his thoughts. His whole body tingled, an experience he usually associated with a thorough round of sex, but Sebastien hadn't done more than kiss him. A cool breeze kicked up as he lay there, still trembling from the exertion of containing and then releasing that much magic. He shivered and sat up so he could zip his coat. As he moved, he felt an unexpected stickiness. "Fuck," he muttered again. "He's not even here and he made me come in my pants. I'm not sure I want to know what actually having sex with him will do to me."

He stumbled to his feet and took a moment to steady himself. He shouldn't have been this shaky, but he felt as if his legs would give out from underneath him at any second. "This is getting annoying. He shouldn't affect me this way."

He needed to go home and take a shower. Then he'd call Raphael and see if his friend had ever heard of anything like what was going on between him and Sebastien. He had never felt out of control like this, even as a newly minted wizard with no experience to draw on. After fourteen years, he had no excuse. He drew his wand and cast a displacement spell, because he had no desire to walk all the way home in soiled trousers. If he was going to cast a spell anyway, better to go home where he could get truly clean than cast a cleansing spell that only worked as an interim measure. When he reached for the doorknob, though, he found empty air. He looked around in confusion, trying to figure out where he was. It was the garden of a small house, but not one he recognized.

"What the hell?"

He looked around more carefully, trying to figure out where he'd ended up, but he could see none of the familiar landmarks that usually dotted the skyline in Paris. Carefully he stretched out with his magic to see if he could determine why he'd been drawn here. As he neared the house, he felt the presence of someone else's spells, old spells, to judge by the faintness of the signature. He traced the lines, searching for anything he could use to identify the creator of the wards, but the layering was thicker than he had encountered anywhere outside l'ANS and l'Institut. Whoever had cast these wards had been both powerful and fearful to have woven such a complex barrier to the outside world. He wasn't sure he would be able to sense if a wizard lived there now, but if one did, he had not adjusted the spells recently.

He walked to the gate and peered down the street. He didn't see anyone, so he opened it quietly and stepped out. He could cast a spell to go home, if it worked this time, but his curiosity was piqued. He needed to know where he was, even if he couldn't figure out why. He walked down the lane toward what appeared to be a larger thoroughfare. Hopefully he would find something there to give him some clue.

He had to wander down several more streets before he found anything to orient him. He stared up the avenue de Paris at the palace of Versailles. "Why Versailles? I don't know anyone in Versailles."

He'd been there, of course, on a school trip when he was in the lycée, but while he had found the palace impressive, he had felt no particular connection to it. Certainly no reason why a spell to go home would bring him here instead of to his apartment. He might have understood if he'd ended up back in Auvergne at the house where he'd grown up, but not Versailles.

His skin pricked again with the feeling of being watched, but when he looked around, the street was empty except for a few patrons of a local café, who were paying no attention to him. The night had gotten decidedly strange. He drew his wand again and cast another displacement spell, this time focusing clearly on Raphael's apartment. To his relief, it worked, and he ended up in the middle of Raphael's living room.

"You can't knock now?" Raphael asked, an amused smile on his face.

"Not at the moment," Kylian said. "It's been way too odd a night for pleasantries."

"What happened?" Raphael asked, instantly concerned. "I thought you had a date."

"I did," Kylian said. "Look, I'll tell you everything, but could I take a shower first?"

Raphael's eyebrows shot up in surprise. "Aren't you always the one talking about not putting out on a first date?"

Kylian glared at him, but he could hardly argue when he knew where he and Sebastien would have ended up if Sebastien hadn't called a halt. Kylian would never have pulled away of his own accord.

"You can yell at me after I have a shower," he said.

"You know where everything is," Raphael replied. "And don't think I won't."

Kylian retreated to the bathroom where he peeled the layers of sticky cloth off his body. He would cast a cleansing spell on them after his shower. It wouldn't be quite the same as clean clothes, but it would have to do for now. He washed mechanically, trying to sort out his thoughts so he could give Raphael a coherent account of the evening—but the more he thought about it, the more inexplicable it became.

With a muttered curse, he got out of the shower and dried off. A quick spell took care of his clothes enough that he could dress and go back into the living room.

"Okay, so spill," Raphael said as soon as Kylian sat down. "What happened?"

"I don't even know how to explain it," Kylian said. "When I try to put it into words, it makes no sense."

"Try," Raphael ordered. "I can't help if I don't know what's going on."

"Something happened when I was with Sebastien tonight," Kylian said slowly. Raphael leered at him playfully. "Not that kind of something. I don't know how to explain it, Raph, but it didn't feel like a first date. The things he told me about himself... I got the feeling he hadn't told anyone some of those things, or almost no one. I suppose Thierry knew them."

"He talked to you about his former partner?" Raphael asked. "That doesn't seem like a good sign for a date."

"Actually I took it as a very good sign," Kylian said. "He was honest about it. If he'd tried to pretend it hadn't happened or wasn't important, I'd be worried, but the fact that he's honest about still loving his deceased partner means he isn't pretending to be ready for something he isn't."

"If you say so," Raphael said. "What happened then?"

"I kissed him, and suddenly kissing wasn't enough, at least not the kind you can do in public, so I suggested we go somewhere else. We got as far as the river, and I kept goading him. It's like I was watching myself from the outside, not able to stop what I was doing as I tried to seduce him. It worked at first. He kissed me back like he wanted to crawl inside me and never leave, and I would have let him. I would have given him anything he asked for, right there on the street where anyone driving by could have seen us. I would've sucked him off. I would've bent over and let him fuck me. Whatever he wanted."

"What did he ask for?" Raphael demanded.

"Nothing," Kylian said. "He left me standing there aching for him, and he ran. I couldn't keep it together. I made it to one of the parks where I could get to dirt instead of concrete and lost all control of my magic and my body. That's why I needed a shower, not because of anything Sebastien did."

"That's not like you," Raphael said. "You've always had better control than the rest of us."

"Not tonight. I'm not done. I tried to go home. I cast a spell because I didn't want to walk home covered in spunk, but instead of ending up at home, I ended up in a garden of some random house in Versailles."

"Why Versailles?"

"That's what I want to know," Kylian said. He scrubbed his hands over his face and couldn't help remembering Sebastien doing the same, albeit far more gently. "I've been to Versailles twice in my life. Once on a school trip and once when my family came to visit and wanted to see it. I don't know anyone who lives there. I don't have any connection to it that I can think of, but I ended up there anyway."

"That's... odd."

"Very. I came here because I figured I could make the spell precise enough to bring me here and maybe you could help. But I guess not."

"Not off the top of my head, but we can try to figure it out," Raphael said. "You said it was like watching yourself and not being able to stop when you were with him. Looking back, did you want to stop? Was he controlling you somehow?"

"Looking back, I know he was right to stop us, but I didn't want him to stop. Even now, if he came in your door, I'd want him the same way," Kylian replied. "If anything was compelling me, it was myself. I know that doesn't make sense, but there you have it."

"Okay," Raphael said slowly. "Now I really don't know what to tell you."

"And you would have known what to tell me if he'd been the one compelling me?"

"If nothing else, you could have stayed away from him," Raphael said.

Kylian contemplated staying away from Sebastien, but every fiber of his being cried out in protest at the thought. "I don't think that's an option. I never felt like someone was missing from my life the way you've always described, but I think I understand the need driving you now. It's an itch under my skin, like if I don't see him again, I'll come right out of my body. Just climb right out of the empty shell, because if he's not there, that's all it is." He shook his head. "This is ridiculous. I can't feel this way about someone I've known less than a week. We've only really talked twice—the first night barely counts, he left so quickly."

He dragged his hands through his wet hair, tempted to tug on it in his frustration. "What is happening to me, Raph? I've never felt like this about anything. It scares me."

"I don't know," Raphael said, "but whatever it is, we'll figure it out. You aren't in this alone, okay? I'm not going anywhere, even if I'm jealous as hell that you found a vampire when I haven't."

"I wasn't looking for a specific vampire. That probably made it easier," Kylian said shakily.

"Do you really think you'd react this way to another vampire?" Raphael asked. "Because from where I'm sitting, it looks pretty damn specific."

Kylian shuddered at the thought of being with another vampire the way he'd been with Sebastien. "Okay, maybe you're right, but I swear I wasn't looking, Raph. I don't know what this is. It doesn't make sense."

"I believe you," Raphael said, "but now that you've found him, you have to decide what to do with him. For better or worse or somewhere in between, you're tied to a vampire. Is he your partner?"

"If you mean does he have the potential to be my partner, yes, but he didn't bite me, if that's what you're asking. The bond hasn't formed yet."

Raphael looked at him speculatively for a moment. "Do you really believe that?"

"But how else could it have formed?" Kylian demanded. "He hasn't bitten me. I think I'd remember that. And that's how the bond forms. The seminars couldn't have been any clearer about it. Until blood has been exchanged, both partners are free to walk away. It's only after the vampire has fed from the wizard that they're linked."

Raphael leaned back in his chair and tapped his fingers on his thigh. "What do you want out of this? When we talked about it a couple of days ago, you kept talking about not rushing and anything worth doing being worth doing right. Now, two days and a few kisses later, you've thrown caution to the wind and all but jumped the man. In public, no less. So what do you want from him?"

"I wish I knew," Kylian said.

"That's the question you have to answer. Once you have an answer for that, you can decide what to do next," Raphael said. "Until then, all I can do is listen if you need to talk. I don't have much other advice to give."

"Then I guess I have some thinking to do. I think I'll walk home. One strange trip per night is more than enough."

"Be safe," Raphael said. "I'll see you tomorrow after work?"

"I'll be there," Kylian said. "See you then."

Chapter 8

SEBASTIEN RACED through the city, ignoring the surprised cries of the people he jostled as he passed. They were of no concern to him. His only thought centered around escape. If he thought about anything else, he'd zero back in on Kylian, and he didn't trust his own control if he let his thoughts wander in that direction. Even now, he swore he could feel Kylian's presence tugging at him. The slightest slip would be enough to turn his feet back toward the wizard, the infuriating, intoxicating wizard who could be his partner if he let it happen. It would have been so easy. A slip of his fangs would have done it, and he could have blamed it on chance, an accident, not his intent, and then he would have Kylian as his own no matter what.

He stumbled into the Père Lachaise cemetery and fell to his knees at the base of Thierry's headstone. He traced the letters with his fingers, focusing on the cool stone beneath his hand. But the letters provided no respite from the maelstrom of emotions coursing through him. He leaned forward and rested his head against the granite. "What am I going to do, Thierry?" he whispered. "I can't do this."

Once the surface would have warmed beneath his touch, but it had been years since he'd felt anything of the sort at Thierry's grave. He tried not to let it bother him, told himself it was a natural progression and not a result of him returning to hunting after a number of years of only feeding at Sang Froid. He missed the comfort of feeling as if Thierry could actually hear him. "I called him like I told you I would. I met him at the café and talked to him. I don't know what came over me, but I told him things I didn't tell you for months after we met. I talked to him like, well, like I talked to you. I've only known him a few days, and I told him some of my greatest secrets. I told him about Thibaut, about the reason Jean hated me for all those years. I even told him about feeling forced into the Aveu de Sang. The only secret I held back was our mating ritual. I talked about losing Thibaut, about losing you. God, you'd have laughed at me, spilling my secrets like that, but I couldn't help myself. The words just came out."

Sebastien paused for a moment to gather his thoughts. "He kissed me this time, not that I complained. He has a beard." He swore he heard Thierry's snort of disbelief. "Okay, he has the scruff of a beard, and this glorious long black hair. It felt so good to kiss him, like it mattered. Like it was more than a means to an end, as it's been since you died. I think I could have kissed him all night, except that he suggested we go for a walk—and as soon as we were alone, kissing him wasn't enough. I couldn't control my beast. I haven't lost control—as opposed to giving up control when you asked me to—since I was newly made, but I couldn't draw my fangs back. He could be my partner if we both decide it's what we want, and I nearly bit him without his permission. I don't act that way. I'm a civilized man. I swore when I was turned that I'd never bite someone without permission. It would be bad enough with some random person off the street who would feed me, and that would be the end of it. With Kylian, if I bit him, the only end would be his death. I can't do that to him.

"Yes, I know what you're thinking. I'm so focused on him and not on myself. But if I did it, I'd have no one to blame but myself. Maybe it wouldn't be any consolation if we ended up like Adèle and Jude, but I'd have brought it on myself. His only mistake would have been trusting me."

He slammed his hand against the stone. "I don't do this. I'm never out of control. I'm never at the mercy of my instincts. I've spent five hundred years refining my defenses so I can deal with anything life throws at me. I even dealt with you when you landed in my lap with no warning. But I can't deal with him. He doesn't fit any expectation I have. I kissed him right there on the street—and when he rubbed against me, every wall I've built to keep myself in check crumbled. I could have taken him right there and not given a single thought to the people who might have seen us."

His gut clenched as he remembered the heat of Kylian's body against his. He'd felt every beat of the wizard's heart as they kissed, and the temptation of Kylian's blood had nearly outdone him. "I'd have stripped him bare and claimed him for all the world to see if I'd let my instincts have their way. What's happening to me, Thierry? I feel like I'm going mad!

"All I have, all any of us have as vampires in this world is the promise first Marcel and then Raymond made about us—that beneath the magical trappings that keep us bound to this world when our bodies should have long since died, we are men and women like any others, capable of rational thought, of self-control, of responsible behavior and civilized choices. If we break that promise, we're no better than the *extorris* Jean banished from the Cour during the war. We're no better than Orlando's maker. We're nothing more than the monsters myth makes us out to be. I won't be a monster. I'll see my body reduced to ash before I let that happen."

The weight of his doubts bent him double. He dug his fingers into the dirt that held Thierry's ashes. He knew nothing remained of them after all these years, but it was the only thing he had left of Thierry besides his memories. "I've failed you," he whispered brokenly. "I promised I'd find a way to go on, true to your memory but not trapped by it, but I haven't done either. There's nothing true to your memory about the way I acted tonight. You might not have been the spokesman for our rights the way Raymond was, but you were always my staunchest supporter. Even when I nearly savaged you, you insisted it wasn't really me, that I was better than that, and then you searched and fought and argued and beat down every wall until you could find a way to give me what I needed. I never deserved it, but you gave it to me anyway. And now that it's gone, now that you're gone, I can't even think straight. I don't know how to do this, Thierry. I don't know how to be with him when even the slightest touch shatters my control. You allowed me to give up control because I knew your touch, your blood, would keep me from rampaging, but your presence never forced my control from me. Without meaning to, he nearly did."

The silence in the cemetery offered no answers, not that Sebastien had expected any, but he didn't have anywhere else to go. He couldn't take his fears to Jean in his current state. Even if Jean could help him, burdening him with these concerns wouldn't be fair. More likely, though, Jean wouldn't have an answer, because Sebastien's bond with Thierry had been unique. They had mimicked as many of the characteristics of the Aveu de Sang as they could, but it had been something totally new in the world. In the long term, he could perhaps talk to the vampires at l'Institut to see if they had learned anything relevant, but they would have little to go on beyond the record of Thierry's studies and Sebastien's description of the ritual they had performed to create the bond, and Sebastien probably knew that material better than they did. The wizards might see some implication in the incantations that Thierry had missed, but Raymond had gone over the spells with them, dissecting every word and phrase to make sure they got exactly the results they wanted and nothing more. He didn't know the current denizens of l'Institut, but he couldn't imagine them finding something Raymond had missed. Especially not with a rite of such importance to him and Thierry. Raymond was never careless, but he was always particularly diligent with matters that touched the lives of his closest friends.

He traced Thierry's name one more time, missing the days when the letters would warm beneath his touch. "I should go. It will be light before long. I love you, and I miss you every day. Even when I don't come here or don't talk to you at my apartment, I think of you. You'd yell at me for saying it, but there's a hole in my heart that won't ever be filled because it won't ever be you. If I can ever trust myself with Kylian, I might have another lover, maybe even another partner, but he won't be you. Nothing can ever replace our bond. Good night, my love."

He pushed himself to his feet and began the long walk toward home.

A POUNDING at the door roused Sebastien from what passed for sleep among vampires. He glanced automatically toward the closed volets to check the hour. He could still see light around the edges of the metal slats that covered the windows, but dim enough that the sun had passed overhead and started its descent on the other side of his building. The frantic knocking sounded again, so he dragged himself from bed and pulled on a pair of jeans.

"Coming," he called. As he crossed to the door, he ran his hand through his hair, hoping to tame it somewhat. He peered through the peephole to see who had disturbed him at such an unreasonable hour for a vampire.

Kylian's best friend stood on the other side.

Sebastien's stomach sank. Raphael could want only one of two things. He'd either come to ask for Sebastien's help in finding a partner—something Sebastien wasn't sure he could give—or he'd come because Kylian had told him what happened between them the night before. Sebastien almost hoped that was the reason. Raphael would yell at him, but it was no more than Sebastien deserved.

He opened the door and gestured for Raphael to come inside.

"Tell me what you did to him," Raphael demanded as soon as Sebastien had closed the door. "I've never seen him in the state he was in last night."

"Nothing," Sebastien said. "I swear. I didn't do anything but kiss him."

"Why not? Is he not good enough for you?" Raphael spat.

"What? No, that's not…. He's too good for me. He deserves someone who can make him happy. All I would do is saddle him with a broken vampire who can barely even control himself," Sebastien said. "I could have hurt him last night without meaning to. I had to get away before I did something we'd both regret."

"That doesn't explain his reaction to you," Raphael said. "He never lets people close this quickly."

"I'm a vampire, not a wizard," Sebastien said. "The only magic in my life is the magic that preserves my body from aging and allows blood to sustain me. Any other magic came from my partner and died when he did. For what it's worth, and maybe that's nothing, the strange reaction is mutual. I don't let people close either."

"I don't know if that makes it better or worse," Raphael said. "If you'd done something to him, I could fix it. I could convince you to stop, or I could find a way to block it. But if you haven't done anything, then there's nothing I can do to help him."

"Was he terribly upset?" The last thing Sebastien had wanted was to upset Kylian—even knowing he had probably done so, running the way he did. He hadn't seen another viable option at the time, but surely he could have handled it better.

"To the point that he lost control of his magic," Raphael replied. "You've spent time with wizards. You know how rare that is."

Sebastien did know. He could count on one hand the times Thierry had lost control of his magic outside their bed. He didn't count the times the earth shook as they made love. He prided himself on those moments far too much to consider them in the same vein as the time Thierry's temper got the best of him as the alliance first formed or the night they lost control of the Rite d'équilibrage and he nearly lost Thierry to a spell gone wrong.

"Is he okay? I mean, he didn't hurt himself with the spell or anything?" The memory of Thierry lying unconscious, possibly burned out by the wild magic, was forever etched into Sebastien's memory.

"He's fine physically," Raphael said, "but I wouldn't say he's okay. Totally freaked out is a better description. He doesn't know what's going on in his head, and he doesn't like it."

"I'm sorry. I don't know what else to say." Sebastien paced the length of the living room as he tried to gather his thoughts. "If I caused this, it wasn't intentional, although I don't know how I could have caused it even unintentionally. We met at the café. We kissed a couple of times. We went for a walk, and suddenly we were making out in the middle of the sidewalk. I couldn't even tell you which one of us started it. Maybe we both did. Maybe it wasn't either of us. He could be my partner if he wanted to be, if I wanted him to be, but that isn't what either of us want, and yet pulling back was the hardest thing I've done in years."

"You live for centuries," Raphael said. "Forgive me if 'years' doesn't impress me."

"It's the hardest thing I've done since I buried my partner and had to leave the cemetery alone," Sebastien said bitterly. "Satisfied now?"

That gave Raphael pause.

"You'd put him on a level with monsieur Dumont?"

"I shouldn't," Sebastien replied honestly. "Over ninety years with Thierry can't possibly compare to knowing someone only a few days, but given enough time, I think I could."

That took the wind out of Raphael's sails. Sebastien could all but see the anger leave him.

"What happens now?" Raphael asked.

"That depends on Kylian and what he wants," Sebastien replied immediately. "I won't pressure him into anything. It has to be his choice as much as mine, or it will be miserable for both of us."

"That didn't answer my question," Raphael said. "What are you going to do now?"

"That isn't what you asked," Sebastien pointed out, but he pondered the question. "It still depends on what Kylian wants. If it were up to me alone, I'd try again, somewhere public, preferably with someone nearby to keep me from making a mistake if I start losing control again like I did last night—but he has to be willing to see me again. If he won't give me another chance, it doesn't matter what I want."

"I didn't peg you for someone who'd give up so easily."

"There's a difference between giving up and not forcing someone into something they don't want, especially if they don't really know what they're getting into."

Sebastien hoped his voice didn't betray his bitterness, but he had wished more than once that he'd found the strength to delay Thibaut when he had rushed Sebastien into an Aveu de Sang. He wouldn't be responsible for rushing Kylian into anything, much less something as irrevocable as a partnership.

"As long as you don't make the opposite decision for him either," Raphael said. "Don't back away on the chance he might not want this as much as you do. Whatever his choice, give him the chance to make it. He's already surprised himself. He might surprise you as well."

Sebastien drew hope from the words. Raphael wouldn't be so insistent if he was sure Kylian would reject him. Sebastien didn't expect it to be easy, but maybe he had a chance after all. He grabbed a piece of paper and jotted down his number. "In case he didn't keep my number," he said as he handed the paper to Raphael. "When—if he's ready to give me another chance, he can call me. I'll be waiting."

"And if he doesn't call?"

"I'll still be waiting."

Chapter 9

"WHAT'S THIS?" Kylian asked when Raphael handed him a folded piece of paper across the table at their favorite bar. They met there every Friday to celebrate the end of another week and to unwind a little before facing whatever they had planned for the weekend.

"Sebastien's phone number," Raphael said. "In case you didn't keep it in your phone."

Kylian frowned at the slip of paper. He didn't like the implications. "And why do you have it?"

"Because I went to talk to him this afternoon," Raphael said. "I needed to know he wasn't playing you. Maybe things will work out, maybe they won't, but at least I know he's as tangled up in this as you are."

"You had no right." Kylian nearly growled in frustration. He shouldn't be surprised Raphael had taken it on himself to interfere, but that didn't make it any easier to deal with. "You yelled at me when I talked to Sebastien about you. What made you think I'd feel any different if you talked to him about me? Or is this revenge?"

"I probably deserve that," Raphael admitted, "but revenge didn't even cross my mind. You were hurting. I've never seen you like you were last night, Ky. I had to know he wasn't just stringing you along."

"Isn't it my mistake to make if he is?" Kylian asked.

"Maybe, but I can't help if I don't know the whole story."

"And now he knows more than I wanted him to," Kylian said with a sigh. "I didn't want him to know I was so upset. I didn't want him to know what he did to me. I wanted to try to get things back on an even footing with him. Instead, I'm at even more of a disadvantage now."

"You're not," Raphael said. "He's as messed up by this as you are." He raised his hands in pacification when Kylian nearly exploded again. "I'm not telling you what to do. You can decide to call him or not, to see him again or not. Just… he's as vulnerable to this as you are, and from what I could tell, he's beating himself up pretty hard because of it."

"So you think I should give him another chance?" Kylian asked.

"I don't know," Raphael answered. "It depends on what you want now that you've had time to calm down, because it's pretty clear from what you both said that if you keep seeing each other, you're going to end up as partners eventually. You might be able to delay it a few weeks or months—but one of these days, one of you is going to lose control and he's going to bite you. Wedded and bedded in one brush of his fangs. If you're okay with that, then yes, I think you should see him again. But if that's not what you want—or even if you want it eventually but you're not ready for it now—then I think you should break it off before you end up in a situation you can't get out of. Because I know one thing for sure—once he has you, he isn't going to let you go."

Kylian shivered at that thought, half-remembered dreams coming back to taunt him with the unimaginable pleasure to be found beneath a vampire's hands and fangs. He could deal with the hands—he enjoyed a good, sweaty bout of sex as much as the next man—but he wasn't so sure about the fangs. He'd been to the seminar. He'd heard the partnered wizards assure the attendees that it was no imposition and indeed could be quite enjoyable in the right circumstances. The secret smiles they sent their partners as they said it had told Kylian more than words ever could. The vampires' smug smiles in return had said even more. They reveled in the effect feeding had on their partners, even if Kylian couldn't quite wrap his mind around it.

"I don't know," he said. "I keep going around and around in my head, trying to make sense of it, and I keep coming up against this wall of ignorance. I don't know if I can let him feed from me the way he would need to if he were my partner. Even if he didn't feed from me exclusively, he'd want it regularly, and given the kind of partnership he had before, I don't know if he'd even consider nonexclusivity. I know vampires can feed from people other than their partners, but they so rarely choose to that it might as well be impossible."

"And the only way to know if you could do it is to try, but trying isn't an option because trying with him equals doing—not just for that time but for always," Raphael surmised. "I suppose you could try with another vampire. It wouldn't matter that you're a wizard. If you aren't that vampire's partner, your blood is no different than anyone else's."

Kylian shuddered. As much as he couldn't decide how he felt about Sebastien feeding from him, the idea of anyone else being that close to him was a hundred times worse. He doubted he could even suggest it without chickening out halfway through. "Not an option. I wouldn't even be able to let someone else close enough to bite me."

"Why not?"

"Because it wouldn't be him." The words came out without conscious thought, but as soon as he'd said them, Kylian felt the truth in them. He was Sebastien's partner, not some other vampire's, and if he had to be with anyone, he wanted it to be Sebastien.

"I think that answers your question, then," Raphael said. "You don't have to let him feed from you right away, if you can stop yourself from asking for it, but I think you have to give a relationship a chance. For both your sakes."

"That's the problem, though," Kylian said. "I didn't even realize I was asking for it last night. I mean, in retrospect I can see how I was, but at the time, I just wanted him. I didn't care what form it took or what the consequences would be. If he hadn't found the strength to pull away, this conversation would already be too late."

"If you think it would help, I could tag along," Raphael offered. "Not to sit at the same table or anything, but just to be there if you start getting carried away. A fail-safe, if you will."

"Kind of puts a damper on exploring anything beyond a few kisses," Kylian said.

"Given what happened last night, I'd say that's a good thing until you both decide what you want," Raphael said, nudging Kylian's ankle beneath the table. "You already know your physical chemistry is explosive. You need to talk to him, get to know him so you can decide if you want to spend your life with him. As young as we are, you could be looking at a hundred years or more. It's nothing for a wizard to live to be a hundred and twenty."

"That's only ninety years," Kylian said.

"And how many wizards, especially wizards with partners, have lived even longer than that?" Raphael asked. "Besides, the difference between ninety and a hundred years doesn't change the point of the conversation. If you do this, you're going to be with him for a long, long time."

"Yeah, I know," Kylian said. "It's the one thing keeping me in my seat instead of searching the city to find him. That's too long a commitment to make on a whim. Unfortunately, I can *say* that, but as soon as we're together, rational thought goes out the window and I'm left with gut instinct—which is telling me to grab on for all I'm worth. Last night gut instinct won."

"Look," Raphael said, "do you want this or not? If you don't, say so, and we'll figure out how to end it before it goes any farther. If you do, we'll figure out how to make it happen at a speed you're comfortable with. You can call him; you can chat with him via video. You have options. I'll support you whatever you decide. You just have to make up your mind."

"It's not that easy," Kylian protested. "If you were the one in my shoes, maybe. You've always wanted a partner."

"No, I've always wanted the missing half of my soul," Raphael said. "I believe I'll find that in a partner, but if I met someone and it didn't feel right, I wouldn't create a partnership."

"But you know the person you're looking for. You have a sense of him to fall back on," Kylian said. "I don't."

"And yet every time you've had a relationship, you've ended it by saying he wasn't right or he wasn't the one you were looking for, or that he didn't measure up, or something like that. No one has ever measured up, whether it was a relationship or a night of sex. Who are you measuring them against if none of them have ever really satisfied you?"

The question drew Kylian up short. He *had* said something like that every time he'd told Raphael why one man or another wasn't right for him, but he'd never stopped to question where that certainty came from.

"Think about it," Raphael said. "You don't have to tell me, but really think about it, and then think about last night. Not about how it ended, but about how it felt when you were together."

"The little we did before he left was enough to make me lose control of my magic and cream my pants," Kylian said. "Nobody else has ever made me feel like that."

"Then maybe he's the one you've been waiting for without realizing it," Raphael said.

"You're taking this a lot better than I expected," Kylian said.

Raphael shrugged. "He isn't for me, no matter what you decide. If he makes you happy, what is there to be upset about? You didn't go looking for him, and it's not a competition where just one of us gets the prize. If anything, it gives me hope. You found your partner, so maybe it's not so farfetched that I'll find mine. So are you going to call him?"

"Yeah, I think so, but I'm going to take you up on that chaperone offer," Kylian said. "Until I'm comfortable with what it would mean if we lose it again, I need to know someone rational is watching."

"No duègne will ever have been more cautious of her charge's virtue," Raphael promised with a wiggle of his eyebrows.

Kylian laughed, as Raphael had intended.

"Just don't overdo it, okay? I enjoyed kissing him, even if I'm not sure I'm ready for more."

"I won't stop you unless you cross the line of what's appropriate for a public place. Unless you want me to."

Kylian suspected Sebastien could cross the line even in public if he nipped at Kylian's lips like he'd done last night. All it would take was one hint of fangs instead of teeth and they'd be lost, but he didn't mention that to Raphael. He didn't want to lose all chance of kissing Sebastien.

THE RINGING of the phone surprised Sebastien. Hardly anyone called him these days. He picked it up and smiled when he saw Kylian's name displayed on the screen.

"Allô?"

"Hi, Sebastien. Do you have a few minutes to talk?"

Sebastien's stomach fell. Kylian's words didn't bode well for the conversation. "Of course. I don't have plans for this evening, so we can talk as long as you want."

"Is it bad that I'm glad to hear that?" Kylian asked. "I was afraid you'd be out hunting or something, and I would just get your voice mail."

"I hunted two nights ago," Sebastien replied automatically. "I'll be fine for another day or two."

He'd be even better if Kylian would let him feed instead, but he wasn't going to bring that up after his spectacular loss of control the night before.

"Good," Kylian said. "Then maybe we could try again tomorrow night? I had a really good time talking to you, despite how things ended last night."

"I'm sorry about that," Sebastien said. "I shouldn't have run the way I did."

"No," Kylian interrupted. "You don't need to apologize. We were out of control. I wouldn't have stopped you last night, whatever you wanted. If you hadn't pulled back, we'd be in a real bind right now."

Sebastien knew most of that from what Raphael had said, but hearing it from Kylian only made it worse. Instead of being alone right now, he could have had Kylian with him. Of course, Kylian would probably hate him for it, but he wouldn't have to be alone.

"Where do you want to meet?" he asked, instead of talking about what they needed to discuss. "The same café again?"

"That works for me," Kylian said. "Raphael is going to come too. He won't sit with us, but after last night, I think we need someone to keep us in line."

"He can sit with us," Sebastien said. "Unless you have secrets you don't want him to know."

"I don't have any secrets from him, but I wasn't sure how comfortable you'd be with him sitting right there."

"I just feel bad about making him come and then sit alone," Sebastien explained. "And maybe it'll feel less like we're doing something we shouldn't be if he's there with us."

"Do you think we're doing something we shouldn't be?" Kylian asked.

"No, but I think we've both proven we aren't very good judges of that. If we were, we wouldn't have left the café last night."

"It's hard to regret something that felt so good."

"And that's exactly why I'm worried," Sebastien said. "It felt too good. Good enough that I don't trust myself not to want it again. And there's no guarantee I'll be able to stop next time. Maybe it won't always be a bad idea—but nothing's changed since last night, which means that right now, it would be bad. So invite Raphael to join us. We'll talk. We'll get to know each other. Maybe he'll be a little less protective if he gets to know me too. And then we'll see what happens next."

"If you're sure," Kylian said. "We'll meet you there at eight?"

"I'll be there," Sebastien said.

"Think of me until then?" Kylian asked.

Sebastien wouldn't be able to think of anything else.

"What should I think about you?" he asked, unable to stop the flirtatious reply.

"I'm not sure I should answer that." Kylian's voice took on the same husky quality that had driven Sebastien mad the night before. "Is phone sex allowed if we haven't had real sex yet?"

"What am I going to do with you?" Sebastien heard the desperate tinge to his voice, but he couldn't modulate his tone. Not with Kylian saying such things to him.

"Keep me, I hope," Kylian replied.

"Don't say that if you don't mean it," Sebastien warned. "Vampires are possessive creatures. Maybe not quite as much as werewolves, but once we've decided something or someone is ours, we don't let go without a fight. I'm trying to keep that instinct in check, to give you space to decide what you want from this relationship, but you can't provoke my inner beast like that and expect me to ignore it."

"I know," Kylian said, "but I can't seem to stop it. I open my mouth to say one thing and another thing entirely comes out. I've never acted like this with anyone. I'd tell you I want to stop, but a part of me doesn't. A part of me wants to grab whatever is building between us and ride it for all it's worth."

An image of Kylian above him, black hair in disarray as he rode Sebastien's cock with complete abandon, flashed through Sebastien's mind. He could practically feel the tight heat around him as he thrust up into every downward motion.

It had been one of Thierry's favorite ways to make love.

"I have to go," Sebastien said hoarsely. "I'll see you at the café tomorrow."

"Wait," Kylian said. "What's wrong? I didn't mean to scare you off."

"Tomorrow," Sebastien repeated. "Good night, Kylian."

He ended the call even as Kylian's repeated protests came through the speaker.

"I'm losing my mind," he said to the empty room. It hadn't been like this when he met Thierry. Thierry hadn't reminded Sebastien of Thibaut. He hadn't compared them or even really thought about them at the same time, but every thought of Kylian evoked some memory of Thierry, and that wasn't fair to either of them.

He had no idea how their date would go, but he had to find a way to focus on Kylian and nothing else. If he really meant to make a go of a new relationship, he couldn't do it burdened with memories of the past.

Chapter 10

SEBASTIEN ARRIVED at the café before Kylian and Raphael and took a seat at the table he was already beginning to think of as theirs. Paul, the waiter from the first night, was working, but he veered away when Sebastien glared at him. He would have to deal with the man once Kylian and Raphael got there. He didn't need to deal with him sooner than that.

He'd probably made a mistake in not going hunting after he got off the phone with Kylian, but he hadn't been hungry then, and he hadn't had time to hunt after sunset before meeting them tonight. Now he had a restless beast to deal with, even without the provocation of Kylian's company. If Raphael didn't join them of his own accord, Sebastien would have to insist. Otherwise he wasn't sure he'd be able to survive the next few hours. He had to keep his beast in check. Any other option was unacceptable. Even if by some miracle Kylian agreed to let him feed, he would have to stay in control. However much Kylian evoked memories of Thierry, he wasn't Sebastien's mate.

"You look awfully pensive. I hope you haven't changed your mind about tonight."

Kylian's voice startled Sebastien out of his dour thoughts. "Not at all. I was thinking about something else entirely." He smiled at Kylian and gave Raphael a nod.

"Good." Kylian leaned in and kissed Sebastien lightly before taking the seat next to him. Sebastien caught himself before he chased Kylian's lips for another kiss. He had to stay in control.

"How are you tonight?" he asked both wizards.

"Enjoying a quiet Saturday," Kylian said. "I've been working crazy hours the past couple of months on a big project, and this is the first time I haven't put in at least some hours on Saturday in longer than I care to remember."

"I don't even know what you do for a living," Sebastien said. "We've talked about all the wrong things."

"Not wrong things," Kylian corrected. "Just not those things. I'm an architect, mostly commercial and industrial design, although I've done some renovation work on old houses too. This project involved rehabbing an old building in the quinzième for commercial use without violating any of the building codes for structures on the city's historical register. The shell of the building was mostly sound, but the inside needed a complete overhaul to be good for much of anything. I swear, the plumbing dated from the nineteenth century."

"That sounds like the perfect job for a wizard with an affinity to earth," Sebastien said. "It took a lot of work to restore l'Institut when l'ANS first purchased it. We could never have done it without the help of a group of dedicated wizards."

He didn't mention Thierry by name, but he remembered watching Thierry after the battle at Notre-Dame as he used his magic and the magic inherent in the church itself to mend the damage. He had fallen more in love by the second as Thierry worked. The repairs at l'Institut had been slower and less dramatic, but Sebastien had never tired of watching Thierry work.

"What about you?" Raphael asked. "What do you do to fill your days, or maybe your nights?"

"I'm retired," Sebastien said. "I shared the responsibility of caretaker of l'Institut for ninety years. L'ANS offered us a retirement package when Thierry grew too old to work there. With some judicious investment of that and other revenues, I'm free to do as I please."

"You don't get bored with nothing to do?" Kylian asked.

"Ah, there's a difference between not working and having nothing to do," Sebastien said. "I spent the last years of Thierry's life caring for him. Then Raymond died, and I've spent the last thirty years caring for Jean. It's gotten a little easier now that he's well enough to take care of himself again, but someone still has to make sure he eats."

"That's...."

"Private," Sebastien finished. "He retired from the Cour, and that's all anyone needs to know. The rest is known only by a select group of friends."

"No one will hear it from us," Raphael promised. "We have too much respect for him to do anything that might reflect badly on him."

Sebastien smiled sadly. "Don't put us on too high a pedestal. We're just as fallible as the next person."

"I was going to say that was very kind of you," Kylian said. "It can't have been easy caring for Jean so soon after losing your own partner."

It hadn't been, but losing Jean would have been worse. "I did what had to be done."

Kylian squeezed his hand, a simple gesture that shouldn't have meant so much—but in that moment, it felt like the greatest accolade Sebastien could have received.

Sebastien cast around for something to say after that, some new topic of conversation to lighten the mood, but he was out of practice. He could sit with Jean for hours without the silence becoming unbearable, the ease of long years of companionship making words unnecessary. It wasn't Jean sitting next to him now, nor Thierry, who had never needed words. He was supposed to be getting to know Kylian and letting Kylian get to know him so they could decide if a partnership between them could work, but a discussion of music or movies felt too banal, and everything else seemed too personal.

"Have you watched any good movies lately?" Raphael asked into the silence.

Kylian glowered at him as Sebastien smothered a laugh at Raphael's choice of topic. "Movies have never been my preferred mode of entertainment," Sebastien admitted. "I've come to appreciate the classics of the Golden Age of cinema, but it's classical theater that has always been my true fascination. Molière, Rostand, even Sartre, although that gets a little too modern for my taste. Is there something out right now that I absolutely can't miss?"

"Not that I can think of," Kylian interrupted before Raphael could reply. "I can't imagine the plays and the actors you must have seen!"

Sebastien could certainly have listed a few, but he wasn't there to drop names. "I think I've seen every production of *Cyrano de Bergerac* since it was first performed. There's just something about that story that calls to me."

"It is a beautiful love story," Kylian agreed. "For me, it was always the films of Jean Cocteau. *La Belle et la Bête* in particular, but I love them all."

"I saw *Le Bel Indifférent* when Édith Piaf was still on stage," Sebastien said. "She was radiant."

"Oh, now I'm jealous," Kylian said. "You really saw her perform?"

"Several times," Sebastien said. "The club where she was discovered was a popular one with vampires at the time. We weren't as welcome at Le Gerny, where she gained her fame, but I slipped in a few times to see her. And of course, once she was on stage, it was easy to see her."

RAPHAEL RESISTED the urge to roll his eyes as he listened with half an ear to Sebastien and Kylian's conversation. He'd brought up movies as a way to make them realize how silly they sounded, tiptoeing around each other, and to break the somber mood that had fallen over them. He hadn't expected it to spark an actual discussion, much less one that kept going beyond the first initial observations.

He should have known better. Even when they were kids, Kylian had appreciated old movies, and every one he mentioned, Sebastien had seen or chosen not to see for one reason or another.

They were sickeningly cute, leaning closer to each other as they got more involved in their discussion, until they'd scooted so close together their chairs were touching. Raphael might have been worried about what they were getting up to beneath the table if he couldn't see their hands gesticulating to emphasize their points or, finally, simply holding hands on the table. Other than that and the first kiss hello, they hadn't made any attempt to touch each other or done anything else he might have needed to object to. He considered leaving—they wouldn't even notice he was gone—but the night wasn't over, and they had been fine while they were in the café last night. The problems only started when they had left and were alone together under the cover of night.

The conversation moved from movies to places they had visited or wanted to visit. He noticed Sebastien had a gap in his trips after carriages, where he could draw the curtains to protect himself from the sunlight, had fallen out of favor. He had only resumed his travel after the war, when his partner's blood gave him the freedom to journey outside during the day once again.

"Not that I always had the money to travel, even when the means were available. There were a lot of lean years in there. I never had to worry about paying for food—but shelter was a requirement, and the resources of the Cour were mostly forbidden to me."

Raphael wanted to ask what that meant, but Kylian nodded as if it was a given and continued the conversation, so Raphael filed it away for later. He was curious, but it wasn't important. This was Kylian and Sebastien's date. He was there just in case, and so far they hadn't needed him beyond getting the conversation started.

That was a good sign, as far as he was concerned. He'd worried they were only compatible physically. That had certainly been the focus of Kylian's description of what had transpired between them. Other than their entwined fingers, nothing about this evening had been physical, but they seemed as happy with each other as Raphael could hope for them to be so soon after meeting. They didn't agree on every movie or every destination, but their tastes coincided more than diverged. As far as Raphael was concerned, they were perfectly matched.

Except he didn't have any say in the matter. That decision was theirs alone. Still, if Kylian asked his opinion, he'd have something to add this time instead of simply asking questions and trying to help Kylian sort out his thoughts.

KYLIAN'S SUDDEN yawn surprised them all. "Wow, I didn't realize it had gotten so late," he said when he glanced at his watch.

"We can call it a night," Sebastien offered. "I wouldn't want to keep you from your rest."

"I don't mean to cut the evening short," Kylian said.

"It's well after midnight. I'd hardly call that cutting it short," Sebastien said. "It's been a lovely evening. Get some rest. We'll have other evenings together."

"I certainly hope so," Kylian said as he stood. Sebastien followed suit and they left the café. Sebastien expected to have to argue with Raphael to be able to kiss Kylian good night. Raphael had left them to talk without joining the conversation, but Sebastien had felt his gaze each time he and Kylian leaned closer to each other. Sebastien was grateful for his previous experience in the public eye for teaching him how to ignore his audience and focus on what mattered—but Raphael's task was to keep them from bonding too soon, and a kiss could do that if Sebastien wasn't completely in control.

He ran his tongue over his teeth as an extra check, though he had not felt his fangs drop. When he pulled Kylian in for a kiss, Raphael turned away to at least give them that much privacy.

"Can I kiss you?" Sebastien asked softly.

"I'd be upset if you didn't," Kylian replied. He slid his arm around Sebastien's waist and pulled him closer. Sebastien moved into the embrace. The smell of Kylian's cologne wafted around them, a fresh scent not at all like the cedar and sandalwood Thierry had preferred. The thought soothed the last of Sebastien's worries. For all that Kylian reminded him of Thierry from time to time, the little differences served to remind him who he was actually with.

"You smell good," he said.

Kylian smiled. "I bet I'd taste good too."

"I'm sure you would," Sebastien said, "but that'll have to wait for another time. We're being responsible tonight, remember?"

"Don't remind me," Kylian said. He tilted his head up for a kiss, which Sebastien gave him immediately. He wouldn't taste beyond that, but he caught a hint of coffee on Kylian's breath.

"You do taste good," he murmured when he broke the kiss. "When can I see you again?"

"Tomorrow night?" Kylian suggested. "I could see if there are tickets to the revival of *Waiting for Godot*. It's not seventeenth-century theater, but it's interesting anyway, and it's supposed to be a fantastic production."

"I'd like that," Sebastien said. "With or without your shadow?"

"He hates theater. It'll just be us, if that's all right with you. Or I could try to find someone else to go with us, if you think we shouldn't be alone."

"We'll hardly be alone in a theater full of people. If we go out after, we can see if Raphael wants to meet us somewhere."

"Or we can try again with just us," Kylian said. "It was fine tonight."

It had been, although now with Kylian in his arms, Sebastien felt the beast stirring.

"We'll see how tomorrow goes." He gave Kylian another quick kiss. "Sleep well tonight."

"I'll dream of you," Kylian said, "if you'll dream of me."

Sebastien didn't tell him that vampires didn't dream. It wouldn't matter. He'd think of Kylian while he was trapped inside by the sun, and that was close enough. "I promise."

"I'll call you when I know if I can get tickets. What time should I call?"

"Anytime," Sebastien replied. "Vampires don't sleep. We rest in a trance of sorts, but it won't hurt me to come out of it to talk to you. As long as we're protected from the sunlight and have the opportunity to feed, we're fine."

"Then I'll call as soon as I know anything," Kylian said.

Sebastien released his hold on Kylian's shoulders, but Kylian didn't back away. "I don't want to go."

"You're tired. You should sleep, and we'll see each other tomorrow night."

"I know," Kylian said, "but that doesn't make it any easier. If you asked—"

"Don't say it," Sebastien interrupted. "Don't tempt me with what I can't have."

"Why can't you?"

"Because your friend is here to make sure we don't do something reckless, and right now, taking you home with me would be the epitome of recklessness," Sebastien said. "There's no way I could have you in my apartment and not bite you. Not the way I'm feeling tonight. I would love nothing more than to take you to bed and make love to you until the sun came up, but until I trust myself to do it without biting you, it's better for you to go home."

"Ky," Raphael said from where he stood a few feet away. "Is everything okay?"

"No," Kylian replied, "but it's nothing you can fix." He kissed Sebastien once more and walked to where Raphael stood. "I'll see you tomorrow, Sebastien."

"Tomorrow," Sebastien agreed. He stayed glued to the spot until Kylian and Raphael had turned the corner and were no longer in view. When they were gone and the spell Kylian seemed to cast on him had lifted, Sebastien realized he was ravenous. He didn't know if Kylian had caused it or if Kylian's presence had forestalled it until now, but either way, Sebastien needed blood and he needed it now. He toyed with the idea of going hunting in one of the clubs, but that struck him as a betrayal of Kylian. At Sang Froid, it was a business transaction, nothing more. In a club, any interaction was fraught with the possibility of more.

He headed toward Montmartre and Sang Froid, hoping Angélique would let him feed without questioning him first.

"I didn't expect to see you tonight," Angélique said as soon as he walked in. "It was my turn to fetch Jean, and he said you'd been hunting."

"I did," Sebastien said, "and tonight I'm not. Is that a problem?"

"Of course not," Angélique said. "You're always welcome here. I just expected you to be with your new man."

"Jean told you."

"He did. He was worried about you, Sebastien. Maybe telling me about your new friend wasn't the best way to show it, but it's the first sign of interest in anything since Raymond died. I wasn't about to discourage him."

"He went hunting with me a few nights ago," Sebastien said.

"Yes, he told me that too. He said he'd never seen you like you were that night, and he was afraid to leave you alone."

"I wasn't that out of control," Sebastien protested. "I just needed the thrill of the hunt."

"And tonight you didn't?"

"Tonight I didn't want it," Sebastien said. "Here it's just a business transaction."

"Even if you always see the same person?" Angélique teased.

"Florence is my friend, nothing more," Sebastien said. "You know that and so does she, but she listens without judging."

"I don't judge," Angélique said. "I may tease. I may ask you if you've lost your mind, but I don't judge. I don't have any right."

Sebastien nodded. "And how is Pascale?"

Angélique flushed at the mention of the young vampire she had taken to her bed after both their partners died. "As innocent as ever," Angélique said. "It seems even I can't corrupt her."

Sebastien shook his head. "I don't need the details of your sex life, please. Is Florence still here?"

"Yes, and I'll let you feed, but when you're done, I want to hear about this new man in your life. And I *do* want details."

Sebastien resigned himself to that conversation, but he already knew Angélique wouldn't understand. She had stayed with David until his death, but of all of them, she had been the least affected by the loss of a partner. Sebastien didn't know how she'd managed to keep that distance, but it meant she wouldn't understand now.

"There's not really much to tell," Sebastien warned her.

"I'll be the judge of that. Florence is in her room."

Chapter 11

SEBASTIEN HEADED up the stairs to the last room on the left and knocked on the door.

"Sebastien!" Florence said as she opened the door. "I didn't expect to see you tonight. How are you?"

"Totally fucked up," Sebastien answered honestly. "I need to feed."

"Of course," she said. "Come in."

"Listen to me," he said as she shut the door behind him. "I'm on edge tonight. I haven't felt this way in… I can't even remember when. I need you to get the emergency buzzer, and I need you to use it. Don't trust me tonight like you usually do. I don't know what's happening to me, but I can't promise I'll be able to stop."

"I do trust you," Florence said, "but I'll do as you asked so you'll be able to relax and not worry about me." She grabbed the buzzer that would ring in Angélique's office and in the entry hall if she needed help and sat down next to him. "Now, wrist or neck tonight?"

Her no-nonsense attitude helped soothe him, but Sebastien opted for her wrist nonetheless. It was safer for her and less intimate for him. She placed her hand in his and smiled at him as he lifted it to his mouth.

"It's fine," she said. "This is just like any other night."

He tried to keep that in mind as his fangs dropped and he bit into her skin. Her blood rushed over his tongue, sweet as always, but it tasted like dust in his mouth. He made himself keep going because he needed the sustenance, but all urge to plunder faded. Her blood would nourish him and prolong his existence for another few days, but it did nothing to inspire his passion. It was a business transaction, exactly as he'd wanted, but tonight the comfort he usually found in Florence's blood and her understanding presence was absent. It was as empty as his apartment, a way to ensure survival, nothing more.

After a few minutes, he lifted his head.

"That wasn't so bad, was it?" Florence said. "See, I didn't need the panic button."

"You were right," Sebastien said, summoning a smile for his friend. "Nothing to worry about after all."

"What's wrong, Sebastien?" she asked. "I've never seen you so on edge."

"I met someone," Sebastien began. "Someone I think could be really special."

"So why are you here with me?" Florence asked. "Shouldn't you be with her?"

"Him," Sebastien corrected, "and maybe I should, but it isn't that simple."

"Nothing worth having ever is," she said. "If it's worth having, it's worth working for."

"We're trying. We went out tonight, and it was really good. It's been a long time since I enjoyed a conversation that much."

"Is he worried because you're a vampire? I'll be happy to tell him you're one of the best-mannered vampires I've ever worked for."

"It's not so much that I'm a vampire, although that's part of it. It's that he's a wizard and we're a match. There would be no going back if he let me bite him."

"He doesn't want that?"

"He doesn't want to go into it blindly," Sebastien specified, "and neither do I. Thus the date tonight, except we keep getting ahead of ourselves. It's like we can't help it. The slightest hint of intimacy, even a kiss, really, is enough to send us spiraling out of control. He offered to come home with me. He even meant it. But at the same time, it's too soon and we both know it."

"Can you really quantify it?" Florence asked. "I know couples who dated for years, and yet after they married, one of them cheated or turned abusive or whatever. I know people who met and married in a couple of months who are still happy after twenty years or more."

"And the opposite is true as well."

"Of course it is, but that's not the point. The point is that time isn't a deciding factor. In the meantime, you're here with me instead of where you want to be. There are no guarantees in life. You're old enough to know that. Sometimes you just have to roll the dice. You're interested in him. You didn't know that much about Thierry before you started with him, and look how that turned out."

"And look how Adèle and Jude turned out," Sebastien replied. "I know you didn't know them, and we don't talk about him much because she was so happy with Pascale, but her time with Jude was a misery. If he hadn't been killed, she would have spent the rest of her life avoiding him if she could and fighting him if she couldn't. Not even Jean and Raymond's influence was enough to keep him away of his own accord."

"But did she even like him?"

"No. They never saw eye to eye."

"Then you're already a step ahead of them."

"I suppose, but he has to be ready too, and he doesn't have the benefit of your wisdom or my experience."

"You can bring him by. I'll happily share my wisdom, as you call it," she said with a cheeky grin. It made Sebastien laugh and broke the tension that had been dogging him all evening.

"This isn't something I'm going to resolve by talking about it, is it?" he asked.

"I don't know. Maybe with someone who sees things from your perspective. I don't have your reaction to the idea of a partnership because it's not an option for me. I might feel differently if I did."

"I guess I need to talk to Jean or Angélique, then, not that either of them had an experience like mine."

"So who did?" Florence asked. "I know they're the ones you see the most, but they aren't the only options. If they can't help you, ask someone else."

That was the problem. The three couples had spent so much time together that Sebastien had fallen out of touch with most of the other vampires in the Cour. Jean had stayed somewhat more in touch because of the Cour, but even that had ended with Raymond's death. He could try consulting the records at l'Institut, but that would give him only names and not any sense of the relationships the partners had. And even if he did find someone else, no one else had the bond he and Thierry had created—not even Orlando or Jean. Thierry had kept the only copy of the spells they had used, and Sebastien had destroyed it at Raymond's insistence after Thierry's death. He remembered the gist of it, but the specific words had begun to fade from his memory. Even trying to explain it to anyone other than Jean, who had been there, would be difficult. Unless….

"Florence, you're brilliant. Now I just have to find time to go to Dommartin."

"I don't know what I said, but you're welcome."

Sebastien kissed her cheek and headed down to speak to Angélique. She was still at the door, where he'd left her.

"You look like you're feeling better."

"Florence has a way of putting things in perspective for me."

"Good. Then you can come into my office and tell me what's going on." She led him into her office. Sebastien had been there often enough to no longer be shocked by the decidedly un-office-like appearance. She took her customary seat on her chaise longue, draping herself over it in a way that might have been provocative if he'd been the least bit attracted to her, but familiarity had taught him that she was most comfortable that way no matter who her audience was. "So tell me about him."

"What do you want to know?"

"Everything, of course," Angélique said, "but you can start with his name and where you met him."

"His name is Kylian, and I met him in one of the clubs you suggested I check out for Jean," Sebastien said.

"That's a good start. If he was at a club, he was looking for someone, even if he didn't know it was you."

Sebastien snorted with laughter. "Oh, that's funny."

"Isn't it a logical assumption?"

"Logical, yes. Accurate, not at all. He was there to keep a friend out of trouble, nothing more. I ran into him again at a different club, same reason, and we got to talking that night, more than the ten words we exchanged the first night. The last thing he wanted was a vampire."

"And yet here you are, all tied up in knots over him."

"He's a wizard, and he would be my partner if I fed from him," Sebastien said. "That's not something to be done lightly."

"I swear," Angélique said, "you make everything into a drama. I know you loved him, Sebastien, but not every partnership has to be a love for all ages. You like the boy. You have fun together. He fires your blood. Does it have to be more than that? More importantly, don't expect it to be more than that. He's not Thierry, and you may never feel that way about another person, partner or not. Expecting every new relationship to be like that one is a recipe for disappointment."

"Is that how you managed your partnership with David?" Sebastien asked. He heard the bitterness in his voice, but he couldn't change it. Angélique wouldn't be offended. She knew him better than that.

"Yes, as a matter of fact. I enjoyed David, and before you ask, I was faithful to him until his death, but I never believed he was the only person I'd ever love."

"And Pascale?"

"We enjoy each other," Angélique said, "but we both feed elsewhere—we have to—and if that turns to more for a night or longer, that's fine. We've shared lovers, and we've each had our own lovers."

"And if one of you found a new partner?"

"Neither of us is looking, but if we did, we would deal with it. As I said, it's not exclusive."

"I can't fathom that," Sebastien said. "I wouldn't know how to start a relationship like that."

"So don't," Angélique said with a shrug. "Just because it's right for me doesn't make it right for you, but you're making it more complicated than it needs to be. Think about it. Think about enjoying the time you have with him instead of worrying about it."

"SO WHAT do you think about him now?" Kylian asked Raphael when he called the next day.

"Honestly, I stopped listening to you two about ten minutes into it. You didn't need my help, and I'd have been in the way. It doesn't matter what I think, anyway. You obviously like him."

"Yeah, I really do. I just wish he wasn't a vampire. Then this would be so much easier."

"How?" Raphael asked. "I mean, I get the whole partnership thing, but is making a commitment really that scary?"

"It doesn't scare you?" Kylian asked.

"No. Maybe it will when I meet my partner, but right now, the idea just seems to fit. So maybe that makes me the wrong person to talk to about this, because if I were in your shoes right now, I'd be jumping for joy. You've got an attractive, interesting man interested in you. I don't think that's anything but a reason to be happy."

"Even if that man is a vampire?"

"Are you really that uncomfortable with the idea of what he is?"

"I'm not exactly comfortable with the thought of him biting me," Kylian said. "Not because of the partnership, but because of the biting itself. It's… disconcerting, to say the least."

"So tell him not to bite you," Raphael said. "You'll have to accept that he's feeding elsewhere, but that doesn't mean you can't have him as a lover. It just means you'll have to share that part of him. He can still feed from others even if you do decide to let him bite you at some point, so it's not like you have to always let him. You'd still be his partner, even if you aren't his only source of blood."

"Everything just gets muddled when he kisses me," Kylian explained.

"Then talk to him before he kisses you. Tell him now what you're comfortable with. Get him to agree to a set of limits, and then stick to it. He's an honorable man. He won't go beyond that."

"It wasn't that simple a couple of nights ago."

"Did you tell him what the lines were?" Raphael asked. "Or did you just agree you weren't ready to be partners without discussing what you did want?"

"We didn't really discuss anything," Kylian admitted.

"So try it my way and see what happens," Raphael suggested. "You'll have your wand with you. If I'm wrong, you'll be able to get away."

If Raphael was wrong, Kylian was afraid it would be too late for that, but he nodded anyway. "It's worth a try."

"Good. Talk to him when you call him to tell him about the tickets. It might be easier if you aren't face-to-face with him."

"It'll be embarrassing no matter what."

"So? It still has to be done. Call him."

Raphael ended the call before Kylian could say anything else. Kylian stared at the phone in annoyance for a minute before deciding Raphael was probably right. He had to call Sebastien anyway to confirm their plans for the evening, and the time between sunset and the start of the show wouldn't give them the opportunity to talk in private before it started. Afterward, if all went well, they would be alone together somewhere, but that was how they'd almost gotten into trouble before.

"I can do this," he muttered. Before he could lose his nerve, he called Sebastien's number.

"Allô?"

"Hi, Sebastien. It's Kylian. I'm not interrupting anything, I hope?"

"Only an afternoon of terrible TV," Sebastien said. "How are you?"

"I'm fine. I got the tickets for tonight. We should probably meet at the theater to be safe on time, but maybe we could go for coffee or something after the show? I took tomorrow off to make up for all the overtime I've been putting in, so I won't be in a hurry tonight."

"I'd like that," Sebastien said. "It'll give us a chance to talk about the show."

"Speaking of talking, I've been thinking a lot about you and us and what that might mean. I really like you, and I want to see how things could be between us, but I'm not ready to let you bite me. Not because of the partnership stuff, but because of the biting stuff. I just...."

"You've never associated blood and sex," Sebastien finished for him. "Believe me, I understand. Most people don't, unless they're vampires or have been with one. So what are you comfortable with?"

"Kissing," Kylian said immediately. "Some petting. Not sure how I'd feel about oral with your fangs and all. That's a little scary to think about."

"I've never bitten anyone's cock without them asking me to," Sebastien said. "Even with people I wouldn't hesitate to bite elsewhere. It's a particular kind of intimacy, but not one most people are comfortable with. But we don't have to go there until you can trust me not to hurt you unintentionally."

"Does that apply to biting me elsewhere too?" Kylian asked. "If I tell you now that I don't want it, can we have sex without it?"

"Yes," Sebastien said. "There might come a point where I'd have to stop kissing you, but even if I can't stop my fangs from dropping, I can control where I put my mouth. If I can't reach you, I can't bite you."

"Then maybe after the show tonight, you'd like to come back to my place for coffee instead of going to a café," Kylian suggested. He alternated between feeling bold and reckless as he said it, but Sebastien's sharp inhale was worth it.

"I'd like that, but tell me what you're offering because I don't want any doubts later."

"Kissing and hands," Kylian said, even as an image of Sebastien hovering above him as he drove into Kylian flashed before his eyes. "We'll start there and see."

"I look forward to it." Sebastien's voice rubbed along Kylian's nerves like velvet, raising goose bumps of anticipation. "I can't wait to see what you look like when you come."

Liquid heat surged through him, but he'd never been a passive lover. "What if I want to see what you look like?"

"I'm all yours."

"Really?" He couldn't stop the sudden burst of hope at Sebastien's declaration.

"As much as you'll take, yes," Sebastien replied. "I still have to feed, but that doesn't necessarily involve sex. If we do this, I won't have sex when I feed unless it's with you."

"Not yet. Maybe not ever. I'm sorry."

"Don't be," Sebastien said. "You have to be comfortable with our relationship, or it will never work."

"You seem a lot more at ease with this than I expected."

"I had a long talk with a friend last night. She reminded me that not every relationship, not even every partnership, has to be the stuff of fairy tales. I'd rather have what you're willing to offer than nothing at all. If the time comes that you want more, we'll talk about it then. For now, I'm going to take what you're offering and be grateful not to be alone."

"Thank your friend for me," Kylian said.

"I will. I'll see you at the show tonight, and we'll see where things go from there."

"I'm looking forward to it already."

They ended the call and Kylian breathed a sigh of relief. Maybe this would work after all.

SEBASTIEN STARED at the phone in his hand and prayed he would be able to keep his promises.

Chapter 12

LATER, KYLIAN would hardly remember a word of the play. He had been totally focused on Sebastien's hand in his, his thumb stroking the back of Kylian's hand. He felt like a teenager on a first date with his first crush, wondering if the night would end in a kiss. Except he'd already agreed to far more than a kiss.

"Relax," Sebastien murmured as they filed out of the theater. "We don't have to do anything you don't want, even if we already agreed to it. You gave me permission to seduce you, not a promise that it would work."

Kylian shivered at the heat in Sebastien's voice even as he marveled that Sebastien could already read him so well. Raphael was the open book who wore his heart on his sleeve, not Kylian, yet Sebastien had nailed the root of his nervousness on the first try.

"That's not fair to you," Kylian protested.

"Neither is pressuring you into something you find you aren't ready for. It's been a wonderful evening so far. I don't want to spoil it by pushing for more than you're ready to give."

"You'll just have to make me want it enough to overcome any misgivings," Kylian said.

"That sounds like a challenge."

Kylian shivered again at the velvety purr in Sebastien's voice. He was halfway to seduced already. "Are you up for it?" he teased, feeling positively brazen.

Sebastien drew closer until his lips brushed Kylian's ear as he spoke. "I'm always up for a challenge. Let's go somewhere private and I'll prove it to you."

Kylian silently cursed the inability of a wizard's magic to affect his partner. If he could, he'd wave his wand and take them straight to his bedroom. As it was, they'd have to endure a Métro ride across town, unless Sebastien's apartment was closer.

"I live near the périphérique in Montparnasse. Is your place closer?"

"About a ten-minute walk," Sebastien replied. "We can go there if that won't make you uncomfortable."

"I don't think it will make a difference one way or another," Kylian admitted. "I'll be nervous either way, but at least at your place, I'll be nervous for a shorter time."

"I hate that I make you nervous," Sebastien said. "I'd hoped our talk this afternoon would help."

"It did." He didn't want Sebastien to have any doubt about that. "This is about me, not you. This means something. I'm not sure anything before this has. There's no way around that."

"Punaise, Kylian," Sebastien cursed as he pulled Kylian down the street. "You shouldn't say things like that. I'm having a hard enough time being a gentleman as it is."

The words touched Kylian deeply. He knew so many men who looked for any excuse not to be a gentleman, not to hold back when what they wanted was on offer; that Sebastien insisted on remaining one despite Kylian's unintentional provocation was refreshing. "Take me home," he requested. "We'll discuss the rest when we get there."

Sebastien pulled Kylian through the streets so quickly that he briefly considered casting a spell to help him keep up, but as he reached that point, Sebastien slowed down. "Sorry, I've gotten out of the habit of walking with nonvampires. Just tell me if I go too fast. I don't mean to drag you down the street."

"Honestly, it's another turn-on," Kylian said.

"How so?"

"You want me so badly you're racing through the streets to get me to bed," Kylian explained. "I don't think I've ever been wanted that way."

"Then the men you've been dating have been real idiots," Sebastien declared.

"Or Raphael is right, and I've been waiting for you all this time without realizing it."

Sebastien froze. "He thinks that?"

"He suggested it as a possibility," Kylian replied. "It explains my instant—and out of character—reaction to you, if nothing else."

"And what do you think?" Sebastien asked.

"I think I've never reacted to anyone the way I have to you. I've been attracted to men before, and I've been involved with some, but never so quickly as with you, and never with the same kind of overwhelming need. Maybe Raphael is right, or maybe it's just coincidence. I've never believed in the idea of one person who's perfect for you to the exclusion of anyone else. It's beautifully romantic but not terribly practical—and it presupposes a greater power at work, in more deliberate ways, than I've ever ascribed to. Plus it negates the choice aspect of a relationship. You choose to be with someone, and you choose to make it work."

"Or you choose not to," Sebastien murmured.

"Personal experience?"

"Not mine, but a couple I knew during the war. He was misogynistic to the extreme and wasn't willing to compromise. She wasn't willing to be his chattel. When the war ended, she left Paris and him," Sebastien recounted. "After he had an unfortunate accident, she found another partner who suited her much better."

"It proves my point, though. If soul mates existed, if the partnership bonds were perfect, then that would have magically solved all their problems," Kylian said.

"Which is why I never wanted another one after Thierry died," Sebastien agreed. "I'd had as near perfect a mate as I was ever going to find. Trying to recreate that wouldn't be fair to anyone involved. It took Angélique knocking sense into me to remind me that expecting anything to be the same as what came before, good or bad, is unfair to you and me both. So instead I'm going to enjoy what builds between us for what it is."

"How much farther?" Kylian asked. "I'm ready to see what builds between us, as you put it."

"Just around the corner."

Kylian followed Sebastien to the door of an apartment building similar to so many others, in yellow limestone from the eighteenth century or rebuilt after the last world war in that style. Kylian wasn't interested in studying the building enough at the moment to determine which. That could wait for another visit, when he was less focused on Sebastien and their destination.

Sebastien led Kylian up the steps to the third-floor apartment. Kylian tested the door automatically for wards, surprised not to find any. "No one spelled your door for you?"

"I never lived here with a wizard and didn't really want anything to do with any of them after Thierry died. Raymond offered, but any magic would have been a reminder I didn't want, even if it wasn't Thierry's magic. I'm hardly a public figure anymore to need that kind of protection, and if someone did try to break in, I'm perfectly capable of dealing with them on my own. There are few things, magical or otherwise, that can truly damage a vampire. A werewolf in its prime might be as strong as I am. A vampire significantly older than I am might be able to overpower me, but there are very few of those in Paris, and the two who are here are my friends, so I'm pretty safe. Closed volets protect me from sunlight, and no spell I'm aware of would be able to protect me if the apartment caught on fire."

"It puts things in a different perspective when you say it that way," Kylian said. "If you ever change your mind, though, I'd be glad to add some protection to the door and windows. I can't stop a fire, but I could slow it down enough to give you time to get out. Earth smothers fire pretty effectively."

"I'll keep it in mind." Sebastien pulled Kylian into his arms, and all the needy prickles raced through Kylian's body again. "For now, though, I'd rather focus on other things."

Kylian started to reply, but he didn't get the words out. Sebastien covered his mouth in a heady kiss that stole his wits immediately. Kylian groaned into Sebastien's mouth and grabbed his shoulders for support. He had the passing thought that Sebastien was more slender than he looked, but it skipped away almost before he thought it. Sebastien ran his tongue over Kylian's lips, urging them to part. When Kylian responded, Sebastien took possession of his mouth, sending tremors of need through Kylian's body. He broke the kiss to gasp for air. Sebastien let his mouth go and nuzzled his jaw instead, making his way back toward Kylian's ear. Kylian shivered with a combination of desire and fear. He trusted Sebastien not to bite him, but the knowledge that it could happen added an illicit danger to the contact. Sebastien nibbled on Kylian's earlobe, and the hint of teeth nearly made Kylian's knees buckle.

"Putain," he cursed. "How do you do this to me?"

"Do what?" Sebastien purred at his ear.

"Make me light-headed with just a kiss."

"If you're light-headed, maybe we should move somewhere you can sit down," Sebastien suggested.

"And where would that be?" Kylian asked coyly.

"I was talking about the couch, but we can move to the bedroom if you'd prefer."

The couch was closer, but it wasn't large and would limit what they could comfortably do. "Bed," Kylian said after only a moment's deliberation.

Sebastien propelled Kylian down the hall and into a small bedroom dominated by a huge bed. Kylian looked at him questioningly.

"It came with the place," Sebastien said. "I left everything behind when I moved here. No one has shared this bed with me, if that's what you want to know."

"It wouldn't matter if they had, so long as no one else is sharing it now." It was true, but Kylian couldn't stop the thrill at the idea of not competing with the memory of past lovers.

"No one but you," Sebastien said. "I'm not asking for a promise of forever, but while we're together, there won't be anyone in my bed but you."

"I'm not in your bed yet," Kylian teased. He gasped when Sebastien lifted him off the floor and tossed him onto the soft mattress as if he weighed nothing.

"You were saying?"

Kylian didn't answer. Instead he held out his arms in invitation. Sebastien joined him immediately and captured Kylian's mouth again. Kylian parted his lips without prompting this time and let Sebastien have control of the kiss. When Sebastien thrust his tongue in, Kylian sucked on it eagerly. He arched into the kiss, seeking more contact with Sebastien's body. He yearned in a way he couldn't explain for Sebastien's weight—against him, over him, behind him, he didn't care, just with him, surrounding him with strength—and how the hell had he ever imagined vampires to be cold? Sebastien burned against him through their clothes, and Kylian burned with him, already feeling like he would go up in flames at any moment.

Sensation burst along his nerves like fireworks under his skin, until he was sure he would come apart from the sheer power of it. His body couldn't possibly contain this overload, and Sebastien was only kissing him. It was the night by the Seine all over again, only this time Kylian was determined to take Sebastien with him.

He slipped a hand between them, reaching for the zipper on Sebastien's jacket. Sebastien leaned back to allow him to undo it and slip his hand beneath the fabric. The thin silk of his shirt did nothing to hide the heat of his skin, and Kylian reveled in the pounding heartbeat beneath his palm as he smoothed his hand over Sebastien's chest. He paused directly over Sebastien's pulse and simply enjoyed the proof of Sebastien's vitality. After a moment, he realized his hand was resting against Sebastien's nipple—his very erect nipple.

He couldn't resist rubbing it through the cloth. Sebastien groaned this time and slid his hands down to Kylian's waist, pulling him closer so he could feel Sebastien's erection pressing against his thigh. Kylian shifted to bring their cocks into alignment so he could rut against Sebastien. Sebastien had already made him come in his pants once, even if he didn't know it. He was determined to return the favor.

"Merde," Sebastien gasped. "Are you trying to make me lose control?"

"The thought had occurred," Kylian replied as he tweaked Sebastien's nipple. "Is it working?"

"You're playing with fire," Sebastien warned. "You really don't want to provoke the beast beyond my control. It's not a pretty sight."

"What's the worst that could happen?" Kylian asked. "You'd bite me, and I'd end up your partner a little faster than we'd planned."

"I could kill you," Sebastien said hoarsely. "I could lose control and gorge myself on you until I'd drained you dry, and you're a wizard, so I couldn't even remedy it by turning you. Please, for the love of all that is good and holy, don't provoke the beast."

Kylian shuddered. "Okay. Tell me if I go too far."

"Just let me lead for now, please."

"As long as you don't keep me waiting for too long."

Sebastien nodded, pinning him to the mattress. "We've already waited too long." He rocked down against Kylian's groin, eliciting a hoarse moan from Kylian's throat.

"Do that again," Kylian begged. "Fuck, please do that again."

Sebastien lifted up onto all fours and grinned ferally down at Kylian. "Oh, I will, but not quite yet. I have plans for you first."

Kylian trembled with need. "What are you waiting for? An invitation?"

"For you to be ready."

"I've been ready," Kylian protested.

"Really?" Sebastien said. "Then why are we just now making it to bed?"

"Because the last time, you ran away," Kylian said.

"And the time after that, you brought a chaperone so we couldn't get carried away," Sebastien reminded him. He sat back on his heels and dragged off his jacket.

The reminder should have sobered Kylian up a little, but instead it only drove him on. Yes, he'd felt that way before, but not now, and he would prove it to Sebastien before the night was over.

"Your shirt too," he urged when Sebastien didn't immediately take it off.

Sebastien cocked an eyebrow at him, but Kylian was having none of it. He reached for the buttons himself, determined to see and touch skin as soon as possible. Sebastien started at the other end and met Kylian's hands in the middle. He left the shirt over his shoulders but offered no protest when Kylian reached inside and ran his hands over bare skin.

Sebastien was even hotter without the barrier of cloth to shield him. Kylian swore he'd combust if things got any hotter. He traced the lines of Sebastien's muscles, enjoying the sounds his touch elicited. The little moans and gasps egged him on, proof that Sebastien was as affected as Kylian was.

"Your turn," Sebastien said after a few moments of Kylian's exploration.

Kylian lifted his arms obediently, letting Sebastien strip his sweater from him. Sebastien's eyes widened, making Kylian's pulse speed up.

"Someday, you'll trust me enough to let me have you, and when you do, I'm going to leave marks on every inch of you." Sebastien flicked Kylian's pierced nipple, his teenaged rebellion against his conservative parents. "For now, I'll have to settle for touching you." He tugged on the ring a little harder. Kylian moaned and arched his back, pushing his chest into Sebastien's hand.

"You like that, do you?" Sebastien teased. He tugged again. Kylian clenched his fists in the duvet, trying not to rush things. Sebastien had asked to be the one to lead, but Kylian wasn't sure how much longer his own patience would last.

"Your mouth would feel even better," Kylian gasped. He'd never been able to explain why he'd chosen to pierce his nipple instead of a more visible form of rebellion, but he was certainly glad of the choice when Sebastien did as he requested and sucked the metal ring into his mouth and teased his nipple with his tongue.

"Please...."

"Please what?" Sebastien prompted.

Kylian wasn't sure what he was asking for. They had set certain limits the night before, and Sebastien wouldn't believe him if he changed them now. When he wasn't burning with need, Kylian would appreciate that fact. For the moment, though, he needed something, anything to quench the fire in his blood. He grabbed Sebastien's hips and pulled, trying to get Sebastien's weight back against his aching cock. That would make twice he'd come in his pants, but at least this time, he had a chance of taking Sebastien with him.

"Not so fast," Sebastien scolded. "I haven't gotten you naked yet."

"What are you waiting for?" Kylian demanded.

Sebastien grinned down at him. "For you to ask."

Kylian scowled at him and reached for his belt. Sebastien pushed his hands away and made quick work of stripping Kylian the rest of the way, shoes and all. Kylian nearly screamed when Sebastien trailed the tip of one finger up the underside of his cock. Sebastien chuckled as he pulled away and rid himself of the rest of his clothing. Kylian's mouth went dry at the sight. Damn, he was one lucky bastard to have a man like this interested in him.

"Last chance," Sebastien said from his spot by the bed.

"Last chance for what?"

"To stop me," Sebastien said. "If I climb back in bed with you, we will be lovers when you leave it."

"We already are," Kylian said. "The rest is just details."

Chapter 13

SEBASTIEN'S BREATH caught in his throat. He had given Kylian every out he could think of, and he hadn't taken them. He stared down at the vision in his bed, all dark hair and pale skin, for a moment longer before sliding back onto the bed next to Kylian. The silver of Kylian's nipple ring winked at him from the dark pelt that covered Kylian's chest. Sebastien couldn't resist leaning down and sucking it into his mouth. His beast had stayed relatively quiescent, so Sebastien felt confident he could keep his fangs out of the way long enough for this. Kylian's skin tasted slightly salty and smelled of his customary cologne, underpinned with the scent of desire. Sebastien wanted to cover himself in Kylian's scent and then cover Kylian in his own scent. It wasn't fang marks in his neck, but it would be enough to mark Kylian as his until he could take the rest of what he desired.

Kylian arched against his mouth, bringing a smile to Sebastien's face. He could do this. He hadn't lost his touch. He'd feared arriving at this point and not being able to please a lover who wasn't Thierry, but Kylian seemed appreciative of his efforts, which he counted as a good start. He sucked harder on Kylian's nipple, wanting him as mindless as Sebastien was rapidly becoming. He needed to come, but he needed to see to Kylian first. He'd never been a selfish lover, but the absolute necessity of that realization surprised him. He could see to Kylian's pleasure as easily after, but his very being protested that thought. He would make Kylian come before he found his own release. He worked a hand between their bodies to find Kylian's erection. Kylian let out a hoarse shout above him, so Sebastien stroked him again, adding a little more pressure. The thick length was hot and hard and perfect in his hand. He wanted to know how it would feel on his tongue and down his throat, but that would have to wait until Kylian trusted him a little more. For now, he would be satisfied with learning the shape and feel against his palm.

Kylian made an aborted move to reciprocate the caress, but Sebastien stroked again to distract him. Kylian could bring him undone with a caress or two, and Sebastien wasn't ready for this to be over. He rocked back on his heels, despite Kylian trying to pull him closer. Kylian was a vision beneath him, legs splayed to give Sebastien space to kneel between them, skin glowing in the dim light, his long hair tousled around his face, his eyes half-closed and his mouth lax with pleasure. Sebastien caressed him again for the pure pleasure of watching Kylian react to it. Kylian's hips lifted and the muscles in his legs and stomach tensed. The tip of his cock glistened, and Sebastien couldn't resist. He licked away the fluid that had gathered, careful to keep his lips and teeth out of the way. Kylian cried out sharply.

"I couldn't resist," Sebastien told him. "You're too tempting, spread out like that. I want to touch, taste, take…." He stopped the flow of words forcibly. He couldn't talk that way. He couldn't feel that way. They weren't at that point yet.

Kylian grabbed his hand and clung. Sebastien tugged until Kylian sat up. Sebastien helped him shift until he was straddling Sebastien's lap. He took Kylian's mouth in a torrid kiss and closed his fist around both their cocks, tugging them together. Kylian moaned into the kiss and gripped Sebastien's shoulders for balance. Sebastien wrapped his other arm around Kylian's hips, settling his hand against the perfect curve of his ass. Another time he'd lavish attention there. For now, given the limits he'd already pushed further than he should have, he would restrain himself to stroking Kylian and bringing him off as they'd agreed.

Kylian's head fell back as he gasped for breath. "Do you know how much I want you to fuck me right now?"

Sebastien couldn't help it. He slid his hand so his fingers brushed Kylian's crease. "As much as I want to fuck you?" Sebastien whispered.

"Putain," Kylian cursed. "Why did I think it was a good idea to decide where we would stop?"

"So that we wouldn't get carried away," Sebastien said. "It's lust talking now, not good sense—yours or mine. If we hadn't agreed, I'd have you every way I could think of, and tomorrow maybe we'd regret it."

He pulled back so he could focus entirely on Kylian's erection and stroked faster, trying to bring Kylian off now. Kylian trembled in his embrace, and Sebastien sped up again. It wasn't enough, but it was what he could offer, and he would offer it with all the care and skill at his disposal.

Kylian cried out as he came, leaving Sebastien's hand gloriously sticky. He caressed Kylian through his climax, prolonging it as long as he could. Absently, he missed the times he and Thierry had made love all night, the passion of one fueling the other until they were completely exhausted. He pushed the thought away. Kylian deserved better than to compete with a man more than thirty years dead.

"Your turn," Kylian said softly, drawing Sebastien's thoughts back to the present.

"I'm all yours," Sebastien said.

Kylian pushed on his shoulders, urging him to his back on the bed. Sebastien let Kylian arrange him as he wanted. Sebastien already had what he desired—he had made Kylian come first. Kylian's touch was tender as he explored Sebastien's body. Sebastien tightened the reins on his beast, determined to give Kylian all the time and space he desired to make love to him in return.

Sebastien quivered with need as Kylian ran his hands over his chest and down his stomach. His cock ached for contact, but Sebastien wouldn't force it. He would rather jerk himself off than push Kylian into something he wasn't comfortable with. They had time to learn each other's bodies and preferences. It didn't all have to happen tonight.

Kylian seemed to have other ideas, though, because he closed his hand around Sebastien's erection and stroked firmly.

"Putain," Sebastien cursed. "You're going to ruin me."

"Is that supposed to discourage me?" Kylian asked against Sebastien's ear. Sebastien turned his head and captured Kylian's lips with his own. He needed the kiss or he'd fly apart. When Kylian took control of the kiss and thrust his tongue deep, running it along the line of Sebastien's teeth, the depth of trust implicit in the gesture sent him flying anyway. He panted into the kiss as he pulsed his hips into the channel of Kylian's fist. It didn't give him the heat or tightness he was sure to find in Kylian's ass, but it came close enough. He threw his head back with a shout as his sac drew up tight. It wouldn't take much. He braced his feet on the bed so he could move more easily against Kylian's hand. Kylian took advantage of it, bringing his other hand to cup Sebastien's balls. The bold touch tipped Sebastien over the edge, mindless with need, helpless to stop the babble that poured from his mouth as he found his release.

Sebastien floated on the cloud of rapture for seconds, minutes, hours—he didn't know. He only knew he felt sated in a way he hadn't in years. He couldn't explain how Kylian had done it, since he'd neither fed from him nor fucked him, but the lack of explanation didn't diminish the feeling of contentment.

He finally managed to focus on Kylian's face and the satisfied smile that graced it. He tugged on Kylian's hand to pull him closer into an embrace. He'd had his share of one-night stands over the centuries of his existence—a quick tumble in bed, in the hay, in an alley behind a tavern, followed by an equally quick dismissal. What was building between Kylian and him couldn't be any further from that, and Sebastien needed to make that clear to Kylian. As far as he was concerned, Kylian didn't ever need to leave.

The thought startled him. He'd been so careful to think only about the moment at hand, to keep from wanting things he wasn't sure he could have or give, but the sense of rightness that imbued him at the moment brooked no discussion. He wouldn't push for more than Kylian was willing to give, but he wouldn't hold anything back. Whatever Kylian wanted, Sebastien would give him.

"I don't want to go," Kylian murmured from his place on Sebastien's shoulder.

"Then don't," Sebastien said. "You said you didn't have to work tomorrow, so stay."

"This is your time to be able to go out." Kylian lifted his head to meet Sebastien's eyes as he spoke. Sebastien smiled and tucked Kylian's head back under his chin.

"I've been out tonight. I saw a fantastic play with a very attractive man. Now I have that man in my bed. What kind of idiot would I be to want to go out again?"

Kylian pressed a kiss to Sebastien's breastbone. "Watching me sleep won't be very interesting."

Sebastien grinned. "Then I'll just have to wake you up again. If you're up for a second round, that is."

Kylian shifted to press his cock against Sebastien's thigh. "I'm sure you could persuade me."

Sebastien ran his hand down Kylian's back until he could stroke the curve of his ass. "What else could I persuade you to do?"

"Anything you want," Kylian replied. "Anything but biting me."

Sebastien's beast stirred inside him. As pleasurable as his orgasm had been, it would take more than that to completely satisfy the demon that drove him. It would take more than Kylian could give.

Sebastien pushed the thought aside. Now was not the time to dwell on thoughts of Thierry. His mate was gone, and no amount of wishful thinking could bring him back.

"Tell me that again in the morning," Sebastien said. "For now, you should sleep."

"I trust you, you know," Kylian said. "You kept your word tonight and didn't go beyond what we agreed to. You won't bite me without permission, and as long as you don't do that, I can handle anything else."

"What if I can't?" Sebastien asked. "I haven't fucked anyone more than once since Thierry died, and you're the first person I will have slept with, assuming you stay after this. I want you to stay. I want you in ways I can't begin to justify, but that doesn't mean I'm ready for it."

"Then maybe it's your turn to set the limits," Kylian replied. "Relationships are one negotiation after another, aren't they?"

"They are," Sebastien agreed, "but no, I don't need to set the limits. I don't know if I'm ready. I don't know if I'll ever be ready, but I also know it doesn't matter. I wasn't ready for Thierry when he exploded into my life, and he turned out to be the best thing that ever happened to me. I'd be a fool to turn you away now."

"You didn't want another partner," Kylian said. "Has that changed? If I gave my permission, would you bite me, knowing what it would entail?"

Sebastien gave the question the consideration it deserved, even though his beast lunged against the chains of his control at the very thought. Kylian was still young, younger than Thierry had been. Biting him now could easily mean a hundred years or more with this man he barely knew at his side. He hadn't known Thierry at all when he'd first bitten him, but he also hadn't known what that bite would mean beyond the alliance and the protection from sunlight that a partner's blood offered a vampire. He hadn't regretted the decision a single day of

Thierry's life, despite how rashly he'd made it. Kylian fired his lust and his heart in a way no one had done since Thierry died. It was already more to build a relationship on than he'd had with Thierry, and they'd made that work. If Kylian wanted it, Sebastien could roll the dice again.

"Yes. As long as you agreed, I would."

Kylian inhaled sharply.

"I'm not asking you to agree," Sebastien said quickly. "I'm not asking for an answer or any kind of a commitment beyond what we already talked about, but I'm not going to lie when you ask me a direct question."

"I did ask," Kylian agreed. "I just didn't expect the answer you gave me. I expected you to still have doubts."

"It doesn't have to change anything," Sebastien insisted.

"It changes everything," Kylian said. "It means I'm denying you something you want if I say no. That's not a good basis for starting a relationship."

"And you giving me something you aren't comfortable with is any better?" Sebastien demanded. "I'm not asking for anything, Kylian. I have exactly what I want right now. You're in bed with me after a round of mind-blowing sex. I'm not greedy."

Kylian pushed out of Sebastien's embrace and hovered over him, his weight braced on his arms on either side of Sebastien's shoulders. "What if I am?"

"Then tell me what you want," Sebastien said calmly, despite the pounding of his heart. Kylian's eyes had taken on a wildness that heated Sebastien's blood, but he pushed that aside. He had to keep his head, because he wasn't sure Kylian could keep his own.

"I don't know, okay?" Kylian snapped. "I don't do this. I don't fall into bed with people I hardly know or stay over when it's done. I don't think about letting people fuck me. I'm the top, not the bottom. I don't lose control of my magic from a kiss. Hell, I don't lose control of my magic when I come, but you touch me and I lose all control. When you left me that night by the river, I couldn't even make it home. I was so worked up I had to let out the magic before I could concentrate enough to cast a displacement spell. I came in my fucking pants without a single touch because of you. And now I catch myself wishing you'd grazed me with your fangs by accident because then it wouldn't be a decision I'd have to make. We'd be partners, and we'd just have to make it work instead of making a choice I always said I'd never make."

"I won't take that choice away from you," Sebastien said. "It would be the worst kind of violation of your trust. I don't take by force. Not blood, not sex, and certainly not something like a partnership. Whatever you can offer freely, I will take gladly. I'm selfish enough to not turn you away. Anything is better than nothing."

Kylian kissed him hard, thrusting his tongue deep into Sebastien's mouth. He shifted so he lay completely on top of Sebastien and rutted against him. Sebastien moaned into the kiss as he twined his tongue with Kylian's. He spread his legs to give Kylian space and braced his feet on the mattress again so he could push up into Kylian's downward movements. In the space of seconds he was hard again.

Kylian lifted his hips and reached between them to take both their cocks in his hand, rubbing them together as he stroked them. Sebastien felt his need spiraling out of control again as he thrust into Kylian's hand. The hot, velvety skin of Kylian's cock rubbed against his own length, leaving him aching once more.

"Bite me," Kylian demanded.

Sebastien shook his head.

"Bite me," Kylian repeated. "Before I change my mind."

Sebastien's fangs dropped despite his best intentions. He clenched his jaw, determined not to let Kylian make a decision of this magnitude in a fit of passion.

Kylian stroked their cocks faster, and Sebastien felt his resolve wavering. He burned with the need to know what Kylian tasted like—but the entire conversation smacked of coercion, and he couldn't do that. He wouldn't do that.

Kylian cursed him roundly, but Sebastien held firm. He was a better man than that. "Bite me, you bastard," Kylian shouted.

Sebastien's patience snapped, and he rolled Kylian beneath him, pinning his arms. "Not like this," he ground out. "Go home. When you can call me and talk about this rationally, we'll discuss us. I won't do it like this."

"You're kicking me out?"

The hurt in Kylian's voice nearly did what his shouting could not, but Sebastien shored up his failing resistance and nodded. "I wanted you to stay, but not like this. Go home and cool off. Call me in a few days if you can forgive me for making you leave tonight. I don't want things to end this way, but this isn't the way to start a relationship, much less a partnership."

He kissed Kylian once more, careful to keep his lips together so he didn't catch Kylian with his fangs by accident. He stood up and gathered Kylian's clothes. "Here. I'll let you get dressed. I'll be in the living room if you want to talk. Otherwise, I'll wait until you leave to come back in."

He grabbed a robe to cover his own nudity and headed toward the door. He opened it, then turned back to where Kylian still lay on the bed. "Don't be too angry at me. I have to do what I think is best."

He left the room, shutting the door carefully behind him. Then he collapsed against the wall and prayed he hadn't ruined things for good.

INSIDE THE room, Kylian dressed mechanically, his thoughts awhirl. When he was clothed again, he found his wand and cast a displacement spell to take him home. To his relief, he arrived in his own living room with no complications. He threw himself on the cold, empty bed and resolved not to cry himself to sleep.

Chapter 14

SEBASTIEN'S HEART leaped when his phone rang two days later. He hadn't heard a word from Kylian since his departure on Sunday night, and he was beginning to wonder if he'd ruined everything by insisting they wait until Kylian could make a decision rationally. If he'd been a little less honorable, he would've had Kylian in his bed and by his side already, but he would have spent months, if not years, worrying that Kylian might regret it and come to resent him for giving in to a moment of passion instead of waiting for a rational choice.

He grabbed the phone, only to see Jean's number displayed instead of Kylian's.

"Where are you?" Jean demanded as soon as Sebastien connected the call.

"I'm at home. Where else would I be?"

"At my apartment, trying to drag me out to feed," Jean said. "You didn't come at your usual time. I got worried."

"Did you go to Sang Froid?"

"Yes, and Angélique hadn't seen you tonight either, so I had to call and check on you. I'll be there in about five minutes."

"You can't get from Sang Froid to my place in five minutes."

"I'm not at Sang Froid. I just got off the Métro."

"And if I hadn't been home?"

"Then I'd have wasted a Métro ticket," Jean said. "Don't leave before I get there."

"I'm not going anywhere."

Not even five minutes later, Sebastien's doorbell rang. He pushed the button to let Jean enter the main door and waited for his friend to climb the steps.

"What's wrong?" Jean asked as soon as he came in. "You haven't missed a night in thirty years. Is it that boy?"

"He's not a boy," Sebastien said absentmindedly.

"Compared to us, he's barely out of diapers," Jean retorted. "What did he do?"

"Compared to you, I'm barely out of diapers, and he didn't do anything."

"Oh, so that's the problem." Jean patted Sebastien's shoulder. "Losing your touch?"

"Fuck you," Sebastien said, but he couldn't put any heat behind the words.

"No, thank you," Jean said. "I'm not the one you want, and I won't be anyone's substitute. What happened?"

"We had a date Sunday night. He came back here afterward. Things got pretty heated, and then he asked me to bite him, but he did it after saying he didn't want it earlier. I couldn't do it. I couldn't risk him not being serious and regretting it later, so I made him leave. I told him to call me when he could ask me for it and mean it instead of asking me to do it before he chickened out. I haven't heard from him since."

"You could call him," Jean suggested. "If he's licking his pride, it might help. So he knows you haven't given up on him."

"I don't want him to feel pressured," Sebastien said.

"Then don't pressure him. Just tell him you were thinking about him and that you want to see him again," Jean said. He grabbed Sebastien's phone.

"What are you doing?"

"Finding his number so you can call him," Jean said. "You won't do it yourself."

Sebastien snatched his phone back. "I can't do it with you leaning over me either."

"Aren't you always telling me that it's been long enough and it's all right to move on?" Jean asked. "Don't be a hypocrite."

"I'm trying!" Sebastien protested. "But I won't trap Kylian into a partnership without being sure it's what he wants. I don't want to end up like Adèle and Jude."

"You couldn't," Jean said. "Even if you had a partner you hated, you wouldn't treat anyone the way Jude treated Adèle. It's not in your nature."

"I'd rather not take that chance."

"So you're wasting time instead," Jean said. "Call him."

"It's the middle of the night. He has to work tomorrow. I'm not going to disturb him now."

"And tomorrow you won't call him because he's at work, and then it'll be night again and it'll start all over again. Don't be stupid about this, Sebastien. If you've found a second chance, you owe it to yourself to take it."

"I already had my second chance," Sebastien reminded him.

"Then give thanks with everything you have that you've been given a third."

Jean left after that, for which Sebastien was grateful. He couldn't talk to Jean about Kylian, not really. It hurt too much to see the pain in Jean's eyes when anything reminded him of Raymond. He wouldn't call Kylian in the middle of the night, but he finally picked up the phone and sent a text.

I miss you.

Kylian would make of that what he wanted, but Sebastien had taken the first step.

KYLIAN SIGHED as he trudged up the steps of the Métro. He'd been distracted at work all day, despite the excitement of starting the restoration he had spent so many hours working on over the past few months. Sebastien's text had made him smile when he first got it, but the guilt over not having called him made it hard to concentrate fully on the spells he had needed to cast. He hadn't thought anyone noticed until his foreman approached him at lunch to ask if he was all right. He'd lied because his team didn't need to hear about his love life or lack thereof, but he'd texted Raphael before going back to work. They'd met at their favorite café, and now, a bottle of wine later, Kylian was exhausted and well on his way to being drunk. He had to call Sebastien—but he had absolutely no idea what to say, even now.

He turned the corner to his street and froze when he saw the figure leaning casually against the door to his building. For just a moment, he thought it was Sebastien standing there, although he'd never given Sebastien his address, but the man was slightly shorter and thinner than Sebastien. When he pushed away from the wall and stood straight, Kylian couldn't help but notice he moved with the same otherworldly grace. That only put him even more on his guard. The man smiled coldly, and Kylian caught a glimpse of his fangs in the light of the streetlamp.

"Kylian Raffier, I presume?"

"You have me at a disadvantage," Kylian said. He closed his fingers around his wand in his jacket pocket. It would ruin his coat if he had to cast a spell through the fabric, but it would be better than falling prey to whatever the vampire in front of him had in mind. "You know who I am, but I don't know you."

"I'm hurt. From everything Sebastien said, I thought you'd recognize me."

Kylian looked a little more closely and felt his heart jump into his throat. "Jean Bellaiche. They say you haven't left your apartment since Raymond Payet died."

"'They' aren't the most reliable sources of information," Bellaiche said. "Just because I choose my own company over that of others doesn't mean I never go out. We need to talk."

Kylian's heart skipped a beat. "Is Sebastien okay?"

"That depends on how you define 'okay,'" Bellaiche replied. "He's not injured or anything, but I wouldn't say he's okay, either. You haven't called him in days."

"It's not that simple," Kylian said.

"That's what he said. I don't believe either of you. However, the sidewalk is not the place for this conversation. Invite me inside, monsieur Raffier."

Kylian hesitated for a moment, but as long as he kept his wand within reach, he could defend himself if Bellaiche turned threatening. With a sharp nod, he opened the door and spelled them both through the wards.

Bellaiche followed him up the stairs to his apartment. Kylian removed his jacket and offered to take his guest's as well. Bellaiche declined and took a seat on one of the chairs in his living room with all the grace of a lounging tiger. Kylian suspected he was just as fast and twice as deadly as one, too.

"You don't need your wand," Bellaiche said when Kylian tried to slip it into his pocket surreptitiously. "I mean you no harm."

"I'll keep it within reach anyway," Kylian said. "You show up at my apartment, make vague comments about my boyfriend, and invite yourself inside without telling me what you really want. I think I'll err on the side of caution."

"As you wish." He gestured for Kylian to take a seat as if it were his apartment, not Kylian's.

"What do you want to talk about?"

"Sebastien, of course. What are your intentions in his regard? I don't take kindly to people who upset my friends."

"If anyone should be upset, it's me," Kylian burst out. "He's the one who keeps pulling back, not me!"

"I know why he pulled back," Jean said, "but I don't think you do."

"What don't I know?" Kylian demanded, his frustration growing with every vague comment Bellaiche made. "That he told me he'd give me anything I wanted and then refused to bite me when I asked? How is that giving me what I want?"

"And now?" Bellaiche asked. "If he were standing here right now, would you still want him to bite you?"

Kylian didn't answer. He'd thought about nothing but that very question since he woke up Monday morning, and he still couldn't say one way or another with any certainty.

"Monsieur Raffier?" Bellaiche prompted. "If he walked in here right now, would you ask him again?"

"I don't know."

"And that's exactly why he pulled back. You made an offer in a moment of passion that has more than momentary consequences. I know you know that, but you haven't lived it once already. You haven't known what a partnership can be to fear having anything less."

"He said he'd decided to take the moment for what it was," Kylian said.

"You can do that with a lover," Bellaiche said. "You can enjoy the moment with the person you're with and walk away in the morning, or days or months later. Or you can stay, but you have that choice. Once he bites you, that choice becomes much more difficult for both of you. Maybe you're ready to make that commitment, maybe you're not. Only you can make that decision, but you need to stop jerking Sebastien around. He deserves better than for you to play games with him."

"I'm not playing games," Kylian insisted. "I shouldn't have done what I did—I get that—but he didn't have to kick me out."

"I think he did," Bellaiche said. "We're dangerous creatures when provoked, you know, and dangling the temptation of blood, sunlight, a normal life in front of him was definitely provocative. If you had stayed, he would have given in eventually, and you would have been stuck with something you didn't really want."

"But I do want it," Kylian said. "I'm just... scared."

"Scared of what?"

"Of him biting me. Not of what it means, but of the act itself. That's why I wanted him to do it before I changed my mind. It's not the partnership, the commitment, any of what that would mean. It's the act of him putting his fangs in my body."

"Then asking for it in a fit of passion is only going to make it worse," Bellaiche said. "If we're in control, we can make it almost painless, but if we're worked up, it's harder to take our time and be careful. If you hurry, you can make it to his apartment before he goes out hunting and have this conversation with him. Before you fall back into bed with him. Unless, of course, you like the idea of his mouth on someone else's body."

Every muscle in Kylian's body tensed at the thought. Bellaiche's expression never changed, but he must have read Kylian's body language because he leaned back a little deeper in the chair and drawled, "When it's done right, it can be a very sensual experience. Why, I've known vampires who could make a lover come from feeding alone."

Kylian's stomach churned at the thought, a mixture of desire and dread so tangled together he would never unwind it. "There's no way."

"My partner is no longer with us to corroborate my claim, but I assure you he wasn't in the habit of lying about our life together. He never let the marks over his heart heal before insisting I feed again."

"But he wasn't just your partner."

"No, he was far more," Bellaiche agreed, "but the marks on his chest were from before he became my Avoué, when they were promises between us, similar to what Sebastien could offer you. There are very few disadvantages to having a vampire as a lover if you see their fangs as a source of pleasure rather than a source of fear, and Sebastien has never been one to leave his lovers unsatisfied."

"And you would know from personal experience?" Kylian snapped.

"No, he's never invited me to his bed, but I spent too many years looking at the face of absolute contentment not to recognize it on another's face when I saw it. Or did he leave you unsatisfied?"

Kylian's cheeks burned, but he refused to give Bellaiche the satisfaction of an answer.

"Call him if you don't feel comfortable going to his apartment, but if you don't hurry, you'll miss him. He didn't feed last night as he should have. If you don't catch him in time, someone else will reap the benefits of his experience tonight instead of you."

"The stories don't mention what a manipulator you are," Kylian said.

"You didn't read them closely enough," Bellaiche replied. "I'm quite sure the history books mention I was chef de la Cour. Manipulation is at the top of the job description. Good evening, monsieur."

Bellaiche didn't wait for Kylian to show him out.

When he was gone, Kylian slumped in his chair. His heart pounded in his chest as he weighed everything Bellaiche had said and implied. He had a feeling the vampire had pulled his punches to some extent, although he had scored more than a few hits on Kylian's heart with his sharp words and descriptions. Jealousy churned in Kylian's stomach at the thought of Sebastien out hunting, feeding from someone else, using his fangs to bring them pleasure. He'd said he wouldn't have anyone in his bed as long as Kylian was there—but Kylian hadn't been there, and the way they'd left things, Sebastien could well consider himself free of those promises.

He didn't want Sebastien to be free of those promises. He wanted to be the one in Sebastien's bed, the one he lavished pleasure on.

He swallowed hard.

Even if it meant accepting Sebastien's fangs.

He scrambled to his feet and ran to the bathroom. After all the wine he'd drunk with Raphael, he needed to brush his teeth before he went anywhere near Sebastien. When that was done, he changed out of his work clothes into something more comfortable, although if he managed to catch Sebastien before he left for the evening, he doubted he'd be wearing much of anything for long—not as worked up as he was. If Sebastien felt anything close to what Kylian was feeling, they'd be fucking like mad within minutes of his arrival.

He needed to get himself under control so he could explain things rationally, but he wasn't feeling rational. The thought of Sebastien with someone else spurred him far beyond control.

He grabbed his wand and focused on the landing outside Sebastien's apartment. He wouldn't invade Sebastien's privacy by arriving inside his apartment without warning or permission, but he couldn't make himself arrive outside the building. If Sebastien didn't ring him in, he'd be stuck on the sidewalk feeling like an idiot. At least on the landing, he could keep knocking until Sebastien opened the door.

The spell took a mere second to send him from one side of the city to the other. He landed with a gasp. Displacement spells and alcohol didn't mix well, but he couldn't be bothered to care. He took a deep breath and waited for his stomach to settle. As soon as it did, he knocked on the door.

Sebastien opened it a moment later, his jacket in his hand like he was getting ready to go out.

"Don't go out," Kylian blurted out. "Please, don't go hunting tonight."

"I wasn't going hunting," Sebastien replied, "but I have to feed."

Kylian held out his hand, palm up, and pulled up his sleeve. "I know. That's why I'm here."

"Kylian—"

"Just let me explain, okay?" Kylian pushed past Sebastien into the apartment, well aware that if Sebastien had wanted to keep him out, he never would have made it over the threshold. "I'm doing this all backward, I know, but I know what I want. I'm scared of it, but that doesn't make me want it less."

"And what do you want?" Sebastien asked.

"You," Kylian replied. "You told me there wouldn't be anyone else in your bed as long as I was there, but that's not enough. I don't want to share you in any way, and if that means letting you bite me, it's better than imagining you feeding from someone else."

"The need for blood isn't ever going to go away," Sebastien said. "Every three days, four at the most, I'm going to need it. Can you really live with that?"

Kylian swallowed hard. The thought made him incredibly edgy, but he couldn't back down. He'd started this. If he walked away now, he'd always regret it, because he was sure Sebastien wouldn't give him another chance. Not to mention he didn't want to think what Bellaiche would do if Kylian came this close and then didn't follow through. The conversation had been mostly affable, but the veiled threat in Bellaiche's mere presence was enough to keep Kylian's hand steady as he held it out.

"I have to try."

Chapter 15

SEBASTIEN STARED at Kylian's outstretched hand. The pale skin of his inner wrist beckoned with the promise of rich, sweet blood, of a few more days of holding on to this world, of walking in the sunlight again. His mouth watered in anticipation as his fangs dropped without any conscious thought. Kylian was offering. Calmly, rationally, and with full awareness of what he was saying. All he had to do was reach out and take what Kylian could give.

He had a brief flash of another hand reached out in similar offering, although the awareness had been different then. Thierry hadn't known what their partnership would bring him beyond an ally in the war. He hadn't been comfortable with the idea of providing sustenance to a vampire, but the end had justified the means in his eyes, and so he'd offered his hand—his wrist already bloody from dozens of bites as he'd searched a room full of vampires for a partner who hadn't been there.

Sebastien almost hadn't gone, even with monsieur Lombard's urging, but he'd given in finally out of sheer curiosity, only to have a complicated, miserable, impossible man hold out his hand in offering. Now, more than a hundred years later, another man, just as complicated but far less miserable, was making the same offer with unblemished skin and full knowledge of what Sebastien's bite would mean.

All he had to do was take it.

His hand trembled as he reached for Kylian's and twined their fingers together. "Then we should go somewhere more comfortable. Standing in my foyer is hardly the best place to do this."

"Better than a waiting room in a train station, I would think," Kylian replied.

The teasing words made Sebastien stumble. "How did you know that?"

"You were part of the first group of partners that formed," Kylian said. "I studied the history of the war and the partnerships along with everyone else when I first came into my magic. I read all about that first meeting. There were a lot of details missing, but I know the instructors at l'Institut credited you and your partner for the discovery that a wizard's magic doesn't work on his partner, so you and monsieur Dumont were there. It was a logical conclusion to assume your partnership formed there as well."

"I forget sometimes how much of our personal lives are also a matter of public record," Sebastien said slowly. "It's disconcerting to have it come up that way."

"I didn't mean to make you uncomfortable," Kylian said. "I was trying to lighten the mood."

"No, it's fine," Sebastien said. "I was already thinking about it, so when you said it, it felt like you'd read my mind. Don't worry about it. That was a lifetime ago and more. It's not important now."

Kylian turned into his arms and kissed him sweetly, the rasp of his scruff against Sebastien's lips a new sensation that belonged to Kylian alone. "Of course it's important. He's important to you. Being with me doesn't lessen that, and pretending otherwise doesn't do either of us any favors."

"I don't want you to feel that you're competing with a ghost," Sebastien explained. "Yes, I loved him in a way I never expected to love anyone, but he's gone now. I've learned to live with that."

"It's harder to live with the elephant in the living room than it is to compete with a ghost," Kylian said. "I'd rather you talk about him and know that you see me too than pretend he never existed and have to compete with him anyway."

"Jean's right. I can't be grateful enough for having found you. I'm not sure I deserve a third chance when so many people never get one, but I'm not going to screw it up if I can help it." He led Kylian to the couch and sat next to him, their joined hands stretched across their bodies. "Tell me if I hurt you. If I do, I'm not doing it right."

KYLIAN HAD imagined many things when he let himself think about Sebastien biting him, but he hadn't imagined the tender brush of Sebastien's lips across his wrist. He hadn't imagined the sweet kisses and licks all over the expanse of skin. He hadn't imagined the tingling along his nerves or the sudden rush of desire in his gut. He'd expected a sharp puncture and having to endure however long it took, like donating blood. This bore no resemblance to the one time he'd tried to give blood and hadn't made it past the needle in his vein.

Sebastien sucked lightly on his pulse point, surprising a gasp from Kylian's throat. They'd hardly started and he was already squirming on the couch, wanting more. The conversation had cooled his ardor and slowed his rush somewhat, but the touch of Sebastien's lips and tongue fanned it all back to life in an instant. His eyes closed as his head fell back to rest on the thick cushions of the couch. As intense as the evening in Sebastien's bed had been, when Sebastien pushed up the sleeve of his sweater to be able to reach more of his skin, Kylian realized he hadn't known what intimacy meant until now.

Sebastien licked Kylian's wrist with such care and thoroughness that Kylian wanted to feel that wicked tongue everywhere. His nipples tightened and his cock throbbed at the thought, sure recipients of that attention, but Kylian suspected it wouldn't stop there. If he gave the slightest hint of approval, Sebastien would cover him in kisses. His ass clenched in need, making Kylian groan with it. He didn't know what magic Sebastien had that made Kylian so eager to be filled by him—fingers, tongue, cock, it didn't even matter—but Kylian didn't know how much longer he'd be able to wait for it.

As if in answer to his thoughts, Sebastien pressed his fangs against Kylian's skin. He drew in a sharp breath, but the anticipated pain never hit. Instead he felt an overwhelming sense of rightness at being pierced by his lover. Then Sebastien sucked, drawing blood into his mouth, and Kylian took back every ounce of silent skepticism about Bellaiche's claims of making a lover come from feeding alone. Sebastien had barely taken the first sip and Kylian was hard as stone.

"Fu-uck," he moaned. "I didn't think it would feel so good."

Sebastien licked around his fangs and lifted his head for a moment. "I can make it even better if you'll let me."

Kylian was pretty sure better would kill him, but he nodded anyway. Sebastien returned to Kylian's wrist, slotting his fangs back into the existing bite marks. Kylian shifted restlessly on the cushion. The precision and repetitiveness of the gesture echoed another way Kylian wanted to be pierced. Sebastien continued to cradle Kylian's arm with one hand, but he stroked up Kylian's arm with the other. Kylian shivered and wondered where that wandering hand would end up. He had a few suggestions if Sebastien needed them.

With unerring accuracy, Sebastien found Kylian's piercing beneath his shirt and tugged at it gently. Kylian cried out and arched his back. "Again," he pleaded. "Harder."

Sebastien did as Kylian ordered, tugging on the ring with more pressure, but the surge of pleasure through his body came as much from his wrist as from his nipple. Kylian struggled to concentrate and separate the sensations in his mind, only to realize that Sebastien had taken the request for harder as permission to suck more deeply on his wrist. Kylian's cock pulsed in time with the rhythm of Sebastien's mouth. Much more of this, and he'd come in his pants again.

"I hate that you can make me come without even trying," he grumbled. Sebastien canted his head so he could look up at Kylian and wink, but he didn't stop his sucking long enough to speak. He did, however, transfer the attentions of his free hand to the waistband of Kylian's pants. Kylian tried to help him, but before he could make his brain work enough to move his arm, Sebastien's nimble fingers had found their way inside his fly and around his cock.

Sensation swamped him then, every pull on his wrist echoed by a stroke on his erection, until he couldn't separate one pleasure from another and everything swirled through him in a mass of seething need. He babbled out praise and pleas and Sebastien's name, incapable of anything more coherent. He rocked his hips into each caress, but it wasn't enough. He needed more. He needed....

The sudden, unexpected brush of fingers over his entrance sent him flying. His vision grayed out and for long, uncounted moments he soared on the wings of bliss beyond any he had ever known. When he finally came back to himself and could force his eyes open, the sight that greeted him nearly made him hard again. Sebastien lay against the other arm of the couch, sucking on the fingers of one hand while stroking the bulge in his pants with the other.

"Was it better than you feared?" Sebastien asked.

Kylian's stomach turned somersaults in his belly as he crawled across the couch to where Sebastien sat. His jeans were still unzipped and his cock was hanging out, but he figured they'd left dignity behind some time ago. If the way Sebastien's gaze lingered on his bare skin was any indication, he agreed completely.

"It was better than anything I've ever felt," Kylian said. "When can we do it again?"

Sebastien laughed at that, but Kylian wasn't joking. He straddled Sebastien's hips and rocked his ass against Sebastien's cock. "How long do I need to recover before it's safe for you to bite me again?"

"It depends on how deeply I feed," Sebastien replied. "A couple of days, maybe a little more. We found the time got shorter as our partners' bodies got used to the demand our feeding placed on them."

"Place as much demand as you want," Kylian offered. "I'm not scared anymore. How do you share something that intimate with someone and walk away from them at the end of it?"

"By not letting it be that intimate," Sebastien said. "I can feed without making love to the person whose blood I'm drinking. I try never to hurt the person I'm biting, of course, but there's a difference between biting someone because I'm hungry and making love to someone with my fangs. Until your body can keep up with my hunger, I may have to feed from others occasionally, but I haven't made love to anyone like that since Thierry died, and I won't do it with anyone but you now."

"Good." Kylian couldn't keep the satisfaction out of his voice. He leaned forward to kiss Sebastien hungrily. Just the thought of having to share Sebastien fired his jealousy and need once more. He rocked down against Sebastien's erection again. "Want a hand with that?"

"If that's all you're offering, yes." Sebastien lifted his hands to curl possessively around Kylian's ass. "But if you're open to suggestions, there are things besides your hand I want more."

"Next time, I get to top," Kylian said even as he melted into Sebastien's touch.

"I'll look forward to it."

Sebastien toppled Kylian onto his back on the couch and crawled over him, reminding Kylian of Bellaiche's assertion that they were dangerous creatures when provoked. He could certainly see the predator in Sebastien's gaze now.

"I haven't bottomed since I was in lycée," Kylian blurted out. "Be gentle with me?"

"As gentle as I was when I fed from you," Sebastien promised. "You should know by now I'll never do anything to hurt you if I can help it."

SEBASTIEN STROKED Kylian's cheek, the scruff tickling his fingers as he brushed over it. He'd be careful with Kylian as requested. As careful as he'd been with Thierry the first time they made love. Fate had to be laughing at him, always sending him virgins, or close enough to make no difference, when all his instincts urged him to plunder. He was no longer ravenous for blood, but sating that need had done nothing to sate the lust inspired by tasting Kylian's release in his blood. It had been far too long since he'd shared that particular pleasure with anyone. He'd fucked and he'd fed, but he hadn't combined them since Thierry died.

Sebastien bent his head to kiss Kylian, determined to make what came next as pleasurable for Kylian as it would be for him. The thrum of need pulsed in the back of his mind, but it was a secondary thought, far outweighed by the bone-deep desire to cherish Kylian as he had never been cherished before. It was ridiculous to be jealous of Kylian's past lovers when they had only recently met, but he wanted to erase every memory of their touch, replace every thought of their kisses and caresses with his own.

Kylian's mouth tasted of mint with a hint of alcohol beneath it, like he'd been drinking and brushed his teeth to hide it before he came to see Sebastien. He didn't want to dwell on whom Kylian might have been with. Kylian smelled of sweat and dust, a scent Sebastien had learned to love as he worked with Thierry restoring l'Institut, not of sex or a fresh shower—so whoever he'd been drinking with, it hadn't resulted in anything other than Kylian coming to him.

The possessive part of Sebastien's soul didn't want to share his partner even that much, but he pushed that thought away. He had Kylian in his bed—well, on his couch—now. Nothing else mattered.

Speaking of beds…. "We'd be more comfortable in the other room," Sebastien said. "Will you come to bed with me?"

The simplicity of the question hid the depth of emotion surging through Sebastien, but Kylian seemed to understand because he stroked Sebastien's cheek in turn. "For as long as you want me there."

Sebastien already knew he'd never tire of it, but Kylian wouldn't believe such a premature declaration, and Sebastien wasn't truly ready to voice it even if he felt it. He could take a page from Jean's book, though, and treat Kylian as if the words were spoken and accepted, so that when they finally came, they would be an affirmation of an established reality rather than a shift in their interaction. It had worked on Raymond. Kylian would be an easy nut to crack in comparison.

He rose from the couch and offered Kylian a hand. When Kylian took it, Sebastien pulled him to his feet and then lifted Kylian's wrist to his lips. He licked over the wounds left by his fangs once more. His saliva had already staunched the flow of blood, leaving nothing but the sealed marks behind, but another application would help them heal even faster. Sebastien counted it a side benefit that Kylian's eyes darkened at the gesture as if he was about to beg Sebastien to bite him again. It wouldn't be the first time a vampire's bite had turned an otherwise innocuous bit of skin into an erogenous zone.

They didn't speak as they walked down the hall to Sebastien's bedroom, the silence thick with expectation and desire but no fear. Kylian might not be in the habit of bottoming, but he wasn't scared of it as he'd been of Sebastien feeding from him. Sebastien would cherish his new lover, but he wouldn't need to seduce him into anything.

When they reached the bedroom, Sebastien pulled Kylian into his embrace, Kylian's back to his chest. He pushed aside Kylian's long hair to nibble teasingly on his neck, but conscious of how much blood he'd already taken, of Kylian's limits and his own, he kept his fangs out of the way. After he and Thierry formed their bond, he'd often bitten Thierry for the pure pleasure of it, trusting in the extra bond to keep them both safe from the effects of overfeeding. But Kylian had no such protection. The partnership alone wouldn't protect Kylian if Sebastien took too much, and Sebastien would risk no harm to his lover, for Kylian was precious to him.

Kylian leaned against him so trustingly that Sebastien nearly pushed him away and scolded him for letting his guard down so completely. He shouldn't trust anyone that way, least of all Sebastien, who could hurt him so badly if he lost control. On bad nights, Sebastien could still see the look on Thierry's face when he had let the beast out of the prison of his mind. Thierry had loved him enough to find a solution to that problem. Kylian had no reason to give him a second chance if he made that mistake again.

"Stop thinking," Kylian murmured. "You've made everything else we've done together wonderful. I know this will be too."

Kylian's words settled something in Sebastien. He focused back on the matter at hand, pushing aside doubts and concerns. He would have time to worry about those later, when Kylian went to work. He slid his hands under the hem of Kylian's sweater and lifted it to reveal his torso. Kylian raised his arms so Sebastien could strip the sweater from him. He lowered his mouth to Kylian's shoulder and bit lightly at the tendon there while he ran his hands over the expanse of Kylian's chest, enjoying the play of wiry muscle beneath furred skin. He was quickly drawn back to Kylian's nipple ring.

"You like that, don't you?" Kylian whispered, his voice low and husky in a way designed to make Sebastien ache with need.

"I do," Sebastien admitted. "I've never had a lover with piercings anywhere other than their ears. Do you mind?" Thierry had toyed with the idea once, but he'd never followed through.

"Not at all," Kylian said. "It feels good."

"What feels best?" Sebastien asked.

"Try and find out," Kylian teased. He stepped out of Sebastien's embrace and pushed his jeans and underwear out of the way. Fully naked, he came back to Sebastien and started undoing the buttons on his shirt. "Take me to bed and play with it until you figure out what makes me scream."

Sebastien ripped his shirt the rest of the way off, uncaring of the buttons that scattered across the room. He advanced on Kylian, backing him toward the bed as he undid his trousers and let them drop to the floor. He grabbed Kylian around the waist and lifted him onto the mattress, then crawled up over Kylian's prone form, feeling every bit the predator as he hovered over Kylian. The sparkle in Kylian's eyes suggested he had Sebastien exactly where he wanted him.

Sebastien couldn't find it in him to mind.

He fiddled with the ring a little more, but while he approved of the way it made Kylian writhe and gasp beneath him, it wasn't what he needed.

He stretched across to the table by the bed, where he kept lube and the toys he used to while away the long, lonely daylight hours, and retrieved the lube. The toys would only be in the way.

Kylian's gaze followed his movements, although Sebastien couldn't tell from his expression if he'd seen the toys. At the moment, Sebastien couldn't be bothered to care. If it was an issue, they could discuss it later, and if it wasn't…. Hell, maybe Kylian was the adventurous kind. He'd taken to Sebastien biting him better than either of them had expected.

"Are you still okay with this?" Sebastien asked. "We don't have to do this tonight."

"You're not getting out of this now, Noyer," Kylian said. "Not when you've got me this worked up again."

Sebastien smiled even as his beast howled in victory inside him. Their lover—Sebastien would ponder that thought later as well—was eager and waiting for them.

He slicked his fingers and stroked Kylian's cock a couple of times, enjoying the way he rocked into Sebastien's touch, but that wasn't where either of them really wanted his hand. He shifted to Kylian's side so he could have both hands free to entice Kylian and still be able to kiss him. Kylian returned the kiss with feral intensity, riling Sebastien's beast even more. It wanted out so it could meet Kylian's need with its own ferocity, but Sebastien had made that mistake once. He wouldn't ever make it again. Instead he concentrated his attention on getting Kylian ready as quickly as thoroughness would allow so he could sate both their desires and send his beast back into hibernation for a few hours.

Kylian spread his legs obligingly when Sebastien moved his hand between them. He kneaded Kylian's sac tenderly for a moment to add another layer of pleasure before he reached for the tight opening that was his ultimate goal. Kylian tensed beneath his fingers, but he didn't break the kiss or pull away, so Sebastien set about gentling Kylian with tender caresses. He softened the kiss so their lips brushed rather than devoured and put his free hand to Kylian's nipple ring again. He hoped it would provide enough stimulation to keep Kylian needy while being familiar enough to ease his nerves. If the way Kylian relaxed into him was any indication, it worked.

Sebastien circled the crinkled entrance, teasing the clenched muscle into relaxing a little. He briefly considered using his tongue to hurry things along, but that would mean giving up Kylian's mouth, and he wasn't willing to do that at the moment. He could rim Kylian into incoherence another time.

Kylian shifted against his fingers, finally seeking more contact, so Sebastien pressed against the pucker, seeking ingress. The guardian ring gave beneath the pressure, and Sebastien slipped one long digit inside. He felt more than heard Kylian's gasp, so he stilled his movements to give Kylian time to adjust.

It took a moment and several long, tender kisses before Kylian relaxed again, but when he did, he sagged into Sebastien's arms, all pliant, giving flesh. Once again, the trust implicit in the gesture stunned Sebastien. He hadn't done anything to deserve the amazing, giving man in his arms, but he would do everything in his power to keep him there. Kylian was an unexpected, unasked-for gift, but now that Sebastien had him, he would hold on for all he was worth.

He broke the kiss as he slid his finger deeper, wanting to hear if Kylian protested or gave any indication of wanting Sebastien to stop or slow down. He had promised to take care of Kylian now as he had done when he was feeding, and that meant not causing Kylian any pain if he could help it. If only he could ease the way now as he had done with his fangs. Unfortunately it didn't work that way, so he would have to settle for patience and copious amounts of lube.

He crooked his finger along the wall of Kylian's passage, looking for the spot that would make any discomfort worthwhile. Kylian nearly came off the bed when Sebastien found it.

"I… fuck… nobody's ever…."

Sebastien didn't share his opinion of whatever boy took Kylian's virginity and didn't even bother finding his prostate, but he'd certainly make up for the other's oversight now. He withdrew for a moment and added more lube to his fingers before returning to the little bump and rubbing it mercilessly.

"One of the benefits of bottoming," he murmured against Kylian's ear.

Kylian didn't reply, but he turned his head so he could kiss Sebastien hungrily. Sebastien gave him control of the kiss and focused on driving Kylian to the brink of release with his fingers. He added a second when Kylian was moving easily against his hand, and then a third. He wasn't overly large, but he didn't want to cause Kylian a moment's discomfort when the time came to join their bodies fully. Besides, Kylian's moans and undulations were pure pleasure for Sebastien.

"Please," Kylian begged, his voice shattered with need.

"Anything you want, mon loup," Sebastien promised as he climbed between Kylian's widespread thighs. Kylian wrapped his legs around Sebastien's waist, pulling him inexorably into the cradle of his hips. Sebastien went willingly until he could rut against Kylian's groin. His cock bumped Kylian's sac and then slipped into his crease to press against his entrance.

Kylian cried out at that, so Sebastien shifted enough to line his erection up and begin the slow press inside. He paused as soon as the head popped through the ring of muscle, but Kylian had lost all patience. As soon as Sebastien breached him, he bucked up against the contact, driving Sebastien fully inside him.

"Easy," Sebastien scolded as he clung to his control with all his might. "I don't want to hurt you."

"You won't hurt me," Kylian said. "Move!"

Skeptical but willing to give Kylian the benefit of the doubt, Sebastien rocked into Kylian's sheath. Kylian cried out again, but his expression revealed nothing but bliss so Sebastien moved again with more deliberation, aiming for Kylian's prostate. He would wring every ounce of pleasure possible out of their lovemaking so Kylian would be eager to repeat the experience in the future. After he'd returned the favor and buggered Sebastien senseless, of course.

He found his target and watched with smug satisfaction as Kylian unraveled beneath him. He thrust harder now, sure of his welcome. It only took moments for Kylian to reach his peak, and Sebastien followed almost immediately. The incredible sense of completion outshone any he had known since he lost Thierry.

He collapsed on top of Kylian, hoping he wasn't too heavy but too strung out to do anything about it if he was. Kylian wrapped his arms tightly around Sebastien's shoulders, assuring him his weight was welcome.

"No one has ever made me feel that good," Kylian murmured.

Sebastien's beast settled inside him smugly at the accolade. Sebastien finally relaxed completely, now that his beast had receded. He nuzzled Kylian's neck. "I'm not sure what that says about the men you've known in the past, but I certainly won't complain about being the one to make love to you the way you deserve."

"It was always just sex," Kylian said. "I don't think anyone's ever made love to me before. I didn't know there was a difference until today."

"I'll enjoy being the one to show you all the differences," Sebastien said. "Stay tonight?"

"As long as you don't kick me out again," Kylian said.

"I'm sorry about that," Sebastien said. "Not that I said no to biting you, but that I made you leave."

"You don't have to apologize," Kylian said. "I had a very enlightening visit from a friend of yours tonight. He explained a few things. We owe him one, because I probably wouldn't have made it over here tonight if he hadn't come by."

"Who came by?" Sebastien asked.

"Bellaiche."

"Jean? What did he say?"

"Quite a few things, but mostly he made me realize I didn't want to share you in any way, even in a way I was scared of. I don't know how he found me, but he was waiting on my doorstep when I got home."

"He's the only link I have left to an incredibly happy period of my life, and I'm the only link to that same time for him, even if his isolation has made that link a tentative thing."

"Then isn't it a good sign that he still cares enough about you to end that isolation to give me a kick in the pants?" Kylian asked. "Even if he goes back into his shell, your happiness matters enough for him to make the effort."

"It's a very good sign," Sebastien agreed. "I just wish I could get him to care for his own happiness. He lost so much so quickly. It's no wonder it gutted him, but he was never as alone as he's felt all these years. He has friends who would welcome him back with open arms. I know Fabienne would gladly hand the Cour back over to him if he showed the slightest interest. It's never easy to lose the one you love, especially when the one you love is as bound to you as Jean was to Raymond, but being alone only makes it worse. I just can't get him to understand it."

"It may be something he has to come to understand on his own," Kylian said. "But I'll do whatever I can to help you with him. Like I said, we owe him one for tonight."

"That's a worry for another night," Sebastien said. He rolled to the side and snuggled Kylian against him. "For now, you need to sleep. You have to go to work tomorrow, but I hope you'll meet me somewhere after work for dinner."

"I always have dinner with Raphael and some other friends on Thursdays," Kylian said, "but you could join us if you'd like. If we're going to do this, you'll need to meet my friends too. Besides Raphael, of course. You know him already."

"I'd like that," Sebastien said. "Just give me the address and tell me what time to be there."

"I'll write it down for you in the morning," Kylian promised through a long yawn.

"Sleep," Sebastien urged. Kylian nodded drowsily and closed his eyes, leaving Sebastien to ponder everything that had happened in the past few hours. A sense of contentment swamped him as he looked at Kylian asleep in his arms. He had missed this. He could feel Kylian's magic wrapped around him like a living shield. It would fade before he'd need to feed again, but it would last through tomorrow evening at the very least. He'd be able to join his partner for dinner before it got dark. He'd be able to meet Kylian's friends. And then, if he was lucky, he could convince Kylian to come home with him again, whether they made love or just slept in each other's arms. He'd go as long as he could without feeding so he wouldn't overtax Kylian's system at first. He could live with spending some days inside until Kylian grew used to the demands of their partnership.

Life hadn't looked this good in a very long time.

Chapter 16

KYLIAN SENT his crew off for a lunch break, watching in silence as they scattered around the work site. Some of them had brought food from home. Others made their way to the cafés and bistros in the surrounding streets. A good restaurant was never more than a few blocks away in Paris, and where they were, near the parc des expositions, Kylian could see a dozen different places to eat without even straining his neck.

"Oh, good, it's lunchtime."

Kylian looked around in surprise to see Raphael standing by the fence that kept passersby out of the construction area. "What are you doing here?"

"Coming to make sure you eat," Raphael replied. "You look better than you did last night, so that's something, anyway."

"About that," Kylian said. "Why don't we go somewhere we can talk while I eat? I may have done something impulsive."

"Impul— Did you go see him last night? Ky, you were at least half-drunk. Please tell me you didn't do anything stupid."

"Not stupid," Kylian said. No, stupid was not a word he would use to describe the night he'd spent in Sebastien's arms. Impulsive, yes, but nothing that resulted in an evening like that could be stupid. "I'll tell you all about it, but it's personal, not something I need my foreman and team gossiping about later."

Raphael eyed him suspiciously but followed him away from the jobsite without further comment. Kylian led him to a restaurant a couple of blocks away from the building they were renovating. The staff had been friendly and discreet when he'd eaten there the first day on the job. Even better, it was just far enough away not to have been discovered by his entire crew yet. He didn't doubt they'd find it soon— and when they did, they wouldn't eat anywhere else—but for now it gave Kylian a measure of privacy for the upcoming conversation.

"What did you do?" Raphael demanded as soon as they were seated and had ordered their lunch.

Kylian held out his hand, palm up, letting the two fang marks on the inner face of his wrist speak for themselves.

"Putain," Raphael breathed out softly. Kylian couldn't decide if the timbre of his voice spoke more of wonder or derision. "I didn't think you'd do it."

"Yeah, well, neither did I, when I left you last night," Kylian admitted. "I'd pretty much decided I wasn't going to see him again."

"Did he come looking for you?" Kylian could see Raphael gearing up to go after Sebastien at the first sign he had coerced Kylian into anything. But if anyone had coerced him, it had been Bellaiche, not Sebastien.

"No. I found a different vampire waiting for me when I got home last night."

"Wait, I thought you were telling me you let Sebastien bite you," Raphael said.

"I did," Kylian replied. "Just let me tell the story, okay?"

Raphael nodded and mimed locking his lips and throwing away the key. Kylian figured that would only last through the revelation of his visitor's identity, but he'd take what he could get.

"As I was saying, I found a different vampire waiting for me last night. Bellaiche apparently decided I was the cause of upsetting his friend—and as he has very few left, he was determined to fix things for Sebastien."

He leaned back and started counting. One, two, thr—

"Bellaiche? Jean Bellaiche? The former chef de la Cour? That Bellaiche?"

"Yes, that Bellaiche. He invited himself in and proceeded to make it very clear that I was not being fair to Sebastien, as far as he was concerned."

"Fucker. What business is it of his anyway?" Raphael muttered. "It's your choice to make."

"Yes, it was, and he acknowledged that, but he also pointed out a few things I hadn't considered from Sebastien's point of view."

"Enough that you changed your mind about him biting you."

"No, he did that by making me insanely jealous at the thought of Sebastien biting anyone else. But the other things he said, before the whole jealousy bit, calmed me down enough to see why Sebastien made me leave the way he did. Then he started in with the bit about how good a vampire could make someone feel just with their fangs, and did I really want Sebastien out biting other people? Because if I didn't, I'd better get to his place before he went out for the evening, since he hadn't fed since Saturday and would have to go hunting. Maybe it was a stupid reason for going, but I don't regret the decision. I only regret that I waited so long to make it." He curled his other hand protectively around his wrist. "He's going to join us for dinner tonight."

"Bellaiche?"

"No, Sebastien. I don't care if I ever see Bellaiche again. He's handsome enough, but it's like watching a pit viper. You can't look away—because you know if you do, you're dead."

"Should you be worried about him knowing where you live?"

"I don't think so," Kylian said. "His primary concern seemed to be Sebastien. Since Sebastien and I are together now, he shouldn't have any other reason to bother with me."

"I still don't like it."

"Raph, he can't get past my wards unless I let him, and I'm not going to let him if I'm feeling threatened. If he finds me anywhere else, I can get away with a displacement spell. I always have my wand with me. Most importantly, though, if he did anything to me, Sebastien would be upset, and the whole reason he came to see me was because he was angry I'd upset Sebastien. He's not going to turn around and do something that would undo his efforts to see Sebastien happy."

"And it was good?" Raphael asked.

Kylian almost teased him about his prurient interest in Kylian's sex life, but he could read the genuine concern on his friend's face. Raphael might ask impertinent questions, but he had Kylian's best interests at heart when he did.

"It was very good. Remember we talked about how no one ever felt good enough?" Raphael nodded. "Everything with Sebastien felt good enough. More than that. Everything with Sebastien felt amazing. I've never felt the way he made me feel last night." And this morning, but Kylian didn't mention that. Raphael was already suspicious. Telling him he'd stayed the night at Sebastien's would only add to it. Even when he'd been in relationships before, he'd always preferred to return to his own bed at the end of the evening. Occasionally he'd let a lover stay with him, but he never slept over at their place. Twice now, he'd considered staying with Sebastien, even if the first time hadn't gone according to plan.

"Lucky bastard," Raphael muttered. "I don't suppose he'll introduce me to any vampire buddies of his so I can find my partner."

"You can ask," Kylian said. "You never know. He might say yes."

SOMEONE POUNDING on Jean's door drew him from his reverie. He wasn't asleep. He hadn't slept since Raymond died. He rested. He let his body relax and his mind drift, but without Raymond's presence to settle his beast, he did not sleep. Even before he looked at the clock, his senses told him the sun had not yet set—which made the knock at his door even more unusual. Unless....

There was only one way to find out.

He pushed open the curtains on his bed and padded barefoot through the apartment to the front door. It opened onto a landing that the sun's rays couldn't reach directly at any time of day, so he had no fear of opening the door to see who was knocking. He could decide to let them in or slam the door in their face after he knew who was there.

He cracked the door open and peered outside. Sebastien stood there, hands in his pockets and shoulders hunched as if he expected to be turned away. Given the hour and all that implied, Jean supposed it wasn't an outlandish worry, but Sebastien was his best friend, the only tie he had left to his old life. He wouldn't turn him away.

"Come in. Some of us don't have partners to protect us from sunlight," he grumbled.

"You don't actually know that," Sebastien said as he came inside and hung his jacket on the coatrack by the door. "You could have a new partner out there and not know it yet."

"That would presume I wanted a new partner," Jean replied wearily. "And I don't, so it doesn't matter if there's someone out there who could be my partner. He wouldn't be Raymond, and that's not something I could forgive long enough to give him a chance. If there is such a person out there, he's better off never knowing I exist. I'd only make his life a living hell."

"You aren't usually quite this bitter," Sebastien said.

"You don't usually show up smelling of sex and the blood of your new partner," Jean retorted. "It's good that things are working out for you, truly, it is, but it changes things."

"First of all, I don't know what you smell, but I showered after he left this morning, and I haven't seen him since," Sebastien said, "so if I really do smell of sex and blood, it wasn't intentional. Secondly, it doesn't change anything that truly matters. After everything we've been through, how can you believe that?"

"I believe you don't want it to change things," Jean said. "I even believe you'll try to keep it from changing things, and I know it's selfish of me, but for thirty years, I've been the most important person in your life. The most important one you can still be with, anyway. And now I won't be anymore."

"Then why did you work so hard last night to get him to come to me?" Sebastien asked. "If you hate the idea of me finding someone new that much, why did you go looking for him? Or push me to call him, for that matter?"

"Because it doesn't matter what I want," Jean said. "He makes you happy when he's with you and unhappy when he's not. If I have to lose you, I'd prefer it to be because you're happy, not because you're miserable over some idiot kid who doesn't know a good thing when he sees it."

Sebastien shook his head and grabbed Jean's shoulder in a half embrace. "You amaze me, you know that? And I swear, the only change having Kylian as my partner will make in our friendship is that he may come around with me sometimes, if that's all right with you. I'm not going to stop dragging you out to feed. And I'm not going to stop being your friend because I've found someone new."

"Bring him if you want to," Jean said. "It doesn't matter to me."

"That's hardly a ringing endorsement."

"It's the best you're going to get," Jean said. "I don't know him well enough to like him or dislike him. I can see the appeal physically, if you go for the scruffy type. The indecisiveness does nothing for me, but he's made his decision now—so as long as he sticks to it, I can forgive him the waffling."

"Now you're being hypocritical," Sebastien said. "How long did it take you and Raymond to decide to make a go of a real relationship? None of us knew what we were getting into, and none of us except

Alain and Orlando embraced it at the start. You and Raymond hated each other for the first few weeks."

"It wasn't that long," Jean said, "and I never hated him. I didn't like him because I didn't trust him, and I certainly gave him no reason to trust me at first, but I never hated him." He'd loved him too much to hate him. He'd hated himself instead for what loving Raymond would mean to the life he'd constructed for himself. It had taken an apparent betrayal and a heavy dose of wild magic to break through enough of the walls he'd constructed around his heart for him to act on what he felt, but he'd never regretted it once he finally let Raymond in.

"You certainly fooled the rest of us, then," Sebastien said. "Orlando worried about it more than once."

"He always was a worrier," Jean said. It hurt less these days to think of the man he'd considered a younger brother from the moment he'd rescued him, but the ache of missing him never truly went away. "He worried for nothing."

"You say that now, but we didn't know that at the time. That's not the point, though. The point is that neither you nor Raymond knew what you'd found when you first met. Thierry and I didn't either. Nor did any of the other partners, successful or failed. Alain and Orlando were the only ones with the sense to see what they brought to each other and jump at it."

"And that only happened because Orlando didn't know what he was doing," Jean said with a small smile at the memory. "He had no idea what he'd unleashed when he formed his Aveu de Sang with Alain. They never regretted it, fortunately, and Orlando's trust wasn't misplaced, but I'm not sure even they would have done it if they'd actually realized what they were doing."

"Which makes it all the more understandable that Kylian would need time to get used to the idea," Sebastien said. "Unlike the rest of us all those years ago, he knows exactly what he's getting into by letting me bite him. He knows it's not some temporary thing to get us all through a war. We leaped before we looked, or maybe we didn't even realize we were leaping. More of us were lucky than not, but there were enough cases of things not working out to give people pause."

"I know," Jean said. "It's why we started l'Institut in the first place. It's not him taking time to make a decision. It's the fact that he led you on in the meantime."

Sebastien laughed. "Jean, I'm more than five hundred years old. I realize that's only half the time you can claim, but it's more than enough to teach me patience. I could have waited for him to make his decision on his own."

"Now you don't have to. And you're welcome."

"I'm meeting him and some friends for dinner tonight. I want to be part of his life beyond just feeding from him, and I want him to be part of mine as well. Will you meet us somewhere another night? I won't ask to bring him here. I know you won't want another wizard in Raymond's home, and I don't blame you. I couldn't have brought another wizard to our rooms at l'Institut, or even to Thierry's house in Versailles before we moved to l'Institut."

"He's your wizard, not mine," Jean said. "I'll meet you wherever you want, but he can come here if he's with you when you come to visit. If nothing else, it'll be amusing watching him try to get through Raymond's wards."

Sebastien chuckled. "Your sense of humor has grown more morbid with each passing year."

"Alain and Thierry were the only two who ever made it through his wards without trouble," Jean said. "I don't know if he showed them the trick of it or if they simply knew him that well by then, but I also know he considered it a test. If someone could make it past his wards, they were worth his full attention. If he had to bring them through, they'd get just enough of him to walk away satisfied without ever seeing behind the mask he always wore. The older he got, the fewer people made it through without help."

"That could be because by the time he died, he'd surpassed the strength of any wizard on record, even Marcel," Sebastien said. "Kind of hard to take that on when you're young and inexperienced."

"It'll be a good test for your friend," Jean said. "We'll see what he's made of."

"And if he waltzes in here like it's nothing?" Sebastien asked.

"Then I'll give him the respect he deserves," Jean said. It wouldn't happen. Raymond's wards were as strong as ever. No one came to his door except Angélique and Sebastien, because so few people could actually get to his door. If they rang for entrance below, he went down to meet them, either to take their delivery or escort them inside if they had a reason to be there. He had two neighbors who sometimes managed to get close enough to knock if they had grown particularly concerned about him, but even they couldn't make it inside without assistance.

"I'll hold you to that," Sebastien said. He glanced at his watch. "I should go if I don't want to be late. I'll find out when Kylian is free and call you to make plans."

"You know my schedule," Jean said. "If I'm not at Sang Froid, I'll be here."

"And you'll only be at Sang Froid if Angélique or I drag you there."

"I went on my own two nights ago," Jean reminded him. "I'm not completely hopeless."

"No, I suppose you aren't," Sebastien said. "I'm glad. I've worried about you too. It's Angélique's turn tomorrow, but I'll see you in another four days, if not before."

"Enjoy your evening." Jean was proud of the way he kept his voice steady as he said it. He even meant it.

Mostly.

Sebastien accepted the words at face value and left to join his new partner for dinner. Jean was sure it wouldn't stop at that. Sebastien might be able to keep his fangs to himself in the interest of keeping his partner healthy, but he'd never manage to keep his hands to himself. Jean remembered those first heady days after Raymond had accepted him as a lover as well as a partner. They'd fucked on every available surface every time they were assured of privacy for more than five minutes. He sighed and returned to bed. He didn't need to feed tonight, so there was no reason to be anywhere but where the memories of Raymond were the strongest.

Chapter 17

KYLIAN SET the phone on the table and stared blankly at the wall.

Mamie was dying.

The one person in his whole fucked-up family who actually understood him, and she wouldn't be there anymore. Not that he saw her often or even talked to her frequently, but he'd always known she was there if he needed her. And now she was dying.

"Kylian? Are you all right?"

Kylian tried to summon a smile for Sebastien when he came out of the bedroom towel drying his hair from his shower, but he couldn't make the expression form.

"What's wrong, mon loup?" Sebastien asked. "I heard the phone ring. Is something wrong at work?"

"No, I wish that were it," Kylian said. "I can fix problems at work. I can't stop my grandmother from dying."

"Oh, I'm so sorry." Sebastien pulled Kylian into his arms, and Kylian let himself be held. The past two weeks had been incredible, spending as much time with Sebastien as work would allow, in bed and out of it. Raphael rolled his eyes and called them lovebirds, but he smiled each time he said it, so Kylian couldn't bring himself to mind.

"I have to go home," Kylian said against Sebastien's chest. "I have to say good-bye."

"Of course," Sebastien said, stroking his hair. "Do you want me to go with you?"

Kylian wanted nothing more, but things were complicated enough with his family as it was, and his relationship with Sebastien was too new. "Will you be upset if I say no? My family is difficult at the best of times. Without Mamie to run interference, it'll be a nightmare. I don't want to subject you to that."

"I'm a vampire, remember?" Sebastien said. "I'm pretty sure I've dealt with worse. But if having me there will make the situation more stressful for you, I'll stay here. Just remember that I'm only a phone call away if you need me. Raphael could bring me to you if it came to that."

He would, without a moment's hesitation. The thought reassured Kylian immensely. "I don't know how long I'll be gone. My aunt didn't give any details. She just told me to come immediately if I wanted to see Mamie again before she died. I could be gone for a matter of hours, or it could take days."

"Stay as long as you need to," Sebastien said. "I can go to Sang Froid if I have to. It won't be the same as having you here, but it will keep me going until you get back. It'll just make me appreciate you more when you get home."

"I could come back if you needed me to, although I hope it won't take that long," Kylian said. "I don't want her to die, but I don't want her to suffer either. If she's really that bad off, it might be a blessing to have it over quickly."

Sebastien shook his head. "No, I can feed from someone else if you're gone that long. You'd never forgive yourself if you were with me instead of her when she died."

Kylian's eyes filled with tears. "Oh God, Sebastien. What am I going to do without her?"

"Remember her," Sebastien said softly. "Cherish the time you have left, even if it's just a few hours, and store those moments in your heart. It's all you can do when those you love leave you."

"I wish you could come with me. Mamie would like you. If she weren't dying, it would be worth the outrage from the rest of them, but I can't do that to her now," Kylian said.

"It's fine," Sebastien soothed. "Worry about getting there in time, not about me. I'll be okay until you get home."

Kylian nodded and took a steadying breath. "I'll call you when I have a better idea of what the situation is."

"I'll keep my phone on me," Sebastien promised. He dipped his head to kiss Kylian so tenderly that the threatened tears finally fell. He clung to that comfort for a few moments longer before taking a step back and drawing his wand.

Words crowded his tongue, but now was not the time to say any of them. When he got back, he'd see how he felt, and maybe he'd say some of them then, but for the moment he had to focus on getting to Auvergne and seeing his grandmother one last time.

SEBASTIEN LOOKED at the empty space where Kylian had stood a moment ago and wished him Godspeed. He went back into the bedroom for his phone and settled down to wait for news.

It was nearly midnight when the phone finally rang. Sebastien snatched it up and answered immediately.

"How's your grandmother?" he asked.

"Hanging on," Kylian said on the other end of the line. "She's weak and in a lot of pain, but she's lucid and as feisty as ever. She ran everyone else off when I got here so we could talk. She took one look at me and knew something was different."

"Is that good or bad?" Sebastien asked.

"It's good. She's the only one in the family I can actually talk to about stuff," Kylian said. "Everyone else has one reason or another to dismiss me or dislike me. We talked for at least an hour. She's happy for me."

Sebastien had a few things to say to the rest of Kylian's family if they were so willing to dismiss him that way, but he would save that for the targets of his ire rather than yelling at Kylian in their stead. "I'm glad you got a chance to see her. Stay as long as you need to. I miss you, but I'll be fine here for a few days longer."

"I miss you too."

The longing in Kylian's voice was almost enough to make Sebastien seek out Raphael and demand he take Sebastien to Auvergne to be with Kylian. Only the knowledge that it would make the situation more complicated held him back.

"Call whenever you want. I'll be here."

"I know," Kylian said. "It's the only thing keeping me sane right now."

KYLIAN FORCED himself to wait until the next morning to call Sebastien again, even though he would have preferred to have his voice as comfort in the dark hours of the night. Sebastien wouldn't have begrudged him the contact, but Kylian was not ready to be that needy with a lover of only two weeks. Yes, things between them had gotten incredibly intense in that time, but not enough to justify clinginess.

"Hi," he said when Sebastien answered the phone.

"Hi, yourself," Sebastien replied. "How are you doing?"

"I've been better," Kylian admitted. "I didn't sleep well last night. I've apparently gotten used to having your arms around me at night."

"Say the word and I'll get Raphael to bring me down there," Sebastien offered. "Even if I just stay in your room and read while you deal with your family, I'd be there to guard your dreams."

"I'd like nothing more," Kylian said, "but I'm sharing a room with my young cousins. Somehow I don't think my aunt would approve, even if all we did was sleep."

"And we mustn't upset your aunt." Sebastien's voice was nearly as bitter as Kylian felt.

"If we do, she won't let me see my grandmother, and Mamie is too frail to get up and come see me," Kylian said. "Once she's gone I'll cheerfully wash my hands of the rest of them, but I don't want to ruin what time she has left when simply biting my tongue and bearing it will give her a measure of peace. Nothing they say bothers me anymore. I've heard it all a thousand times before."

"That doesn't make it right."

"No, but it's only my burden to bear for a few more days. After that, I can walk away and never look back."

"I hope your grandmother knows how much you love her," Sebastien said.

"She does," Kylian said. "She told me I didn't have to stay if things got ugly, but in this one thing, she's wrong. I do have to stay. Otherwise I let them win."

"Just remember you have people who care about you, even if your family doesn't."

"I know," Kylian said. The alarm on his watch beeped. "I have to go. It's my turn to sit with Mamie. I'll call later."

"Anytime you want."

Kylian disconnected the call and took a moment to be grateful he'd found Sebastien when he had. If he'd had to face his grandmother's death with only Raphael to return to, he wasn't sure he'd be handling it as well as he was. Not that it was easy, but Sebastien was his rock, a solid presence in the back of his mind even when they weren't on the phone together. He knew Sebastien would support him, no matter what. Raphael would do his best, but it wouldn't be the same.

KYLIAN SAT at his grandmother's bedside, holding her hand as she slept. He didn't know what was holding her here. Over the past three days, they'd all told her to let go, that she could rest now, but she hadn't listened to any of them. Not that he was terribly surprised. She'd lived her whole life not listening to people when they told her to do the opposite of what her heart told her. Kylian had never stopped being grateful for that.

Night had fallen a couple of hours ago, leaving the soft glow of the lamp to illuminate the room. In another setting it would be romantic. For Kylian, it was the reminder that his shift would end soon. At least he'd be able to call Sebastien. He might even be able to go see him for a few hours, although with Mamie so near death, he wasn't sure he dared to leave. Mamie wouldn't mind if he called now—or even if he went—but if anyone came in, it would give them more ammunition to use against him, and he didn't want that. They'd held their tongues in Mamie's room so far. He wanted to keep it that way. She'd stopped eating, so it wouldn't be long now. Another few days at the most.

He was keenly aware of the passing of the days. Sebastien would have to feed before Kylian got home. He'd known that was a risk when he left, but his aunt had made it sound like Mamie had hours left to live. If he'd realized the situation wasn't quite that dire, he would have insisted Sebastien feed before he left so it would give them a few extra days before he would have to seek blood elsewhere. As it was, it was probably already done.

He wanted to pace and give vent to the jealousy raging inside him, but he didn't want to disturb Mamie. She'd finally managed to get comfortable for a few hours, maybe her last. His irrational emotions were his problem, not hers. He kept his grip on her shriveled hand firm enough for her to feel it without squeezing hard enough to hurt.

A sudden wave of nausea hit him as he thought of Sebastien feeding from someone else. He growled silently at himself for letting his thoughts work him up to the point of feeling ill. He wasn't some callow child to give in to jealousy this way. No, he didn't want

Sebastien to feed from someone else, but this wasn't a case of Sebastien cheating on him. Sebastien wasn't in Paris making love to some other person with his fangs. He was getting the blood he needed to survive, nothing more. If Kylian had been there, he would have come to Kylian for what he needed, and Kylian would have given it gladly, as he had done for the past two weeks. If Mamie weren't in such a fragile condition, he could go home for a few hours and take care of it himself. The marks on his wrist and neck had healed, the combination of Sebastien's saliva and his own magic speeding the process along, and he wanted them back, damn it.

He choked back the bile that rose in his throat a second time. He was being ridiculous, but he couldn't shake the sudden feeling that something was wrong with Sebastien.

He grabbed his phone and sent a text to Sebastien, asking if he was all right. When five minutes passed with no answer and his own premonition grew worse, he texted Raphael.

Something is wrong with Sebastien. He isn't answering his phone. Find him and make sure he's safe.

Raphael's reply came with gratifying speed. *Okay, but you get to explain why I barged into his house in the middle of the night.*

Kylian held his grandmother's hand and waited, his trepidation growing with each minute that passed without news from either Sebastien or Raphael.

"WHAT'S WRONG with Sebastien?" Jean demanded as he strode into Sang Froid.

"I don't know," Angélique said. "That's why I called you. He came to feed because his partner has been gone too long. Everything seemed fine, and then suddenly Florence came running downstairs saying Sebastien was sick and to get help. I figured if anyone would know what to do, it would be you."

"Which room is he in?" Jean asked as he took the stairs two at a time.

"This one."

Jean looked up to see one of Angélique's employees standing in the doorway. "I've never seen him react this way before, and he's visited me many times."

"Tell me what happened. Don't leave anything out."

"He came in about an hour ago, maybe a little less. I could tell he needed to feed because he looked a little ashen, but he wanted to talk first," she said. "We talk a lot when he comes to visit. I don't think he has a lot of friends."

"Go on," Jean said, hiding his guilt beneath his impatience. Sebastien should have been able to talk to him instead of having to go to some girl at Sang Froid for advice.

"He explained about his new partner, about how now, more than ever, this was nothing but a business transaction and a chat with a friend. That's all it's ever been, but I thought it was sweet he felt the need to make it clear."

Jean remembered how it felt to feed from someone else after feeding from Raymond the first time. They hadn't even been lovers at the time, and the betrayal had eaten at him. He could imagine how much worse it would be for Sebastien when he and Kylian had become a couple.

"After we'd talked, he bit me. Everything seemed just like always, and then suddenly he started retching. I didn't know what else to do, so I called Angélique."

"How soon after he bit you?" Jean asked. Vampires didn't get sick, but the only other explanation that came to mind defied all possibility. Sebastien had formed an Aveu de Sang once. He couldn't do it a second time. But Jean knew of nothing else that would cause a vampire to get sick on blood that had always nourished him before.

"A few seconds, a minute at the most," she said. "He stopped throwing up, but he has hardly moved since then."

Jean nodded and went into the room where Sebastien lay on the couch, his eyes closed. His face was indeed ashen, as the woman had said. The last time he had seen a vampire that color, it had been Orlando as he staggered out of Serrier's lair and into Alain's arms. It had been the one time in Jude's miserable life that Jean had been glad to see him, because no one else could have brought Orlando back. If Jean couldn't get Sebastien's partner here in time, Sebastien would be lost. Only his maker or someone of his line could bring him back, and Jean knew of no one from that line still alive.

"Where's his phone?"

"I don't know."

Jean cursed and started rifling Sebastien's pockets, but they were empty.

"Bordel de merde. He must have left it at home." Jean hoped he'd left it there and not lost it. As good as Jean's memory was, he couldn't remember Kylian's phone number—and he'd deleted it from his phone, thinking he'd never need to call the wizard now that he and Sebastien had cemented their partnership.

He had been wrong.

"We've got to get him home and hope I can find his phone," Jean said.

"Go," Angélique said. "We'll gather him up and meet you at his place. You can move faster without him, and maybe have his partner waiting for him when we get there."

Jean waved his thanks and ran like the hounds of hell were snapping at his heels.

Chapter 18

RAPHAEL POUNDED on the door to Sebastien's apartment but got no response. He was tempted to tell Kylian he'd tried and failed, but Kylian would just tell him to keep looking. Hoping he wasn't making a monumental mistake, he drew his wand and cast a spell to open the lock. If Sebastien had wards in place, he'd be in trouble, but he hadn't felt any when he'd visited.

"Sebastien?" he called as he stepped inside. "Are you here? You aren't answering your phone and Kylian's worried."

He heard only silence in reply. Feeling like the worst kind of intruder, he walked down the hall toward the bedroom. He'd check to make sure the apartment really was empty, and then he'd call Kylian and ask for other suggestions of where to look.

The bedroom was as empty as the rest of the apartment. He walked back into the living room only to be grabbed from behind, his arms pinned above his head as he was shoved face-first against the wall. The grip on the side where he held his wand was so tight he couldn't feel his fingers.

"Drop it," the man behind him ordered.

Raphael considered trying to cast a spell even in that awkward position, but he couldn't guarantee it would hit his target. Conceding defeat, he let the wand slide from his fingers.

"Who are you, and what the fuck are you doing in Sebastien's apartment?"

"My name's Raphael," he said slowly. "I came because Sebastien's boyfriend is a worrywart who's convinced something is wrong with him. I didn't mean anyone any harm."

The man released his wrists and took a step back. "Why didn't he come himself?"

"He's in Auvergne. His grandmother is dying."

"Fuck. Do you have his number?"

"Of course I do," Raphael said.

"Good. Get him here. Now."

"I just told you his grandmother is dying," Raphael said, rubbing circulation back into his hands.

"If he doesn't get his ass back here, his boyfriend will be dead too," the man spat as he advanced on Raphael. "Call him. Or give me the goddamn phone so I can."

Raphael blanched. "Okay, I'll call him. My phone is in my pocket. Are you going to freak out on me if I reach for it?"

"There isn't anything you could pull out of your pocket that could hurt me," the man replied. "You're wasting time."

Raphael pulled his phone out and flipped to the contacts. "Care to tell me your name so I can let him know who gave me the message about Sebastien?"

"Bellaiche. Now call him."

Kylian had compared Bellaiche to a pit viper. The comparison didn't do the vampire leader justice. Hands trembling, he called Kylian and hoped his friend would answer.

"Did you find him?"

"No," Raphael said, ignoring the lack of greeting. Under the circumstances, they had more pressing things to discuss. "I'm at his apartment, where a vampire by the name of Bellaiche says Sebastien's dying and you need to—"

Bellaiche grabbed the phone from his hand before he could say more.

"I don't know what you did, you fucker, to make him get sick from drinking someone else's blood, but get your stupid fucking ass back here right now and fix it or there will be nowhere on God's green earth for you to hide."

Raphael snatched the phone back. "Are you all right, Ky?"

"Have you seen him?" Kylian asked. "Is it as bad as Bellaiche says?"

"He's not here," Raphael said. "I don't know where he is."

"He'll be here in a minute," Bellaiche said. "Before your excuse for a friend gets here, that's for sure."

"Bellaiche says they're bringing him here," Raphael relayed.

"What do I do, Raph?" Kylian asked.

"Kiss Mamie for me," Raphael replied. "She'll understand."

Raphael ended the call before Bellaiche could grab the phone again. He stuck it back in his pocket and turned his full attention to the vampire in front of him. Now that he wasn't caught off guard, he had a few things to say to the man.

"He's on his way," Raphael said. He didn't actually know that, but if Kylian's grandmother had any lucidity left, she'd order him to Sebastien's side in a heartbeat. Raphael hadn't seen her in ten years, but she couldn't have changed completely in that short a time. "I hope you realize what he's giving up for your friend. His grandmother is the only real family he has."

"If he hadn't done whatever he did to cause other blood to make Sebastien sick, we wouldn't be in this situation," Bellaiche retorted. "If anyone is to blame here, it's him."

"Where do you get off?" Raphael demanded, advancing on Bellaiche. "Accusing him of… of what? Trapping Sebastien somehow? Cursing him with this sickness and then abandoning him? I don't know who the hell you think you are, accusing him that way, but think again. You're nothing but a dried-up shell of a vampire who used to be someone important. Your word doesn't carry any weight anymore."

"There are only two known causes for Sebastien getting sick the way he did," Bellaiche fired back. "One is if a vampire with an Avoué feeds from someone other than that person. Sebastien's Avoué died more than four centuries ago, and that spell only works once. The other was the result of a spell it took four of the most powerful wizards in France to cast a century ago, and that spell was destroyed after it was used. I don't know where he found it or how he convinced Sebastien to agree to it, but I will end your friend if I find out he did it against Sebastien's will."

The sound of frantic footsteps outside the apartment forestalled Raphael's retort. Raphael didn't recognize the people carrying Sebastien, but he could tell Sebastien was in bad shape.

"Put him in the bedroom," Bellaiche ordered. "If his partner gets here in time, they'll need the privacy."

"I thought you didn't trust him," Raphael said.

"I don't," Bellaiche replied, "but some things are not meant for anyone else to see."

"Where is he?" Kylian shouted as he popped into the kitchen.

"Bedroom," Bellaiche said. "You'll have to break your skin and dribble blood into his mouth. He's unconscious. He won't be able to bite you."

Kylian grabbed a knife from the drawer and ran toward the back of the apartment. Raphael started after him, determined to keep Kylian from doing any permanent damage, but Bellaiche caught his arm. "Private, remember?"

"And if he kills himself trying to save Sebastien?"

"Then good riddance to him," Bellaiche muttered.

Raphael nearly snapped, but he held his temper in check. Kylian wouldn't appreciate him killing Sebastien's best friend, no matter how much he deserved it. He'd save that for later, when Sebastien wasn't in danger anymore.

KYLIAN STUMBLED into the bedroom and fell to his knees at Sebastien's side. He had eyes only for his partner. Sebastien's skin was gray, even more than his grandmother's had been, but his chest still rose and fell slowly. Pinning his hopes on that, Kylian slashed the knife across his palm. He'd bleed more from his wrist, but he ran more risk of injuring himself that way too. He'd have to hope this would be enough. If it wasn't, he'd try something more extreme.

He held his fingers over Sebastien's mouth so his blood would run down them and between Sebastien's slightly parted lips. With his other hand, he massaged his wrist, trying to speed the flow of blood out of the cut. He hadn't needed to worry about that before. Sebastien had managed it with his fangs and tongue, but Sebastien was lying unresponsive on the bed.

"Don't leave me," he pleaded. "I can't do anything for Mamie, but I can help you. You just have to hold on long enough for my blood to work."

If his blood worked. Sebastien had been fine all the times he'd fed from Kylian up until now, and Jean seemed to think it would cure Sebastien, so he had to try. The first droplets fell into Sebastien's mouth. Kylian studied his face for any sign of improvement, but Sebastien remained unconscious.

"Come on, Sebastien. You faced worse than this in the war. This is just a little bit of blood from the wrong person. Take some of mine and you'll be fine. You have to be fine."

The droplets had turned into a steady stream now, thin, but flowing into Sebastien's mouth. His throat worked reflexively, the first sign Kylian had seen of any returning life. He pressed his palm against Sebastien's lips, hoping it would entice him to suck the blood himself instead of having it dribbled into his mouth.

Some of the ashy patina on Sebastien's skin faded. Kylian wouldn't call his color healthy yet, but he looked marginally better. Now if only Sebastien would show some sign of intentional movement, instead of just the reflexive swallowing Kylian had seen so far.

"Come on, Sebastien," Kylian cajoled. "From the sound of things, Jean and Raphael are going to kill each other if you don't get better and help me put a stop to it. I don't really want to go out there and kill both of them."

Sebastien finally stirred, his eyelids fluttering although they didn't open yet. Kylian nearly sobbed in relief. He'd come in time.

WARMTH DRIFTED through his body, chasing away the clammy chill that had dragged him down into darkness. He chased after the source of that warmth, sucking life-giving blood into his mouth. He knew that taste, the comfort and safety it represented. He sought more of it, wrapping his senses in the power and passion of his partner's blood. His beast purred within him, content now that it had the right blood again.

He clawed his way back to consciousness, one word crystal clear in his mind.

"Thierry."

The soft sob that greeted his voice did not match with the voice in his mind. He forced his eyes open to a different face, a different man.

A different name.

"I'm—"

"Don't say it," Kylian said. "You're still weak. Even I can tell your color is off. You need to feed more. We can talk later."

Sebastien knew a reprieve when he heard one. He brought Kylian's hand back to his mouth and drew as much blood from the wound as he dared. He only prayed he still had a partner when this was done.

As satiation approached, exhaustion overwhelmed him, and he let the darkness claim him again.

KYLIAN STARED down at Sebastien's dark head. His eyes had closed again, and he had stopped sucking on the cut across Kylian's palm, but his breathing was steady and his color had returned to normal. Sebastien had told him that vampires didn't sleep, but maybe the near-death experience had been enough to force him to rest.

His chest ached even more than his palm as he freed his hand from Sebastien's slack grip and went to the bathroom to find something to cover the cut. He tried telling himself that Sebastien had been insensible when he came to, that the whisper of another man's name— even *that* man's name—had been disorientation more than anything else. He tried telling himself it didn't mean anything, that he'd known from the very beginning he'd never have the same place in Sebastien's life as his former partner had, but it hurt. God, it hurt to hear someone else's name on Sebastien's lips when it was Kylian's blood that had saved him.

He washed the cut on his hand and searched the cabinets for anything he could use as a bandage. It hadn't mattered before now. Sebastien had always closed the wounds his fangs had made with his tongue, adding to the sensual pleasure of his feeding. He hadn't done that tonight. He'd been unconscious again. Kylian had watched him struggle to stay awake and take care of the injury, but it added to the sting. If Thierry had been there, would Sebastien have managed to hold on to consciousness a little longer? Of course, if Thierry had been there, Sebastien would never have gotten sick the way he'd done tonight, because Sebastien wouldn't have gone to anyone else to feed.

Sebastien hadn't said it, but he hadn't needed to. He'd accepted Kylian's absence, offered to come with him, told him not to worry when Kylian declined—but underneath it had been a thread of confusion at the separation, as though Sebastien didn't comprehend a separation between partners once the bond had formed.

Now, with Thierry's name between them, it made sense. Thierry would never have left Sebastien for three days. He would never have let Sebastien go to someone else to feed. He would never have let Sebastien get sick on someone else's blood.

He slammed his hand against the counter. Sebastien had promised Kylian he wouldn't have to compete with a ghost. Kylian had thought that meant Sebastien was ready to move on. Now he understood what Sebastien had really meant. Kylian wouldn't have to compete with a ghost because there was no competition. Thierry had already won.

He finally found a roll of gauze in the back of a drawer and wrapped it tightly around his hand. He had no idea how old it was, but it hadn't been opened, so it would still be sterile. When he couldn't find any other reason to delay, he walked back toward the living room with all the enthusiasm of one going to the guillotine. Raphael and Jean had been shouting at each other when he arrived. For all he knew, they were still shouting. It didn't matter. If he had to deal with them, he wouldn't be dwelling on Sebastien. Maybe it would hurt less if he had something else to think about.

He'd only taken one step into the room when he was assaulted from both sides. Raphael's worried "What's wrong?" was nearly overshadowed by Jean's demands to know how Sebastien was.

"He's fine," Kylian said to Jean, "or he will be. He woke up long enough to feed. Now he's asleep again."

Jean frowned but didn't say anything else. Instead he headed down the hall, presumably to check Sebastien's state for himself.

"What's wrong?" Raphael repeated. "You said he's okay."

Kylian tried to smile, but he doubted he'd managed a convincing one. "It's nothing, really. I'd hoped he was starting to feel as much for me as I feel for him. I was wrong."

"What are you talking about?" Raphael asked. "You weren't in there for very long. What happened?"

"He woke up," Kylian said, "but it wasn't me he called for. He tried to cover it, but I'm not stupid. I know what he gets from being with me. He gets the freedom to walk in the sun and a steady supply of blood and sex. There's nothing wrong with that. I'd just hoped for more."

Raphael said nothing for a moment, only drawing Kylian over to sit on the couch. "Look, I don't know what was going on in his head when he came to, but something strange is going on. According to Bellaiche, he shouldn't have reacted the way he did to someone else's blood unless there was a much deeper bond than just a partnership. He wasn't kind about it, but I'm trying to believe that was worry over Sebastien rather than his real opinion of you. Did you do anything that might go beyond a typical partnership?"

"No, nothing," Kylian said. And if he had, if it had even occurred to him to think of it, it wouldn't have been another man's name Sebastien spoke when he woke up.

JEAN MARCHED into Sebastien's bedroom like he had every right to be there, even if he'd never actually been invited. Sebastien had never told him not to come in.

Sebastien lay quietly on the bed, his chest rising and falling steadily, as Kylian had said. Jean examined his color carefully, but he saw no sign of any lingering gray tinge. Other than Sebastien's unconsciousness, it appeared the bastard had managed to save him. Jean supposed that ought to make him grateful. Instead it only made him more suspicious.

"What did he do to you?" he asked Sebastien. He didn't expect a reply.

Taking a seat at the foot of the bed, he prepared to sit sentinel over Sebastien for as long as it took for him to wake. As he waited, he racked his memory for any case of anything even close to what had happened to Sebastien that didn't involve an Aveu de Sang. He wanted there to be another explanation. He didn't want to have to tell Sebastien he'd been tricked into a deeper bond, but he drew a complete blank. Unless Sebastien had an explanation that hadn't occurred to him, the boy would rue the day he met Sebastien.

Chapter 19

SEBASTIEN WOKE slowly, weak and disoriented. He vaguely remembered voices, maybe even Kylian's, although that wasn't possible because Kylian was in Auvergne. The rest was a blur. "Where am I?"

"At home," Jean said from his perch on the end of Sebastien's bed. "You went out to feed. It didn't end well."

Sebastien frowned, trying to match Jean's words with memories of the night, but he couldn't get past the chaos in his mind. "Was I hurt? Is that why you're here?"

"You weren't attacked, if that's what you mean by hurt," Jean said. "You got sick on the blood you drank at Sang Froid."

Sebastien's frown deepened. That made no sense. The only person he went to at Sang Froid was Florence, and he'd drunk from her dozens of times without it ever bothering him. "Are you sure?"

"Angélique called me because you were vomiting all over her floor seconds after starting to feed," Jean said. "Yes, I'm sure. We got you back here, got your partner back from Auvergne, and got his blood into you in time. I was afraid we'd lost you like we almost lost Orlando."

"Kylian came back? But he was with his grandmother. She was dying."

"As were you," Jean said. "His friend called him and he came. Sebastien, why did that woman's blood make you sick? What did you let that wizard do to you?"

"Do to me?" Sebastien repeated, still feeling sluggish. "What are you talking about?"

"If Thierry were alive, it would make sense. The spell duplicated as many of the attributes of the Aveu de Sang as Thierry and Raymond could put in. In exchange for you being able to feed as much as you wanted, anyone else's blood would have made you sick. But Thierry has been gone for more than thirty years, and you've been fine all that time. If it were some side effect of the spell, you should have felt it immediately."

"Could it be that the spell latches onto whoever my partner is?" Sebastien asked. "I got a new partner and the spell somehow carried over? While I had no partner, it was dormant, but the introduction of Kylian's magic triggered it?"

"I'm not a wizard. I don't know if that's even possible."

"Raymond's wards are as strong as the day he cast them," Sebastien said. "Spells don't just disappear because the wizard dies. We saw it enough during the war, even if we hadn't learned it since."

"But that spell was specific," Jean said. "Raymond and Thierry wrote it to force your beast to recognize Thierry as your mate. It shouldn't carry over."

"'Shouldn't' doesn't mean 'didn't,'" Sebastien pointed out. "Unless you have another explanation?"

"I've spent the past hour trying to come up with one and failing," Jean said. "And without Raymond here, I don't even know who to ask."

"Kylian might know," Sebastien said. "And if not, the director at l'Institut should be able to recommend someone."

"I'm not leaving you alone with him until I know he didn't trick you into this."

"His magic doesn't work on me, remember? That's why it took Alain, Raymond, and Eric to complete the spell. The four elements wound together to create something so far beyond any of the four of them that it could reach inside to an abomination and tame it to Thierry's hand. Do you really think Kylian could have managed that without me realizing it? If it is the spell carrying over somehow, Kylian is as much a victim of it as I am. And if it's something else, he's as clueless about it as I am. Either way, he's not to blame. Is he here?"

"Too trusting for your own damn good," Jean muttered. "And he'd better still be here."

"His grandmother is dying. I wouldn't blame him if he went back to her as soon as he knew I wouldn't die on him too," Sebastien said. "I don't know the whole story, but she's the only person he considers family anymore."

Jean scowled, but he rose and headed for the door. Sebastien counted it a victory.

"Raffier, get your ass in here!" he shouted down the hallway.

Sebastien flinched at that. He knew Jean was upset, but he hadn't realized quite how much.

Kylian appeared a moment later. "What is it? Is he getting worse?"

"I'm fine," Sebastien said, struggling to sit up. "Or at least I'm better than I was."

"That's good." Kylian's tone was off. Sebastien didn't know what had caused it, but he would find out and he would fix it. "I guess I'll be going, then."

"Going?" Sebastien said. "No, wait. How's your grandmother?"

"She's gone," Kylian said. "She died while I was trying to help you. My aunt will send the funeral arrangements after they've made them."

"I'm so sorry, Kylian," Sebastien said. "Jean, give us a minute, please."

Jean glared at him, but he left the room. Sebastien would have preferred he close the door behind him, but he'd take what he could get.

"Come here." He held his arms out to Kylian. Kylian took a few steps into the room, but he didn't cross to the bed as Sebastien expected. "Kylian?"

"You don't have to pretend anymore," Kylian said. "I get it, okay? You can feed as often as you need to so you can go out and have a normal life again. Just don't act like it means more than it does, okay?"

"What are you talking about?" Sebastien said.

"You said his name," Kylian cried. "When you were coming to. You were feeding from me, but it wasn't me you called out for. I know I'll never be half the wizard he was, but you didn't have to rub it in."

Sebastien's breath caught in his throat at Kylian's accusations. He struggled with his memories, the vague sense of homecoming he'd felt those few moments he'd been awake.

"No," he whispered, although he couldn't have said if he was talking to Kylian or to himself. "Kylian, please. I was so far gone I didn't know where I was or who I was with. I lived with him, relied on him for so long, that it came out without thought."

"But that's exactly the point," Kylian said. "When you were dying, it wasn't me you wanted. It was him."

Sebastien scrubbed his hand over his face as he tried to figure out how to explain. "What do you know about the Aveu de Sang between a vampire and a wizard?"

"What does that have to do with anything?" Kylian asked.

"It has everything to do with it," Sebastien said. "Just answer the question."

"It's a bond a vampire forms with someone special."

"It is," Sebastien agreed, "but there's a lot more to it than that, at least when your partner is a wizard. Unfortunately for Thierry and me, I'd already formed an Aveu de Sang once, and so all those benefits were denied to us. Being as hardheaded as the stone he worked with for a living, he decided that wasn't acceptable. Maybe I couldn't make him my Avoué, but we'd have another bond. He researched for months. My stonemason, who'd never set foot inside a library of his own free will, spent months scouring everything he could find about the Aveu de Sang, about soul bonds, about anything that might be relevant to us. He talked to the werewolf pack about their mating rituals. He was determined to find another route to give us as many of the benefits of the Aveu de Sang as possible. And by some miracle, he did it. He created a spell that forced the beast inside of me to recognize him as its mate. He linked our hearts and bodies in as close an approximation of an Aveu de Sang as possible. So when I was at my weakest, nothing more than that mass of instincts inside me, it makes sense I would call out for him. A part of me will always call out for him, because when he died, he took a part of me with him. But that's in the past. I can't undo it, nor would I, but I've accepted it. I fed from you, I made love to you, and I formed a partnership bond with you because I want to be with you. You, not anyone else. You aren't a replacement for Thierry. You're my new partner and my new lover. I'm sorry I upset you. Now, will you come here?"

Kylian moved closer and let Sebastien pull him into his arms, but while he made no effort to pull away or hold back, he also didn't turn his head for a kiss or snuggle closer, as he usually did. Sebastien smothered a sigh. He'd promised himself he'd never let his relationship with Thierry interfere with his relationship with Kylian, and he'd failed after only a few weeks. He pressed a kiss to Kylian's temple.

"Think what you want, but it wasn't Thierry who saved me just now. It was you, and I'm grateful for it," Sebastien murmured against his ear. He'd reached for Kylian's wrist, thinking to kiss the bite marks there, when he saw the bandage around Kylian's hand. "What did you do to yourself?"

"I cut my hand so it would bleed," Kylian said. "You weren't in any state to bite me. I had to get the blood in you somehow."

Sebastien lifted Kylian's hand to his mouth and pressed a tender kiss to the bandage. "Will you let me take care of it?"

Kylian nodded after a moment's hesitation. Sebastien unwrapped the bandage and licked the wound thoroughly. He wasn't sure his saliva would speed the healing of an injury he hadn't inflicted, but it couldn't hurt to try. When he was finished, he wrapped the bandage back in place.

"I don't know what's going on," Sebastien said without releasing Kylian's hand. Kylian would have to pull away first. "Jean has all kinds of wild theories, but whatever the explanation is, I'm glad you're the one I'm with now."

"I swear I didn't do anything," Kylian said. "Raphael said Jean made some pretty harsh accusations—but I didn't do anything to trap you, or whatever he thinks."

"Jean has learned not to trust anyone over the years," Sebastien said. "When he finds someone he does trust, he's fiercely protective of them. At this point, I would guess there are three, maybe four people in the world he trusts, and of those people, I'm the only one he also calls his friend. Don't judge him too harshly for whatever he might have said."

"He didn't say much of anything to me," Kylian said. "He seems to have shouted it all at Raphael instead. I don't know how to convince Jean I'm not at fault here."

"Until we know what happened, I'm not sure anything will convince him," Sebastien said. "We're both out of touch with l'ANS and the wizard community. Do you know anyone who might be able to help us figure out what's going on? Raymond would be all over it if he were still alive. He loved nothing more than a magical problem no one else could solve."

"I don't really know many academics," Kylian said. "Raphael might be able to help you find someone. He's at the Sorbonne working on a doctorate in sociology."

"Shall we go ask him?" Sebastien suggested. "We can set him searching for someone for us and then send him and Jean somewhere else so I can try to make up for hurting you earlier."

Kylian smiled. It wasn't his usual smile, but it was better than the pain that had been on his face when he first came into the room.

Sebastien stood slowly, not entirely steady on his feet. Before he could stumble, Kylian was there, his shoulder beneath Sebastien's arm, his arm around Sebastien's waist. "Lean on me," he said. "I won't let you fall."

Too late for that, Sebastien thought. Sometime in the past two weeks, he'd fallen hard for Kylian.

Jean and Raphael were both still in Sebastien's living room, and judging by the looks on their faces, Sebastien counted himself lucky that nothing was broken. His opinion of Raphael went up a few notches. Very few people could deal with Jean when he wore that expression without giving in or running away in fear.

"Good to see you up and about, Sebastien," Raphael said. "You didn't look so good when they carried you in here."

"I heard," Sebastien said. He took a seat on the couch and pulled Kylian down next to him. "Kylian says you're at the Sorbonne. I'm hoping you might know someone who can help us."

"Help with what?"

"Figuring out why I got sick tonight," Sebastien said. "The explanations we came up with aren't possible, but Jean and I aren't wizards, so we don't know what other explanations there might be."

"What are the impossible explanations?" Raphael asked.

"That Kylian somehow cast a spell on me that made everyone else's blood act as poison on me, even though his magic doesn't work on me, or that a spell cast over a hundred years ago has suddenly transferred to him, even though it has nothing to do with him," Sebastien said. "Did I miss anything, Jean?"

Jean shook his head.

Raphael's face fairly glowed with his excitement. "What kind of a spell?"

"A private one," Jean said before Sebastien could reply. "One that was used once and then destroyed, because none of the wizards involved in casting it felt comfortable having anyone know what they had done, or how. Do you really want to tell them about it now, Sebastien?"

"You're the one demanding explanations," Sebastien reminded him. "If the explanations don't exist within our lore, maybe they exist within wizard lore. Or even werewolf lore. The spell came as much from Adenet as it did from our wizards."

"Adenet?" Raphael asked.

"The shaman of the werewolf pack in le Morvan," Sebastien said. "He mated with a wizard. When we were researching bonds, he shared some of their lore with us."

"Damn, I wish I'd known about this six months ago," Raphael said. "I'd have proposed it as my dissertation topic."

"What's your degree in?" Sebastien asked.

"Sociology of the magical races," Raphael said. "This spell sounds like the perfect case study for the power of blending traditions."

"Sebastien is not a case study," Jean spat. "This is serious."

"So are my studies," Raphael retorted.

Sebastien ignored them both. "Do you think you'll be able to help us?" he asked Raphael.

"I don't know, but I'd love to try. Maybe not tonight, though. You still look like you don't feel well. I could come by tomorrow and we could talk about it."

"That's fine," Sebastien said.

"Then I'll say good night." He shook Sebastien's hand and then Kylian's. "I wish I could say it's been a pleasure, Bellaiche, but we both know it would be a lie."

"You can leave too, Jean," Sebastien said.

"I'm not sure that's a good idea."

"I have two plans for the rest of the evening," Sebastien said. "Making love to Kylian until he forgets everything but my name, and then holding him until he wakes up. Neither of those requires your supervision."

Jean scowled, but he could hardly argue. When he was gone, Sebastien pulled Kylian into a tighter embrace. "Let me make it up to you?"

Chapter 20

"TELL ME about this spell," Raphael said when Raphael came by his apartment a few days later. Sebastien recognized that look in his eye. He was doing well to have gotten through the pleasantries first.

"This is not for some paper or thesis," Sebastien said before anything else. "A lot of what I'm going to tell you is secrets all three races hold incredibly close to their vests, the kinds of things they don't share with outsiders under normal circumstances."

"I know why the vampires would share that kind of thing for your ritual, but you said the werewolves helped too," Raphael said. "How did you get them to agree to that?"

"By helping them solve a problem of their own," Sebastien said. "The shaman, Adenet, ended up mated to a wizard, Marc. Marc convinced Adenet that they owed it to us to help if they could. But that's one of the reasons the spell was destroyed. It contained lore we shouldn't have had access to. They trusted us because of Marc, but that's as far as it went. As long as Raymond was alive they remained cordial to l'Institut since he was the one they first went to for help, but that was as far as it went. I don't know if they've had any contact since he died. I don't want to cause problems for anyone now because I told you about something that was meant to die with the wizards involved."

"Let's start there, then," Raphael said. "Which wizards were involved, and why?"

"Werewolf magic is more nature magic than elemental magic, and Thierry's magic alone wouldn't affect me, so we had four wizards, one for each element. We discussed whether we needed a fifth, another earth wizard, since Thierry's magic didn't work on me, but they decided that his magic blended with the others would create something sufficiently unique that it wouldn't matter. And since we were doing this in secret, the fewer people who knew, the better."

"Thierry was the earth wizard. Who else?"

"Alain for air, Raymond for water, and Thierry and Alain's friend Eric for fire. He didn't have a vampire partner, so he didn't understand the way Raymond and Alain did, but before the war, the three of them had been inseparable. The war strained that, but things were getting better. I think it was Eric's way of proving he would still do anything for them."

"Alain Magnier, I assume. I don't know an Eric, but if he didn't have a partner, there'd be no reason for him to come up in my studies."

"Eric Simonet," Sebastien said. "Marcel Chavinier's spy throughout the war."

"Oh! He fell completely out of the history books after the war. I never knew what happened to him."

"He wanted it that way. He stayed friends with Thierry and Alain, as I said, but he preferred to stay out of politics and public life. After all he'd lost and suffered, no one argued with him. He helped out at l'Institut occasionally when we were doing the restoration. His lover was an earth wizard like Thierry, and those are few and far between."

"Okay, a combination of the four elements," Raphael said. "That's already a powerful mix, and three of those wizards are renowned for just how strong their magic was. What was the goal of the spell?"

"To create a bond between Thierry and me that mimicked as many known aspects of the Aveu de Sang as possible," Sebastien said. "I had an Avoué soon after I was turned, when I was too young to know better. I'd learned to live with the loss and the fact that I would only be Thierry's partner, nothing more, but it tortured Thierry that he couldn't give me the same benefits Jean and Orlando got from their Avoués when he'd gotten so much from me. I told him that was ridiculous and that I got plenty from him in return, but he was as stubborn as stone and determined to find a way around the fact that the Aveu de Sang only works once."

"I know the term, but what benefits specifically?" Raphael asked. "The more I know, the more I can try to figure out if the spell has somehow carried over to Kylian."

"The ability to feed from the Avoué without limits and without fear of hurting him or her, a connection to the Avoué's emotions that lets both parties sense what the other person is feeling, and the ability for the vampire to let go of all control of the monster inside him without hurting his Avoué," Sebastien said. Stated that way, it seemed so little, but Sebastien remembered the nights with Thierry, the way they could make love and feed for hours as long as they didn't come at the same time, until Sebastien was so gorged on blood and sex that he could actually sleep for a few hours. Even more than the ability to walk in the sunlight, it was that soul-deep connection with Thierry that Sebastien missed.

"Deceptively simple and yet terribly delicate all at once," Raphael said. "I wouldn't even know where to begin. How does it work for an Aveu de Sang?"

"The Aveu de Sang is the one bit of magic a vampire can actually do," Sebastien said. "There's an agreement of the two parties, usually before witnesses, a brand to the flesh of the mortal, and then a consummation of the bond. I never wondered where the magic for it came from until I took up with wizards and came to understand a little more about how that works. Raymond postulated that a wizard must have created the spell at some time in the past, but he could never find any record of it. Thierry always argued that we had to be missing something that would explain why it only worked once and why it tied the two people together in such a way that the Avoué could never be turned, thus ensuring the lovers would be separated at the end of the mortal's life. The bitter irony of the Aveu de Sang, they always said. Raymond couldn't figure that one out either."

"So the Aveu de Sang ceremony was no help in itself," Raphael concluded.

"No. The only thing we knew about the magic of it was that it was incredibly ancient and powerful magic. Marcel was present when Alain and Orlando made their bond. He felt the magic and said it wasn't something he could undo. I watched that old man do magic. If he couldn't undo it, it couldn't be undone. Raymond surpassed him before the end, but it wasn't about strength of magic. It was about the magic itself."

"Once done, it couldn't be undone," Raphael mused. "Magic isn't supposed to work that way, you know. There are very few spells that don't have a counterspell." He made a note on his tablet. "And most of those that don't are considered the very darkest of magic."

"The *Abbatoire,* for example?" Sebastien asked. "We encountered it a few times during the war."

"Yes, and blood magic or sex magic," Raphael replied.

"Raymond always argued it was the intent that made a spell dark, not the spell itself. Certainly the werewolves have a very different opinion about sex magic than we do. I've never seen Raymond so animated as when he got deep into a discussion of different kinds of magics with the werewolf shaman from the US who came to help the werewolves here. Tristan was a witch before he became a werewolf, and his philosophy of magic was very different from Raymond's."

"Interesting," Raphael said. "From what little you said, the Aveu de Sang sounds like a mixture of blood magic and sex magic, since I would imagine the consummation includes feeding as well as sex. And while the brand wouldn't bleed, it would still leave a scar—frequently a hallmark of blood magic—which means it predates those taboos, if it indeed came from a wizard and not a witch."

"We never even considered that," Sebastien said with a short laugh. "But then, we'd gone beyond searching for the origins of the Aveu de Sang and into looking for ways to recreate its effects. And as you said, the new spell was indeed a mix of blood and sex magic along with the kind of esoterica Raymond reveled in—and that was so far over my head I couldn't repeat it if I tried. Jean might be able to. He shared Raymond's fascination for the old lore, although his focus was always the vampire lore rather than wizard lore."

"If I don't get anywhere with what you've given me, I'll ask him," Raphael said, "although I don't know if he'll tell me. We didn't get off to the best start yesterday."

"I'd tell you Jean is all bark and no bite, but that's not true," Sebastien said. "He is generally controlled enough to wait until he's sure of the situation before carrying out his threats, though. He might not discuss it for the sake of discussing it, but if you take him specific questions, he will probably answer them, if only to help me."

"I'll keep that in mind. So we have a spell using blood magic and sex magic to imitate the effects of another blood magic spell, performed by three incredibly powerful wizards, plus a fourth who must have been reasonably strong—if he wasn't, the spell wouldn't have worked, because the balance would have been off. Did you perform the spell somewhere in particular?"

"In the crypt of Notre-Dame," Sebastien said. "The priests were properly scandalized, but they couldn't deny access to the heroes of the war—especially Thierry, since he had repaired the church after a battle left it in danger of collapse. Raymond insisted the natural power there would add to the chances of success for the spell. We wanted it to work, but I'm not sure he really believed it would until it did."

"And the rite itself?" Raphael asked.

"I don't remember the words they used to summon the magic. I'm not entirely sure it was even in French. There may have been some Latin and Greek in there, or other things even older. When the time came, Raymond instructed me to bite my own wrist and offer it to Thierry like I would if I were trying to turn him. It wouldn't have that effect, of course, but the idea was to leave a trace of my blood in him so that when I fed from him, my beast would recognize it and thus him as its mate. When that was done, I fed from him to seal the bond. I knew the minute I tasted his blood that it had worked. That part of it, anyway. I hadn't felt the kind of inner peace I knew in that moment since I was turned, when I discovered I had this monster inside me that only constant vigilance could control. It took longer to know if the rest worked, because even for a vampire with an Avoué, the sense of each other's emotions develops over time as you learn to read each other."

"That's the blood part," Raphael said. "I assume sex followed."

Sebastien's face flamed as he remembered it. He'd never been an exhibitionist. It had been the one part of the ritual he'd argued against. He could deal with feeding from Thierry with the others watching. As intimate as it was, he'd lost some of that reticence as often as they had done it during the war, when privacy wasn't always available. The thought of spreading Thierry out on the cold stones of the crypt and making love to him with the others in the room had nearly been the breaking point. They had compromised by setting up a screen to give the illusion of privacy. The others could hear every gasp and moan as they maintained the flow of magic around them, but at least Sebastien hadn't had to deal with their gazes on him. "Yes. They kept the spell going. I guess by that point Thierry's magic was entangled in it enough that they didn't need his conscious participation."

Raphael chuckled. "It's sex magic. He participated, even if he wasn't consciously casting a spell. His magic would have been the strongest at that moment because he was the one actually having sex. The others would have been there to provide the mix that let his magic work on you. Isn't that what you said they were there for in the first place?"

"That and to make up the full complement of magic that a witch or shaman would have naturally at their disposal," Sebastien said.

"Do you remember anything about the wording of the spell?" Raphael asked. "Any loophole that might have let the spell carry over to Kylian after Thierry's death?"

"I don't," Sebastien said, "but as I told you, I didn't pay a lot of attention to the wording because it didn't matter to me. I trusted Thierry and Raymond to create the ritual. All they needed from me was my agreement, my blood, and for me to make love to Thierry. But it was Thierry I bound myself to. He was the one who took my blood into him so my beast would recognize him. He was the one I fed from and made love to. I don't see where there could be any ambiguity in that."

"No, I agree," Raphael said. "That does sound quite specific, which makes this all the more puzzling. I'm going to see what I can find out. There is research available to me that Raymond wouldn't have had access to when you did the ritual. Maybe I can find something."

"I appreciate it," Sebastien said. "I need to know what's going on, because if there are other effects of whatever this is, I'd rather not get caught off guard again like I was when I went to feed from Florence. If you hadn't reached Kylian, or if he hadn't been able to get here in time, I would be gone. The only way to restore a vampire who has gone too long without food is with the blood of a vampire farther up the line. I'm the oldest of my line. There would have been no bringing me back."

"Then I'm glad he got here in time," Raphael said. "For your sake and for his. I'll call when I have more questions, or any answers. Say hi to Kylian for me if you see him tonight."

"I will," Sebastien said.

Raphael left and Sebastien slumped back onto the couch. He hadn't talked about the ritual in that much detail since they'd decided on how it would go. He ached with missing Thierry, the bond that had soothed his beast and added such richness to his days and nights. He didn't dare hope that his illness the night before meant he could find any of the rest of it with Kylian. He didn't even know for sure if he would've gotten sick off anyone's blood but Thierry's while he lived. Even before they pledged their troth, he hadn't fed from anyone else in years. He certainly never did after that night. They could be pursuing this for nothing, and the explanation could be something as mundane as a second partnership. Sebastien didn't know if any other vampire had found a new partner after losing their first, so he had no one to ask. He supposed he could contact someone at l'Institut, but surely if such a thing were common, Raphael would know, given how entrenched he was in his studies.

With a sigh, he went to the liquor cabinet and poured a glass of cognac. He wouldn't taste it, and it wouldn't affect him, but the routine would soothe him.

He took a sip and nearly dropped the glass.

For the first time in thirty-three years, the smoky flavor of the liquor exploded on his tongue.

Chapter 21

SEBASTIEN PACED around the living room, his heart pounding in his chest and his breath coming in shallow pants. This couldn't be happening. He shouldn't be able to taste the cognac. Only Thierry had ever given him that, and Thierry was dead.

He ran through a list of all that had changed after their ritual, the things Thierry had brought him that no one else had. Tasting the cognac was a side effect, not anything intentional. They had intended the rest. Thierry's blood soothed his beast. Thierry's emotions mingled with his. Thierry's passion fired his own. None of those things had happened until after the bonding ceremony, not the way they did later. Thierry's passion had always aroused him, but after they consecrated their bond, it was a physical effect, cycling between them until they were mindless with need.

He couldn't feel Kylian that way. Whatever this was, it wasn't the same as his bond with Thierry. Maybe the ritual had made him more susceptible to a new partnership, making it more powerful than a typical partnership.

He closed his eyes and focused inward, trying to find the place where Thierry's emotions had always dwelled in his heart, but it was as barren as it had been since the day Thierry died. He felt no connection there. He was going in circles for nothing. Without that connection, the passion wouldn't cycle between them, and without that, he wouldn't be able to let go of his control and sate his inner beast. And that had been at the core of their bond. Thierry had brought him peace. Only being able to feed from Thierry, if that was even a side effect, being able to taste the cognac, those were secondary. They didn't matter in the grand scheme of things. What mattered was the connection they had forged that night in the bowels of Notre-Dame.

His phone rang, drawing him from his thoughts.

"Hi, Kylian," he said when he saw Kylian's number on the screen. "Is everything okay? You don't usually call during the day."

"I don't know," Kylian said. "I got the strangest feeling. It happened when you were sick too. I called Raphael to check on you because you weren't answering your phone. Are you feeling okay? Not weak or sick or anything?"

"I'm not feeling sick," Sebastien said. "But I'm not sure 'okay' is the right word. I had a long talk with Raphael this afternoon, and it's left me feeling unsettled. Lots of old memories stirred up and all that."

"Are you sure that's all it is?" Kylian pressed.

Sebastien felt something unclench inside him at Kylian's concern. "No," he said honestly, "but I don't know how to explain the rest. What time do you get off work?"

"In another three hours," Kylian said. "Do you want me to come by when I'm done?"

"Yes. I need to see you."

"I'll be there as soon as I can," Kylian promised. "Probably around six thirty."

"I'll be here," Sebastien said.

He ended the call and returned to his pacing. He hadn't known about Kylian sensing it when he had been sick. And now Kylian had called when he was upset.

He'd just tried to find Kylian's emotions in his own heart and failed. So why was Kylian sensing things about him? He couldn't test the rest even if he wanted to, even if he believed some part of his bond with Thierry had carried over to Kylian. If he was wrong, he would end up attacking Kylian the way he had attacked Thierry. Even if they took all the same precautions, Sebastien feared losing Kylian if his beast took the upper hand again. Thierry had stayed, although Sebastien never did fully understand how he could forgive that night. He had no guarantee Kylian would react the same way.

His restlessness increased until the four walls of his apartment seemed to close in around him. It took a minute to remember he could leave anytime he wanted now. He grabbed a jacket and headed outside. Without thinking about where he was going, he found himself at Thierry's grave.

He buried his hands in the dirt, not that he expected to feel the connection he'd once felt with his lover when he sat there. He had felt it for a few years after Thierry had died, but it was long gone. A breeze ruffled his hair, making him think fondly of Alain. Alain would often summon a breeze on a warm day to make them all more comfortable. This breeze was a natural one, he was sure, but the memory of it made him smile nonetheless.

He sat there a few minutes longer, but the location gave him no more peace than his apartment had done. He ran his fingers tenderly over the headstone and walked toward Alain and Orlando's grave. He hadn't had many reasons to visit it over the years, but it hadn't changed in that time. He rested his hand against the stone for a moment. "What would you think of all of this?" he asked softly. "Besides telling me I was a fool for worrying about it when I could be focusing on what I do have."

The breeze picked up as he spoke, and his heart stuttered as he heard laughter on the wind. It nearly broke him, to still be able to sense Alain and Orlando when he could no longer sense Thierry, with whom he'd had a far deeper connection. What held their souls here when Thierry's was gone?

Unless....

He tried to push the thought away, but once it had formed, it wouldn't leave. It was beyond crazy to think that the ritual or their bond had managed to bring Thierry back somehow. He didn't know where souls went after their bodies died. He'd never really subscribed to any specific beliefs, although he knew what Jean would say.

Jean would laugh him out of the city if Sebastien suggested it, and yet it would explain so much. Why Florence's blood had made him sick, why he couldn't sense Thierry at his grave anymore, why he'd fallen for Kylian so hard and so fast.

There had to be another explanation. He couldn't be lucky enough to have Thierry come back to him in the body of the only man who had held Sebastien's interest for more than a few minutes since Thierry died. Of course, if he was right, that could be why Kylian held his interest.

"No," Sebastien said to the empty cemetery. "Even if it's true—it can't be true, but even if it's true—Kylian isn't Thierry. I know that. Thierry was never that innocent, not by the time I knew him. He was snide and sarcastic and cynical. Kylian can be snide, but he's not cynical. He's not hard the way Thierry was. They don't look anything alike. They don't taste anything alike. The only thing they share is a magical element, and there are only four of those, so the chances of that aren't that low."

He couldn't believe he was actually considering this. It was beyond far-fetched, and yet it made more sense than anything else he'd come up with. He needed to talk to someone, to bounce his ideas off someone who might be able to offer some insight. He couldn't ask Jean about it, though. He was too tied up in his Christian upbringing and the years he'd spent in a monastery to consider any other option for life after death, but the Aveu de Sang dated from well before the advent of Christianity. Monsieur Lombard had lost his Avoué in the battle that had resulted in Clovis converting to Christianity along with all his army in 496 AD, and the Aveu de Sang had been an old spell even then. He didn't know if monsieur Lombard would open the door for him after living in seclusion after he turned the Cour over to Jean centuries ago, but it was worth a try. He had three hours before Kylian arrived. That was enough time to get to île St-Louis and back if he hurried. And if it was all for naught, at least he'd know he tried.

"IT HAS been a long time since you darkened my door," Lombard said by way of greeting after Mireille had shown Sebastien into the library. If anything, Sebastien swore Lombard was more intimidating now than he had been when they first met. Then, he had been the one to provide the means of finding Orlando. Now, he was the only hope Sebastien had of confirming his wild theory. The oldest vampire in Paris, the vampire even Jean deferred to when it came to vampire history and lore. If anyone could shed light on his situation, it would be Lombard.

"It has. I hope you don't mind that I've come now."

"That will depend on why you're here," Lombard said. "And during the day on top of that."

"I found a new partner," Sebastien said. "I wasn't looking, but it seems fate had other plans in store for me. I stumbled across him while I was trying to help Jean."

"You came to tell me you found a new partner?" Lombard asked.

"No. Well, not entirely. When you were turned, did people believe in reincarnation?"

"That is quite a question, young man. I was not a priest among our people, so I cannot give you all that many details of our beliefs, but yes, we believed a soul could be granted a second life. Could be, mind you, not would be."

"Were there conditions for that boon?" Sebastien asked, his heart pounding in his chest. He loved Kylian already, and he would love him no matter what the answer was, but if it was true, if it could possibly be true...."

"The priests had many explanations for those conditions, but I always believed it came down to one thing," Lombard said. "A tie to this world that had not been broken, something so strong it could drag the soul back from the other side. For some, that was a task unfulfilled. For others, it was to right a great wrong."

"Or to rejoin a love left behind?" Sebastien whispered.

"Now that is an interesting supposition. For most, certainly when I was alive, a loved one wouldn't live long enough for a soul to be reborn and grow to adulthood to be rejoined with a lost lover. Even if the person died quite young, they were more likely to be reunited in the hereafter than on this plane. But you are a vampire. The span of your years is unlimited. And so you're wondering if somehow you've dragged the one you lost back into this world because you're still here."

"Is it possible?" Sebastien asked.

"That is a question I cannot answer," Lombard said. "I am old by every definition of the word, and I have seen many things in my long years, but I am not omniscient. Is it possible? Many things that have been said to be impossible have since come to pass. We have flying machines, devices that project our voices across continents and into outer space, access to information in ways we have never had before. If you had told me that one day I could sit down at a box and have the collected knowledge of the world at my fingertips, I would have called you mad. Is it possible? Perhaps. The better question is, does it matter?"

"In some ways, it doesn't," Sebastien said. "What I feel for Kylian won't be lessened if I'm wrong, although it might be increased if I'm right. But I will stay with him one way or another. That isn't in question."

"Then what is in question?" Lombard asked.

"Thierry wasn't just my partner. We... had another bond."

"Yes, I'm aware," Lombard said. "I told Jean then it was a bad idea, because you were dealing with magic you had no hope of understanding or controlling. Go on."

"The bond had multiple effects," Sebastien said. "I've started feeling some of them again with Kylian over the past few days. If I'm right and the other effects have carried over as well, I would like to know. Getting sick because I drank someone else's blood was not pleasant. I'd rather avoid any other complications if I can."

Lombard's already cool expression hardened to ice. "Do not toy with me, boy. I have lived for over two millennia. I think if a bond as all-consuming as the Aveu de Sang couldn't reunite a vampire with his lover on this plane, then your bond has no hope of matching it." Sebastien caught the momentary grief that crossed Lombard's face, a reminder that Lombard had loved and lost just as Sebastien had, but he could not let Lombard's grief sway him from his mission.

"With all due respect, monsieur," Sebastien said, "your Avoué wasn't a wizard."

"And what difference would that make?" Lombard demanded.

"Jean and Orlando had experiences with their Avoués that I didn't have with mine," Sebastien said. "The sense of connection was a hundred times stronger than I ever had with Thibaut. Even the connection I had with Thierry, as bastardized as you think it was, was a hundred times stronger than what I had with Thibaut. If your people were right about it being a tie to this world that was not yet broken, I can't think of much that would be stronger than the bond we shared with our wizards."

"Get out," Lombard said. "You meddled in things you had no business meddling in. You will face the consequences of it, whatever they may be, alone. Do not look to me for false hope, for I will give you none."

SEBASTIEN HAD returned to pacing when Kylian knocked on his door at six thirty, as promised. Sebastien let him in and kissed him hard as soon as the door closed behind them.

"Not that I'm complaining, but what brought that on?" Kylian asked when Sebastien finally released his mouth.

"It's been a trying day," Sebastien said. "Talking with Raphael first, and then I started feeling trapped, so I went for a walk and then to see an old mentor of Jean's, hoping he'd be able to shed some light on the situation."

"Could he?" Kylian asked.

Sebastien considered his answer carefully. "Yes and no. He thinks I'm on the wrong track, but I'm not sure how much of that is because my logic is wrong and how much of it is because I'm the one making the leap of logic."

"Why would that be a problem?" Kylian asked.

"He never approved of Thierry and me forming a bond," Sebastien said. "Not the partnership, but the other bond. He had an Avoué a long time ago. For him, that bond is sacred, and to try to duplicate it with someone else was the height of arrogance. He'd meet any suggestion that the bond might have any kind of positive effect with disdain. On the other hand, he didn't tell me it was impossible."

"What was impossible?"

"The ancients believed a soul could be reborn if it had a strong enough tie to this world—unfinished business, so to speak."

"And you think your bond created that kind of tie," Kylian said slowly. Sebastien watched nervously as the implications of the words sank in. Kylian's face twisted with anger and betrayal when it did. "Are you so desperate to have him back that you can't be happy with me as I am?"

"That's not it at all," Sebastien exclaimed. "But things are happening that don't make sense unless you have Thierry's soul."

"I'm not Thierry. I'm Kylian," Kylian insisted. "I don't have any memories but my own. I've never had any hint of a previous life. I don't even have Raphael's sense of a missing half. I'm sorry, Sebastien, but this is impossible."

"Is it?" Sebastien asked. He'd had many of the same thoughts that Kylian had just voiced. "I didn't say you were Thierry. I know you're not. You're different from him in so many ways, but I got sick on someone else's blood. I could taste the cognac this afternoon when I had a glass. You sensed when I was sick, and then today when I was upset. Those are all things that have only happened between bonded pairs. If the bond we made caused his soul to be reborn in you, then it changes things. It allows us things we wouldn't otherwise have."

"Like what?" Kylian asked. His expression was still wary, but he was listening. That was all Sebastien could ask for at this point.

"Like feeding from you without fear I'll drain you," Sebastien said. "Like not having to fear the loss of my humanity if the monster inside of me gets loose. Like being able to let go knowing that your touch, your blood will control that monster for me. I don't expect you to act like him, to think like him, to have his memories. I fell in love with you, not a replacement for someone I lost."

"You fell…."

Sebastien flinched when he realized what he'd said. That wasn't how he'd intended to tell Kylian about his feelings, but he'd said it now. Trying to backtrack would only make things worse. "Yes, I fell in love with you. I know it's too fast for you to feel the same, but that seems to be a habit of mine. I'd only known my Avoué a week when I claimed him. It took a little longer to claim Thierry as anything other than a partner—but that was because he'd never been with a man before and had to get used to the idea, not because I questioned my feelings. So two weeks with you is pretty much the right time frame."

"You called his name when you came to," Kylian said.

Sebastien dredged up the hazy memories of that moment. "If anything, I think that proves my point. In that moment, there was nothing of the human in me. I was too far gone. All that was left was the vampire. When we rescued Orlando from Serrier, he was gone, completely inanimate. Jude pulled him back and Alain offered his wrist to feed him. Orlando was on him like a wild thing until the taste of Alain's blood called him back to himself and calmed the beast enough for Orlando's humanity to surface again. When the vampire doesn't have someone like that, it takes another vampire to hold him back so he doesn't drain the first person he feeds from. Even a vampire who would normally never act that way loses control when he's that far gone. I came back without the beast going wild. Yes, I said his name, because he's the only one who could ever tame the beast. His is the only name my beast has ever recognized as anything other than prey."

"Not even your Avoué?"

"I don't know," Sebastien said. "It never occurred to me to test the limits of my control when he was alive. I only tested it with Thierry because he insisted after some things Alain had said. And when we tested it, I lost control and tried to attack Thierry. It took a long time before I trusted myself after that, but after we bonded, we tested it again and it worked. He represented a kind of peace I hadn't known since I was turned. So yes—when I felt that peace again as you brought me back, his name came out. But he wasn't the one who brought me back, because he isn't here. You're the one who brought me back. If it bothers you, I won't look into it anymore. I'll tell Jean it doesn't matter. I'll have Raphael stop his research. Having you is more important than having an explanation."

"No, you're right. We need to know. I don't want something happening to you again because we pretended it didn't exist."

"There's not much else that could happen," Sebastien said. "Getting sick because of feeding from someone else is pretty much the only negative effect of the bond."

"But there are positives you would be denied if we don't take it any farther," Kylian said. "When Jean told me you were dying, I couldn't think. I couldn't breathe. Mamie took one look at me and asked what I was still doing there with an old woman when you needed me. I love you too. It'll just take some time to get used to the idea that I'm somehow your bondmate reborn."

"We don't know that you are," Sebastien said. "It's a supposition at best."

"Do you have any other explanation?"

"No."

"Then I think we have to go with the idea that I am, until we can prove that I'm not." He fell silent for a moment, going back over all the strange incidents that had occurred since he met Sebastien. They had explained most of them, but he hadn't ever figured out the house in Versailles. "Did you ever live in Versailles?"

"No," Sebastien said. "Well, not really. Thierry had a house there that we used a few times toward the end of the war. Why?"

"Because the night you left me on the riverbank, I cast a spell to go home, but I ended up in Versailles instead. I couldn't figure out why. I don't know anyone there, and the house wasn't at all familiar."

Sebastien frowned, clearly lost in memories. "Thierry and I spent his recovery there when the Rite d'équilibrage went wrong." He hesitated for so long that Kylian thought he wasn't going to say anything else. "We made love for the first time there."

Kylian's heart missed a beat. "Does that count as proof?"

"It certainly points in that direction."

Chapter 22

KYLIAN LET himself into his apartment. Sebastien had asked him to stay, but despite his brave words about acting as if Sebastien's wild idea was right, he needed his own space tonight. Sebastien had let him go without protest.

He poked at the idea, seeking flaws to debunk it. It was riddled with them, as far as he could tell. He had no memory of a past life. He had no particular connection with Thierry beyond his fascination with all the heroes of the war. He knew nothing about strategy or any of the things Thierry had been renowned for except where card games were concerned. The only thing they had in common was being earth wizards.

And falling in love with Sebastien.

That didn't prove anything, though. Kylian was sure lots of people had fallen in love with Sebastien over the course of his existence. There had been at least one other, because Sebastien had an Avoué somewhere in his far distant past. So that made at least one person unrelated to this whole nightmare who had fallen in love with Sebastien.

It was absolutely insane, and yet when Sebastien laid it out with all the details, it made an alarming amount of sense, even more so when they added his own unintentional trip to Versailles. Many of the hallmarks of the bond were already there—and the ones that weren't might be there without their knowing, since they hadn't tested them. He shivered as he imagined what testing Sebastien's control would entail. He wasn't sure he was ready to be faced with the inhuman core of Sebastien's vampire side. He'd known it was there, but it was one thing to know and another entirely to see it and possibly have to defend himself from it.

Raphael had talked about soul mates from time to time, had even considered using that as the topic for his postdoctoral research, but Kylian had never paid much attention. He'd had no use for that kind of romantic nonsense. It was all well and good for Raphael, but Kylian had always been too grounded to believe in such a thing. Now... now he needed to talk to Raphael.

"TELL ME about soul mates or soul bonds," Kylian asked Raphael when they met for lunch the next day.

"Are you talking legends about them or actual research done on the topic?" Raphael asked. "Because they aren't the same thing."

"I don't know," Kylian said. "Maybe both."

"Werewolves believe in the concept of a mate," Raphael said. Kylian could practically see him putting on his professor cap. The thought tickled him, but he pushed it aside to concentrate on what Raphael was saying. "The idea is that when they meet the right person, they know instantly. Of course, there's a difference between knowing and accepting, but from what little I know of it, the wolf usually gets its way unless the one the wolf picks as a mate doesn't feel the same pull. To my knowledge, no studies have been done on how or why that works, beyond the instinct of the animal inside the person. The mating ritual is intended to solidify or formalize that connection, but the formation of the connection doesn't require any action or even conscious thought on the part of the individuals involved. That's probably the most concrete example of a soul mate, although I'm not sure it's actually anything as highbrow as a soul that's involved since it's usually the wolf half, not the human half, that recognizes the mate first. Beyond that, there are various cultures with legends of souls split in two at birth and destined to find each other again in life, but they're even less verifiable than the werewolf lore. That doesn't mean they're wrong, just that the only way to study them is through anecdotes—and those are notoriously unreliable from a scientific perspective. They're interesting sociologically, certainly, but not enough to base predictions on."

"What about creating a soul bond?" Kylian asked. "Something that would tie two souls together? I'm not talking about promises between two people. I'm talking about an actual link that couldn't be broken just because one of them changed their mind."

"This is about Sebastien, isn't it?" Raphael asked.

"Yes," Kylian said. "You didn't answer the question."

"That's deep, dark magic. Ancient magic, the kind we don't practice anymore," Raphael said slowly. "I think it could be done, but I'm not sure at what cost. I can't imagine what would be worth the risk."

"Not spending eternity alone?" Kylian suggested. "It's just a guess, and not one we could ever really test, but it fits the facts. Sort of, anyway."

"You're going to have to start at the beginning," Raphael said.

"Sebastien told you about the bond he formed with Thierry, right?"

Raphael nodded.

"They did it to force the beast inside him to recognize Thierry as its mate," Kylian continued. "And they did it at least in part using werewolf lore. They created the same kind of bond that exists between a werewolf and its mate. Then Thierry died, and Sebastien didn't. And for more than thirty years, he's been without that mate. He expected it, he's coping with it, that's not the problem. But if you take the werewolf lore and push it to its extreme, would that bond be strong enough to drag his soul mate back? Not his body, but his soul."

Raphael stared at him, speechless. "I can't... I don't... Kylian, have you thought about what you're suggesting?"

"I haven't thought about anything else since Sebastien brought it up yesterday," Kylian said. "Thierry died a little over thirty years ago. I'm twenty-eight. We're both earth wizards, despite how rare those are compared to the other elements. That night I ended up in Versailles, I was probably at Thierry's house. He lived there before the war. My blood soothed Sebastien's beast and helped him hold on to his humanity when he nearly died. He said usually, when a vampire is that far gone, it takes another vampire to keep the sick one from killing the first person they feed from because their need is so strong. But Sebastien came back in control of himself and calling Thierry's name. He thinks it's because his beast recognized his mate in my blood the same as it did in Thierry's."

"I think you're both insane," Raphael said with a shake of his head. "This is dangerous shit, Ky. The kind of shit that gets people tried for misuse of magic, and not just misdemeanors, either."

"Then it's a good thing the people who cast the spell are all beyond the reach of any tribunal, isn't it?" Kylian said.

"Do you think they knew what they were doing when they cast the spell?" Raphael asked. "Do you think they realized how deep they were delving to create that bond?"

"I don't know," Kylian replied. "I do know they would have done anything for each other."

"Sebastien and Thierry?"

"No. Well, yes, but that wasn't who I meant. I meant the wizards. Payet, Dumont, Magnier, and Simonet, I guess. If Thierry wanted the bond, the other three would have moved heaven and earth to make it happen. And we know one of the reasons Payet sided with the dark wizards at the beginning of the war was because he disagreed with a lot of the laws on the use of magic and what constituted dark magic. He wouldn't have hesitated to use forbidden magic for a good cause. If they knew, though, they didn't tell Sebastien."

"A pretty damn selfish cause, if you ask me," Raphael said.

Kylian huffed bitterly. "That's easy for you to say. You aren't in the position of watching your best friends give something to their lovers that you can never give, through no fault of your own."

Raphael swallowed hard and leaned back in his chair. "Now you're scaring me."

"What do you mean?"

"The way you said that. I don't know how else to explain it, but that wasn't something you're repeating from Sebastien. You said it like you'd lived it." He buried his face in his hands for a moment before looking back up. "I need to see that spell."

"Sebastien said they destroyed it," Kylian said.

"There are a few who remember it."

"Sebastien doesn't remember the words. He never even really paid attention to them. Asking him won't do any good."

"Maybe not, but he wasn't the only one there. Bellaiche was as much a driving force behind the research at l'Institut as his partner was. I'd put money on him knowing more about the spell than he's letting on," Raphael said.

"You're taking this better than I expected," Kylian said. "I expected you to tell me we were both crazy."

"Oh, I think you're crazy," Raphael said. "But that doesn't make you wrong. It's worth asking a few more questions, anyway."

"If Jean will answer them."

"I think he will," Raphael said. "If they were all as devoted to each other as you say, he'll want Sebastien to be happy again."

"We'll have to talk to Sebastien about that," Kylian said. "I don't know where Jean lives." Kylian finished his lunch and started to stand.

"Wait," Raphael said. "Scientific explanations aside, are you okay with this? I mean, that's a hell of a bombshell to drop on someone."

"I don't know," Kylian replied honestly. "He says he's not comparing me to Thierry. That he sees me for who I am, and that he loved me before he had the slightest hint something was different."

"Love?" Raphael said. "Moving a little fast there, isn't he?"

Kylian shrugged. "Sometimes time doesn't matter. I haven't wrapped my mind around it all the way. I want to say it's a load of bullshit, but then I think about how I felt when he got sick, how I knew something was wrong. Given the timing of when you got to his apartment and when Jean did, he couldn't have been sick for long before I called."

"Can you feel him now?" Raphael asked.

"Not really, but he said the connection was something that developed over time—that strong emotions came first and the normal, everyday kind of contentment came later. I didn't ask what 'later' meant, but he didn't seem concerned."

"You do realize you've stumbled into what I've spent all my life dreaming about, right?" Raphael said. "I don't know if I'll ever feel comfortable with the reincarnation piece of this, because that kind of magic is dangerous beyond telling, but I would give anything to find someone who looked at me the way Sebastien looks at you. Has always looked at you, by the way. In case you were entertaining any thoughts of him using you as a replacement."

"I know," Kylian said, "and we talked about the fact that I'm not Thierry, that he can't expect me to have Thierry's memories or react to things the way Thierry did. And he hasn't. He's never criticized anything I've done or said for being different than Thierry. And we don't look a thing alike, so that's not an issue."

"Okay, good," Raphael said. "I'd hate to have to yell at him for mistreating my best friend."

Kylian laughed. "I should get back to work. Come by Sebastien's apartment tonight around seven? We can talk to him about getting more details from Jean."

"I'll be there."

THE GATHERING in Sebastien's living room was somber. Kylian sat quietly at Sebastien's side, but Sebastien could feel the tension rolling off him in waves. Mentally he prodded at the sensation, trying to send soothing thoughts to Kylian, as much to see if it worked as to calm Kylian down. He couldn't tell if it helped, but Kylian did turn and smile at him.

"I take it Kylian told you what we think might have happened," Sebastien said to Raphael. "What do you think?"

"I think you're both insane," Raphael said, "and furthermore I think the wizards who created that spell were insane, but it doesn't matter what I think. As an explanation, it fits the facts, other than the whole bit about it being illegal and possibly immoral and generally a terrible, terrible idea. I'm not sure how I feel about my heroes having been involved in it."

"Illegal, I understand," Sebastien said. "I knew we were dabbling in some gray areas, but how can you say it was immoral if everyone involved agreed to it? We didn't hurt anyone. We didn't deprive anyone of their freedom or any other rights."

"Not in their lifetime," Raphael said, "but no one asked Kylian what he wanted. No one asked him if he wanted to be born with another man's soul in his body, if he wanted to be saddled with that man's lover despite his own preferences to the contrary. No one asked him if he wanted this connection. For that matter, no one asked you if you wanted to have and lose your lover generation after generation. Once was hard enough."

"Once was excruciating," Sebastien said. "The second time was even worse, and yet I went looking again. Whether it's the same soul or different ones, I'll never have a lover I can keep as long as I want unless I take a vampire as a lover. So maybe they didn't ask me if I wanted to have Thierry's soul reborn, but I knew I'd lose him and would have to go on without him."

"Kylian didn't have even that much choice," Raphael said.

"That's not true," Kylian said softly. "No, I didn't ask to be born with this soul, but I had a choice with Sebastien. I didn't have to agree to be his partner. I wanted to agree, but I didn't have to. I could have said no."

"Could you really?" Raphael asked.

"Yes," Kylian insisted. "It might not have been easy, but I could have done it. If it hadn't been right for me—not Thierry's soul in my body, but me with all my experiences and needs and desires—I would have said no. The fact that my soul—and it *is* mine, colored by my life, even if we're right and it was Thierry's before—calls out to Sebastien's is an added benefit. So maybe I didn't choose it then, but I choose it now, whatever that means."

"I need to talk to Bellaiche," Raphael said. "I need to know more about the spell. If the spell couldn't have done this the way you've postulated, I need to find another explanation."

"Need?" Sebastien asked. "I can understand wanting another explanation, but why do you need it? If we've accepted this explanation, why do you need one at all?"

"Because I've spent my entire life feeling as if my soul was torn in half," Raphael said. "As much as it scares me to consider it, maybe your explanation applies to me too."

"There's no way someone else cast the same spell," Sebastien said.

"Unless someone else got ahold of your spell without you knowing it," Raphael said.

"No one else had access to it," Sebastien said. "I saw the wards Raymond put around the safe he kept his research in. Even if Jean hadn't destroyed it after Raymond's death, no one could have gotten into it without his knowledge. We didn't go into this intending to have the spell extend beyond Thierry's lifetime, you know. Whatever the reality of what they did, nobody set out to create a soul bond that would extend beyond Thierry's life."

"You cast the spell to imitate the Aveu de Sang," Raphael said slowly. "But it couldn't have worked exactly the same, since this isn't any side effect of an Aveu de Sang I ever heard of."

"It isn't," Sebastien said. "I had an Avoué. I never found him again. Nor did Lombard."

"Then I guess I'll have to suck it up and talk to Bellaiche," Raphael said. "If they truly didn't intend the soul bond, then something went awry, and I want to know what."

"He's not as bad as that," Sebastien said.

"You didn't hear the things he said when he thought you were dying," Raphael muttered.

"No, I didn't," Sebastien agreed, "but I can guess how it went. I'll let you in on a little secret. Jean has a tender heart, but he hides it from all but a select few. I'm one of the few who gets to see it anymore, and to have that threatened was more than he could handle. It was that way with Raymond as well. Nothing sends Jean into a rage faster than believing those he cares about are in danger. If any of his accusations had been true, or if I hadn't recovered, he would have followed through on his threats, but Kylian got to me in time. He may not be happy, but he won't be as threatening the next time you see him."

"I'm hoping that will be soon," Raphael said. "Will he come here, or do I need to go to him?"

"I think it would be best if we all went," Sebastien said. "He should be there tonight. He'll be less combative if we wait and go after dark. It will be less of an affront that I've found a new partner and he hasn't."

"Has he looked?" Kylian asked.

"No, but that doesn't change the fact that I seem to be moving on," Sebastien said. "He's afraid that will affect our friendship somehow."

"I'd never try to come between you," Kylian said.

"I know you wouldn't, but after Raymond died and Jean shut down, my world revolved around keeping him from starving himself out of existence. Now that isn't the only thing on my priority list. He's still my best friend, but he's not the only person I have now. I'm still the only one he has."

"Maybe if he made less of a habit of threatening people, he'd have more friends," Raphael grumbled.

"That's probably true," Sebastien said, "but then he'd have to worry about losing them too, and he's lost too many people already—vampire and mortal alike. The last thing he wants is someone else to lose."

"That's no way to live," Kylian said.

"No, it's not, but I'm not what he needs to make him see that."

"That's why you were at the clubs those two nights, isn't it?" Kylian said. "You were looking for a place to take Jean, to try to get him out again so maybe he would find someone new."

"I wasn't that ambitious," Sebastien said. "I was hoping for somewhere he could go to hunt on his own without me having to drag him out every few days. Instead I found you. So far as trades go, I'll take it."

"What are we going to tell him?" Raphael asked.

"The truth," Sebastien said. "Everything that's happened, everything we've guessed, everything we've extrapolated. You'll never get a lie past him. You'll be lucky if you get an omission past him. I know you've only seen the out-of-control protector, but he held the Cour in Paris for hundreds of years. That didn't happen accidentally or because no one tried to take it from him. He's as shrewd as anyone you'll ever meet and a hundred times more ruthless. If we're going to tell him anything, we have to tell him everything. I'm not sure he can help us, but if we don't trust him with what we know, he won't help us even if he can. Before we do that, though…."

"What?" Kylian asked. "What were you going to say? I know you think I won't like it, but tell us anyway."

"There's one test Jean couldn't dispute," Sebastien said slowly. "If I can tell him that I let go of all control and you calmed my beast, he'd have no choice but to accept that somehow the bond has snapped back into place."

Sebastien felt Kylian's emotions go haywire next to him.

"We don't have to do it," Sebastien said. "Now or ever, if you don't want to. We can still talk to Jean. He'll be harder to convince, but we'll work around it."

"What would it entail?" Kylian asked.

Sebastien snorted. "Tying me to the bed and seeing what happens when I let go of my control. Either your blood will soothe the beast or it won't. If it does, we have the closest to proof we'll ever get. If it doesn't, you run like hell and call Jean to come deal with me."

Chapter 23

KYLIAN STOOD at the door to the bedroom, every muscle in his body tense. Sebastien truly believed this would work out for the best, but while Kylian trusted him, he had much less confidence in the outcome of the proceedings. Other than the sense of Sebastien's illness and a few stray emotions, he felt no sign of a bond between them. Maybe things had been different before, but Kylian couldn't imagine planning and carrying out a ritual of that complexity, only to have no tangible benefits for the one who planned it in the first place. He knew what Sebastien got out of it, but what was in it for Kylian? What had been in it for Thierry?

"We don't have to do this."

Kylian looked at Sebastien spread out on the bed, still fully clothed, his hands secured above his head. Raphael had cast those spells, so they ran no risk of Kylian's magic losing its hold on Sebastien. He lay there with such a trusting look on his face, like the answer to all the world's problems—or all his problems, anyway—lay with Kylian. He didn't know if Sebastien was right, but he couldn't get past the hopeful look on his face.

"We really do," Kylian said. "It's the only way to know for sure."

"Okay, we don't have to do this now. We can wait until you're more comfortable with the idea."

Kylian doubted he would ever be comfortable with the idea. It was fear of the unknown as much as anything else, and he could only conquer that by turning the unknown into the known.

"I'm afraid of what will happen if you're wrong," Kylian admitted.

"If I'm wrong, it will be like it has been the past two weeks. I'll be careful of how much I drink from you, and I'll keep the monster under control when we make love, but we'll still be together. We'll still be partners."

"And you'll spend the rest of my life being disappointed I'm not Thierry," Kylian finished. The words Sebastien used to describe the vampire side of himself didn't help with Kylian's nerves. Beast, monster, demon… they were the stuff of nightmares, yet Sebastien had always been a gentleman with him. He found it hard to believe such a creature lurked beneath the surface, but if he agreed to this, he would find out up close and personal just how accurate Sebastien's descriptions were.

"No," Sebastien said firmly. "I didn't fall in love with you because I thought you were Thierry. I fell in love with you, Kylian. Just you. If it turns out it's the same spirit in a different body, that's an unlooked-for bonus, but it's not a requirement. I told you last night that we could forget about it. We could let the idea go completely if it bothered you that much. That offer still stands, and it will always stand."

Kylian hesitated. The words warmed him, but they were only words, and what they were talking about doing went far beyond words.

"Close your eyes," Sebastien said. Kylian did as Sebastien said. A moment later a wave of love and sincerity flooded his mind, easing his fears. "Can you feel that? Can you feel how much I love you? I won't ever be able to lie to you. You'd know."

Kylian's eyes fluttered open, and he met Sebastien's gaze across the room. "I feel it. Not just some vague sense of you, but actual emotions."

"Then you know I mean everything I've said," Sebastien said. "The choice is yours."

"We have to try," Kylian said. "We have to know." His grin turned mischievous. "Besides, you're already tied to the bed. After traumatizing Raphael that much, we have to follow through."

"Oh, I don't know," Sebastien said with a matching grin. "He might prefer it if we didn't. Much easier to come untie me than to sit in the other room while we make love."

"You really believe this will work."

"I really do," Sebastien said, "but if I'm wrong, if the first bite doesn't calm me down, promise me you'll leave. Don't let me hurt you."

Just like that, Kylian was back where he started, nervous about what exactly Sebastien would turn into if they continued this. He reminded himself Sebastien had done this before, and with far less assurance it would work out—and that what he turned into had driven Thierry to create their bond, but not to end things. If the worst happened, he would leave. Sebastien wouldn't be able to get loose from Raphael's spells, and he would be safe.

"I won't," Kylian promised. "If it comes to that, I'll leave and get Jean."

Sebastien closed his eyes and took a deep breath. Kylian felt the emotions inside him begin to change, the love and concern fading far too quickly. Rage and lust took their place, shaking Kylian to his very core. He understood the lust. They'd shared enough nights in Sebastien's bed for that to make sense. The rage took him aback, though. Sebastien was a gentleman. He'd been careful with Kylian at every turn. The creature on the bed whose emotions now invaded his mind would have no such care, because it had no such humanity. He couldn't help but wonder what could cause such unfettered fury. Was it being tied to the bed? Kylian could see that frustrating as primal a being as the vampire.

He swallowed hard. He was supposed to cross the room and offer his blood to the monster straining against its bonds. He had learned to appreciate the feeling of Sebastien's fangs in his skin, but Sebastien took the time to prepare his skin and soothe his entry as much as possible. *It* wouldn't give him the same courtesy. Being bitten by the creature on the bed would be the realization of all his fears.

He had to try. He had promised Sebastien he would try. If it didn't work, it didn't work, but if he walked out of the room now, Sebastien would have done this for nothing. He took a couple of steps closer, then froze when the vampire raised its head and fixated on him.

"Come closer, pretty," it purred. "I'll give you what you need." If Kylian hadn't seen its lips moving, he wouldn't have believed the voice came from Sebastien's body. Sebastien had never sounded like that, had never spoken to him in that tone. He shuddered at what it might think he needed. Nothing it could give him, certainly.

If Sebastien was right, though, there was something he could give it. Peace, Sebastien had said. That's what Thierry's blood had given him, more than anything else. That's what Kylian's blood would give him if he was right. And if he could give the beast peace, maybe it would give him Sebastien back.

Resolve set, he crossed the rest of the way to the bed and offered his wrist. "Here," he said to draw its attention, not that it had looked anywhere else since it locked gazes with him.

He braced himself for the bite, and it was every bit as rough and painful as he had feared. This was what he had dreaded when he thought about letting Sebastien feed from him, back before he'd finally agreed. Sebastien hadn't lunged at him this way, driving ruthless fangs into his tender flesh with no warning and no preparation, but this creature did. It tore into his skin, leaving him gasping with the pain and struggling not to snatch his hand back. It wouldn't be able to stop him, no matter how much it fought the magic around its wrists. Kylian knew what Raphael was capable of when he put his mind to it.

The pull of the vampire's mouth on his skin was just as rough as the entry had been, hard and fast and ruthless. Sebastien had said it would work or it wouldn't, no waiting around to see, no wishful thinking if it didn't happen quickly. He hadn't said how quickly, though. Would a single swallow do it? Would it take a minute? Two? Five? He should have asked for more precision.

He started to pull away, and then he felt it. The vampire licked the area around his fangs, soothing the entry wounds, and in the space beneath his heart that Sebastien filled, a sense of peace started to unfurl. Lust was still there near the forefront, but the rage faded—and with it, Kylian's fear.

He relaxed against Sebastien's mouth, letting Sebastien's tongue soothe the sting, and waited to see what would happen next. He knew feeding and sex frequently went together for vampires, and he could certainly feel the need throbbing through their bond. Now that his fear had faded, his own desire was rising to match it. He only needed a sign from Sebastien that he should continue.

A moment later, Sebastien pulled back from Kylian's wrist.

"It worked." His voice trembled as he spoke, and Kylian appreciated the effort it must have cost him to stop feeding for even that long.

"It did," Kylian agreed, because he hadn't needed Sebastien's words for that. "What now?"

"Now you let me show you the rest of the benefits of our bond."

"*Our* bond," Kylian repeated slowly. He hadn't thought of it that way. It had always been Sebastien and Thierry's bond, somehow transferred to him. Now, though….

"What else would you call it?" Sebastien asked hoarsely. "It's your emotions I feel beneath my sternum. It's your blood that brought me back when I let the beast go. Maybe the bond didn't originate with us, but it's our bond now."

Kylian lunged forward to kiss Sebastien, his heart pounding in his chest as the truth of Sebastien's words soaked into him. No more worry about competing with a ghost. No more fear of not measuring up. He *was* the ghost, and he had already given Sebastien the same elusive peace he had thought forever lost to him. Everything else was easy in comparison.

Sebastien strained against his bonds in an effort to meet the kiss, but Kylian pulled back and grinned at him. "None of that, now," he teased as he worked the hem of Sebastien's sweater up as far as it would go. "You said my blood and my touch would control the beast, which means you're going to stay right there and let me use that control to both our benefits."

Sebastien groaned, and Kylian felt the surge of rage beginning to rise again along with the lust. He wanted the untamed lust, but he wouldn't accept the rage. He wouldn't deny them what they wanted. He just intended to drag it out as long as possible so their release, when it finally came, would be worth all the fear and tension that had come before. He countered it with as much love as he could push back through their bond. He only half expected it to work, but Sebastien arched into his hands when Kylian ran them over his torso.

"Don't free my hands," Sebastien gasped. "I'm not enough in control to let you take charge if I'm loose."

"That's the whole point," Kylian said. "I'm the one in control, so you don't have to be. Trust me. Let go."

SEBASTIEN STRUGGLED with the request. He wanted to do as Kylian asked, but letting go of control over his beast meant letting the beast have control. It calmed to the blood of its mate, but that didn't mean it accepted said mate's control. On the contrary. He couldn't think of a single time he'd let go of his beast and then bottomed for Thierry.

One more way Kylian is different, Sebastien thought. If he could do as Kylian asked, that was.

The burst of Kylian's blood across his tongue had soothed the beast enough to let Sebastien's consciousness reemerge, but it was a delicate balance to have that awareness without putting the cage back up. It was anyone's guess how long he could manage it without getting more blood to drive home the feeling of safety that was so essential.

Kylian's hands felt so good against his skin. He was burning from the inside out, and the cool brush of Kylian's skin calmed the flames. He arched into the touch, wanting to encourage Kylian to continue, but words were beyond him again as the bloodlust rose. He tried to channel it into desire for sex, because he knew Kylian would give him that. Maybe not the way the beast wanted, but it would be sex. It would be release. And if Sebastien was lucky, Kylian might be up for a second round so that Sebastien could ravish him the way he wanted to.

Kylian traced across his pecs and down his breastbone, avoiding Sebastien's nipples. Sebastien tried to protest, but then Kylian found the spot beneath his ribs that made him gasp and mewl. Thierry had loved those sounds—and judging from the satisfaction Sebastien could sense through the bond, Kylian felt the same. He thrashed against his bonds, trying to get free so he could hold Kylian's head to that spot, so he could flip Kylian over and fuck him senseless. The bonds held, though, and he cursed the magic that held him in place. He had to be projecting his need because Kylian suddenly lifted his head, eyes nearly black with equal need. Sebastien inhaled sharply. This was what he had missed, the cycling of emotions that fired his blood and made it possible to finally find true satiation.

Kylian shifted to his side so he could continue to explore Sebastien's chest with one hand, while offering the other back to Sebastien to feed. He lunged for it as much as his bound arms would let him, but the moment the skin touched his lips, he calmed. He needed blood, but not if the cost was his partner's pain. He sucked on Kylian's wrist, letting his saliva ease the marks he'd already left and prepare it for the new bite. When he punctured Kylian's skin this time, he felt no pain echo back through their bond, and his beast crowed in triumph. It could bring pleasure to its mate. Sebastien settled for being happy not to have to fight for control.

As the blood eased Sebastien's turmoil, Kylian lowered his head and brushed his stubble over the sensitive spot. Sebastien moaned against Kylian's wrist.

"Where else?" Kylian goaded. "Where else can I touch you to make you moan like that?"

Sebastien didn't bother releasing Kylian's wrist to reply. Kylian would find his sensitive spots or not. Sebastien had other things to worry about, like making love to Kylian with his fangs, since that was the only contact he could control.

He worked his jaw slowly against Kylian's wrist, moving his fangs in and out deliberately. He might not get to fuck Kylian's ass tonight, but he'd find other ways to give him pleasure, even if it meant fucking him with his fangs instead.

A wave of comfort and love met the rising aggression in his mind as Kylian kissed his way across Sebastien's stomach to the other side. Sebastien could have told him it wasn't nearly as sensitive, if he'd been in the mood to make things easier for his mate. As it was, he took a perverse pleasure in making Kylian work for each needy sound he made.

Then Kylian popped open the button on his jeans and reached inside to caress him through his underwear. Sebastien moaned and bucked into the contact. Kylian laughed at him as he moved his hand away, leaving Sebastien cursing silently. He would show Kylian what happened to people who teased him.

He bit harder into Kylian's wrist.

"Relax," Kylian urged as he circled Sebastien's navel with one finger and dipped inside teasingly. Sebastien moaned despite himself, swamped with the conflicting need to take and the wanton desire to be taken. He tore his head away from Kylian's wrist, intending to beg for what he needed if that was what it took.

"You hate being out of control, don't you?" Kylian asked before Sebastien could speak. He continued to dip his finger in and out of Sebastien's navel in that maddening promise of things to come. "Or is it that half of you hates being controlled while the other half can't let go?"

"Both," Sebastien said breathlessly.

"You don't have to be in control tonight." Kylian reached up and tapped the bonds holding Sebastien's wrists in place. "You can't be in control tonight. You have to let go, both halves of you, and trust me."

"I do trust you," Sebastien said. The moment he said the words, he realized how true they were. He had trusted Kylian for weeks now, but he had kept his beast carefully caged, never letting it loose. Now that he had, now that it had recognized Kylian as its mate, the trust went to his very core, beyond his humanity, even to the depths of the nightmare he lived with every day. "Both sides of me."

"Good," Kylian said. He released the bindings on Sebastien's legs and tugged on the waistband of Sebastien's jeans until he lifted his hips so Kylian could strip him. "Remember that while I make love to you."

Sebastien nodded and tried to focus on the sense of love and comfort that radiated from Kylian as he stroked Sebastien's cock. He was already fully hard and leaking, but the touch of Kylian's hand made it worse. He closed his eyes and let his need subsume him. He couldn't do anything but lie there and take it, anyway. Better to enjoy it than to fight it.

His beast didn't agree—but every time it reared its head to try to wrest back control, Kylian met it with another surge of comfort, interspersed with blood, until nothing was left but heat and need and the yawning emptiness inside him begging to be filled.

Kylian soothed the emptiness with fingers first, and then, when Sebastien had learned to accept that, he replaced the digits with his cock. Sebastien's beast howled in protest at having to submit, until Kylian covered him completely and offered his neck. The moment Kylian's blood slid across his tongue again, the beast quieted and let Sebastien enjoy the feeling of his mate inside him.

When they finally reached their peak, minutes or hours later, and Sebastien released Kylian's neck, he marveled at how calm he felt, all the wildness of their lovemaking replaced by satiation. He had expected to still need to take after Kylian was done with him, but his beast dozed within him.

"You are a wonder," he murmured against Kylian's hair. "Will you let me hold you?"

Kylian smiled and released the spell holding his wrists. "All night long."

Sebastien shook his arms to bring feeling back into them and pulled Kylian into a tight embrace. As Kylian settled against him, Sebastien thought he could stay like this forever and be happy.

Chapter 24

THE BUZZER at the building door roused Jean from the book he was reading. He had kept in touch with the bouquiniste who had always saved books for Raymond, and now his granddaughter ran the stand. She had called a couple of days ago with a new book she thought he might be interested in and had brought it by when he decided to buy it. It hadn't given him any answers about what had happened to Sebastien, but he hadn't finished it yet, either. It *had* given him quite a different view on so-called dark magic, though. Apparently the moral injunctions against blood and sex magic were not as entrenched in the Middle Ages as Jean had been led to believe. The book in his hand was a sixteenth-century reprint of a tenth-century treatise by a monk in Paris, on the role of magic and the effects of blood and sex on a spell's effectiveness. To hear the monk tell it, adding a drop of blood when casting a spell would increase its effectiveness significantly.

He set the book aside when the bell chimed again. "Who is it?" he snapped when he reached the call button.

"It's Sebastien. I brought Kylian and Raphael with me. Can we come up and talk?"

Jean searched for a reason to say only Sebastien could come up, but Sebastien would see through any excuse. He pushed the buzzer to let them in. He could laugh at the wizards' attempts to make it through Raymond's wards, if nothing else. He opened the door and stood back to watch. Sebastien waited with the wizards as they reached the edge of the magical barrier.

"This is amazing work," Raphael said immediately, tracing the edge of the spell with his hands. "I've never seen one like this."

"You can see it?" Kylian asked.

"Yes. Can't you?"

"I can feel it, but I can't see the threads of the magic," Kylian said. "You shouldn't be able to see it either."

"Why not?" Sebastien asked.

"It's not his magic," Kylian explained. "Most wizards can only see their own spells or spells that the casting wizard intended people to see, unless they're tracing a spell. But that would require casting a spell of your own, and Raphael didn't do that."

Jean didn't trust the look that passed between the two, but he was even more taken with the fascination on Raphael's face.

"It's…. Oh, wait. I see."

And just like that, the kid Jean wanted to hate stepped through Raymond's wards like they weren't even there."

"How did you do that?" Jean demanded.

"It just made sense," Raphael said. "It was a puzzle, yes, but once I saw the whole thing, it was obvious. Something intended to welcome friends and trip up everyone else."

"Yes," Jean said slowly, "that's exactly what it was, but only two people ever figured it out without help, and they were those friends you mentioned. Everyone else was supposed to trip so we could decide if we wanted to let them in."

"He had a wicked sense of humor, that's for sure," Raphael commented. "Kylian, are you coming?"

"I'm still trying to figure out if I can come in," Kylian said.

"Stop thinking. Just feel the wards," Raphael said.

Jean watched as Kylian's face screwed up and then suddenly relaxed as he stepped through. "That is a wicked sense of humor. It's all backwards, but not 180 degrees backwards. It's more like every centimeter you move through, it shifts a few degrees."

"Yes," Raphael said. "I don't know what it represents, but once you see it, it's easy to follow. Do you have a piece of paper?"

Jean nodded and retrieved a sheet from the nineteenth-century rolltop desk in the living room. He could feel Raphael's eyes on him, a befuddled expression on his face, but he ignored it. Raphael could feel whatever he wanted. It wasn't Jean's problem. Raphael took the paper and drew an image on it.

"This is…." He studied it. "This is your medallion. The one you always wore during the war."

"The medallion that marked me as chef de la Cour," Jean said. "I gave it to Fabienne when she took my place."

Raphael stared at it a little longer, then looked back at Jean. "That isn't it. That isn't why the symbol wards your apartment. I don't know what it is, but it's more personal than that."

"How can you tell?" Sebastien asked when Jean didn't say anything.

"There's too much emotion in the magic for it to be just the symbol of an office that could pass to anyone."

Jean flinched and sought to change the subject. "As glad as I am that you appreciate the elegance of the protection on my apartment, I'm sure that's not why you came."

"No, it isn't," Sebastien said. "Promise me you'll hear me out. You can rant all you want when I'm done, but promise me you'll let me finish first."

Jean frowned but nodded. Sebastien wouldn't upset him for no reason.

Sebastien took a seat near the fireplace. Raphael moved to the other chair, and Kylian perched on the arm of Sebastien's chair, leaving the couch for Jean.

"Okay, I'm listening."

"You accused Kylian of finding a way to transfer my bond with Thierry to him. I think the reverse is actually true."

Jean opened his mouth to ask what that meant, but Sebastien stopped him with a sharp look.

"When we did the ritual, we used everything we could put our hands on to force my beast to recognize Thierry. When he took that bit of my blood, I became a part of him and he part of me. It worked, Jean. My beast knew him from then until his death, and it was more than eighty years of bliss. But I think we did something we didn't intend that night. I think we did more than bind Thierry and me. I think we created a bond between our souls that not even death could break. And I think that bond dragged Thierry's soul back to life in Kylian."

"How can you say that?" Jean exploded.

"You said you would listen. Anyone's blood besides Kylian's makes me sick. He knew when I was sick. He knew when I was upset. I can feel the nerves radiating off him right now, as clear as it was with Thierry. I can't feel Thierry when I go to his grave anymore. I can get a sense of Alain and Orlando, but I haven't felt Thierry in almost thirty years. When Kylian lost control of his magic because of me one night and tried to go home, he ended up in Versailles—where Thierry and I rode out the wild magic. But most important of all, my beast calmed to his blood and his touch. I can only come up with one explanation for that collection of facts—that Kylian and Thierry are the same soul."

Sebastien fell silent.

"Are you done?"

"Yes."

Jean tried to gather his thoughts, but they flew around his head like so many wasps, stinging him at random but never landing long enough for him to catch them or send them away.

"I can't even begin to list all the ways in which that is wrong," he said finally. "Twisted and sick and just… wrong."

"As much of an abomination as a vampire is?" Sebastien asked. "Or as a gay couple? As loving someone enough to die for them? Why is a soul bond any worse than anything else that defines us? You're thinking with your seminary upbringing, not with everything you've learned since then. The Aveu de Sang, the werewolf lore we borrowed, how much older are those than the arrival of Christianity? It's not a Christian bond, yours or mine. Don't subject it to the limits of one spiritual view."

Jean tried to separate the beliefs of his youth from the studies of a millennium, but this challenged the very core of who he was. "If I accept what you're saying…." He shook his head, unable to finish the sentence.

"So don't accept it," Raphael challenged. "You know more about the spell that bound them than anyone else. If it can't be, then tell us what in the spell makes it impossible. Prove us wrong."

"You think they're right?" Jean asked.

"I don't know," Raphael said. "I wasn't there. I can see how it could be possible from what Sebastien has told me and from the proof before our eyes, but I can see how it wouldn't have to be. I don't have another explanation right now, though I'm not opposed to looking for one. But I can't do anything until I know more about the spell."

"What do you want to know?"

"The words," Raphael said. "What did the spell do?"

"You know what it did."

"Yes, but I don't know *how* it did it, and without that, I don't know if there could be side effects."

"Are you suggesting we overlooked something?"

"You suggested it yourself when you asked what Kylian had done to make the bond jump to him," Raphael countered. "Despite everything you've said, if you didn't think it was possible, you wouldn't wonder if Kylian had somehow managed it."

"Raymond always said magic was 90 percent intention and 10 percent execution," Jean said slowly. "He and Alain argued about it when they were constructing the ritual. Never when Thierry was around, because neither of them had the heart to discourage him in any way, but Alain wasn't comfortable with a lot of what they drew on. He always said it was too risky, that we didn't know how the werewolf lore would affect a wizard or a vampire, that some of the arcane wizard lore fell out of use for a reason, even if we didn't know what that reason might be. Raymond always countered that we would perform the ritual with the best intentions of connecting two consenting adults who understood what they were doing, and that would forestall any potential negative consequences from the same kind of magic with different intent."

"None of that is wrong," Raphael said, "but it is still 10 percent execution, and that leaves room for error and unintended consequences."

"Before the ritual, Raymond mentioned publishing an article about it. After the ritual, he locked the spell away and never mentioned it again. He made me promise to destroy it after he died. He never told me why."

"So you've spent all these years wondering if something went wrong."

"Why didn't you say something?" Sebastien asked. "If not then, later."

"I didn't say anything before because Raymond was convinced it would work as planned. I didn't say anything later because from what I could see, it had worked and you were happy. And if there were side effects, it was too late to do anything about them. There was even less reason to say anything after they died. I destroyed the spell and all their notes as Raymond asked and let it go. Until you got sick."

"Could Raymond have known?" Kylian asked. "Would he have told you if he did?"

"I'd like to think he would have, if it had been more than a feeling," Jean said, "but I don't know for sure. He could have kept his silence for the same reasons I did."

"You said magic was all about intent," Sebastien said slowly. "The thing we feared—all six of us, not just Thierry and me—the thing we feared most was being separated at the end of our partners' lives. Orlando solved that problem in his own way, but that wasn't a choice for you or me, and at the time of the ritual, we didn't even think of that as an option. With three of the four wizards and both of the recipients of the spell fearing that, could it have mutated the spell to reduce those fears? We were creating a bond anyway. Could it have gone beyond the original intention to create a soul bond that survived beyond Thierry's death and brought his soul back to be reborn in Kylian?"

"Damned if I know," Jean said bitterly. "And the only person who might have been able to tell us is long gone."

"It would take a spell of immense power to create that kind of bond," Raphael interjected, his voice measured, as if he was analyzing every word before speaking. "Immense power. But I know who was involved and I know where you did the ritual. I assume you and Orlando augmented your partners' power. I know Sebastien fed from Thierry during the ritual. With that, plus the power inherent at the locus, not to mention the evidence before us, I don't think the question is whether they created a bond between Sebastien and Thierry. I think the question is what other effects it had."

"Like what?" Kylian asked.

"Sebastien said he could still sense Alain and Orlando at the cemetery. He shouldn't be able to sense them at all, even if we could come up with a reason why they're there in the first place."

"It's not really sensing them as much as it is always feeling a breeze there, even on the calmest days, and hearing laughter when I'm there," Sebastien said.

"Still not explainable," Raphael insisted.

"You think the spell expanded out to connect Sebastien to the other wizards as well?" Jean asked.

"I don't think anything at this point," Raphael said, "but your Avoué wasn't the only student of magic. Something strange is going on. I want to understand what."

"But if that's the case, where's Raymond?" Kylian said. "If it affected Thierry to bring him back as me, and Alain and Orlando enough to keep them close enough that Sebastien can sense them, then Raymond should be somewhere too."

"Get out," Jean snapped. "Take your stupid fucking theories and get out. Raymond is gone. I have accepted that. I don't need it all dragged back up."

The two wizards did as he demanded, but Sebastien lingered.

"Please," Jean said, his façade dangerously close to shattering. "Just go."

"I'm sorry, Jean. I didn't know he was going to say that. I wouldn't have brought him with us."

"It doesn't matter. Just go. I need to be alone now."

He could tell Sebastien wanted to argue. He had long since learned to read Sebastien's thoughts on his face. Because they were friends, damn it, not because of some far-fetched theory about a spell having stronger and deeper effects than intended. Raphael could take his notions and shove them up his ass. Jean was done listening to him.

"I'll go, but I'm coming tomorrow to take you to Sang Froid."

"It's Angélique's turn. And I don't need a babysitter."

"I'll come anyway," Sebastien said. "Call me if you need me."

"Good-bye, Sebastien."

Sebastien sighed and left. Jean waited until the door shut before doubling over. He had said his good-byes to Raymond. He had accepted that he would be alone. Sebastien had recovered after losing his Avoué, but not until he met Thierry. Jean couldn't imagine opening himself up again the way he had to Raymond. Raymond had been his lover, his partner, his best friend, the perfect match for him in every way that mattered. They had argued as hard as they loved, and it only made them stronger. The thought of even trying to replace that struck him to his very core, and his beast raged within him. Raymond might be gone, but he was still and would always be Jean's perfect mate. Anyone else would be a pale imitation at best. Better to be alone than to settle for second best.

He wished Sebastien all the best. He really did. If Sebastien could make peace with a new partner, Jean wouldn't criticize. His life and his choices were his own, even if Jean couldn't fathom them. As long as Sebastien didn't expect him to make the same choices, nothing had to change.

Except it already had. He'd had wizards in his apartment tonight for the first time since Raymond died. Wizards who had walked through Raymond's wards with a minimum of effort. They had complimented the complexity and deviousness of the wards, but they'd still walked right through.

He wondered what Raymond would think of them. They were so young. All mortals were, compared to him, but they seemed like children after his years with Raymond. Raymond hadn't been more than ten years older than they were when they met, but Raymond's life had been anything but easy at that point, and it showed in his outlook on the world. Kylian and Raphael had never seen war, had never lived through that kind of hell. Jean had seen enough senseless killing for a hundred lifetimes, but Kylian and Raphael had a certain innocence that had been lacking in the early days of the alliance and the partnerships. It had given Raymond depth, even if Jean had not trusted him at first. He had learned, and once he had, they'd been inseparable.

He forced his hands to pick up the book he'd been reading and his mind to focus on the text. Raphael couldn't be right—but on the off chance he was, Jean needed now more than ever to understand what they had wrought all those years ago.

Chapter 25

"HOW MUCH of what you said in there do you actually believe?" Kylian asked.

Raphael looked up in surprise. He still didn't know why Kylian had sent Sebastien on his way with the promise of meeting him later, only to follow Raphael home. Honestly, it didn't matter why Kylian had followed him home. He needed Kylian to go away. He needed to think, and he couldn't do that with Kylian jabbering at him. "What?"

"All the stuff you said to Jean," Kylian repeated. "Do you believe it?"

"I don't know," Raphael said slowly, "but it's not unreasonable."

"Not... Raph, listen to yourself."

"How is it any more far-fetched than being Thierry's soul reborn?" Raphael demanded. "It would explain so much."

"Explain what?"

Raphael hesitated. Kylian was right in a way. None of this was reasonable. But reason had flown out the window the moment he had walked through those wards and seen Jean's apartment. The rest of the evening had only added to that feeling of recognition. As they had sat there talking, Jean had grown more and more familiar. The timbre of his voice, the way he moved, the way he argued—Raphael knew those things. He had lived with them in his dreams. He had to tell Kylian, though. Of anyone, Kylian was the one who would understand.

"Why I recognized Jean," Raphael said. "Not the first time—emotions were running high when we met before—but sitting in his apartment tonight. I always told you my partner was out there."

"You think Jean Bellaiche is the partner you've missed your whole life," Kylian repeated incredulously. "Are you insane?"

"Probably," Raphael said, "but that doesn't change what I felt when I walked through his wards or when I sat in his apartment. I've dreamed of that room. The desk he got the paper from—I've dreamed of sitting there writing."

"That's crazy."

"I always thought it was an overactive imagination," Raphael said. "Rooms like that don't exist outside of museums, so I dismissed it as a fanciful backdrop to the important reality of my other half, but I'm not imagining the similarities. It's the exact same room. I can tell you what the bedroom looks like too. I've had enough wet dreams about what might go on in that room that it's burned into my memory. And the symbol on the medallion that makes up the wards—I've seen that too."

"In photos in history books," Kylian said. "You said it yourself. He wore it at press conferences during the war."

"Maybe," Raphael said, "but it was in my dreams too. Only in my dreams it was on fire."

"Okay, say I believe this for a minute. Say I accept everything you've said tonight as the truth. Do you really want Jean as a partner? I mean, I know he's an incredibly old and powerful vampire, but you'd be out of your mind to want to take on that kind of attitude. He'd kill you for suggesting it."

Kylian was right, and that was the crux of Raphael's dilemma, the reason he hadn't said anything when Kylian asked where Raymond was if Raphael was right. "He probably would. He hates me, and he probably has reason to. I haven't exactly set out to make friends with him. I don't know the answer. I've always wanted my missing half, and if my dreams are more than just nighttime imaginings, if there's a kernel of truth to them, he could be everything I've wanted, because he's already been everything I wanted. The question isn't whether I want him. The question is whether he'll ever want me."

"You're breaking my brain," Kylian said with a shake of his head. "Are you saying your dreams are memories of the past? Memories of a previous life?"

"Why not?" Raphael asked. "Jung suggested it centuries ago."

"Jung suggested a lot of things," Kylian countered. "That doesn't make them right."

"Maybe, maybe not," Raphael agreed, "but you know as well as I do that some things defy rational explanations. As much as we want to believe there's a pattern and an order to the world, sometimes there isn't. Sometimes we just have to accept things on faith."

"You're taking this better than I expected you to," Kylian said.

"I've had a lot longer to get used to the idea," Raphael said. "Not the whole reincarnation thing, but the idea of having a soul mate out there. The only part of this that's new to me is the question of how he became my soul mate. Well, and what to do about the fact that he currently hates me, but that may be one of those things I can't do anything about."

"You've spent your whole adult life searching for him—and now that you've found him, you're just going to give up?"

"Not give up," Raphael said, "but maybe adjust my expectations a little. Sebastien was starting to move on when he met you. He'd accepted Thierry's loss and was open to a new relationship. Right now, if Jean saw me at all, it would only be as Raymond reborn. I'm not a fool. I'm not going to set myself up for that comparison, because there's no way I can come out of it looking anything other than puerile, weak, and stupid. Raymond Payet was his world, and no one will ever match up to that for him. Maybe eventually he'll be able to see me for who I am, but until then, it's better not to bring it up."

"Do you want me to keep it a secret from Sebastien too?" Kylian asked. "He's Jean's best friend. I'm not sure he could keep quiet if he knew."

"No," Raphael said. "It's not worth having a secret between you. If he tells Jean, I'll deal with the fallout."

"I have one more question and then I'll stop, I promise," Kylian said.

"Ask all the questions you want," Raphael said. "Maybe one of them will help this all make sense."

"Why didn't I ever dream of Sebastien or of the past?" Kylian said. "We know I have this connection to Sebastien, the core connection, if your theory is right, but I have no memory of before, even in dreams. When we met, I didn't recognize him. Yes, things moved a lot faster than I would usually allow, but that's not the same as what you've always described."

"I don't know," Raphael said. "None of this makes sense in any but the wildest ways. Something about Raymond? Something about Jean? Something about how strong their partnership made them? Something about the fact that they already had one bond, and the ritual for Thierry and Sebastien added a second one? It could be any of those things or none of them, and I'm not even sure how we'd go about trying to figure it out."

"It's not important," Kylian said, though Raphael could tell it was more important than he wanted it to be. "I was just curious."

"I wish I could get my hands on a copy of that spell," Raphael said. "There are so many questions it might answer."

"And it might not answer any of them," Kylian reminded him. "That whole intention idea. We know the ritual went beyond what was on the page, because they didn't set out to bring Thierry back. Sebastien surely would have known if that had been planned. If Sebastien is right and their fear changed the ritual beyond what was spoken, the words wouldn't help."

"I know, but my curiosity is killing me."

"You have some memories," Kylian said. "You don't have that one?"

"No, it's all centered around my partner and our life together," Raphael said. "Almost always in the apartment—Jean's apartment, I guess, although occasionally there's another set of rooms. Maybe Raymond had an apartment of his own?"

"They lived at l'Institut for a while, didn't they?" Kylian asked. "Maybe it's those rooms you're seeing."

"Maybe. I don't suppose it matters. As you said, he's too wrapped up in the past to see the present, much less a future. It was a lovely idea, but not really a practical one."

"If you could get him to bite you, I bet he'd change his tune," Kylian said. "If you're right about being Raymond, your blood would call to him on a level he'd have a hard time resisting."

"And he'd hate me even more for trapping him," Raphael said with a shake of his head. "No, as appealing a thought as it is to have the partnership I dreamed about, that won't happen until he's at least willing to entertain the idea."

"I'm sorry, Raph. I feel like I've stolen your dream."

"No," Raphael said, even though it felt like that to him sometimes too. "You are living the life you were meant to live."

"Maybe, but you aren't."

"You aren't keeping me from it," Raphael insisted. "Nothing about your happiness keeps me from mine. Bellaiche is doing that quite well on his own."

"He might come around."

He might, but Raphael wasn't holding his breath. He'd made the worst possible first impression on the vampire, and his second impression hadn't been much better.

"We'll see, I guess."

KYLIAN LET himself into Sebastien's apartment—although he supposed he ought to start thinking of it as theirs, since he'd only gone back to his own place for clothes since they started sleeping together. Something else to discuss when they had time.

"How's Raphael?" Sebastien asked when Kylian came into the living room.

"Pretty messed up," Kylian replied. "He's trying to hide it because he doesn't want me to worry about him, but we've been friends too long for that. He didn't say it at Jean's apartment, but when I asked where Raymond was…. I told you Raphael has always felt like he was missing half his soul."

"He thinks Jean is that partner?" Sebastien asked. Kylian nodded. "He knows he's setting himself up for disappointment, doesn't he?"

"That's why he's so messed up," Kylian said. "He says he recognized Jean's apartment from his dreams, but now that he's found the vampire he's always dreamed about, it's someone who won't ever be interested in him. If he doesn't tell Jean about his dreams, about the sense of connection he felt, Jean won't give him the time of day. If he does tell Jean, assuming Jean believes him, Jean will only see him as a replacement for the one he lost. Neither of those is the happy ending he always believed he'd have. He's always believed in happy endings, even when they seemed impossible. He believed, and I got one."

"And he didn't. This isn't your fault."

"He keeps telling me that," Kylian said. "I just wish I didn't feel so guilty."

"You can't change who he loves," Sebastien said.

"But he doesn't love Jean," Kylian said. "He doesn't even know him."

"That's probably for the best right now," Sebastien said. "Jean is not an easy man to love, even on his best days. And he hasn't had a good day since Raymond died."

"And if Raphael is the one who could give him back those good days?" Kylian asked.

"They have to figure that out for themselves," Sebastien said. "Neither of them would thank us for interfering."

"No, I suppose not," Kylian said. "I just wish there was something we could do."

"We can be their friends, no matter what happens," Sebastien said. "Anything else would just make matters worse."

Chapter 26

SEBASTIEN DIDN'T bother going to Jean's apartment the next night. Given the way their conversation had ended the night before, Jean wouldn't answer even if he did show up. Better to catch him at Sang Froid after he fed and was hopefully in a better mood.

"I didn't expect to see you when Jean showed up alone," Angélique said. "I'm not letting you feed after what happened last time."

"I don't need to feed," Sebastien said. He'd taken care of that this morning, before Kylian left for work. The memory made him smile despite his audience. "I need to talk to Jean, and I figured he'd be in a better mood when he was done here."

"He was in a state when he came in," Angélique said. "What happened?"

"It's a long story," Sebastien said. "I'll tell you another time, when I have a better idea of how it ends."

"I'll give you a week," Angélique said. "Then I'm coming for answers."

Sebastien laughed. "Deal. I don't know if anything will change that quickly, but I'll tell you then if not before."

The sound of Jean's voice as he came down the stairs interrupted their conversation. "But for now, I have a vampire to corner."

"Don't let him hear you say that. You know he's always been at his most volatile when he feels trapped."

"That's what I'm counting on." It was the only way he would get any honest answers.

"What are you doing here?" Jean said when he came into view of the entrance.

"Looking for you," Sebastien said. "We didn't finish our conversation last night."

"We aren't finishing it tonight, either," Jean snapped.

"Why not?" Sebastien said. "If it doesn't matter, why not talk about it?"

Jean's eyes narrowed in a look that had struck fear into the hearts of many vampires and even more mortals, but Sebastien had grown immune to it. "Not here," he said finally, when it became clear Sebastien would not back down.

"Wherever you want," Sebastien replied easily. "As long as you talk to me."

Jean glared once more and then stalked out of Sang Froid, leaving Sebastien to follow if he chose. Sebastien let Jean have that little victory. The night would be his.

He didn't recognize the dive Jean led him to, but there were enough tables and few enough patrons that they could talk undisturbed.

"What do you want me to say?" Jean demanded when they'd found a table and ordered espressos so the waiter would stop hovering.

"Whatever you need to say," Sebastien replied. "You were upset last night."

"Do you blame me?"

"No, but understanding why you're upset doesn't make me less worried about you," Sebastien said. "Even if everything he said is wrong—"

"It is," Jean interrupted. "Don't you think I'd know if Raymond were out there somewhere?"

"I didn't," Sebastien said. "I had to get sick on someone else's blood before I started wondering, and even that wasn't enough to convince me it wasn't a fluke until more evidence started piling up. Why should you be any different?"

"Because he was my everything," Jean said.

"And Thierry wasn't mine?" Sebastien said. "We moved heaven and earth to form our bond. Compared to that, you had it easy."

"I'm sorry. I didn't mean to imply—"

"Yes, you did, but that's beside the point. What are you going to do about Raymond?"

"Nothing," Jean said. "Even if I found this person, whoever it might be, it wouldn't be Raymond. You told me yourself how different Kylian is from Thierry. I don't want different. I don't want a replacement. I want Raymond."

"Is having someone different, and yet the same in so many ways, really worse than being alone?" Sebastien asked. "You've been miserable since Raymond died, and I get that, but he didn't want you to suffer. He wanted you to move on and find someone new. Hell, the way things have been going, he probably knew what happened with the spell and said that so you'd be open to the possibility of finding him again."

Jean smiled, though the expression didn't reach his eyes. "He would do that, wouldn't he?"

"He would. And he'd think it was all a great joke. You've mourned, Jean, but it's time to let that go. Maybe that someone won't be Raymond. Maybe he isn't even Raymond reborn. That doesn't mean you have to be alone."

"If he's out there, he wouldn't ever forgive me for not finding him."

"No, he wouldn't."

"I wouldn't even know where to start."

Gotcha. Sebastien tried to keep his expression neutral as he crowed internally.

"You can start by going out again," Sebastien said. "Not to hunt, necessarily, but just so you're around people who aren't Angélique and me. You think Raphael is wrong. Start there. Raymond wasn't the only one who researched the ritual. Go back over what you studied back then. Prove him wrong, like he said. If nothing else, Raymond would approve of the academic pursuit."

"Raymond would like him," Jean said. "I don't, but Raymond would. He'd see a kindred spirit in the thirst for knowledge, even if the kid needs to learn tact."

"Raymond needed to learn tact too," Sebastien reminded him. "He was blunt to a fault."

"Only with people he trusted," Jean said. "You didn't see him that much early on, and by the time you did, you'd become his friend. I watched him on the public stage. He guarded his words like gold when he was in the spotlight."

"Pretty sure he learned that from you," Sebastien said. "You should try teaching Raphael that too."

"You're awfully fixated on him. Is there something you're not telling me?"

"He's the one nonvampire other than my partner who you know at this point," Sebastien said. "And someone you have a reason to talk to. He seemed like a reasonable choice for remembering how to interact with the world again."

Jean frowned. "Only so I can vindicate Raymond and his research on the ritual. I don't know how Kylian and Thierry are one, but it wasn't because Raymond missed something in his research."

"By the time you're done with that, you'll be out and about again," Sebastien said. "That's what I care about. You don't have to take up the mantle of chef de la Cour again. I just want to see you living again instead of merely existing from feeding to feeding because Angélique and I won't let you starve to death. If you find someone new, Raymond or not, partner or not, that's as it will be. It's not what matters to me."

"Orlando wouldn't have, even if we'd managed to keep him alive after Alain died," Jean said.

"No, but you aren't Orlando. Orlando had a bastard of a maker and so much abuse to get over it's a miracle he ever let Alain close. Even if we'd managed to convince him he'd get Alain back, he wouldn't have gone for someone new. That was Orlando's choice, and if the laughter I hear on the wind every time I go by their tomb is any indication, they're together and happy. What more can we wish for them?"

"Nothing," Jean said, with a more genuine smile this time. "It took me a long time to forgive Orlando, but you're right. He wouldn't have survived long enough for Alain to come back to him, even if it were possible."

"But I did, and you have, if you're willing to look," Sebastien said.

"You're assuming Raphael is right," Jean said.

"I haven't seen any reason to believe he's wrong," Sebastien countered.

"I'm working on that," Jean said. "I got a couple of new books, and Marie-Pierre, the bouquiniste, is keeping an eye out for anything else that might be useful. You know her grandfather always found things for Raymond. Anyway, she found a book that's really interesting. All about blood magic, with a little conjecture on sex magic thrown in."

"And?" Sebastien said. "Does it say anything relevant?"

"It says all kinds of things," Jean said. "I'm not a wizard, though, to know how much of it is accurate and how much of it is tenth-century mysticism getting mixed in with actual magic."

"Don't look at me. I wasn't alive back then, and I'm not a wizard. I'm not going to be of any use to you in figuring it out."

"I know," Jean said. "I'll either have to call l'Institut or get Raphael to look at it."

"Raphael would be closer," Sebastien said. "Not to mention you could keep the book in your possession the whole time instead of having to send it to l'Institut. Unless you've changed your mind about going back."

"No, I won't ever go back," Jean said. "It's hard enough to be in my apartment, where I have memories other than my life with him. There's nothing at l'Institut that isn't completely steeped in his presence or his magic. I wouldn't last a day."

Sebastien understood that. He'd sold the house he and Thierry had shared in Dommartin. For Sebastien, the clean slate had been welcome when they started their lives together, and creating a clean slate again had kept him sane when he'd moved back to Paris after Thierry's death.

"I have Raphael's number if you want to call him," Sebastien offered. "Or you could meet at my place if you don't want him at your apartment."

"Why would it bother me more to deal with him there than elsewhere?" Jean asked.

"Because it's your sanctuary?" Sebastien asked. "You barely tolerate having me there, and you like me most of the time."

Not to mention the way Raphael had passed through Raymond's wards so easily, but Sebastien wouldn't bring that up unless Jean did. He could explain why Kylian could pass through, since Thierry had known the trick and their magic was the same, but that would beg the question of how Raphael could. Sebastien would wait to open that can of worms for as long as he could. He wasn't above a little manipulation to get Jean to spend time with Raphael, but he really hoped they'd do the rest on their own.

"The conversation will probably make me furious no matter where it happens," Jean said. "He's too sure of his explanation, and he doesn't seem like the type to listen to alternate arguments. At least if

I'm at home, I'll have the option of kicking him out. Anywhere else, I'd have to leave instead."

"And that would be admitting defeat?" Sebastien teased.

"I never admit defeat," Jean said haughtily.

Sebastien just laughed. "That's not the way Raymond told it."

"I won his trust, his love, and the right to call him my Avoué," Jean countered. "I even convinced him to stop keeping it a secret after a time. I wouldn't call that defeat."

"Then don't let Raphael defeat you either," Sebastien said. "Convince him of your view, or find a compromise explanation somewhere in the middle. I don't know if he's right or wrong. I don't know that it even matters in the grand scheme of things. What's done is done, and it's how we move forward that's important to me, but I know having an explanation is important to you. If you understand what we did, even if it turns out he's right, you'll be able to accept it more easily. You never had any trouble accepting my bond with Thierry, even when some other vampires did."

"Because I would have done the same if our positions had been reversed. I never did thank you for stealing Thibaut from me, did I?"

Sebastien laughed. "I wish you'd kept him. Then maybe we wouldn't be in this situation."

"Or maybe we would be, only I'd be the one at the heart of a mystery we may never solve."

"I thought you didn't admit defeat," Sebastien said. "Whatever the answer is, you'll find it."

"But so much has been lost," Jean said with a sigh. "Books or manuscripts that are referred to but that we don't have copies of. Rituals that originated before we have any records to draw from. The Aveu de Sang is the perfect example. We know it was already an old ritual when monsieur Lombard was turned. We don't know when it was created, by whom, or even really why. We know what it does, but that's about it."

"And we have no real way of finding out," Sebastien finished.

"Exactly. Unfortunately, so much is like that. We can experiment, study, document, but there are always limits. Raymond taught me that. We push to those limits. We might even push those limits. But at some point, we have to accept that some things simply are."

"Talk to Raphael anyway," Sebastien said. "A lot of research has been done since Raymond retired from l'Institut. He might have information that was unavailable to us back when we planned the ritual. And even if he doesn't, he's a set of fresh eyes. He may think of something in hindsight that didn't occur to us at the time."

"Fine," Jean said. "I'll talk to him. Just don't expect miracles."

As far as Sebastien was concerned, he'd already gotten one.

Chapter 27

JEAN FROWNED down at the faux marble tabletop in the little café around the corner from his apartment. Despite his words to Sebastien, he hadn't invited Raphael back to his place when he'd proposed meeting to discuss the ritual and Raphael's wild theories. He'd decided neutral ground would put them both more at ease. He wasn't entirely sure why he cared if Raphael was comfortable during their conversation. He'd chosen to focus on his own comfort instead. He might not have the option of kicking Raphael out at the café, but he also wouldn't have to deal with another wizard and his magic in Raymond's space.

"Sorry I'm late," Raphael said as he approached the table. "The Métro was packed after work, so I was late getting home, and that put me behind for our meeting."

Jean didn't ask why he bothered taking the Métro when he could simply cast a displacement spell. Raymond had done the same thing after the war, only using magic when he needed to, not just to make his life easier. He frowned at the thought of any similarity between his current annoyance and the love of his life, but he already knew they were both scholars. Maybe that attitude toward using magic came from their studies.

"I haven't been waiting long," Jean replied. He didn't offer his hand for Raphael to shake, and he noticed the wizard didn't initiate the gesture either. "Do you want something to drink? I'm told the coffee here is excellent. Their selection of liqueurs is also quite extensive."

"Do you have a favorite?"

"You forget," Jean said. "I can't taste any of them."

"Not now, but you could when your partner was alive. Or is that an effect limited to the second ritual, rather than one shared with the Aveu de Sang?"

"It applies to both," Jean said, "but that was years ago. The vintages I enjoyed then are no longer available. I don't know how the newer vintages measure up."

"Then I'll have a coffee." He caught the waiter's eye and placed his order. "You said you had questions."

"A few. Your conjecture—or maybe Sebastien's reason why your conjecture might be right—is that either something in the ritual that we didn't understand or the subconscious fears of the participants in the ritual pushed the bond beyond what was planned into something powerful enough to bring Thierry's soul back from heaven to be reborn in Kylian's body."

"In a nutshell," Raphael said. "It's probably not quite that simple when you get into the details of how it would work, but that sums it up as well as anything."

Nothing about this was simple, but Jean saw no point in arguing semantics this early on.

"I'm not a wizard, but I've spent a lot of time with them, one in particular—enough to have a general understanding of how magic works and to have a fairly specific understanding of the ritual we performed," Jean said. "And none of what I know or have read supports the idea of the subconscious interfering with the conscious intention behind a spell."

"That would depend on how strong the subconscious is compared to the conscious and how at odds those intentions are," Raphael replied. "If the conscious intent was to create a bond and the subconscious fear was that the bond would be too deep or wouldn't work or wasn't desired, it might not have any effect, especially if they weren't deeply seated fears. In this case, though, the fear of being separated played into the desire for a bond. Everyone wanted the bond, either because they were the recipients of it or because they wanted it for their friends. So the subconscious fear was working in concert with the conscious intention. Given that the ritual was successful, nobody would think to look beyond that to see the rest, until circumstances arose that forced a reexamination of the ritual itself."

"Okay, that makes a certain amount of sense," Jean conceded. "If you want a ward to protect something and you're truly afraid of what will happen, your fear may make the spell stronger than you intended—but since it achieves the end of protection, you may not ever realize you did anything beyond what you set out to do."

"Yes, exactly. And while it's not a phenomenon that's been studied extensively, anecdotally it's been observed in a few cases. Enough to allow it as a possibility in this case," Raphael said. "Of course, all we can do with the ritual in question is discuss it anecdotally and theoretically, since we aren't in a position to study either the words or the ritual directly."

Jean could probably have recreated the bulk of the ritual, words and all, from memory, but his promise to Raymond held him back. "For the sake of argument, then, let's say it worked. The bond between Thierry and Sebastien went deep enough that it brought Thierry's soul back. At this point, my own spiritual beliefs aside, I'm almost willing to accept that part however it happened. How do you go from there to the idea that it affected the rest of us?"

"What should have happened to Alain and Orlando after they died?" Raphael said by way of reply.

"Their souls should have found their way to heaven," Jean said automatically. "Neither of them was perfect, but they lived good lives."

"You won't hear me arguing with you," Raphael said. "By that line of belief, there shouldn't be any trace of them at the cemetery other than their ashes. Yet Sebastien insists he can still sense them there."

"Not just Sebastien," Jean said. "I don't go there often, but the few times I have, I could hear their laughter on the wind as well."

"How do you explain that?"

Jean started to bristle at the question but realized Raphael was truly looking for an answer. "I don't," he replied. "I've never tried. I've taken it as a blessing and left it at that."

"A blessing? In what sense?"

"That they're together," Jean said. "We kept the worst of Orlando's past out of public record because it had no bearing on the war or anything that came after, but Orlando was both the strongest and the most fragile of us all. The things he survived would have killed a lesser man, but it made his relationship with Alain a miracle in and of itself. Partnerships, alliance, war, and everything else aside, the fact that he could love Alain and let himself be loved in return—that he could open himself up to an Aveu de Sang and commit himself to a relationship that would last for as long as Alain lived—was a miracle like I have never seen. Most vampires either choose to socialize exclusively with other vampires, viewing mortals as nothing more than a means to prolong their existence, or they learn to live with loss and move on. The span of our years forces us into one option or the other. Orlando had taken the first option right up until he met Alain, but the second option wasn't open to him. No amount of time passing would have let Orlando move on. Alain was it for him. His one and only. When Alain died, Orlando did too, in all the ways that really mattered. The night we buried Alain, Orlando asked me if we were damned because we'd been changed, and I told him no. I'm not sure I believed it, but I said it because it was what he needed to hear. And then the sun rose and all that was left of my best friend, my little brother in every way that mattered, was a pile of ash. But then something happened that I hadn't expected and couldn't explain. The soil turned again beneath the ash, even though none of the wizards present cast a spell. Orlando's name appeared on the grave marker next to Alain's, and I heard laughter. Their laughter. They were together and happy and no longer trapped by aging bodies or painful pasts. So yes, a blessing, because I didn't have to worry about them. I had plenty of other things to worry about, but not that."

"That is a blessing," Raphael said quietly. "And I don't want to diminish that in any way, but rationally, doesn't it seem odd to you that you can still hear them? I can understand when it first happened. Their bond was a deep and exclusive one, and their deaths were close together. But now? It's been, what, thirty years?"

"Thirty-four," Jean said.

"Thirty-four, then. Why can you still hear them?"

"Because I still need to," Jean replied.

"That's your faith talking, not your reason."

"I never felt the need to separate them," Jean said.

"That doesn't work for me," Raphael insisted. "I need an explanation beyond blind faith."

"I don't have one for you."

"No, but I have one," Raphael said, "one you're trying to dismiss. I'm open to discussing it because it's a hypothesis, but the discussion can't be my reason against your faith. That won't get us anywhere."

"Putain, you're almost as infuriating as Raymond was," Jean snapped. "I already told you I don't have an explanation beyond my faith. What more do you want from me?"

"For you to put your mind and your considerable experience to the job of finding one, or at least proving me wrong," Raphael snapped back. "So you don't have an explanation right now. Find one. Or punch holes in mine. Just *think* about it."

"Fine. If you're right, then what about Eric and Vincent? There were eight people in the crypt that night. We needed Eric for fire, and his husband came as well to add his strength to Eric's. Even without us feeding, Raymond, Alain, and Thierry had outstripped Eric's abilities by then. With us added to the equation, the ritual would have been completely unbalanced if he'd been alone. With Vincent there, it brought Eric up to a level Raymond could work with. If you're right and the ritual spiraled out and bound all of us, why aren't they still here somewhere?"

"Are you sure they aren't?" Raphael asked. "Have you gone to their grave to see?"

"Not since their funerals," Jean said, "but there was nothing then like there was with Alain and Orlando."

Raphael finished his coffee. "Let's go. We can be at the cemetery in fifteen minutes, depending on the trains. We can see if they're there or not."

"Fine," Jean said. He pulled enough cash from his wallet to cover the tab and nodded to the waiter on his way out. He stalked down the street toward the Métro stop, not waiting to see if Raphael followed him. This was all his stupid idea. He could just keep up.

From l'Opéra, it was a straight shot to Père Lachaise. They rode in silence, Jean unwilling to make small talk. Raphael's reasons for staying silent were his own. Jean refused to care what they were.

The gates of the cemetery were closed, but Jean had spent years bypassing them when he needed to get in. At times he had done so officially, but many other times he had simply scaled the walls and been done with it.

"There's no need to climb," Raphael said. "It's a simple lock with no magical protection." He pointed his wand and said something Jean didn't catch. "There, no reason to ruin your trousers."

Jean glowered at him but walked through the open gates and toward the area of the cemetery where the veterans of l'émeute des Sorciers were buried. To a one, they had refused military honors unless they had served in one of the other branches before or after the war, but the city had set aside a plot of land for them nonetheless. Eric and Vincent had been buried next to each other. Jean hadn't been to their graves since their funerals, but he remembered where they were.

Far enough from Raymond that Jean didn't have to be haunted by the lack of Raymond's presence.

"Here they are," he said to fill the pregnant silence. "I didn't know them all that well, but they were always there if we needed them. Vincent helped with the restoration of l'Institut because he was also an earth wizard, and even with Sebastien's help, Thierry couldn't do it all by himself. At least not at the speed we needed it done. And Eric... before the war, Eric, Alain, and Thierry were the three musketeers."

"And Raymond was their d'Artagnan?"

"Not really," Jean said. "The war put a strain on that friendship. They always invited Eric and Vincent to special occasions, but they only came if they were sure there wouldn't be any media—and our lives were rarely less than a spectacle, no matter how hard we tried to keep them private. If anything, Raymond became the third musketeer."

"Do you get any sense of them at all?" Raphael asked.

Jean shook his head, but in the interest of fairness, he ran his hand over the two gravestones and then knelt and touched the earth at the base. Sebastien said he'd felt the connection with Thierry there, and since Vincent had been an earth wizard, it made sense the same would hold true for him. He focused all his attention on the point of contact. He didn't want Raphael to be able to say he hadn't tried his best when he finally said he couldn't feel them.

"Nothing," he said after a few minutes. "But they didn't have vampire partners. They didn't have the same fear driving them. If that's what really changed the bond, maybe it wouldn't have affected them, since they didn't share the emotion."

"That's not an unreasonable supposition," Raphael said slowly. "Where are Alain and Orlando?"

"Over there," Jean said with a wave of his hand.

"Do you mind if we go see their grave as well?"

Jean had no desire to go that way because doing so would take him past Raymond's grave, but he didn't see a way to refuse gracefully. "After you."

Jean kept his eyes on the path as they walked toward Alain and Orlando's grave. He couldn't look at Raymond's headstone. It would tear him to pieces again, and he'd never manage the rest of this conversation. Yet not looking felt like the worst kind of betrayal of Raymond's memory. He'd send Raphael on his way after they visited

Alain and Orlando, and then he'd come back and break down. Raymond would understand the delay. If anyone had ever been suited for this debate with Raphael, it was Raymond.

The gentle breeze, unseasonably warm, picked up as they neared the marker. Jean couldn't stop the smile when he heard soft laughter echoing along the eddies of air. "Bonsoir," he murmured to them.

"I didn't believe you," Raphael said, drawing Jean's attention back to him. "I took it at face value and accepted that you and Sebastien felt something when you were here, but I didn't think it would be this strong."

"We're only half-crazy," Jean retorted. "Although, if the connection is to Sebastien and me, why can you feel it too?"

"Probably because you're here," Raphael said quickly. Almost too quickly, as though he'd expected the question and prepared an answer ahead of time, but Jean didn't question it. He had other worries at the moment. Like not having a nervous breakdown this close to Raymond's grave. "Your presence triggers the effect, but anyone around can feel it once it happens."

"So if I left, the wind would die down and you wouldn't be able to hear them laughing anymore?" Jean asked.

"Yes, although I don't know how far away you'd have to go," Raphael replied. "Or how long the effect would linger if you left completely. Magic doesn't always turn on and off like a switch. It has an existence of its own."

Jean could attest to that. He remembered all too clearly the night the wild magic had broken loose of the Rite d'équilibrage and nearly destroyed Thierry. They had learned two things that night—that a vampire feeding could help heal his partner, and that even the most rational of them were susceptible to the sexual pull between them if given enough incentive. He had held back from ravishing Raymond by force of will alone. He suspected it was even more Raymond's willpower than his own that had kept them in check that night, though neither of them had held out much longer.

"Come back sometime when I'm not with you," Jean said. "Just for curiosity's sake."

"I will," Raphael said. "Do you want to go back to the café or find somewhere near here to continue our conversation? It would be more comfortable than the middle of the cemetery."

Jean shook his head. "Another time. It's getting late, and you undoubtedly have classes to teach in the morning. You should go. I'll close the gate behind me."

"Are you sure?" Raphael said. "I could wait for you."

"I'm sure. I'm hardly defenseless, and I know my way home from here."

Raphael looked like he was about to say something else, but Jean didn't give him the chance. He turned and walked away from all the familiar names, hoping Raphael would take the hint and leave. When he'd completed a circle and returned to the same spot, Raphael was gone.

He knelt down next to Raymond's grave and touched the stone, but it was bone dry. When Jean had come more frequently in the months after Raymond's death, a mist had always hung around the stone, keeping it damp and enveloping Jean's hair and clothes whenever he came to visit. He had stopped coming after a while, too torn up to do anything, and when he finally returned, the mist had disappeared.

"What a mess I've gotten myself into now," he murmured. "You'd like the kid. Even better, you'd understand the kid. I get the feeling not a lot of people have. He's a little too smart for everyone else to handle. But oh, the conversations you could have had with him. If he'd been alive then, Olivier wouldn't have taken your place at l'Institut. You'd have promoted this kid, even if he was the youngest candidate, with no qualifications other than the size of his brain. I want to hate him, but I can't. He reminds me too much of you. Not in the ways that really matter, but in little ways that still hit home. You should have heard him read me the riot act tonight. I haven't been scolded like that in years."

The familiarity of it all broke something in his chest. He had loved this kind of discussion with Raymond. They had spent hours upon hours in just this kind of conversation, debating nuances of words and how meanings had changed over time, dissecting old spells and abandoned rites. Every new discovery Raymond made, he brought straight to Jean for him to pick apart. And Jean had done it, not because he doubted Raymond, but because if he did it in private, Raymond would have all the answers when the critics tried to do it in public.

"It hurts," he said, his voice cracking with sorrow. "If I do nothing, if I shut out the world, I ache with your absence, but getting out doesn't help either because everything reminds me of you. Why did you make me promise to stay? Why couldn't you have let me follow you? I miss you so much. I thought it would get easier with time, but whoever said time heals all wounds lied. The wound hasn't healed. It's festered until it's eaten every part of me. I should hate you for it, but that would be like hating myself, because you always were the best part of me. Maybe that's why there's so little left without you here."

His eyes prickled with tears that would never fall. For once, in the safety of the darkness, he let his façade crack and sobbed his despair. Dry shudders racked his shoulders, but no comfort came. None could come with Raymond's ashes buried beneath his hands.

RAPHAEL TOOK an involuntary step forward when he heard Jean's cry, but his presence would be an intrusion, not a comfort. He'd hoped Jean would recognize him or at least feel some sense of connection as they talked, but he'd given no sign beyond intellectual curiosity. Seeing him like this, though, Raphael knew he couldn't wait much longer. His heart ached at the sight of his partner in pain. He owed it to Jean to give him some hope of surcease.

Chapter 28

"YOU LOOK like you've seen a ghost," Kylian said when Raphael walked—stumbled, really—into his apartment. Raphael didn't know why Kylian was there instead of at Sebastien's, but when he'd texted a frantic note, Kylian had said to meet him there.

"Not a ghost," Raphael said slowly, "but the breaking of the strongest man I've ever known. And I did it. I didn't mean to, but I still did it."

"Jean?"

Raphael nodded.

"What happened?"

"We met at the café to talk about the ritual and magic and whatever else came up, although nothing else really did. The other two wizards who helped with the ritual, the ones who had each other instead of a vampire partner, came up as a flaw in my theory of a wider bond formed by the ritual, so we went to the cemetery to see if we could feel any trace of them."

"Could you?"

"No, but then we went to Alain and Orlando's grave, and there.... Merde, Ky, I've never felt anything like it. We're standing there, and all of a sudden there's this warm breeze, warmer than it should be, and there's laughter and this incredible sense of well-being. Like there will never be another moment of sadness."

"For them, there won't be," Kylian said, "and that is a beautiful thing."

"Unfortunately, that only seemed to make Jean worse," Raphael said.

"Are you surprised?" Kylian asked. "His best friend is buried there, which has to be hard enough. Then add to it that he lost his Avoué too. As much as he wants to be happy for them, they represent everything he lost. It's salt in an open wound."

"I know. He asked me to leave after that. I did, but before I got to the gates, I had this nagging feeling I needed to go back. When I got close, I could see him at a different grave."

"Raymond's grave."

"Yes, and he was sobbing. Hoarse, dry heaves of breath and sound. I wanted to say something, to find a way to comfort him, but he wouldn't have taken any comfort from me seeing him like that."

"Would you want him to see you like that?" Kylian asked.

"I didn't say I blamed him for feeling that way," Raphael said, "but it drove home to me that I want to earn the right to comfort him. Whether I'm Raymond reborn or whether I'm just another wizard with a desperate crush, I want him."

"It won't be easy," Kylian warned. "He's not like Sebastien, open to the idea of someone new. He's still firmly fixated on Raymond and may always be. This may not be a battle you can win."

"Maybe not, but I won't know if I never try."

"Do you have a plan?"

"Not even the beginning of one," Raphael said with a sharp laugh. "Any kind of announcement of being his partner, his soul mate, Raymond reborn, whatever, will seem like I'm either trying to take advantage of the situation or like I've been keeping secrets because I waited until now to tell him. Not that I could have told him sooner, as volatile as he's been. He wouldn't have wanted to hear it then either."

"You could try getting him to bring it up," Kylian suggested.

"Like he'd ever do that," Raphael replied. "He doesn't believe it's possible. He's not going to look at me and see it. At best he'll start to think of me as a friend, but that's not what I want or what he needs."

"Careful," Kylian said. "He won't appreciate you making decisions about what he needs. If it's not what you want, that's fine. You're entitled to your own desires, even your own needs, but don't fall into the trap of trying to dictate his. I know you feel like you've known him your whole life, but he doesn't know you that way—and you can't know how many of those dreams are real and how many are fantasies. Don't let them give you a familiarity you haven't earned."

Raphael chafed at the suggestion that he didn't know Jean as well as he thought he did, but he could admit the validity of Kylian's concerns. His dreams felt real, especially now that he'd seen Jean's apartment, but once the bedroom had become a recurring setting for his dreams, he'd allowed his conscious mind to wander there as well, playing out fantasy scenarios in his head. He had to push all that aside and work only with what Jean had chosen to share with him.

"Then I guess it's back to another academic discussion," Raphael said. "It was a good discussion until we went to the cemetery and he shut down. There's still plenty of ground to go over, so it's not unreasonable that I'd want to talk to him again."

"That's a start," Kylian agreed, "but don't let him think it's just about the academics. Ask him how he is. Tell him you were worried about the state he was in when you left him at the cemetery. Something to give it a personal edge too. If you want him to see you as anything other than the researcher who turned his world upside down with his crazy ideas, you have to take the first step."

"How do you seduce a man who doesn't want to be seduced?" Raphael said sadly.

"With things that don't appear to be seduction," Kylian replied. "From what Sebastien has said and what I've seen, he's isolated himself almost completely. Human contact is probably a form of seduction in itself after all these years. Intellectual stimulation is the same. If you don't want to keep going over the same ground, get his opinion on your thesis research. He could probably give you some insight. If nothing else, he's lived long enough to see attitudes change. Talk about primary sources."

"It's worth a try," Raphael said. "Even if I don't get anything new for my thesis out of it, we would have something else to talk about."

"And we know he was as much a driving force behind the research at l'Institut as Raymond was, so I think he'd appreciate it once you piqued his interest. Give it a try. What do you have to lose?"

Raphael was afraid to answer that question, but at the same time, he didn't have anything now except hopes and dreams. They were poor company in the dark

"I'd better wait until tomorrow to call him. Even if he's home by now, he won't want to talk to me tonight."

"Maybe not, but a message telling him you hope everything is okay and that you hope to see him again soon wouldn't go amiss, whether he's home or not," Kylian said. "How is it that you're the romantic and I'm the one giving you advice?"

"I'm the romantic, but it's all been in my heart and head until now. I haven't had a lot of chance to practice. It always seemed pointless when I knew the person I was talking to wasn't the person I was waiting for."

"Maybe you should tell Jean *that*," Kylian teased. "It might catch his interest."

"Unicorns are the ones attracted to virgins, not vampires," Raphael corrected automatically.

"I wasn't thinking about the vampire. I was thinking about the man," Kylian replied. "Vampires are known to be possessive. The thought that you've waited for him all this time… I could see it appealing to him."

Raphael flushed. "Fuck off."

"If we're done, I will," Kylian said with a snarky grin. "Sebastien is waiting for me."

"Espèce de con," Raphael said, but he grinned back. "Go get laid. I'll call Jean and see where things go from there."

Kylian sobered for a moment. "I hope it goes exactly where you want it to. You know that, right? I may tease, but underneath it, I want everything to work out for you."

"I know," Raphael said. "It will or it won't. Only time will tell."

"Call or text me if you need me."

"I will," Raphael promised. He took his leave and cast a spell to take himself home.

Raphael's apartment felt emptier than ever. It was a place to keep his things, a roof over his head, but it wasn't home in any way that mattered. When he dreamed at night, home was a place of love and laughter and warmth, filled with personal touches and the collected detritus of a lifetime. He could imagine Jean's apartment filled with laughter, though it had been filled with anger and tension the one time he had actually been there. He'd caught glimpses tonight of the man Jean had been and could be again if Raphael managed to break through his walls. It was probably wishful thinking, but the memory of Jean hunched over and crying at Raymond's grave haunted him. He couldn't leave it like that. He had to do something. He had to try.

RAPHAEL'S HEART pounded in his chest and butterflies churned in his stomach as he waited for Jean to show up. He'd made a point of arriving early this time. He didn't want Jean to think he was always running late.

Jean had seemed back in control when Raphael talked to him that afternoon. More importantly, he'd accepted Raphael's suggestion of meeting again immediately. Whatever demons had driven him the night before, Jean didn't seem to blame Raphael for it. It wasn't much, but Raphael would take what he could get.

When Jean came in and joined him, Raphael smiled, hoping to put the conversation on a more casual footing. Jean looked surprised, but he smiled back stiffly, as though he was out of practice.

"I talked to the waiter," Raphael said when Jean sat down. "He recommended the Rémy Martin, if you like cognac. He said the current vintage they have is very smooth."

Jean's surprise increased, but the smile became more natural. "Thank you. That wasn't a brand we drank often, so I'm not familiar with it. I suppose I should have a glass since you went to the trouble for me."

"Only if you want to," Raphael said. "I know you can't really taste it, but I thought you might enjoy it anyway."

"I'd like that," Jean said. The wonder in Jean's voice made Raphael glad he'd taken the time to ask. He suspected no one had made any kind of effort for Jean in a long time. Sebastien and Angélique had kept him fed, but that wasn't the same.

The waiter came and Raphael ordered two glasses of cognac for them.

"How are you tonight?" Raphael asked when the waiter left.

Jean looked as surprised at the question as he had at everything else tonight. Raphael was going to have words with Sebastien if even the simplest of kindnesses left Jean stunned.

"I'm…."

"I'm sorry," Raphael said. "I didn't think when I suggested we go to the cemetery last night. I didn't mean to upset you."

"I know that," Jean said. "I didn't expect to be as bothered by it as I was. I haven't been affected like that in a long time. It brought back emotions I'd thought myself long beyond."

"We don't have to talk about them tonight," Raphael offered.

"Then what do you propose we talk about?" Jean replied. The droll humor in his voice made Raphael want to cheer.

"You could suggest something," Raphael said.

"You said you were studying the sociology of the magical races. What does that mean, exactly?" Jean asked.

"That depends on who you ask," Raphael replied with a laugh. "For me, though, it means looking at how the magical races interact with each other and with society as a whole, and how and why that has changed over time."

"That's very broad."

"That's the field as a whole," Raphael clarified. "Like any field, individuals have a narrower focus that contributes to the understanding of the whole."

"So what is your focus?"

"Well, I have two," Raphael said. "My thesis research is on attitudes toward dark magic and how that progression led to the start of l'émeute des Sorciers. Serrier's official platform before the war was that the government had labeled too much as dark magic and that a nonmagical body shouldn't have that kind of control over the practice of magic. I know it got twisted beyond that later, but that's how it started."

"If it hadn't started that way, he would have found another platform," Jean said. "He wasn't after justice or fair representation. He was after power."

"I know that," Raphael said, "and nothing in my thesis suggests otherwise. It's not about Serrier at all, really. More about what forces in society allowed him to attempt to seize power using the specific arguments he did."

"It's the intent versus execution debate again," Jean said, leaning forward. "Laws made certain kinds of spells illegal, no matter what they were used for, instead of focusing on the intent or the outcome. That was one of the big pushes l'ANS made after the war was over—to make the laws about the outcome, not about the method."

"Yes, but the question I'm looking at is how societal attitudes changed to the point that those laws got passed," Raphael said. "What were the defining moments of thought that made blood magic or sex magic illegal? When did we start thinking that any spell that included animals was wrong? I'm not condoning cruelty, but there is significant evidence that some ancient civilizations used animals as familiars as well as sacrifices. Even if modern sensibilities prohibit the sacrifice element, why should familiars be forbidden? Those are the questions I'm looking at."

"Because the use of animals smacked of the occult," Jean said. "The cabals in the sixteenth and seventeenth centuries were viewed as a threat by the kings at the time. Whether they were fomenting rebellion or simply amusing themselves, it didn't matter. As far as the kings were concerned, it was dangerous, so they sent people to infiltrate them and to discover their methods. A number of them during the reign of Louis XIII, especially, used animals in their rituals. I don't know when the laws themselves changed, but it became more and more secretive after that."

"Do you remember any of the names?" Raphael asked. "Either of the cabals or of the people who infiltrated them?"

"I didn't pay that much attention," Jean said. "I'm sorry. I was aware of it because it made it harder for us as well. If we ever had problems finding a willing person to feed from, we could feed from animals in a pinch, but that's almost impossible to do without killing the animal. Before that time, nobody questioned the body of a dead animal, but once they started cracking down on the cabals, it became harder to dispose of them without drawing unwanted attention to ourselves."

"I knew about the cabals, although I don't have a lot of research on them, but I didn't know about how it affected the vampires. See, this is why it's about all magical races, not just about wizards, for all that the question focuses on them on the surface."

"Angélique opened Sang Froid around that time too," Jean said. "She saw the struggle vampires were having to find enough to eat and figured she could solve the problem and earn her living at the same time. She wasn't wrong."

"Fascinating," Raphael said. "I'll have to add a section about how this affected the vampires. What about blood magic or sex magic?"

"That's more likely to have affected the werewolves," Jean said. "Vampires don't do magic. The law concerning animals only affected us because we used it as a cover, not because it was essential to our existence. I did find a book the other day that might help you."

"Really? What book is that?"

"It's at home. It's a treatise from a tenth-century monk about blood and sex magic. It's a first edition from the fifteen hundreds. I was lucky to get my hands on it, so I'd prefer if you didn't take it with you, but you'd be welcome to study it at my apartment," Jean said.

"Where did you find something like that?" Raphael asked, feeling excitement bubbling up in his chest. "And do you have anything else like it?"

"I donated most of Raymond's library to l'Institut, and I'm sure you've seen what's there," Jean said. "I still have my own library, of course. A friend still looks out for books she thinks I might find interesting. She was just a child when Raymond died, but we'd been getting books from her family for years."

"It's strange to hear you talk of him so casually," Raphael said. "I grew up hearing his name, and yours, of course, in school as heroes of a war and great contributors to the cause of equality for all magical races. I idolized him."

"Just him?" Jean teased, surprising Raphael.

"No, of course not. But you have to understand, my relationship with vampires, or with the idea of vampires, was different." He took a deep breath. This was his chance. "I grew up dreaming about vampires, not as some mythical, magical creature, but as a friend, a playmate, and then later, when I got older, as a lover. For as long as I can remember, there's been a vampire in my head, and the older I got, the more detailed those dreams became."

Jean frowned, but Raphael pressed on. "I could never see a face, but he was a presence in my head. As a child, I took my scraped knees and hurt feelings to him, and he kissed them better or reminded me that words were a tool I could use too and that playing the long game took more patience but made me stronger in the end. When I got older, I brought him other concerns, and he was there for me then too. I botched my first kiss because the poor kid I was with wasn't as smooth as the lover in my dreams."

"That hardly seems fair," Jean remarked with studied calm.

"It wasn't," Raphael said, "but it didn't matter, because it proved I didn't want anyone if I couldn't have him."

"That's a tall order for a man to live up to," Jean said, "vampire or not. Even if you somehow found the vampire you've spent your whole life dreaming about, how could he ever be as perfect as your dreams?"

"Maybe he isn't, but he's still mine," Raphael said. "That's the part nobody ever understood until Kylian met Sebastien. This isn't something I chose, but it *is* something I have lived with and accepted my whole life. He's the other part of me. I hope someday I'll be the other part of him too."

"How do you propose to find him?" Jean asked.

Raphael swallowed hard and looked Jean square in the eye. "I already have."

Chapter 29

JEAN STARED at Raphael blindly for a moment as the import of the words sank in. The evening had been unusual enough already, between talking about Raymond—which he normally only did with Sebastien, and even then only if he couldn't help it—and flirting with Raphael. He didn't know where *that* had come from. He wasn't even sure he liked the kid. There was no excuse for leading him on. And now... now Raphael was saying he'd spent his entire life dreaming about Jean.

"I'm not the lover in some fairy-tale story. You've mistaken me for someone else."

"I know you're not a fairy-tale prince," Raphael said. "The first time we met, you threw me up against a wall and threatened me. Believe me, I have no delusions in that regard."

"Yet you think I'm the vampire you've spent your life dreaming about."

"That doesn't make you a fairy-tale prince," Raphael replied. "It just makes you the one I've been waiting for."

"You can't know that."

"I didn't that night," Raphael conceded. "Emotions were so high, and neither of us was at our best. But I knew it the night we came to your apartment. I knew *you* that night."

Jean shook his head, unable to concentrate in the face of Raphael's unwavering determination. He couldn't be right. And if he was, the implications were too much to face. "You expect me to believe you're Raymond reborn?"

"No, I don't expect anything. I hope you'll hear me out. I hope you'll give me a chance to show you we could be good together, but I don't expect anything. My dreams were predicated on my vampire being willing to be with me. I've seen enough over the past few days to know you aren't at that point."

"This is insane."

"That seems to be a common thread in our conversations recently," Raphael said with a smile. "And yet we keep coming back to the same things. I think I can prove I'm not mistaken about the identity of the vampire in my dreams. Probably not much else, but I think I can prove that."

"How?" Jean asked warily. He wasn't about to bite Raphael to test it the way Sebastien had done.

"When I got older and my dreams went from being play dates to more adult interactions, they almost always took place in one of two rooms. Whichever room it was in, one thing never changed—it had a four-poster bed with black draperies. The posts were carved.... "

Raphael kept talking. Jean could see his lips moving, but he couldn't hear the words over the buzzing in his ears. No one should have been able to describe his bed. He hadn't allowed anyone but Raymond in his bedroom in hundreds of years. Even in the midst of his grief, he had always come out to Sebastien rather than allow Sebastien to cross that threshold. No one could have given Raphael these details.

"How do you know that?" Jean asked hoarsely. "What spell did you cast—"

"You know I didn't," Raphael interrupted. "You were there the whole time I was in your apartment. You know I couldn't have cast a spell to see inside your room, even if I would do such a thing. The bed is always in the dreams, but sometimes it's in a room with stone walls and floors covered in rugs and tapestries. Other times it's in a room with hardwood floors and silk paper on the walls."

"Stop," Jean said. "That's enough. I don't want to hear it."

"Do you believe me now?"

Jean wanted to shout no and order Raphael to leave, even though they were on neutral ground. He wanted to pretend he hadn't heard any of what Raphael had said in the past few minutes, but that wouldn't get him anywhere. Raphael knew things he shouldn't know. Whether that meant he was Raymond reborn or just that he had the Sight, as his mother used to call it, Jean didn't know. He couldn't deny the evidence of Raphael's words, though. He knew things he couldn't possibly know.

"Does it matter? You said yourself I don't want a new partner."

"It matters to me," Raphael said. "It doesn't obligate you to anything. I'm not going to take you believing me as permission to move into your life or your bed or anything, but it would be nice to have the one person, besides Kylian, who has been a constant in my life believe that I'm not mad."

"I'm pretty sure we're both mad," Jean replied. "Fine. I believe you. But it doesn't change anything. It can't change anything."

"All right. It doesn't change anything," Raphael said. "We'll still meet for coffee or cognac sometimes. I'll tell you about my research, and you'll point out all the things I've missed because you lived what I can only read about. And at the end of the night, we'll go our separate ways."

"That's it?"

"What else should there be?" Raphael asked. "I've done fine without you until now. If all I can have is your friendship, it's still more than I had last week. And if I can't have even that, I'll be content with my dreams."

"I don't believe you."

Raphael's eyes narrowed. "What don't you believe?"

"That a young man like you—attractive, intelligent, personable— would be content to spend your life alone because I said no."

"I told you I bungled my first kiss because he wasn't you. The more I experimented, the worse it got. I gave up because it wasn't worth making myself or my lover miserable. I'd rather be alone with my dreams."

Jean tried not to imagine Raphael, blond and beautiful, alone in his bed, eyes closed as he dreamed of Jean and pleasured himself to those dreams. He didn't want those thoughts in his head, but Raphael's words had planted a seed he couldn't uproot.

"Damn you. How am I supposed to think of anything else now?"

"You don't want a lover, remember?" Raphael said. "You had the perfect man already. I get that. I told you I idolized him. Why do you think I went into academics? It wasn't for the money, that's for sure. No, I wanted to be just like him. That he'd had a vampire for a partner only made that dream seem more attainable. I never imagined I'd end up here with you."

"I did have the perfect man," Jean said. "Perfect for me, anyway. I don't know why you dream of my bedroom when only he was ever there, but you aren't him. I'm not trying to be cruel. I just need you to understand that I can't give you what you need."

"I haven't asked for anything," Raphael reminded him, "except a few hours of your time now and then to discuss my research. You offered to let me look at the book you just found. It doesn't have to be anything more than that."

"And how long will that last?" Jean asked bitterly.

"Until you tell me there's a possibility of something more," Raphael said. "I know you don't believe that, but it's the truth. Give me a chance to prove it to you. If I can't, you can kick me out at any time."

"I need some time to think about this. I haven't had years to get used to the idea."

"Take all the time you need," Raphael said. "I'm not going anywhere."

Jean knew that was a lie. They might not live in a war zone like when he met Raymond, but accidents happened every day. People stepped off the sidewalk to cross the street and got hit by buses or cars, or they stumbled in the Métro and fell onto the tracks. Or they choked on pieces of hard candy or fell asleep at the wheel. Tomorrow wasn't guaranteed for any of them. He could say good-bye to Raphael tonight and never get a chance to see him again.

"Come to my apartment in three days. You can look at the book, and we'll talk then."

"I'll be there," Raphael promised. "If you're free sooner, you can always call."

Being free wasn't the problem. The problem was being ready, and no amount of time would cure that. He had three days to wrap his head around everything Raphael had said.

"I'll see you in three days."

When Raphael had left, Jean slumped in his chair, struggling to reconcile the conflicting thoughts and emotions racing through his head like so many buzzing gnats. Somewhere, somehow, this all made sense, but he couldn't even find a thread to pull to start unraveling the knot. He had resigned himself to being alone because he had no choice. Raphael was resigned to being alone because of Jean's choice.

Yet what could he offer Raphael besides the empty, brittle husk of the man he had once been? Raymond would kick his ass from here to heaven and back to hear him say that, but it was true, no matter how much Raymond would argue with him. Raymond's death had broken him, and Jean didn't know if anything would be enough to put him back together again.

Raymond would flick his ear and tell him he had just let his best chance walk out the door, and Raymond would probably be right, but that didn't mean Jean was ready to take it. It would mean reaching down into the barren recesses of his soul and finding something else to give. He was a selfish man—he knew and accepted that about himself—but he couldn't allow anything to develop with Raphael if he could give nothing in return.

The moment that thought crystallized, he recoiled. When had he gone from rejecting the idea to considering whether he had anything left to give a lover? Like the moment of flirtatiousness, the thought had come unbidden and unwelcomed, but it set off a landslide inside him that he could not hold back or ignore.

He signaled the waiter for the check so he could pay and get out of there. He wasn't sure how much longer he could sit in the little café and pretend to be normal.

"Your friend took care of the check," the waiter said when he reached the table.

"Thank you," Jean said automatically as he rose and headed for the door. Something else to take up with Raphael when they saw each other again. Jean knew the poor-student type well. Raphael didn't need to spend what money he had on Jean.

When had it started mattering what Raphael spent his money on? For that matter, when had the assumption that they would see each other again become so automatic? Jean had agreed to let Raphael look at the book Marie-Pierre had found for him, but that was a far cry from what Jean was feeling. No, this felt as if Raphael belonged there, would always be there—and Jean didn't like it, because he couldn't remember accepting it. It had snuck past his defenses. Intellectually, two evenings in a café did not equate to a lifetime together. Apparently intellect had no say in the matter.

He considered going to the cemetery to talk to Raymond, but he'd proven all too well how empty that consolation was when he had been there a few nights previously. Besides, he'd never needed to be at Raymond's tomb to hear his voice giving him a kick in the pants. Even more than that, Raymond's voice in his head didn't know any more about the situation than Jean did. Sebastien was the only person who could even come close to understanding what he was going through. His pride protested automatically, but he pushed it aside. He wasn't chef de la Cour any longer. He didn't need to be bound by le jeu des Cours.

He was less comfortable discussing the situation with Kylian around, since Raphael was his best friend. He wondered if that was coincidence or more proof of Raphael's supposition that the spell had created a bond among the six of them, but it wasn't a question he could answer. Probably no one could answer. Raymond, maybe, given how his attitude changed after the ritual was over, but Raymond wasn't here to ask. Raphael might know some things he shouldn't, but he obviously didn't have all of Raymond's memories, or he wouldn't need to ask so many questions about the ritual itself.

He thought about calling, but Sebastien's apartment was only a few blocks from his. If he got there and they were out, he would hardly have gone out of his way. Then he could call Sebastien and ask him to come by when he could, preferably without Kylian.

Sebastien buzzed him in almost immediately after he rang.

"What's wrong?" Sebastien said as soon as Jean walked in.

"Is it that obvious?" Jean asked. "I must be losing my touch."

"It wouldn't be to anyone else," Sebastien assured him, "but I know you too well. What's wrong?"

"Is Kylian here?" Jean asked.

"No, Raphael called and asked if Kylian would meet him," Sebastien said. "I didn't ask why."

"Because of me," Jean said. "Or something like that, I would imagine."

"He told you?"

"You knew?" Jean exclaimed. "Why didn't you say anything?"

"For the same reason he didn't until tonight," Sebastien said. "Because we all knew this is how you would react."

"Is it that unreasonable a reaction?" Jean demanded.

"I didn't say that," Sebastien said. "It's not unreasonable at all, but Raphael's heart is on the line. He was understandably worried about how you would react, and really, I'm surprised he said anything this quickly. He'd talked about letting you get to know him and get used to him being around so that it would just come naturally instead of being a revelation with a huge fallout."

"It would have been worse if he'd waited," Jean said. "I already feel betrayed that he didn't say something the moment he knew.

Dragging it out longer would have only made that worse. And I know, emotions were too high that night for him to say anything, and then the time after that, we ended up at the cemetery. I know he couldn't have really said anything sooner, but it doesn't make it feel less like everyone was keeping secrets."

"Well, now you know. So what are you going to do about it?"

Jean sighed. "I don't know. I don't even know where to start thinking about it."

"Ask yourself this, then. What do you have to lose?"

"He says he's dreamed of me his entire life," Jean said. "How am I supposed to live up to that? And what happens when I don't?"

"You remind him you're not a dream," Sebastien said. "He's not going to measure you against a fantasy."

"He's measured everyone else against it," Jean muttered.

"What was that?" Sebastien asked.

"Nothing. He doesn't know me well enough to know if he wants me," Jean said. "We've talked a total of four times, and one of those times consisted of me yelling at him because you were sick. Not the best first impression."

"And yet he told you about his dreams tonight," Sebastien said. "That first impression obviously isn't holding him back. You're miserable now, and don't deny it. We all know you are. If you take a chance with Raphael and it doesn't work out, you'll still be miserable, but it won't be any worse than it is now. If it does work out, you could have a chance at being happy again."

"It would be worse than it is now," Jean said. "Because if it doesn't work out, I'd still be stuck having to drink only his blood for the rest of his life. You proved that pretty conclusively with Kylian."

"I wasn't suggesting you go straight to feeding from him," Sebastien said. "I meant getting to know him, trying to see how a relationship would work. Before you do anything you can't undo."

Jean flushed. His mind had already jumped far beyond the getting-acquainted stage to feeding and fucking, but Sebastien was right. He had waited with Raymond. Not on the feeding part—but they hadn't had sex until their partnership was well established. Surely he could resist Raphael without even the lure of blood to draw him in.

"How?"

"Are you asking me how to keep from jumping him the next time you see him or how to get to know him?" Sebastien asked with a grin.

"Maybe a little of both," Jean replied honestly. "Raymond and I didn't start an intimate relationship right away, but we also didn't start off on the best footing. Not to mention I was somewhat involved with someone else. It wasn't as serious as she wanted, but it was an outlet at first. As for the getting to know him part, it's been so long since I was the pursuer. When I was chef de la Cour, people came to me."

"What makes you so sure you'd be the pursuer this time?" Sebastien asked. "I'm pretty sure Raphael will keep finding excuses to see you until he doesn't need excuses anymore. This isn't some passing fancy for him. As long as you let him, he will be around."

Unless I drive him away.

"That's not fair to him either. He shouldn't have to do all the work."

"That doesn't sound uninterested," Sebastien said. "What do you want, Jean? Short of Raymond magically coming back to life, what would make you happy?"

"That's just it," Jean said. "I'm not sure anything else could."

"Then what would make you the least unhappy?" Sebastien said. "What would make things better for you right now?"

Jean didn't have an answer to that.

"Do you enjoy talking with him?" Sebastien prompted when Jean didn't answer. "From what I've seen of him, he's got a brain to rival Raymond's. You should be able to have all kinds of debates with him."

Jean thought back to their recent conversations. They had not been easy, but mind-blowing revelations aside, they had been stimulating. He hadn't talked that way with anyone since Raymond died, and even before that, their conversations had rarely included anyone else. No one else could keep up with them. Raphael could have, if he and Raymond had lived at the same time.

"'Enjoy' might not be the right word, given the way all of our discussions to date have ended," Jean said, "but he challenges me and makes me think in a way I haven't done since Raymond died."

"So if the topic were less fraught, there's a good chance you really would enjoy the conversation," Sebastien said. "That's a good start. Do you think he's attractive?"

"I have eyes, don't I?"

"That's not an answer," Sebastien said. "He doesn't look a thing like Raymond. For all I know, you could hate blonds on principle."

"I don't hate blonds," Jean said.

"Then that's another good thing," Sebastien said. "You're at least somewhat attracted to him."

Jean wouldn't have thought it before tonight, but tonight had been full of unexpected epiphanies. Finding he was attracted to someone for the first time in thirty years was actually the least startling one.

"There are worse places to start," Sebastien said when Jean looked up at him again. "It's not a guarantee, but we both learned a long time ago that life doesn't come with guarantees. I know you haven't been ready to hear it, but you've mourned Raymond for a long time. Longer than he would have wanted. Honor his memory by giving this a chance. If it doesn't work out, then it doesn't work out, but not even trying because you're clinging to memories of Raymond isn't what he wanted."

"Do you think he knew?" Jean asked.

"Knew what?"

"That the ritual had gone beyond what we planned," Jean explained. "Even if he didn't know the full effects."

"I don't know," Sebastien said, "but it's possible. You said his attitude toward his work changed completely after we completed the ritual. He never mentioned publication or any of that to me, so I didn't see it, and he was as happy as everyone else when Thierry and I announced that it had worked. I don't think he could have feigned that."

"No, he was happy for you," Jean said. "Whatever he may have known or suspected, it didn't change his pleasure in your happiness. The friendship among the six of us was one of the great joys of his life. He never quite understood how or why it happened, but he never stopped valuing it."

"Then in the name of that friendship, trust me," Sebastien said. "I don't know a lot of things in this world, but I know your happiness was Raymond's primary concern. If Raphael can make you happy, or even if he can just take the edge off your unhappiness, Raymond would approve."

That wasn't the problem, but Jean couldn't put the rest of his concerns into words any more clearly than he'd already done. Even now, he couldn't completely let go of the habits ingrained from his years as chef de la Cour.

"Thank you. I guess I'd better figure out the rest, then."

"I'm here if you need me."

"I know," Jean said, "and I appreciate it, but ultimately this is something I have to decide on my own."

"Whatever you decide, I'll support you."

"Even if you don't agree with me?"

"Even if I don't agree with you."

Chapter 30

"HOW DID it go?" Kylian asked as soon as he arrived at Raphael's apartment.

"Well enough, I guess," Raphael said. "He didn't storm off or say he never wanted to see me again or anything like that."

"That's encouraging," Kylian said.

Raphael smiled weakly. "It's better than it could have been. He doesn't know what to make of the idea, and I don't really blame him. I've lived with it my whole life, and sometimes it still trips me up."

"You always knew there was a possibility you'd find the person you were looking for and he wouldn't feel the same way," Kylian said. "Maybe you didn't want to think about it, but you knew."

"Yes, I knew," Raphael said. "I just didn't expect the resistance to be because he was grieving the loss of someone else. I can't compete with his memories of Raymond Payet. Jean worshipped him. It's clear every time he says his name. It's too much to expect him to want me."

"Hey, that's my best friend you're talking about," Kylian said. "Give yourself a little credit."

Raphael shook his head. "I can't. If I push him, he'll bolt. I told him I wasn't asking him for anything and that I wouldn't ask for anything other than a few hours of his time now and then to talk about my research. That's something he can do, something we can do. Anything else would drive him away."

"Can you really live with that?" Kylian asked. "All your life you've dreamed of the relationship you would have when you finally found your soul mate, and now you're going to settle for the occasional research debate?"

"I don't have any other choice," Raphael said. "You didn't see him tonight, Ky. If I'd given even the slightest hint of wanting more, he would have been gone before I finished the sentence. At least this way, I'll have something."

"You do have a choice," Kylian insisted. "Maybe you didn't tonight, but you do for the long term. If you want him, you have to fight for him."

"I know it doesn't look that way to you, but that's what I'm doing," Raphael said. "The only way I know how. The only way that has any hope of working. The moment I ask for more without some sign from him first, he'll take away even our discussions. By staying around, by proving I'll keep my word, I'll win his trust. The rest will come, if it comes, from there."

"Are you okay with that?"

"What do you think?" Raphael said with a bitter laugh. "Of course I'm not okay with it, but that doesn't change it. You're right. I wanted everything. I wanted a partner and a lover—hell, maybe even an Aveu de Sang. I had it all worked out in my head, but instead I have Jean with all the associated baggage. But even with that, he's who I want. If all I can have of him is his mind, it's still better than nothing."

"He'll come around," Kylian said.

"I wish I could be so sure," Raphael replied. "You didn't see his face tonight. It was all he could do to stay seated when I told him. He was ready to bolt right then. I'm not sure that's something he'll ever get over."

"You could meet someone else."

Raphael snorted, though he felt no amusement. "Yeah, right. That's gone so well when I tried it before."

"Before, you were still clinging to the dream of finding your partner," Kylian said. "Maybe now that you have, it will be easier to let that go and stop comparing everyone to your ideal."

"Easier?" Raphael repeated. "Who exactly is going to come off well in comparison now that I've met Jean?"

"I can think of a lot of people," Kylian insisted. "He hasn't exactly been nice to you."

He hadn't. Raphael couldn't argue with that, but there was just something about him. "Maybe not, although he was nicer tonight before I dropped this on him. He was even nicer the first time we met without you and Sebastien. It's when something upsets him that he stops being nice, but nice or not, he's got this charisma to him, this harnessed power that is as seductive as it is deadly. There's no way anyone else can compete with that."

"Even if you can't have it?"

"Even if I can't have it."

THREE DAYS later, Jean was no closer to making a decision. He had gone round and round in his head, the same questions and concerns raised each time without any conclusive answers. He wanted and yet he didn't. He was interested despite himself and horrified because of it. Sebastien had asked him what he had to lose. He'd avoided putting the answer in words, but he feared opening himself up to the pain of loss again. Raymond would demand to know if the loss outweighed the happiness of their lives together, and Jean would say no, but that didn't mean he was ready to go through it again. Raphael was younger than Raymond had been when they met, but he was still mortal. They might have a hundred years together instead of ninety, but one way or another, it would come to an end. Losing Raymond had crippled him. Adding another loss on top of that seemed the very height of folly.

He hadn't called Raphael to tell him not to come. He couldn't. As much as he feared what having Raphael around would mean, he couldn't bring himself to sever all ties with him.

When the buzzer rang shortly after sunset, he let Raphael in the main door and left his door open in invitation. He couldn't stand there and watch Raphael walk through the wards again, but he'd invited the wizard. He could hardly lock him out now. Besides, as easily as Raphael had negotiated the wards, he could probably unlock the door with a quick spell too.

"Bonsoir," he said when Raphael walked into the living room.

"Bonsoir," Raphael replied absently. "Where does the Aveu de Sang come from?"

Jean blinked in surprise. "I thought you wanted to look at the book I found."

"I do in a minute, but this is more important. Where does it come from?"

"I don't know," Jean said. "No one does. The oldest recorded histories and legends all speak of it as something established before anyone could remember."

"Merde. I suppose that means you don't know what the original intent of it was either," Raphael said. "So much for that line of thinking."

Intrigued despite himself, Jean leaned forward. "What line of thinking?"

"It's nothing," Raphael said. "A wild hare I figured you'd disprove in the blink of an eye. But if you don't know anything about the origins, it'll have to stay a random guess."

"If you tell me what it is, I might be able to provide some insight," Jean said with a shake of his head. "Just because I can't answer those two specific questions doesn't mean I know nothing about the rite."

"Don't laugh," Raphael said firmly. "I just got to wondering why someone would create a spell like the Aveu de Sang and why two people would agree to it that first time. I mean, I see the advantage to the vampire and even to some extent to the Avoué, but there had to be something behind it. To create a spell so powerful that a vampire can now perform it, even though you lot keep insisting you can't do magic, would require a hell of a lot of effort on the part of a wizard somewhere. The kind of investment that not many wizards would be willing to put into something out of the goodness of their hearts."

"You're not the first wizard to ask that question," Jean said. "Thierry asked it more than once. We never came up with an answer."

"To your knowledge, has any vampire in previous generations had a wizard for an Avoué?" Raphael asked.

"Not to my knowledge, but the rite is not much in favor among my kind," Jean said. "Orlando chose to face the dawn rather than go on without his Avoué, and my choice was not much better. Vampires look at that and decide it would be easier not to make the bond than to live with losing it."

"What if," Raphael said slowly, "and this is a huge leap of logic on my part, but what if the Aveu de Sang only works the way it's supposed to if the Avoué is a wizard?"

"It worked fine for Sebastien," Jean replied. "He never tested the part where the Avoué can calm the vampire's beast, but he was able to feed from Thibaut at will without draining his Avoué. He could sense his emotions. He got all the other benefits I did from my Avoué except immunity to sunlight, but any vampire with a partner can have that. It doesn't require an Aveu de Sang."

"And then his Avoué died, and he was left tied to a person who was no longer there," Raphael said. "Unless the wizard who created the rite intended it as a curse—and that would be a pretty shabby curse if it was one vampires could avoid by simply not doing the rite—then it doesn't make sense. Why would you create that kind of spell?"

"You're driving at something," Jean said. "I recognize that look. Raymond would get it too when he thought I was being particularly dense."

"What if… you're going to kick me out for saying this."

"Just tell me," Jean said impatiently. "Whatever it is, you're not going to relax until you've said it."

"What if the point of the Aveu de Sang is to create a soul bond?" Raphael blurted out. "Only if the Avoué isn't a wizard, the vampire's inherent magic isn't strong enough to complete it."

Jean opened his mouth to reply, but nothing came out. He felt like he'd been kicked in the stomach, all breath knocked out of his lungs. He shook his head in automatic denial, but it made so much sense. Thierry had argued against the bitter irony of the Aveu de Sang until he was blue in the face, but they'd only had Sebastien's and monsieur Lombard's experiences to judge by, and for them, there had been no other end. But Raymond had been a wizard. Had they created a bond deep enough to span the distance between worlds without even realizing it? If so, then he had to face the very real possibility that he was looking at Raymond all over again.

"I told you you'd hate the idea," Raphael said, turning away.

"No," Jean croaked out. "No, just give me a minute to think about it. We never considered it. We couldn't have. We didn't have anything to suggest it was even possible." He shook his head a couple of times. "Wishful thinking aside, tell me the truth. Is it possible?"

"If you believe the evidence of Kylian and Sebastien, then yes, it's possible," Raphael said. "And you and Sebastien both said the ritual that bound them—well, Thierry, but that's semantics at this point—was intended to mimic the Aveu de Sang as closely as possible. Whether it was the fear of being separated that created the soul bond or something in the imitation of the Aveu de Sang, I couldn't say."

"But if we didn't even know it was possible, how could the creators of the spell have known it?" Jean said. "With all the knowledge we have available to us, we didn't have even a hint of it."

"It's easy to discount ancient wisdom because nothing in current thinking can account for it—but modern engineering models all say the cathedral in Chartres shouldn't stand, yet it's been there for close to a thousand years," Raphael said. "It's amazing what faith and ingenuity can achieve."

"So some ancient shaman fell in love with a vampire, and rather than be parted from him or her, created a spell to bind their souls so that they would find each other again?" Jean summarized.

"I'd be laughed out of the Sorbonne for even suggesting it," Raphael said, "but it's better than any other explanation I can come up with. It's better than believing it's a spell destined to leave a vampire destroyed and alone for the rest of his existence."

"Or dead because he can't go on alone," Jean murmured.

"Or that," Raphael agreed. "I don't expect this to change anything. I meant what I said when we talked about it before. I'm not asking you for anything, but I couldn't keep it to myself, either."

"Because if you're right, it changes things," Jean finished for him. "The problem is there's no way to know if you're right."

"Well, there might be, but that would ask something of you, and I promised I wouldn't do that."

Jean couldn't stop the huff of laughter at that. "Yes, that would indeed ask something of both of us. I don't know if I can do that. I don't know if I can let down those guards again. When Raymond died, I locked everything away inside me because it was easier to feel nothing than to live with the pain. I built a cage around the beast inside me so strong that nothing could break it, because I knew if it got loose, I'd never rein it in again. I don't know if I can undo that."

"Then don't," Raphael said. He covered Jean's hand with his own. "Just don't send me away. I can live with anything else."

The innocent contact surprised Jean. No one had touched him that way since Raymond died. Sebastien had held him in check, but no one had held his hand or touched his cheek or given him any kind of physical affection. He knew it was because he hadn't invited it, not because they were unwilling to show it, but his breath caught in his throat now. He stared at the place where they touched. He could feel the warmth of Raphael's hand against his skin and realized he hadn't felt anything but cold even on the hottest summer nights in so long. He yearned for that warmth. He closed his eyes and turned his hand beneath Raphael's so their palms met and their fingers could tangle together.

Raphael squeezed his hand gently. "So where's this book you were telling me about?"

RAPHAEL SMILED absently as Kylian and Sebastien talked about their days. He'd come home with Kylian after work instead of having drinks out, thinking to talk with them in a more private setting, but watching them together made the empty space at his side all the more obvious. Jean should be there with him, with all of them, but he wasn't and might never be.

"Are you going to see Jean tonight?" Sebastien asked when he handed Raphael a kir cocktail.

"Not tonight," Raphael said. "I dropped another bombshell on him last night. I thought he might like a night without me."

"What bombshell was this?" Kylian asked as he joined them in the living room. Raphael envied the easy way they shared each other's space. He didn't know if he'd ever have that with Jean.

"I haven't been able to stop thinking about the Aveu de Sang," Raphael said. "I asked about its origins, hoping to make sense of the spell, because it doesn't make sense."

"No," Sebastien agreed, "it doesn't. I can't tell you how many times Thierry insisted we had to be missing something. I take it you thought of something?"

"Maybe," Raphael said. "Kylian is here after you and Thierry did a ritual designed to imitate the Aveu de Sang. I'm here, having spent my entire life believing I was born to be Jean's mate. I wondered if maybe that was the point of the Aveu de Sang in the first place, to make sure the Avoué and the vampire are reunited. It's not something we can prove. We can't travel back in time to the moment the spell was created to know what the original participants intended, or even hoped for."

"It would explain so much," Sebastien said. "Certainly it would explain why Orlando and Alain are still together. Orlando made an incredible leap of faith when he stayed at Alain's grave rather than fleeing the rising sun. Anything could have happened in that moment. He believed he and Alain would be united."

"And he was right," Kylian interjected.

"Yes, he was right, but he had no way of knowing that," Sebastien said. "His courage in that moment can't be overstated. I've known more than one vampire who thought to give up only to be unable to follow through at the last minute. As tedious as it can be at times to live for centuries or more, choosing death is not easy."

"With an Aveu de Sang and a wizard for an Avoué, the vampire would have the promise of multiple lifetimes with his loved one to help break up the tedium. Twenty or thirty years between incarnations is nothing compared to decades together each time," Raphael said. "And at the time the spell was created, cultural norms might have allowed that time to be even shorter. The Egyptians married younger than that, didn't they?"

"Not just the Egyptians," Sebastien said. "When I was turned, many couples married when they were fifteen or sixteen. It's not very long when weighed against centuries."

Now if Jean can just accept it, Raphael thought sadly. If not, his future looked very bleak indeed.

Chapter 31

JEAN SAT at his desk, pen in hand, studiously ignoring the quiet presence in front of his fireplace. Raphael had taken to coming over most evenings to continue studying books from Jean's library. Some nights they discussed what he read. Other nights, he read in silence until he needed to leave. Tonight seemed to be one of the silent ones. That was fine with Jean. He had grown used to Raphael's company, but more nights than not it still left him unsettled how easy it was to sit together, each occupied with his own pursuits. Like they had spent a lifetime of evenings together in just such a way.

They hadn't discussed it since that night. They'd discussed other things, even the blood magic on which the Aveu de Sang was surely based, but they had avoided the topic of the bond itself like the plague. It hadn't stopped Jean, though, from imagining scenario after scenario of an ancient shaman or priestess dying and the vampire lover who begged them to stay—and of a hasty, perhaps ill-thought-out ritual to bind them so the wizard would be reborn to be reunited with the vampire. Of the vampire watching their loved one fade and having the agony of the wait as he held vigil over the years to see if it worked. In some ways Jean thought that would be even worse than the situation he was in now. To have such a tentative hope and such a high risk of having it dashed was surely harder than believing his mate to be gone, only to learn that perhaps he was not as lost as he had believed.

Shaking his head to chase away such thoughts, he reached for the bottle of ink to refill his pen, but his distraction was greater than he realized and he fumbled the bottle. He cursed and grabbed for the cloth he kept to clean his pen after he'd filled it. Raymond had found this desk for him. He couldn't stand to see it ruined.

He had only started to soak up the ink when he felt the brush of magic in the air. It raised goose bumps on his skin and then it was gone. When he lifted the cloth, so was the ink.

He turned to face Raphael, far too conscious of the ink on his hands and all that implied. His unease must have shown on his face, because Raphael looked instantly abashed.

"I'm sorry. I should have asked, but the ink would have ruined the wood, and it's too beautiful a piece to see it damaged that way."

"Thank you for keeping it from staining," Jean said, his tone forced. "It was a gift from Raymond, for our first anniversary, actually." One of their first anniversaries, since they had more than one date to count from, depending on what they felt like commemorating. "However, we have another problem now."

"We do?"

Jean dropped the cloth, revealing his ink-stained fingers. Raphael gasped, answering Jean's question of whether Raphael would understand the impact.

"I see."

Jean turned awkwardly back to his desk. Anything to escape the question in Raphael's eyes. He had no answer to give.

"It doesn't have to mean anything," Raphael said. "We already knew it was likely the case. It doesn't have to change anything."

"I know that," Jean said, keeping a tight rein on his temper—but however much he pretended it didn't matter, he knew it would change everything. As long as there had been a doubt, he could hold back, but Raphael's spell had removed what little doubt remained. He was Jean's partner, and given Sebastien's experience, being Jean's partner meant so much more than it once had.

"Do you want me to leave?" Raphael asked.

It would have been easier to say yes, but that was the coward's way out. "You still have at least an hour of reading time left. No reason to waste it."

"Thank you," Raphael said.

"Don't mention it."

Jean forced his attention to stay on the volume in front of him. The leather-bound notebook had been a gift from a well-wisher many years ago. He'd never found a particular use for it, but when talking with Raphael had sparked a desire for reading again, Jean had pulled it out to record his thoughts. Raphael had laughed at him for being old-fashioned, but Jean preferred the feel of a pen in his hand and the scratch of the nib across fine paper to the impersonal touch of more modern recording devices. He could use them if he needed to, but chose not to for anything that really mattered.

He resisted the urge to glance over his shoulder at Raphael, but it didn't solve the problem of his thoughts returning constantly to him. His partner.

The reality had grown too complicated for such a simple word. It had suited all those years ago, when they had formed an alliance to win a war, and the fastest way to do that was to match vampires with wizards whose blood could protect them from sunlight. They were partners then, going into battle at one another's sides and protecting each other's backs. Alain and Orlando had taken it far beyond that, but they had a name for their relationship. They were Avoués. The term "partner" only applied to them in the strictest of senses, for they did fight together. Then the wild magic had happened, and everything had gotten so much more complicated. What had been a simple military arrangement became sexual, and what became sexual became personal. And then it had become everything.

Despite everything it had become, despite the Aveu de Sang that bound them, they had continued to use the word "partner"—because for several years, the Aveu de Sang was a secret known only to a few. By the time they told people the truth, using the term was so ingrained that they didn't change their terminology. Raymond had been Jean's partner for a hundred years. To apply that term now to someone else felt so empty.

Yet at its root, that's exactly what Raphael was. His magic didn't work on Jean. If Jean fed from him, he would be able to go out in sunlight again. If Jean fed from him, the ensuing shockwaves would destroy his whole world.

"WHEN YOU asked me to meet you at the cemetery, this isn't the grave I expected to find you standing in front of," Sebastien said when he came into view. Jean summoned a smile for him, no matter how forced it felt.

"For once, they're the ones on my mind instead of Raymond. As much as I miss them, as much as it hurts to think about never seeing them again, I sometimes think this is the most peaceful place in Paris."

"I have always loved it here," Sebastien agreed. "A lot of my happiest memories include them."

"Yes," Jean said. "I wish we'd known. We could have stopped Orlando if we'd been able to promise him Alain would come back to him if he just held on for long enough."

"Except that even now, we don't really know," Sebastien said. "I mean, it worked this time, most likely. Unless you've fed from Raphael and not mentioned it yet?"

"No, but I think we have enough proof to be fairly confident in our suppositions," Jean said. He glanced down at the ink stains on his hands. "I spilled a bottle of ink tonight. Raphael cleaned it up before it could stain the desk."

"But not before it could stain your hands, I see," Sebastien said.

"The spell didn't work on my hands, no," Jean replied. "And before you ask, no, it doesn't change anything. I can't do this."

"If you can't, what makes you so sure Orlando could have?" Sebastien asked. "You always said it was a miracle he'd trusted Alain. There's no guarantee he could have trusted a second time, even if we could have convinced him that person was Alain reborn."

"I'm not sure at all. In all honesty, he probably wouldn't have trusted again, no matter what we said," Jean said. "It's selfish of me. I know that. But I miss them, and I feel guilty that they didn't know they had the choice."

The breeze picked up, ruffling their hair.

"They'd both kick us in the ass for that," Sebastien said. "I miss them too, but Orlando did have a choice. Do you remember what he said that night, about being happy he had found someone he loved so much?"

"I do," Jean said hoarsely. "Every word is etched in my memory."

"Then you know he's at peace. He wanted one thing, and that was to be with Alain. And now he is. All you have to do is close your eyes to know that. They didn't need the evidence we have before us to know their souls were bound. They knew it the first time Orlando fed from him. He wouldn't have lasted the thirty plus years it took me to find Kylian. He wouldn't have lasted past the first feeding. It might not have made him sick, but it would have killed him."

"I know," Jean said. "I've always known. It doesn't make it any easier, but I know."

"Just keep reminding yourself he's happy," Sebastien said. "No one with any sense could stand here and doubt it."

Jean closed his eyes and pushed his grief aside as much as he could. It was easier than he expected it to be, and when he did, a sense of contentment washed through him. Sebastien was right. However much Orlando's choice rankled because it felt like Jean had failed to keep him safe, Orlando had made the choice that was right for him.

Chapter 32

JEAN GLANCED across the room for what felt like the hundredth time that night. Raphael wasn't doing anything different than any other evening, blond head bent over one of Jean's books as he read, occasionally stopping to write notes on his tablet. The light didn't catch his features any differently, because it was the same lamp in the same spot as every other time he had sat there to study. Nothing had changed.

So why was he so restless tonight? He'd called Sebastien and told him not to come because he was staying in tonight. He'd go to Sang Froid tomorrow. He'd gone longer than that without feeding, both before and since Raymond. Not often, perhaps, especially since, but he had gone longer. He should not have so much trouble keeping his eyes to himself.

Raphael was just so damn available. He never said anything. He'd kept his promise of not asking anything of Jean beyond the discussion of his research, but Jean knew. He could still feel the brush of Raphael's magic over his skin. The ink stains had finally faded that morning, but even that hadn't been enough to put the thought from his mind. If he asked….

He wasn't going to ask, so it was a pointless train of thought. He'd gone down that route. He wasn't going there again.

Raphael shifted in the chair, drawing Jean's attention again. He set the tablet and book aside and stretched, arching his back and kneading at the muscles to release the tension there. Jean clenched his fists against the desire to replace Raphael's hands with his own. He would do a much better job because he wouldn't be fighting an awkward angle.

Oblivious to Jean's thoughts, Raphael settled back in the chair and picked up his things again, going back to his studies. Jean turned back to his book as well, trying to erase the image of Raphael's arched body—and the many things he could do to make Raphael react that way—out of his head. He was a fool to have allowed Raphael to come over tonight, knowing he would be hungry. His beast was restless within him, wanting blood. It made it harder than it should have been to ignore the temptation Raphael presented.

He could still go to Sang Froid tonight after Raphael left. He usually only stayed until ten or eleven unless it was a weekend night, since he had classes to teach, often early in the morning. Sunrise did not come so early that Jean would be in danger going out after Raphael left, even if he chose to hunt instead of going to Sang Froid. Now he understood Sebastien's edginess from a month ago. Feeding would take the edge off, but the thrill of the hunt would offer so much more.

Not as much as Raphael could, a traitorous voice whispered in his head.

It didn't matter what Raphael could offer. Jean couldn't take it.

"Don't come tomorrow night. I won't be here."

"Why not?" Raphael asked, looking up from his work.

"I don't owe you an explanation." The belligerent words were out before he could stop them. He didn't want to antagonize Raphael. He just wanted to be able to breathe again.

"Why not, Jean?"

"Because I have to feed," Jean snapped. "If I don't, there's no point in your coming ever again."

"So you'll hunt, or you'll go to Sang Froid and pay for blood, but you won't take what's freely on offer here," Raphael said bitterly. "Fine, but did you have to rub it in my face?"

"You're the one who asked," Jean retorted. He struggled to pull himself back under control. He didn't want to fight with Raphael, but he couldn't stop the anger welling inside him. He rose from his seat to pace the room restlessly. If he couldn't control the surge of emotion, maybe he could channel it into movement so he didn't do something rash. "You're the one who wouldn't let well enough alone. You said you wouldn't push. Nice to see how you keep your promises."

"I didn't ask you to flaunt your feeding from someone else in my face." Raphael rose as well to approach Jean angrily. "Am I that unattractive to you that you'd go somewhere else when it would mean so much more right here?"

"Maybe that's what I want," Jean replied. "Maybe I don't want it to mean anything."

"What are you afraid of?" Raphael demanded.

Jean's temper snapped. He drove Raphael back against the wall. "I'm not the one who should be afraid."

"I'm not afraid of you," Raphael replied.

Jean smiled cruelly. "You should be."

Never letting go of Jean's gaze, Raphael tilted his head to the side. "Stop fighting yourself."

Those words.... How many times had he heard those exact words from Raymond when Jean would get it into his head to "spare" his lover the full force of his attentions?

Jean lost control, and the beast lunged for Raphael's throat. He tried to slow the attack, but it had the scent of blood now—Raphael's blood, hot and sweet and rich with life and love and determination to take anything Jean could throw at him.

He didn't prepare the skin the way he should have. That would have meant holding back, and he had no more chance of doing that than he had of learning to fly. Raphael's blood tasted as sweet as he'd known it would. Raphael's magic wrapped around him, as he'd known it would. He hadn't known Raphael's blood would give him back the patience to do this right. Not enough control to stop, but then, he could taste Raphael's willingness, his sheer delight in the feeling of Jean's fangs in his skin, Jean's body against him. He couldn't stop, because Raphael wanted this as badly as Jean's beast. His own fears could not override them both.

He sucked hard on Raphael's neck, needing the marks of his fangs to be so deep no one would be able to contest his claim. Raphael cradled his head, holding him in place as he drowned himself in the rush of blood that flooded his senses as it filled his mouth. As good as it tasted, as right and rich and *familiar,* Jean knew it could taste better. He reared back, searching Raphael's face for any sign of hesitation. When he found none, he grabbed the collar of the T-shirt he wore and pulled. The fabric gave beneath his hands, and he fell on Raphael's chest like a starving man. He licked the patch of skin over his heart quickly and then bit down hard.

There.

That was the flavor, the connection that had been missing for so long. He heard Raphael's gasp, but it wasn't fear he tasted in his blood. It was need as great as Jean's own.

He tried to hold back, to remind himself he had never done this with Raphael before, but his beast paid no heed to his warnings. It had the taste of its mate in its system again after being denied for so long, and nothing would do but to gorge.

He lifted his head long enough to meet Raphael's eyes. Tasting desire in his blood was all well and good, but for his own peace of mind, Jean needed explicit agreement. "If this isn't what you want, you need to draw your wand and leave now, because if this goes any farther, I won't be able to stop."

Raphael's eyes were dark with lust, only the faintest rim of blue visible around his dilated pupils. He leaned against the wall, his shirt hanging open, blood staining his chest and neck where Jean had bitten him, everything about his body language screaming at Jean in invitation. But Jean needed the words, or if not the words, then some incontrovertible proof that Raphael wanted this as badly as he did.

Raphael smiled and pulled him into a kiss.

It was all the permission Jean needed. He grabbed Raphael's ass and lifted, pinning him against the wall as Jean returned to his chest. Raphael wrapped his legs around Jean's hips to press himself closer. He rocked his hips against Jean's stomach, letting Jean feel his erection.

He reached for Raphael's pants, using his weight to keep Raphael in place.

"You already owe me a shirt," Raphael said hoarsely. "Don't ruin my pants too."

Jean was tempted to tear them just because he could, but he let Raphael's feet fall to the ground so he could strip away the remaining barriers to golden, naked flesh.

He was every bit as beautiful unclothed as fully dressed, the hints of muscle Jean had refused to notice beneath his clothes on full display. He took a moment to simply look, letting the image settle into his soul. As hard as he had fought, that was in the past. This man, this beautiful, amazing man, was now his, and he fully intended to enjoy it.

"Like what you see?"

"Do you even have to ask?"

"Just checking," Raphael said with a grin. "When do I get to see you?"

Jean stripped as quickly as he could. He was slender by modern standards, a legacy of the monastic poverty of his youth, but Raymond had never complained. He hoped Raphael would be equally satisfied.

He stood still as long as he could stand, but his beast, soothed momentarily by the taste of its mate, was growing demanding again. The moment Raphael reached for him, the beast surged back to the fore. Jean let it loose, guiding rather than curtailing it. Raphael was inexperienced at best, and the beast was single-minded in its focus. Jean hoped that by keeping the thought of not hurting Raphael in mind he could draw this out long enough to avoid scaring Raphael away.

RAPHAEL TREMBLED when Jean pinned him against the wall again, skin touching skin this time. He'd dreamed—mon Dieu, had he dreamed!—of what it would feel like to be the sole focus of his vampire's attention. The dreams had gotten even more intense after he'd met Jean and had a face to put on his phantom lover—but those dreams hadn't come close to preparing him for the intensity of Jean's stare, the power of his deceptively slender body, the overwhelming intimacy of his fangs against Raphael's throat or, heaven help him, over his heart. His body filled with liquid heat, making him melt into Jean's embrace, receptive to any advance, any caress.

His skin burned everywhere their bodies touched, and when Jean reached down to lift him again, Raphael shuddered at how right it felt to trust Jean's strength, to give him the lead. Jean's hands were hot and hard against his buttocks as they supported him. The position left him open, his legs splayed wide around Jean's hips, but the brush of Jean's fingers along his crease as he shifted his grip only added to Raphael's need. He should have felt vulnerable. He had never felt safer. Here, in this apartment, with Jean between him and the world, nothing could touch him. Nothing but Jean, the vampire lover of his dreams made flesh, and that touch could never hurt him.

Jean shifted, bracing his thigh beneath Raphael to take part of his weight. He lowered his head and fitted his fangs to the incisions he had left when he had ripped Raphael's shirt open and fallen on him like a starving man. Right over the two little freckles that never faded, even in the deep of winter, Raphael noticed vaguely. This time Jean's movements were more controlled but no less mesmerizing.

Since Raphael grew old enough to understand, he had dreamed of a vampire's fangs in him. The reality surpassed his most cherished fantasies. The prick of pain at the moment of penetration was completely outweighed by the sense of connection that had slammed into place at the first touch of Jean's fangs. Jean had said he was no fairy-tale prince, but Raphael couldn't have proven it. Jean was everything he'd dreamed of and so much more. He was *real.*

He threw his head back with a loud moan when Jean closed a hand around his erection. It felt nothing like the touch of his own hand. Jean's hands were smaller, with calluses in different places. Most importantly, though, they weren't his own hands. He couldn't predict or control their movement. Jean was doing this to him, touching him, pleasuring him.

Making love to him.

The thought swept through him. He had no experience to speak of, but this wasn't just fucking. He could feel Jean's heart pounding in time with his own. Jean's fangs pulled on his skin, more intimate than any kiss. He was surrounded, protected, cherished in Jean's arms. He knew it like he knew his own name. Like he knew his mate. He could feel his orgasm bubbling through his system, building up pressure. He tried to hold it back. A few strokes of Jean's hand shouldn't have been enough to make him come like a teen, but it was so much more. It was Jean's fangs in his skin, the incredible sense of finally being complete, the knowledge that this was only the beginning.

Jean released his grip on Raphael's chest. He licked Raphael's nipple teasingly, then looked up at him. "Let go. I want to see what you look like when you come."

Raphael's eyes closed as he gave in to Jean's urging. He cried out as every muscle in his body tensed. His climax seemed to go on forever before he finally relaxed into Jean's embrace. Even then, desire simmered beneath the surface, just waiting to be brought back to a boil. When he finally forced his eyes to open, he met Jean's glittering gaze.

"Ça va?" Jean asked.

"Never been better," Raphael replied.

"Good." Jean moved his hand, slick with Raphael's release, between his legs, probing along Raphael's crease. He couldn't stop the reflexive flinch at the burn when Jean pressed the tip of his finger against his entrance.

Immediately, Jean withdrew.

"Don't," Raphael said. "I… I want—"

"Yes, and you'll get," Jean said, "but you don't deserve your first time to be against a wall. Will you let me take you to bed?"

Raphael had barely started to nod when Jean swung away from the wall, keeping Raphael surrounded by his embrace, and walked into the bedroom. The bed from his dreams, Raphael realized, as Jean set him tenderly on the black-and-gold counterpane. The mingled scents of jasmine and sandalwood surround him immediately.

"We'll need something to ease the way," Jean said. "I won't hurt you."

"I can…." Raphael's voice cracked. He swallowed hard, trying to make his voice work. "If you bring me my wand, I can get something from my place. If you don't have anything here, I mean."

"I don't," Jean said. "It's been many long years since I needed it."

Raphael's heart went out to Jean, so lost in grief for so long. *No more,* he swore. He didn't expect Jean to forget Raymond, but he would find a way to help him be happy again.

"Don't move," Jean said. Raphael was pretty sure his legs wouldn't support him if he tried.

Jean returned in moments, Raphael's wand in hand. As he climbed back onto the bed, he pulled the ties on the bed curtains, cocooning them in heated darkness. Enough light filtered through the place where the black drapes met for Raphael to see Jean up close, but it gave the illusion of being the only two people in the world. Raphael took a moment to concentrate and picture his bedroom and the lube next to the bed. It would have been easier if Jean wasn't kissing his collarbone. He hadn't bitten Raphael again, a small blessing, because Raphael would never have managed the spell with Jean's fangs in him. When he thought he could complete the spell, he cast the spell and hoped for the best. A moment later, the tube appeared on the pillow next to him.

"You are a wonder," Jean whispered and transferred his attention from Raphael's chest to his mouth. It should have been disconcerting to taste his blood in Jean's mouth, but the thought that he had nourished Jean, had provided him with this most basic of needs, thrilled him to the core. Jean was *his* now. His partner, his lover, his soul mate, and woe to anyone who sought to challenge that bond. He might not have

Jean's mark the way Raymond had, but Raphael would stand at his side as faithfully as Jean's Avoué had done.

Kissing Jean bore no resemblance to those awkward kisses of his teenage years. Jean was sophistication personified, and his kisses reflected it, smooth and hot with just a hint of wild underneath. Raphael thought he could lie in Jean's arms and do nothing but kiss him for hours. Jean seemed to sense his mood. He settled in next to Raphael, aligning their bodies, and kissed and kissed and kissed him—long, lingering, particularly filthy kisses. Raphael felt positively possessed from the devastatingly thorough claiming of his mouth. When Jean finally lifted his head, Raphael could swear he'd already been fucked. It couldn't be any more powerful than those kisses.

Then Jean was back, proving him wrong as he stole Raphael's senses even more completely, so much that Raphael barely felt the fingertip teasing his entrance and working past his guardian muscle. Only when Jean was in past the first knuckle did he release Raphael's mouth again.

Raphael shuddered at the exquisite sensation of Jean's finger inside him.

"What now?" he asked breathlessly.

Jean smiled, though Raphael knew it only by the crinkles around his eyes. "Now we play."

Raphael shivered at the heat in Jean's voice. He didn't know what "playing" entailed, but he was sure it would be as devastating as everything else Jean had done to him. To judge by the smug satisfaction on Jean's face, they had barely gotten started, and Raphael's wanton inability to resist Jean's charms only added to Jean's determination to wreck him. Raphael couldn't wait. He pulled Jean back into another kiss, hoping to signal his agreement.

Jean moved easily to join their mouths again, but he kept the contact lighter this time, allowing Raphael to focus on both the kiss and the feeling of Jean's finger inside him. Raphael had tried the same maneuver on himself once or twice, but the angle was awkward enough he had abandoned it as not worth the effort. Jean's fingers weren't awkward at all, sliding in and out of him with ease, teaching Raphael the movement and rhythm to come. Within moments, Raphael had started meeting each ingress with a lift of his hips, fucking himself on Jean's hand as Jean moved into him. Then Jean stopped moving, his finger buried deep inside Raphael's body. He twisted it so the pad ran along the inner walls until it hit... something. Raphael yelped at the sudden burst of pleasure inside him.

"I did promise we would play," Jean purred in his ear. He latched onto the patch of skin beneath Raphael's ear as his finger tortured that sweet spot. Raphael thrashed on the bed, nearly insensate. He needed Jean's kiss to ground him or he'd fly apart right there.

Jean bit him instead. Raphael screamed at the explosion of sensation. He couldn't... he needed.... Only one thought coalesced.

"Jean!"

"I'm here," Jean whispered. Raphael whimpered at the loss of Jean's fangs. "Do you trust me?"

Raphael nodded, unable to make his voice work.

"Then don't hold anything back. Come if you need to, shout if you need to, tell me what you need if I'm not doing it. Whatever it is, I'll be right here."

The words seared through Raphael down to his soul. Jean would be there. Raphael no longer faced a future alone. He turned his head, seeking Jean's lips with his own. Jean met him halfway in a torrid kiss to seal their promise.

Finally Jean pulled back to look Raphael deep in the eyes. "What do you need?"

Raphael tried to formulate an answer, but they had gone so far beyond the scope of his dreams that he didn't know where to start. Add to that the constant pressure of Jean's fingers against his prostate, and Raphael could only manage one word. "You."

"You have me," Jean said, and Raphael thought he'd never heard more beautiful words. Jean kissed him again, so tenderly Raphael felt like he would burst from the emotion. He wondered if any of it was Jean's, but if so, it was too close to his own to distinguish. A second finger joined the first. Raphael lifted his hips into the contact. He could feel Jean, hot and hard against his hip. He wanted that inside him, and that meant letting Jean stretch him.

Jean twisted his fingers, working Raphael open. The sensation burned a little, but Raphael ignored it in favor of sucking Jean's tongue into his mouth. Jean used his free hand to cradle Raphael's head. Raphael leaned into the support, wanting every connection he could get.

As if in answer to that thought, Jean kissed his way down Raphael's throat. He sucked lightly at the hollow there, then moved lower, lingering over one nipple. Raphael arched up into the caress. He could feel the barest hint of Jean's fangs and had the wild thought that he'd end up pierced like Kylian if Jean wasn't careful. Jean had more control than that, though, because they didn't so much as scratch the areola. Raphael buried his hands in Jean's dark hair, the long strands wrapping around his fingers. He held Jean there as he sucked in time with the rhythm of his fingers.

The scent of musk wafted around them, wreathing Raphael's senses and mixing with the already intoxicating smell from the covers. Between that and Jean's attentions, he couldn't catch his breath. His head swam with desire and desperation. Jean's fangs surprised him, driving deep again into the bite marks from before. The pinch sent him tumbling, a second climax spilling out of him. Jean drank deeply through his release, his fangs and fingers and tongue never easing their assault on Raphael's senses.

He needed to breathe. He needed a moment of respite, but Jean was relentless, dragging out Raphael's orgasm until every sensation was an exquisite agony, his overstimulated body dreading each new touch as much as he craved it.

He whimpered.

Immediately Jean withdrew his fingers and lifted his head. Raphael shook his head in protest. They couldn't be done yet. Despite his climax, desire still churned restlessly in his belly. He tried to pull Jean back against him, but his strength was no match for Jean's.

"Turn over," Jean urged. "I'm not done with you yet."

Raphael shivered in anticipation. The silk counterpane that had felt so good against his back was rough against his still hard cock. He didn't know how he was still hard. He'd come twice in quick succession, but he showed no sign of softening. He lifted into Jean's hands when he felt them spreading him. He tensed as he waited to feel the tip of Jean's erection against him. He got a puff of breath instead. Oh, putain, was Jean going to…? He keened when Jean laved his entrance. When Jean pushed his tongue inside him, all wet heat and strong muscle, Raphael scrambled to get his knees under him so he could press back into Jean's mouth.

Jean lifted his head to help steady him as he moved, then froze.

"Your back," he said in a strangled voice.

"I was born with it," Raphael said, sure Jean was talking about the purple-black birthmark across his spine. "The doctors called it a Mongolian spot. They said it would fade, but it never did."

Jean traced the edges of the mark. "It's not a Mongolian spot. It's...."

Worried at the conflicted emotions—these were definitely Jean's—Raphael rolled onto his back again so he could see Jean's face. "It's just a birthmark. Nothing to worry about."

"When I couldn't answer your questions about the Aveu de Sang, you assumed we'd never be able to prove it," Jean said. "I'm looking at all the proof we'll ever need. I know that mark. Half of it is my medallion, the same one you recognized in the wards. The other half is the mark Serrier left on his lieutenants. No one could have duplicated that because no one else ever saw it. Welcome home, my heart."

Something in Raphael unclenched. He wasn't crazy. All the years of fearing ridicule for his "flights of fancy" were over. Jean believed and accepted him.

"Do I get a welcome-home kiss?" he asked hoarsely.

"Oh, you'll get more than that," Jean said, "as soon as I'm sure I won't hurt you."

"Then you'd better hurry up," Raphael said, reaching down to stroke Jean's cock. "I'm getting lonely."

Jean grinned and fell on him, driving his fangs deep into that spot on his chest. Raphael would have to ask about that later. He had other things on his mind at the moment. Jean's fingers were back, pumping hard and fast, stretching him wide. A third finger joined the first two, but Raphael was too high on endorphins from his earlier releases to care about the burn. All veneer of sophistication had disappeared, leaving wildness in its place. Raphael found that even more arousing than the suave lover had been.

Jean ended the bite with a light lick and moved between Raphael's thighs. Raphael wrapped his legs around Jean's waist in eager welcome.

"Another night, I'll take my time," Jean whispered against Raphael's skin. "I'll lick and kiss every inch of you, leave you covered in bites, and I'll suck you and rim you and make you come so many times you'll pass out from the pleasure of it, but I don't have the patience tonight. I need to be inside you. I need to claim you again."

Raphael pulled Jean's head to his for a kiss. "I want it too. It's all I've ever wanted."

The tip of Jean's cock nudged his entrance.

"Breathe," Jean ordered. Then he stole Raphael's breath with another torrid kiss. Raphael melted into the kiss, all tension gone. Only then did Jean press forward, joining their bodies. Raphael moaned into the kiss. Jean's ingress was inexorable, filling Raphael until he couldn't take another centimeter, but his body knew its mate even when his mind protested. The sense of communion was stronger than the momentary discomfort. Then Jean was fully seated within him, and contentment washed through him, filling the hole he had lived with his whole life. He had found his mate. He had come home.

As amazing as Jean's kisses were, as unbelievably perfect as it felt to have Jean's cock inside him, one thing was missing.

"Bite me," he begged. He tilted his head and bared his neck in offering. Jean's gaze flicked down to his chest for a moment before returning to his throat. He nuzzled Raphael's jaw until he tilted his head in the other direction. "Trying to leave as many marks as you can?"

"I don't want anyone to doubt how fully you are mine."

"I don't see anyone else lining up to challenge you," Raphael said.

The surge of jealousy and fury that hit him had to come from Jean. It shook Raphael to the core to know Jean felt so strongly about him already.

"There's no one else I would let stake a claim," he hastened to add. "You are the one I want. The one I've always wanted. Now claim me properly."

Jean stared down at him for a moment before he shook his head. "The Cour is in my past. This is the only claim we need."

That was something else to ask Jean about at another time, when they'd had a chance to settle into their new relationship. Raphael wouldn't complain about having Jean's attention all to himself, but he would never deny Jean a life of his own if he decided to return to a position of prominence within the Cour. He didn't get a chance to voice that thought, though, because Jean took his offer and bit his throat. Slowly, almost painfully slowly, he started to move inside Raphael.

Long, deliberate strokes, aiming for Raphael's prostate with each pass. The sensation built and built, a maelstrom of need and want and lust and love inside him, his emotions and Jean's so tangled together he couldn't separate them. He lost track of the noises he made, the words he babbled in desperate pleas for more, for the pinnacle of rapture that towered over him, threatening to crash down over them both. He could drown in the possessiveness that swamped his mind, Jean's for him and his for Jean—for if he was Jean's lost love reborn, Jean was the embodiment of Raphael's dreams, everything he had never let himself hope for in one seductive package.

It was all too much. He couldn't contain it anymore. His release stole his breath and then his consciousness.

He came to some minutes later to the sight of Jean lying next to him, hair damp with mist, stroking his cheek tenderly. He shifted experimentally to feel the proof of their lovemaking, just in case it had been one more dream, but no, he felt an unfamiliar ache, testament to how thoroughly Jean had taken him.

"How are you feeling?" Jean asked.

Raphael smiled. "Like I might never move again. How are you?"

"I am well. I may never let you leave our bed."

"As long as you figure out how to feed me, I can live with that," Raphael said. "Although you'll have to explain to the Sorbonne why I can no longer teach my classes."

"I'm sure I can come up with an excuse they'll accept," Jean said.

Raphael chuckled. He was sure Jean could charm the skin off a snake if he chose to.

"I don't know by what miracle I found you," Jean said softly, burrowing his face into the crook of Raphael's neck, "but I will never take that for granted."

"I know you won't," Raphael said. "You forget. I know you already. Most of my dreams were dreams, not memories, but you were never a fantasy. You were always and indisputably you, even when I couldn't see your face. I don't know what the future holds, but I know where my place in it will be."

"Where is that?" Jean asked.

"At your side," Raphael replied. "For whatever length of years is given to us this time around and for as many lifetimes as we're granted, my place will always be at your side."

"Raymond made a promise to me once," Jean said softly. "Before he knew Marcel intended to make him his successor, he promised to support me in every way he could. He thought he'd be a burden to me because he'd sided with Serrier at the start of the war. When Marcel made him president of l'ANS, I promised that same support in return." He found Raphael's hand and lifted it to his lips to kiss it softly. "It's not the end of a war, and you're not the president of l'ANS, but that promise stands. I will support you in every way I can."

"As I will support you," Raphael said. A thought occurred to him. "Do you suppose we'll hate each other on sight in every lifetime?"

Jean laughed, the first time Raphael had ever heard the sound from his lips. "Next time I'll know to watch for you. I won't mistake you for anyone other than my soul a second time."

Raphael kissed him. "We should let Kylian and Sebastien know. I would have given up if it hadn't been for their support."

Jean's grin turned wicked, sending a thrill racing down Raphael's back. Never mind that they'd just finished making love. One look from Jean and Raphael was ready to go again. "They'll still be there in the morning. I've waited too long for you to let you get away so soon."

He rolled to his back and pulled Raphael on top of him. Raphael went easily, eager to see what else life with Jean had in store for him.

Enjoy this bonus short story
in the Partnership in Blood series

MY PARTNER,
MY MATE,
MY HEART,
MY SOUL

Partnership
Reforged

A Companion to the
Partnership in Blood series

ARIEL TACHNA

Partnership Reforged

THE SPIRES of Notre-Dame rose tall and solid against the night sky as they gathered on the parterre outside. Sebastien swore he could feel the confluence of magical elements that made the cathedral a locus, as if the stones themselves hummed in anticipation of the ritual to come. He pushed aside the fanciful notion, but no amount of determination could stop the feeling of static electricity raising the fine hairs on his forearms and the back of his neck. It might be a fanciful notion, but *something* was in the air tonight. When they had all assembled, four wizards to represent the four elements, three vampires as their partners, and Vincent to support Eric, who had no vampire lover, Raymond gestured toward the church. In silence, they filed into the nave, pausing long enough for Jean to pay his respects before descending into the crypt. Sebastien didn't know who Jean and Raymond had bribed, begged, or bullied into letting them use the crypt, but the nave and crypt were both deserted, giving them complete privacy for their ritual.

The wizards took their places: Thierry, Alain, Eric, and Raymond at the respective points of the compass, the vampires and Vincent aligning themselves behind them to complete the circle. The magic snapped into place around them even before Alain began the chant that would provide the foundation for what they were about to do. Sebastien had left the details to Jean and Raymond. They would understand the nuances and implications of the spell more than Sebastien could. He knew all he needed to know. At the end of the night, he would be Thierry's, and if the ritual worked as planned, Thierry would be his.

"Last chance," he said softly to Thierry. "We don't have to do this."

"Maybe not," Thierry said, "but I want to. Unless you've changed your mind?"

"Never," Sebastien swore. "I don't need it, but I do want it."

Thierry smiled. "Then let's begin."

He nodded to Alain on his left, who began the chant, the air around them stirring at his command. Eric's voice joined in a moment later, every candle in the crypt flaring as he summoned fire. Raymond followed, calling on the power of water that surrounded the island outside. Thierry came last, earth to ground them and the focus of the ritual. Thierry's magic had always been a cloak for Sebastien, a layer of protection against sunlight and war. Now, though, he felt it more deeply, surrounding him, invading his senses, exploring the edges of his soul. He tensed automatically, but before he could pull away, Thierry joined their hands and steadied him. At Raymond's sign, Vincent moved in behind Eric, fitting their bodies together as closely as he could. He rested his hands on Eric's wrists. Orlando and Jean took their own places, their fangs in their partners' necks, increasing their power. Then only Thierry and Sebastien remained.

Holding Sebastien's gaze, Thierry stripped down to his underwear. Sebastien had protested this step, insisting they weren't forming an Aveu de Sang and so it was a pointless invasion of Thierry's privacy to force him to prove he was unmarked, but Thierry had overridden him with the reminder the others would be witness to far more intimacy than that in order to seal their bond. Proving he was unmarked and thus available for Sebastien's claiming seemed a little enough nod to the vampire lore they had subverted to their own ends.

"He is unmarked," Alain proclaimed. Normally that would have been Jean's role, but Jean was in no position to talk, and Alain was Thierry's best friend. They had agreed he would be an acceptable substitute since their bond would never be recognized by the Cour. No one outside the crypt would know they had gone beyond a typical partnership.

"I claim him before the witnesses here as mine for as long as he lives," Sebastien intoned. "He is my partner, my lover, and my mate. I will have only him until he is no more."

They weren't the traditional words, but they served well enough for a ritual cobbled together from vampire, wizard, and werewolf lore.

"I accept him as my partner, my lover, and my mate," Thierry replied in turn.

"Then claim him," Raymond said.

Sebastien loosened his grip on Thierry's hand long enough to lift his own wrist to his mouth and puncture the skin there. He had questioned this step in the ritual, fearing what his blood might do to Thierry, but Jean and Raymond had agreed it was necessary. A few drops of his blood in Thierry's veins to help Sebastien's beast recognize Thierry as part of him long enough for the magic to forge the bond. Thierry took the offered blood without hesitation. When Thierry released Sebastien's wrist, Sebastien moved so he stood directly behind Thierry, their bodies aligning completely. Thierry tipped his head, offering his neck to Sebastien. Sebastien closed his eyes for a moment as Raymond and the others resumed the soft litany of words that made up the spell. He could feel the magic permeating him, flooding through him in a way nothing but Thierry's blood ever had. It wrapped around his very soul until he felt alternately exposed and protected by it, as if his every secret were laid bare for all to see. He nuzzled Thierry's jaw and licked across his pulse point, preparing the patch of skin for his fangs. As many times as he and Thierry had done this, he felt the import of the movement like never before. Even with Thibaut, it hadn't been like this. He hadn't known what might be with his Avoué, so he hadn't worried about what might not come to pass. Now, with Thierry, he knew what they hoped would happen, but this ritual had never been performed before. The chances of failure were at least as high as the chance of success. If they failed, nothing would change, but Thierry would be crushed, and that was unacceptable in Sebastien's eyes. This had to work.

Thierry turned his head, craning to look over his shoulder when Sebastien didn't immediately bite him. Sebastien covered the hesitation with a last lick and another nuzzle before he unsheathed his fangs and bit deep into Thierry's neck. Hot, sweet blood flooded his mouth, rich with magic and desire. Sebastien reveled in the joy he could taste, Thierry's euphoria at finally being able to perform the ritual they had struggled for two years to perfect. The image of Thierry—rough and ready, always poised for action Thierry—hunched over books older than Sebastien as he tried to find anything to help would never cease to awe Sebastien to the depths of his being. If Thierry could work so hard to bring this moment to fruition, Sebastien would commit to it with his whole heart. Thierry and Raymond had both said more than once that magic was 90 percent intention and 10 percent execution. Sebastien would do his part in making the intention as clear and pure as the sunlight Thierry's blood allowed him to experience again. If the ritual failed, it would not be because of his doubts and fears.

Mine, he intoned silently as he drank deeply. *My partner. My mate. My heart. My soul.*

He felt the beast inside him stir in response to the magic. Instead of pushing it down like he had always done before, locking it behind iron bars as strong as his will, he channeled his need and desire in its direction. *My mate, my heart, my soul.*

The beast subsided, giving Sebastien hope. It had never retreated on its own before. The true test wouldn't come until he dropped all control and let the beast loose, but Sebastien no longer feared that moment. He sucked harder on Thierry's neck to imprint the flavor of Thierry's blood on his memory. His conscious mind would never mistake Thierry for another. Now he needed to ensure his beast felt the same recognition. Only then would the bond be complete.

Thierry shuddered in his arms as need built in his blood. Sebastien knew what he wanted, but the time hadn't yet come. Not until he was as gorged on blood as he dared. Satiation would slow his beast down, giving Thierry the chance to get away if the worst happened. And if the best happened, if all they hoped for came to pass, they would never have to worry about limits again.

He let his hands begin to wander over Thierry's body as he arched and ground back against Sebastien's groin. Sebastien's cock pulsed in time with his feeding, and his beast grew impatient. Blood was all well and good, but it needed more, and everything in Thierry's taste and body language proclaimed his willingness. Sebastien pushed it down. He hadn't understood much about the ritual preparation, but one thing had been clear: the longer he could make the ritual last, the more likely it was to work. He had not followed the reasoning behind the statement, but he had no reason to question it. His control was key, and he refused to be the reason the ritual failed.

Magic eddied around them and through them, although Thierry no longer chanted with the others as he had done before. The words that fell from his lips now were pleas, not incantations.

"Fuck me, Sebastien, please. I need you."

The words enflamed Sebastien's beast almost to the point of defeating Sebastien's control. Praying it had been long enough, Sebastien lifted his head and turned Thierry in his arms to kiss him deeply—a mortal's kiss.

One of the wizards took that as his cue to erect a screen to give them some semblance of privacy. They would still hear everything that transpired as they maintained the magic that formed the ritual, but they would not be able to see as Sebastien gathered Thierry into his arms and made love to him. He despaired momentarily the lack of bedding to protect Thierry from the hard floor of the crypt, but almost as soon as the thought formed, a mattress appeared at his feet. He'd have to thank whichever wizard read his mind later. For now, he focused on Thierry. He guided Thierry down onto the mattress and stretched out next to him.

"You're still dressed," Thierry said as he pulled Sebastien in for a kiss.

"It's easier to stay in control that way."

Thierry nodded but reached for Sebastien's shirt anyway. "It's time."

Sebastien let Thierry strip his shirt from him, but he caught Thierry's hands when he started on his belt. "Do not let me hurt you. You remember what it was like last time. If the same thing happens again, call for help. Get away from me, whatever it takes."

"I will, but it won't come to that. Can't you feel the difference?"

He could, but that didn't mean it would be enough. Raymond's words about his intentions rang in his head, so he pushed those doubts aside and for the second time in his existence consciously dropped his control of his beast. It roared within him, wild with need, but unlike the last time, it had a single focus. Sebastien nearly sobbed with relief. Instead of being trapped behind the beast's madness, they wanted the same thing this time. They wanted Thierry.

The clothing that had once been a layer of protection and modesty was now an unacceptable barrier. Sebastien stripped himself and Thierry as quickly as he could and all but fell on Thierry as soon as he was naked.

"Sebastien?"

"I'm here," Sebastien replied, relief thickening his voice. "I think it worked."

"Then make love to me to seal the bond."

Sebastien could think of nothing he wanted more.

THIERRY BRACED himself for what came next. Sebastien had answered him, which was already a huge improvement over the first time they had tried this, but the beast was still loose. It was what he had wanted—for Sebastien to be able to set his beast free without turning into a monster—but now that he had it, he had to see it through.

Keeping Raymond and Alain's advice in mind, he concentrated on how much he loved Sebastien and how much he wanted his vampire to make love to him. No one knew how quickly the emotional bond between them would develop, but if anything got through, he wanted it to be the right things. He wanted Sebastien as his mate, and that meant embracing all of him.

He met Sebastien's gaze, searching for a cue. The hungry expression decided him. If Alain was right, once wouldn't be enough between the beast's need for sex and blood and the magic coursing through him. If he could take the edge off for Sebastien, the next round would be slower and more intense, the better to seal their bond. With that in mind, he reached for Sebastien's erection and stroked it just the way he knew Sebastien liked.

"I'm supposed to be making love to you," Sebastien protested.

Thierry shook his head. "We're supposed to be making love to each other. And right now, you're wound so tight you wouldn't last a minute. Let me take care of you now, and then you can make me scream until you're ready to go again."

"Promise?" Sebastien's gaze darkened with hunger. Thierry grinned. Sebastien liked the idea of taking Thierry apart.

"I promise."

Thierry urged Sebastien to roll to his back, but that was more than his beast would tolerate. He hovered over Thierry, gaze fixed on the punctures on Thierry's neck. "Go on. Bite me. It can't hurt me now."

The ability to feed as much as Sebastien wanted had been one of the two things their partnership alone hadn't given them—that and the chance for Sebastien to finally drop his control without losing himself to his demon.

"You don't know that," Sebastien said breathlessly. Thierry could feel him struggling to hold back, all the proof he needed that the ritual had worked.

"Yes, I do. It *worked*, Sebastien." With his senses heightened by the magic still resonating through the crypt, he traced the bond between them. He wouldn't be able to see it so clearly on his own, so he cherished the glimpse of it now, shimmery gold threads tying them together in an unbreakable bond. He stroked Sebastien's cock with his hand as he stroked the bond with his magic. Sebastien shuddered above him, whether from one touch or both, Thierry didn't know.

"Bite me," Thierry said as he set up a rhythm designed to push Sebastien over the edge as quickly as possible. His vampire was seething with impatience, and it spilled over into Thierry's mind as well.

Sebastien leaned over Thierry so he could reach Thierry's neck while still leaving room for Thierry's hands to work their magic. The minute Sebastien's fangs touched his skin, Thierry gasped and arched into the contact. He had long ago learned to love the feeling of Sebastien's fangs in him, but this went far beyond anything that had come before. He tightened his grip around Sebastien's erection and matched his strokes to the pull of Sebastien's lips on his neck. Within seconds, Sebastien spilled over his fist and onto his stomach, and the swell of passion Thierry could feel through their bond knocked the breath out of him. He trembled with his own need now, hoping Sebastien would recover his composure quickly, because he didn't know how long he could wait.

Sebastien licked around his fangs and lifted his head, his eyes glittering in the low light. Thierry shivered from the feral intensity.

"My turn."

Thierry nodded and let his hand drop to the side. He wouldn't stay still for long—he never could when Sebastien started touching him—but he would hold back as long as he could. Sebastien lowered his full weight onto Thierry's body. As slight as he was compared to Thierry's breadth, Thierry could have dislodged him if he'd wanted to, but the contact felt too good, especially when Sebastien started nibbling his way down Thierry's neck and over his chest. His fangs never broke the skin, but Thierry felt the scrape of them with every kiss. He opened his mouth to beg Sebastien to bite him properly, but before he could form the words, Sebastien latched on to one nipple, sucking hard. Any words disappeared into a sharp cry of need. Sebastien started to lift his head, but Thierry grabbed his hair, holding him in place.

Sebastien sucked harder, leaving Thierry moaning and writhing beneath him.

"You like that," Sebastien said, his voice hoarse and harsh in a way Thierry had rarely heard it. He lifted his head so their gazes met. Sebastien's pupils were blown, his irises nearly black, and from the look in his eyes, Thierry suspected he was seeing Sebastien's demon more than Sebastien himself.

"I do," he replied.

"You'd like it even more if I bit you, wouldn't you?"

"I've never said otherwise."

Sebastien's lips twitched into something anticipatory as he lowered his head again, keeping Thierry's gaze. He scraped his teeth over the same nipple he'd sucked so enthusiastically earlier. "And if I bit you here?"

Thierry shuddered but made no effort to pull away. He wouldn't have thought of it until Sebastien brought it up, but now that he had....

"Do it."

Sebastien sucked harder, pulling the teat into his mouth, and sank his fangs into the tender flesh. A hoarse shout escaped Thierry's throat. He could feel Sebastien hesitate, not at all the reaction he wanted. He wanted Sebastien to let go. With the magic of the ritual pervading him, Thierry's doubts had faded to nothing. All that remained was proving to Sebastien's beast that Thierry would revel in whatever it chose to dish out. "You promised to make me scream," he goaded.

"You're playing with fire," Sebastien groaned.

"I'm an earth wizard. I won't get burned."

Thierry felt the surge of lust deep in his gut. He met it with his own need and felt the final vestiges of Sebastien's control snap. He reached for Sebastien and pulled him into a deep kiss. Sebastien's beast met the kiss, all teeth and tongue and wild energy to match the magic still surging around them. Thierry grabbed for it, channeling it through every point of contact between their bodies. He grabbed at Sebastien's back, scraping his nails down the pale flesh. They would leave marks, but if anything, that would only spur Sebastien's beast on. With his other hand, he reached for the ground. If he could touch stone, the power inherent in the locus would increase his strength exponentially. He would ground his magic so deeply in Sebastien that nothing would ever break their bond, not even the mindless fury of his beast.

The kiss gentled, though when Thierry met Sebastien's gaze, he saw the same wild hunger in it. When Sebastien nuzzled his ear, Thierry relaxed. The beast might be in charge, but Sebastien was there guiding it.

The swell of magic around them grew as Sebastien kissed his way down Thierry's body until it glutted Thierry's mind. He shouldn't have been able to channel that much power, but in the locus, with his friends as support on the other side of the screen and Sebastien doing wonderful wicked things to his body, it seemed like child's play. Every fiber of his being cried out for Sebastien's touch, and the teasing kisses and nibbling love bites were no longer enough. He needed to be claimed, to be savaged until his body proclaimed their bond as fully as he already felt it in his soul. "In me," he gasped.

Sebastien looked up, their gazes locking, and Thierry shivered at the possessiveness on Sebastien's face. This wasn't fondness, not even love. This was instinct, an animal's desire to stake its claim and defend it against any and all challengers. "Fuck me."

Sebastien shook his head, but he reached for the lube in his trouser pocket anyway.

"You aren't screaming for me yet."

Thierry barely recognized Sebastien's voice, but when Sebastien pressed slick fingers against Thierry's entrance, he did so with the utmost care, perhaps even more than he normally showed. As often as they made love, Thierry didn't need as much preparation as he once had. Sebastien touched him now like he had their first night together, when Thierry's inexperience had made him especially careful.

"Hurry," he pleaded.

Sebastien growled deep in his chest in reply.

Thierry shivered again. If words didn't work, perhaps body language would. He rolled to his stomach and arched his back, pushing his ass against Sebastien's hand. Sebastien fell on him like a man possessed, his fangs penetrating deep into Thierry's glutes as he drove his fingers inside Thierry's passage.

"Yes," Thierry sobbed. "More, fuck, more, please."

Sebastien pumped his hand faster, dragging the tips of his fingers over Thierry's prostate with every pass until Thierry was mindless with need. He curled his fingers around the edge of a stone on the floor and let every barrier drop so that he was completely open to Sebastien and the magic cycling between them. The very earth shook with it, rocking the crypt and the church above them, but Thierry couldn't do more than hold on as his orgasm gutted him. He gasped for breath, trying to steady himself, but the onslaught of Sebastien's passion sent him reeling again. He cried out as Sebastien mounted him from behind, driving into him wildly. This, fuck, *this* was what he wanted, to be joined with his mate in every way possible, to have the beast as fully as he had Sebastien. Sebastien reared back and pulled Thierry up to sitting so he could reach the juncture of Thierry's neck and shoulder. He licked the skin swiftly and drove his fangs as deep as his cock, spearing Thierry from both ends. Thierry scrabbled for something to hold on to, some way to ground himself, but the stone floor was out of reach. He gripped the only thing he could find—Sebastien's thighs—and held on for dear life.

At that angle, Sebastien couldn't pound into him as hard or as deeply as before, but Thierry didn't suggest a change in position. He wouldn't do anything that might make Sebastien move his fangs from his body. As good as a long, thorough fuck would feel, they had gone beyond that now, to a kind of desperation Thierry had never felt. Sebastien reached around and stroked Thierry's cock, sending him soaring again. He wanted to protest and remind Sebastien that the longer they could keep the magic spiraling between them, the stronger their bond would be.

It's the depth of the connection that matters.

Thierry hoped that was a memory and not Raymond's voice in his head, but he would worry about it later. For now, he focused on the connection, on burrowing his magic so deeply into Sebastien's heart and soul that nothing would ever separate them. Sebastien came hard inside him, shaking his whole body to the point that his fangs tore the skin of Thierry's shoulder. Thierry roared out his pleasure and collapsed forward onto the mattress. Darkness beckoned, and with Sebastien's comforting presence tucked firmly in the back of his mind, he surrendered.

WARMTH, A stinging in his shoulder, and the stickiness of a long fuck greeted Thierry as he slowly regained consciousness. He blinked a few times to get them to focus, but the light from one candle on the far side of the crypt did little to dispel the darkness. He took stock of the situation. Sebastien was still curled around him from behind, one arm tucked firmly around Thierry's waist. A blanket covered them, preserving their modesty and keeping them warm in the coolness of the crypt. All other evidence of their ritual was gone. They were alone in the room with only the background magic of the locus itself tinting the air. Thierry snuggled deeper into Sebastien's embrace, feeling the quiet hum of contentment between them. They would have to get up before the sun rose and the cathedral opened to visitors again, but they had hours still. They could sleep a little longer.

Don't miss how the
story started!

Alliance in Blood

Partnership in Blood:
Volume One

By Ariel Tachna

Can a desperate wizard and a bitter, disillusioned vampire find a way to
build the partnership that could save their world?

In a world rocked by magical war, vampires are seen by many as less
than human, as the stereotypical creatures of the night who prey on
others. But as the war intensifies, the wizards know they need an
advantage to turn the tide in their favor: the strength and edge the
vampires can give them in the battle against the dark wizards who seek
to destroy life as they know it.

In a dangerous move and show of good will, the wizards ask the leader
of the vampires to meet with them, so that they might plead their cause.
One desperate man, Alain Magnier, and one bitter, disillusioned
vampire, Orlando St. Clair, meet in Paris, and the fate of the world
hangs in the balance of their decision: Will the vampires join the cause
and form a partnership with the wizards to win the war?

http://www.dreamspinnerpress.com

Don't miss what
happens next in

Covenant
in Blood

Sequel to *Alliance in Blood*
Partnership in Blood:
Volume Two

By Ariel Tachna

The wizards and the vampires have forged an alliance based on blood and magic, hoping to turn the tide of the war against the dark wizards. A few wizard-vampire bonds are as successful as Alain Magnier's and Orlando St. Clair's, but some are much less so, leading to arguments, resentment, and outright fights between the allies despite their mutual goals.

Following his best friend Alain's example, Thierry Dumont determinedly forms a partnership with vampire Sebastien Noyer, despite the wizard's discomfort with being so close to a vampire—a man—so soon after his wife's death. But they find that desperation may be the key to forming a covenant that works: Thierry and Sebastien are almost immediately devoted to one another's safety.

With new strength behind it, the Alliance's leaders move to announce its existence to the whole world, hoping to rally support against the dark wizards who threaten to destroy life as they know it. Struggling to find its way in the expanding war, the Alliance discovers that despite its advantages, the partnerships are affecting the balance of magical power in the world, which may be an even bigger threat than the war itself.

http://www.dreamspinnerpress.com

The story continues in

Conflict in Blood

Sequel to *Covenant in Blood*
Partnership in Blood:
Volume Three

By Ariel Tachna

As the Alliance wizard-vampire partnerships grow stronger, the dark wizards feel the effects and become increasingly desperate to find enough information to counter them, unaware of the growing strain of the blood-magic bonds on the wizards and vampires alike.

The conflict is spreading. The strife of uncomfortable relationships, both personal and professional, is threatening to tear up the Alliance from the inside, despite the efforts of Alain Magnier and Orlando St. Clair, Thierry Dumont and Sebastien Noyer, and even Raymond Payet and Jean Bellaiche, leader of the Paris vampires, who is fighting to establish a stable covenant with his own partner so he might lead by example.

As the war rages on and heartbreaking casualties mount on both sides, the dark wizards keep searching for clues to understand and counter the strength of the Alliance, while the blood-bound Alliance partners hunt through ancient prejudices and forgotten lore to find an edge that can turn the tide of the war once and for all.

ARIEL TACHNA lives outside of Houston with her husband, her daughter and son, and their cat. Before moving there, she traveled all over the world, having fallen in love with both France, where she found her husband, and India, where she dreams of retiring someday. She's bilingual with snippets of four other languages to her credit and is as in love with languages as she is with writing.

Visit Ariel at her website: http://www.arieltachna.com or on Facebook: https://www.facebook.com/ArielTachna, or e-mail her at arieltachna@gmail.com.

www.ingramcontent.com/pod-product-compliance
Lightning Source LLC
Chambersburg PA
CBHW070053030726
47506CB00002B/455